Two Strand River

Two Strand River

Keith Maillard

■ HarperPerennial
HarperCollins*PublishersLtd*

For Hibou, who reminded me that "alle Anfang ist
Schwer"; for Ferron, Nena Boax, Bonnie Johnson,
Jim Silverman, and Michael Williamson; and for
Judi, who brought me a pomegranate.

http://www.harpercollins.com

First published in hardcover by Press Porcépic: 1976
First published in paperback by General Publishing Co. Limited: 1982
First HarperCollins Publishers Ltd paperback edition: 1996

Canadian Cataloguing in Publication Data

Maillard, Keith, 1942-
    Two strand river

ISBN 0-00-648143-4

I. Title.

PS8576.A49T86 1996   C813'.54   C95-933322-3
PR9199.3.M345T86 1996

---

96 97 98 99 ❖ HC 10 9 8 7 6 5 4 3 2 1

Printed and bound in the United States

Part I

There was an old woman toss'd up in a basket,
Seventeen times as high as the moon;
But where she was going no mortal could ask it,
For under her arm she carried a broom.
Old woman, old woman, old woman, said I!
Whither, ah whither, ah whither so high?
To sweep the cobwebs out of the sky.
Can I come with thee?
                    Aye . . . by and by.

                                        Mother Goose

THE FIRST HOUR OF LESLIE'S DAY WAS SPECIAL, linked to the same hour of the day before, linked into the future: so that these times would continue, one after another, day after day, and no matter what else might be happening in her life, they would remain consistent and compelling. It's like a ritual, she thought, the same thing, carefully, the same thing . . . again and again. Like those moments before falling asleep when she'd remember what she'd forgotten, that she would fall asleep like that every night of her life, be hung a moment in a suspended dreamy state and then in the midst of activity the next day she would forget about it. And it would go on and on into the future . . . until it stopped. What would it be like, that dissolving? Something very simple? An old woman goes to sleep at night not knowing if she'll waken in the morning. No, she thought, not that. (And the fear, for a moment, was more than an idea; it was a ripple of movement over her skin.) No. I would want to see it coming. I would want to know, want to fight it. Like death by drowning. It would be right . . . and fitting . . . that I should drown. But it would take one hell of a water to do it, the sea off the coast, or those icy channels and inlets. Water so cold I'd freeze to death in minutes.

But the first hour of Leslie's day was special; for one thing it was her only time to think about such things as old age, or drowning . . . dying . . . the only time she allowed it to happen. This time is set aside to think about life and death, she thought, teasing herself as her father would have done. She was walking in her ritual clothing—jeans and runners and sweater—following the unvarying route: from her apartment to the corner, turn left and walk the three blocks past the shops, turn right and through the park to the school. It was dark now this time of year when she arrived on the street, and she watched the dawn beginning as she walked. The street lights were always still on, the streets were deserted, and none of the shops were ever open. But there were small variations day to day. This morning was charged, beaten with a tense wind and smelling like the sea . . . that perhaps the strange prolonged autumn heat might finally be broken and Vancouver return to character with rain. Now she was passing the Danish bakery and the record store. The street lights threw yellow cones, contrasting with the dark sky. But the sky was beginning to lighten; she saw it happening over the vacant lot.

Now she was passing that absurd little beauty salon— "somewhat sick," she thought of it—called the Page of Cups. Named, she supposed, for the mannequin in the window, a child dressed up as a page. She could never decide whether the child was supposed to be a boy or a girl, and that ambiguity was irritating . . . symptomatic of everything that seemed to be collapsing around her ears, the collapse of values, beginning of the end, North America turning effete like the last days of Rome. But lately she had begun to wonder if those values weren't collapsing inside herself as well, declining just as quickly. She had not turned out to be the person she had thought that she would be, could no longer stand the pain of a good stiff workout the way she'd been able to ten years before. And now, far from going energetically about her business in the world, she wasn't sure any longer that she *had* any business there, in fact spent much of her time escaping into the fantasy realm of children's literature. (Am I, she thought, really the same person who used to pin up notes to herself that said: REST IS RUST?) And so she'd come, if not exactly to liking the page, at least to accepting him . . . or her. She would permit others their fantasies. Good morning, Page. We with our values collapsing salute you.

She was reminded by the beauty salon, as she was every morning, that she wanted to get her hair cut. (But not there!) Thinking, this is the way things happen with me . . . or to me . . . even something as simple and trivial as getting my hair cut. I can't just decide to do it. It's got to take its own sweet slow time, like mental soil erosion, has to shift forty tons of psychic dirt before I'll act. Even the way she was still hanging onto swimming (to move from trivia to something important) must be out of this same ponderous inertia. Knowing that at twenty-four she was too old, should have retired after Munich, that there were several sharp, bright-eyed teenage girls in B.C. who could take her any day of the week and a dozen or so more in the rest of Canada, didn't seem to stop her, didn't seem to make a dent. Well, a dent maybe . . . the first bite of the soil crumbling away. (And now she was waiting on the corner for the light to change even though there was no traffic.) And eventually, she thought, I'll just get up one morning and I won't be able to do it. I won't be able to get dressed and walk out the door with no breakfast in me and walk up the street and over to the pool and do it. It will be as simple as that. As simple as an old woman not knowing each night when she goes to sleep if she'll waken in the morning.

She was crossing the park. Going to rain, she thought. Gulls. They flew in circles, calling. She pulled the key ring out of her jacket and unlocked the main doors of the Sherwood Senior Secondary School. Inside, she pulled the doors shut behind her, listened for the sound of the lock falling back into place. She walked past the rows of silent lockers, down the darkened empty halls; the small padding sounds her feet made were echoed back to her. The stairs at the end of the hall led down and around to the left; it was dark there. She had to find the keyhole by touch. She swung open the doors of the gym, turned and locked them behind her. The dawn was by then usually throwing just enough light through the windows for her to be able to cross the gym floor without bumping into anything, the oddments that might have been left from classes the day before: a badminton net or trampoline or side horse.

Gyms always smell the same, she thought. It's more than just years of accumulated sweat; I could recognize it blindfolded. She unlocked the door at the far end of the gym, locked it behind her. The stairs down now were perfectly lightless, and she stepped down carefully, one hand against the wall. But what would I do, she thought, if I quit swimming? Take a ballet class once a week with a bunch of fat housewives? Go to those yoga classes that Ted keeps pushing at me? Take up jogging? Again touch found her the keyhole and she let herself into the weight room. A slit of light, filtering down from somewhere above (she was now below ground level), was just enough to bring up the outlines of the barbells. Funny toys, all fitting neatly together. A child might play with them . . . if they were tiny. And she unlocked the last door, checked to make sure it had locked behind her. Then down the last flight of stairs to the pool.

Like going down in a bathysphere, or sinking to the bottom of a dirty aquarium . . . this remote murky light. And then she flipped the switches, one for the dressing room, one for the pool, and for the moment, as it always did, the bright work-a-day illumination seemed too bright. She stripped, dumped her clothes into the bottom of the locker she always used, pulled her bathing cap out of the pocket of her jacket and began to tuck her hair into it. And was reminded again that *this* was why she wanted to get her hair cut. Not that it had been over a year since she'd overcome

her distaste, walked into a beauty salon, and had her hair styled
into a shag . . . that the shag was now grown out and unmanage-
able and always in her eyes. But that she had to wear a bathing cap,
and she hated bathing caps. Not only were they tight, uncomfortable things, but she'd come to associate them with the period in
her life ("my China Doll Period," she thought of it) when she'd in
all seriousness been planning to be a model. When she'd set her
hair every day, worn a bathing cap every time she'd gone near the
water, and the damn thing had never worked well enough to keep
the curl in. If I'd kept it up, she thought, hadn't blown the
Olympics, just think where I could be today. Like Karen
Magnussen. Could have my face on every drugstore in Vancouver.
She laughed inwardly at the absurdity of that picture: herself made
up and smiling, plastered to the glass of a hundred windows.

She closed the door of the pool behind her, walked to the edge.
If I didn't wear a bathing cap, she thought, my hair would be wet
all the way home and wet all the way into work and I'd have a cold
all winter. Could buy a dryer, one of those little blower things . . .
But spend money on something like *that*? OK, get a haircut. Yeah,
ten or twenty bucks. She curled her toes over the edge of the pool.
I draw magic rings of impossibilities around myself, she thought,
even around simple things, and can't do this because of that, but
when I look at it carefully, it all comes down to nothing. Some
people are conscious, know why they do things. Even Ted, as
wishy-washy as he is . . . (the old joke from school: librarians are
aggressively wishy-washy) . . . even Ted knows why he does things.
But I don't even know why I'm still swimming. Because I wasn't
successful, blew the Olympics? Because I was *too* successful, held a
world record for a week? Well, anyhow it's just about the only
thing in the world that means anything to me.

The smell of the pool. Chlorine, the bright twist in the nose.
This little short-course pool, "the slim pit" the kids in the club

called it . . . its bottom once painted aquatic blue, the paint now flaking off, the black lane markers flaking off. The water was so still that she could see herself reflected: a lean hard girl, not tall, with small breasts and small hips, naked except for the bathing cap. With her hair hidden in that white tight helmet, she seemed to herself all smooth lines . . . like a seal. There's too much muscle now to make a good model, she thought. Clothes designers like you fragile and emaciated.

She looked up at the clock on the far wall where she timed herself. When the minute hand moved to five-after, and the sweep second hand to twelve, she would go. She stretched her arms upward, shook her hands, let her fingers go limp. She breathed deeply, hyperventilating . . . an old sprinter's habit that she'd always kept even though she hadn't been a sprinter since she'd been fourteen. And it wouldn't help her a bit, as she well knew, about to swim three thousand meters. But it was part of the ritual. The minute hand moved: Click. A minute to go.

Her toes were curled over the edge of the pool and holding. She stopped the deep breathing, let her hands fall to her sides, and stood, simply waiting. Her reflection stood, simply waiting. The water was still, no motion, no slap in the gutters. The clear, steady smell of the chlorine. It doesn't matter, she thought. It doesn't matter that I don't know what I'm doing. And her thoughts were beginning to scatter away as they always did now. She was becoming quiet. For years her mind used to race along with her body, passing through a hundred-and-one silly things while she was swimming, but in the last year that had stopped. Nothing was left now but the water, the pull of the muscles, the wall, the turn, the water, the pull of the muscles. She didn't know if other swimmers stopped thinking; she had never bothered to ask another swimmer. She sank down into the starting position. Tense. Her entire body was holding . . . tense, tense. She was carefully aware of her toes

6

gripping the concrete. And then the second hand was at twelve and she was gone, released, shot forward and stretched into the racing dive. And for a moment, a particle of time so short she almost missed it, as she hung there drawn out over the water, fast, unbelievably fast, her reflection was racing up to meet her.

ALAN HAD BEEN TOLD THAT HIS EYES WERE GREY. He had also been told that they were green or hazel. But now, although the broad forceful light was presenting a colour to him that was clear and unmistakable, he couldn't find a name for it. Walking to work, he'd been caught by the sky above the buildings and power lines; the morning had been pulling in on itself, black and to the point of rain. A furious wind had been driving street debris in circles; he'd felt the air yanked in tight, had felt something inside himself yanked in tight. And now the shop seemed as tense and quiet as the day, was in some obscure way reflecting his disquiet back to him. It was in the mirrors. It was also in the dry mechanical hum of the fluorescent tubes, a continuous sound that seemed not separate from their light as it usually did, but an extension of it. It was particularly in the light itself, specially designed, warm to bring up the skin tones, but pitiless: light to put on makeup by. His mind had been circling in familiar patterns; he'd been thinking, only a young face could stand up to this light. My face stands up to it. But what had stopped him had been the colour of his eyes, that he couldn't find a label for it. No, he thought, no face could stand up to this light.

His eyes. He was appalled by the clarity in the mirror. A dark ring around each cornea as precise as if painted by Manet. The whites not white but marked with a minute tracery of blood vessels. He could see pores, hair, veins. So perfection is a painted doll? he thought, startled at something he'd just discovered in himself. The Page in the window is perfection then; I'm not perfect. Well then *any face* could stand up to this light. But how easy to forget, become a caricature of himself, in memory a blank oval, anything but human with pores and blood vessels. And could he stare into the mirror long enough to see himself? But (and this was most important) if he saw himself finally, would he remember?

People are mirrors as much as glass, but he didn't trust either glass or people. All of those things he'd been told: "You look young." "You look like a kid." "You could be fourteen." The teenager who'd picked him up hitch-hiking had asked, "Hey, man, where do you go to school . . . Eric Hamber?" I do look young, he thought. I *could* be a school boy. And it was equally true, as he'd been told often enough, that he looked like a girl. He traced the line of his lips with a thumb nail, imagining the nail painted a muted scarlet, imagining lipstick of the same colour. Outline the lips with a brush, unobtrusive brown, slick them with gloss . . . Oh, I know how to do it, he thought angrily. I could be a real Barbie Doll. If he were a girl, his face could be in *Vogue*: fine model's bones, milky translucent skin, straight nose, delicate neck like a Modigliani. I am beautiful, he thought. He'd heard that often enough too, and he'd never known what to do with it. But now he'd found something else, come upon it with panic. Am I *merely* beautiful? As though his face were indeed a blank oval, a technical problem. Nothing there beyond what could be made of it.

He turned away from the mirror. He collected the coffee pot from the reception room, carried it to the small pink lavatory at the back. Usually he enjoyed those few minutes alone in the morning before Kurt or Trish arrived; he always made it a point to get there first. This morning he was not enjoying it. He was thinking once again of the great plan he'd entertained since high school. He knew he'd never do it. He wasn't sure it would even be possible for him to do it, although God knows he'd worked hard enough to gain the technical expertise. But he thought of it every day, and it was simply this: that he would vanish from Vancouver, would tell no one he was going, and when he rebuilt his life in Toronto or Montreal, he would be a girl. Not Alan but Ellen. But meanwhile here he was as he'd been all of his life, intentionally bland, a slender boy in muted clothing. He wore his straight blond hair in high hippy style, parted in the centre and hanging below his shoulders, dressed invariably in plain unbleached cotton shirts, flared pants that were not too tight, and hand-made dark-brown boots with not much of a heel. Isn't this the age of liberation? he thought. What am I waiting for? He saw himself now as suspended, like the day waiting for the rain. But the rain never came. He never jumped. And time passed. He carried the coffee pot into the waiting room, and plugged it in.

What he'd loved about the shop, what had pulled him in off the street to ask for a job in it, had been the sheer blatant outrageousness of the place. A wooden sign like that of an English inn swung above the street. Trish had painted a crude but pleasantly archaic version of the Page of Cups from the Tarot deck, and in bold spidery letters: THE PAGE OF CUPS—UNISEX HAIR STYLING. A second page, like a reflection of the first, stood inside the window, an old-fashioned little boy mannequin that Kurt had salvaged from a bankrupt children's clothing store. Trish had sewn him a black velvet Little Lord Fauntleroy suit, jacket and knee britches. She'd painted the little boy face, lining in doe eyes, rouging his cheeks, giving him weirdly scarlet Marilyn Monroe lips, glossy with a coat of lacquer. And she'd finished him with a wig of blond curls tumbling halfway down his back, with an antique pair of lady's white kid evening gloves, with black stockings, with black patent leather shoes in the forties prostitute style . . . six-inch heel. The page stood in a graceful static pose, one languid gloved hand holding a silver cup. In the silver cup was a silver fish. Alan didn't know whether by intention or lack of skill on the part of the jeweller friend of Kurt's who'd made it, but the fish wore a mildly demented expression. It poked its head clear of the cup and fixed the customers with a blank walleye like a petulant cod.

The page in the window seemed to draw in the customers, but once in, they were embarrassed by him. Some took him for a girl, and then, although bizarre, he was manageable. But Kurt had supplied a clue to his gender by hanging directly behind him a photograph of a genuine Victorian, Little Lord Fauntleroy boy posed prettily in front of a mirror. And for those who caught the clue, saw him as a boy, he became alarming; they could not meet his eye. The women customers could escape into the back issues of *Vogue* and *Glamour* lying on the glass-topped coffee table, but the men were stuck looking around the room, and nothing there was of much help: not the blue Maxfield Parrish androgynies nor the antique dressmaker's dummy with a sixteen-inch waist and, where her head should have been, a philodendron trailing.

Kurt and Tricia had planned (as they'd told Alan) a small intimate shop catering to gay kids. "My dear," Kurt had said, "I didn't think we could have made it any more obvious if the sign out front had said 'Faggots' Hair styling.'" They did, it was true, have a small gay clientele, but the majority of their customers were straight: school girls, young housewives, stylish secretaries, college kids, the occasional teenage boy and, most amazingly, an incredible number of hip young businessmen. "I swear I'm losing my grip on the Zeitgeist," Kurt had said. "Things are changing so fast. You see advertisements on the buses for 'clothes for all sexes' . . . and that's a department store, mind you. It's the straight kids they're after. And now they're all coming to us. We're supposed to be 'groovy' or something. What do you suppose it is? Camp rock? David Bowie?

"No, my dear, I don't think so. No, I think it's here to stay. And just think of the *implications*. In another five years the straight boys will all be in dresses, and then what will the gay boys do? Wear suits and ties?"

Alan had been working for them now for three months. Kurt had told him eventually, "I'm glad we hired you, my dear. Your work is beautiful. But do you know why I hired you? So quickly? It's because you were so pretty. You walked through the door, and I actually thought to myself, 'My God, Kurt, it's our little page!'" Both Kurt and Tricia had taken Alan for gay. Now that they knew him, they thought he was gay and refusing to admit it to himself.

Alan drew a cup of coffee, opened the appointment book. His first customer: 9:00, Susan Mackenzie, *Cut—Style—Perm*. Oh, he thought, she's finally going to do it. She'll be in hysterics. He sank into one of the brocade-covered chairs where he could look out the window. It had been a long sunny autumn, out of character for Vancouver. Today it looked as though the pattern would break; the light was uncanny, more green than anything else. The edge of the horizon, across the street over the vacant lot (where a high-rise would go up) was as black as if India ink had been poured onto wet water-colour paper and allowed to spread.

Tricia walked in quickly, the long skirt of her forties' raincoat swirling dramatically. She carried a folded red umbrella. Usually she and Alan would have chatted, but now, strangely, neither of them spoke. She nodded in his direction, carried her raincoat to the back, returned to draw herself coffee. She sank heavily into a chair opposite him. "What's the matter?" he said.

She briefly rested two long fingers (pointed pink-frost nails) on her forehead. "Head," she said. "Scotch."

"Take anything?"

She nodded. There was nothing about Tricia that proclaimed her as gay. She was not a flashy dresser, looked like a well-kept housewife or somebody's executive secretary. She wore a grey dress with the new *Vogue*-decreed hemline . . . below the knee. She lay slumped in the chair in a wholly inelegant pose, her legs spread, the heels of her shoes resting on the floor, her feet tilted back. She looked to him like a doll that had been dumped unceremoniously. "Oh, God," she said, touching her head again. "I'm getting old."

"What? At thirty?"

"Thirty-*two*, love . . . thirty-two. Oh God, I'm glad I'm settled down . . . Straight people are right to get married, you know. Not much fun in being liberated when you're over thirty." She looked at Alan darkly over the edge of her styrofoam coffee cup. "Can't drink the way I did when I was a kid."

He didn't answer.

"Rain," she said finally.

"Yeah," he said.

She stood, walked to the desk and looked at the appointment book. "It's a bloody full day," she said. "Another one." Lit a cigarette, stood with one hip cocked and stared out the window.

"Those heels bother you?" he asked her. "To work in?"

"No . . . Well, they used to, but not anymore. Wear heels every day and your legs adjust to them. Can't wear low shoes now. They hurt." Then she gave him a quick malicious smile. "Jealous?"

"Yes," he said.

She walked into her station, began to fluff her hair in front of the mirror. "You'll have to come out one of these days, Alan," she said.

"Come out into *what*?" he said.

"Yeah," she said, "I know a lot of kids don't like the old gay scene . . . and you're right I guess, it's a mess. But for us, for years, it's all we had . . . But there are a lot of kids like you, Alan . . . who are just kids . . . you know, just ordinary kids except that they're gay."

"I'm not gay," he said.

"Oh, come on."

"I'm not straight either, but I'm not gay."

He had come to stand next to her in front of the mirror. They were each speaking to the reflection of the other. "I'd be delighted if I were gay . . . at least then I'd be something," he said.

"Have you ever been to bed with a woman?"

"Yes."

"Well?"

"It didn't work."

"With a man?"

"Yeah . . . and that didn't work either . . . I mean it did in a way. Because I didn't have to do anything I was the . . . ah . . . the receptive partner . . . And I liked the physical sensation, I mean once it got started, I liked it. But it wasn't . . . I mean . . . I didn't feel fulfilled."

At first Trish had been remote and distant with Alan. Then she had loosened up, become chatty. But this was the first time they'd ever said anything to each other of any seriousness. Perhaps, he thought, it was the odd, tense day that had made it possible.

"So you took it in the ass, eh?" she said suddenly. They simultaneously turned away from the mirror to look at each other; inexplicably they both began to laugh.

"Yeah," he said. "Jesus, Trish, I know this is going to sound naive, but it hurt like a son-of-a-bitch . . . until he got in. And then it was . . . well . . . delicious. But it wasn't . . . well, I could have had a better time jerking off. At least then I wouldn't have involved another person, someone I didn't care about."

"Maybe you haven't met the right person. I don't know what I'd be doing if I hadn't met Donna . . . Yes, I do. I'd be hanging around the bars. And that's no kind of a life. You're right if that's what you want to stay away from."

"Men don't turn me on," he said.

"Who does?"

13

"Girls. Usually teenage girls, but . . . I don't know . . . thin fashionable girls with small breasts . . . But when I go to bed with them, nothing happens. I get more excited looking at them."

"How about boys?" she said.

"Sometimes . . . if they look like girls . . ."

"Somebody like you," she said.

Kurt arrived, as he always did, with a bang. Slam of the door, shouting, "Well, children, end of summer, eh?"

"Must be nine," Trish said.

Kurt's only gay mannerism was a swish voice he could turn on and off at will; when he wanted to, he could come on as straight as new-drawn wire. He looked now, Alan thought, in blue blazer . . . with his short sandy hair and huge brush of a moustache . . . like some dotty Scot yachtsman. "I'd almost forgotten it was B.C.," he said, "Too good to last, eh? . . . Well, children, what's on the agenda? Another full day, oh my God! I never wanted to be rich, my dears. Trish, did you? Well, successful in spite of ourselves. Ah, Alan, dear boy, you have the coffee on. How nice . . . such a lovely boy! My favourite sexual fantasy. We should photograph you before you get any older." He stood grinning at them, blowing on his coffee, moustache quivering over the steam. His pale blue eyes were dancing cheerfully.

"Oh God, I can't stand you in the morning," Trish said.

"We can't all be sour in the morning," he said. His voice dropped into the baritone register, "Scare away the customers."

Suddenly it began to rain. It was like an explosion; water struck the pavement and bounced. The view from the window was a roaring white haze, like a Turner, Alan thought. He found that he'd inhaled sharply.

A girl shot through the door, spraying water and laughing. "Oh far out!" she said. She wore a red plastic raincoat, was swinging a red plastic purse like a missile. She shook herself, dog-like, looked back at the torrent in the street, and said again, "Oh far out." A rosy, bouncy, pink-cheeked lady, Alan thought, all in the exuberance of her teen years: his customer. "Let me take your coat, Susan." She wore a very short dress, white tights, and very high heels. She seemed coltish, all legs. He thought that she walked in her fanciful shoes as gracelessly as a boy would have done. She'd been in often enough now that he knew her, and he'd never seen her before in anything but blue jeans. He was charmed.

The phone began to ring. "Here we go," said Trish. She picked it up. "Page of Cups . . ."

Kurt turned on the stereo, the top-forty rock station.

"Coffee, Susan?" Alan was saying.

"Oh yes, please. Cream and sugar."

". . . not today I'm afraid. Who usually does your hair? . . ."

"How nice to see you again, my dear boy. Oh my God, what weather, eh?. . ."

"Next Tuesday?"

Alan had led Susan into the shampoo area, settled her into the chair. He was fastening the pink cape around her neck. "So you're finally going to do it?" he said.

"I'm scared," she said tensely.

"You could wait."

"Oh no. I can't wait forever. Besides, I'm being late for work to get this done. Now I *have* to do it." He saw that she was grinning at him in the mirror. "I'm changing my image," she said, and giggled. "Go ahead, Alan. I trust you."

The door opening and closing, the phone ringing . . . "Oh God! . . . Page of Cups . . .," the music, the steady pounding of the rain, Alan was happy. "Here, scoot down a bit. That's right." He adjusted the temperature of the water, swept her hair into the shampoo basin. And she was lying passively on her back with her eyes closed. He looked down at her lovely teen-age face, well-scrubbed and pink and not a blemish on it. With the hair out of the way, it could be a young boy's face. Susan Mackenzie, he thought, a little Scot. So high coloured that makeup would be redundant . . . well, maybe a touch of mascara and a muted lip gloss. It was another young face. And her burnt sienna hair streaming out behind her in the basin; then the perfume of the shampoo, the lather, his fingers on her scalp. He could see the faint blue veins in her closed eyelids. She was lying there so passively and sweetly, like an obedient doll, that there wasn't the slightest sign on her face that she was waiting for him to finish. He rinsed her long thick hair in the warm water. The pleasures of my occupation, he thought. He was happy.

Kurt was nattering at his customer, another gay gentleman, and Trish was saying: "Do you want much off? . . . Oh yes, love, some coffee of course . . . Alan dear, aren't you about finished there? . . . Oh, look at it rain!"

Susan was seated upright at Alan's station. "Oh, all the hair that's coming off!" she said. "Do you really think it's going to be right for me? . . . I never know."

"Of course it will. All curls. It will be lovely on you . . . show off your neck . . . You have a beautiful long neck."

She giggled and dropped her eyes. And her neck, as though responding to the compliment it had received, began to turn pink. The colour rose in her cheeks and mounted to her forehead. Her face was flaming. He was touched; he smiled.

This is *my* space, he thought. It's my studio now . . . all these familiar things: scissors and styling combs and tail combs, curling irons, blow dryer, brushes, trays with rollers and pins and do-alls, the manicure tray with small nail basin, all the little delicate bottles, bright lacquers, the clear viscous shine of the base coat and sealer, the pots and tubes of makeup . . . and all of these lucent things, my tools and colours (my palette) doubled in the mirror under the bright working light. "These don't really go with the dress, do they, Alan?" Susan was asking him, holding up a foot: navy-blue shoe, ankle strap, five-inch heel.

"Well," he said carefully, "it depends on the statement you want to make."

"I was just looking at *her*." She pointed at Tricia. "And I thought, well, dummy, *that's* the right length skirt . . . I never know what's right for me . . . And my mother's no help at all anymore . . . Sometimes I think I must look . . . silly."

He thought a moment, choosing his words. Then he said, "Trish certainly looks elegant, but it's an older woman's look. And the emphasis now is on a lean tall look . . . You can get it with heels and a long skirt like hers . . . or with heels and a short skirt like yours. But if you try it with a short skirt, you've got to be young. On older women, it looks absurd. But on you . . . I think it looks charming." And Susan was staring at her hands. Her face had coloured again.

How else, he thought, could I get to talk to a teenage girl about her clothes? The pleasures of my occupation. He liked all of his young girl customers, and they knew it; they came back to him. He was happy.

But soon after he'd begun to wind her hair onto the rods, she startled him by announcing flatly: "I think my mother's going crazy." She giggled nervously. "It's no joke . . . I mean really crazy."

"How crazy?" he said uneasily. "What kind of crazy?"

"I don't know what kind of crazy. Just crazy. It's like I don't know her anymore . . . You see, my dad died, oh, let's see . . . I guess it was two years ago. And mom was really screwed up. And I thought . . . I guess everybody thought that she'd just get over it. But she hasn't gotten over it. She's just gotten worse . . . I don't know what to do, Alan. I don't even know who to talk to about it . . ."

So you pick your hairdresser, he thought. "Well, what's the matter with her?" he said.

"Well, mom and dad had a camper, and they used to go away every summer in it . . . and on weekends sometimes. And they'd planned . . . after he retired, they were going to take long trips, go up north. See, dad did something or other up north in the war, and he always wanted to go back. But he didn't even get to retire, because he had a heart attack and died . . . And mom just . . . she just never got over it, eh? She just started driving all over in that camper. I mean she goes away for weeks at a time . . . I mean once it was six weeks or more. And I never know where she is or when she's going to come back. She just goes out into the bush, eh? And I don't know what she *does* out there . . . It's like I don't have a mother anymore. You know what she says, Alan? She says, 'You're grown up now. Sue. You've got to look out for yourself.'"

I wish *my* mother would say that, Alan thought. "Maybe she just likes camping," he said.

"Yeah, but all the time? I mean even in the middle of winter when it's raining every day? And she's just let herself get all sleazy, eh? She wears these ratty old clothes, and her hair hangs down every which way . . . and she *smells* . . . And you wouldn't believe what she brings back. Our house just looks crazy, Alan. I'm ashamed to bring people home . . . She's got plants everywhere drying out, I mean everywhere, not just a little bunch in a corner or something . . . but like she's got half a tree hanging upside down in the front hall. And one time she brought back this great big fish. I mean it was gigantic, Alan. Just this huge fish . . . And you know what she did? She went out into the garage and built some kind of contraption and *smoked* it! How do you think the neighbours liked that? And now we've got fish hanging all over the house . . . I mean can you believe it? Smoked fish hanging on the walls?

"And she won't eat meat anymore . . . doesn't even like to have it in the house. And when she's home, she cooks up these big incredible pots of gruel . . . this strange slop, and she expects me

18

to eat it. And whenever I have boys over . . . You know, boys like to meet your parents . . . I just don't know what to do. I don't know what she's going to say to them. She told this one boy . . . It's a good thing I didn't like him that much, eh? She told him he was in great danger. That's exactly what she said: 'You're in great danger.' She said he was 'leaking energy' . . . And I was upstairs getting dressed and wasn't even around so I could pass it off as a joke. And he said to me later, 'Hey, Sue, your mother's kind of a weirdo, isn't she?' I could have died . . ."

After he'd put Susan under the steamer, Alan went for his second cup of coffee of the morning. Passing Trish, he said into her ear, "I'm going to hang out a sign: Psychiatrist is in."

The day must be turning cold, he thought. The windows were steamed; he could no longer see outside. He sat down in the chair next to the Page. The girl's story had bothered him . . . well, not the story, rather that she had chosen to tell it to *him*, and in this setting. These oddly prescribed and stylized encounters with young girls were the emotional centre of his job (the pleasures of my occupation, he thought again), but that centre was proving to be hollow. He could not call up Susan tonight and ask her how she was getting along with her mother; she'd be horrified. He was not her friend, he was her hairdresser, and must stay in role. He didn't know how it was for them, but for him it was always sexual, at times uncomfortably sexual . . . even more than that, he had to admit, it was the closest he was getting to sex these days . . . celibate now for over a year.

It was much the same feeling that had finally paralyzed him in art school after he'd begun to produce a series of lovely and decorative Art Nouveau ladies, long-legged and boyish and iconic (and as well-dressed as fashion advertisements), and had found that he'd been falling in love with them, with his own drawings and watercolours. He'd dropped out, turned to a study of what the Vancouver Institute of Technology so charmingly called "Beauty Culture," thinking that if he were obsessed with the creation of beautiful objects, at least those objects should be alive. And the satisfaction in that had lasted; he still experienced it daily, and perhaps in the real world that satisfaction was the best he could ask for . . . impossible to do the only thing that would have genuinely satisfied him, to *be* one of those beautiful objects himself, a friend and sister, and at the same time, magically, to be able to sleep with them.

Returning, he said to Susan, "Did you think I'd forgotten you?"

"No," she said.

He unwound one of the rollers at the back of her neck. "Perfect," he said. He slid the steamer away, neutralized the perm solution, and began to remove the rest of the rods.

"I'm scared now," she said.

"It's perfect," he said. "It's going to be just fine."

He washed her hair, rinsed it with tomato juice to kill the smell of the chemicals, set her up before huge hot lights to let the hair dry naturally into curls, began to work through it with a wooden afro-comb, fluffing it. "Oh, wow," she said, staring into the mirror, watching her wet hair as it began to dry, to rise about her head, to assume the imagined and preconceived form. "Oh, wow. It's really strange."

"It's going to take a while to dry. And I've got to cut it a bit too . . . Do you want a magazine?"

"No. No, that's OK ... Alan?" He saw her eyes on him, in the mirror searching. "Could you . . .? Do you think you could . . . show me how to put on makeup?" He didn't answer immediately. "Do you do that sort of thing?" she said.

He smiled. "I'd be glad to, Susan. Don't worry, it's a gift . . . For your new image . . . OK, what do you want? Your face doesn't need much makeup, you know."

She frowned slightly. "But I wanted to see . . . If I really wanted to . . ."

"Oh, fancy, eh? All right." He looked at her thoughtfully. No, she doesn't want it complicated no matter what she says. I'll give her a sketch. He began to work quickly, sure of himself. "You don't need much of a foundation," he said, "you haven't got a line on your face . . . try a frosted moisturizer. You need to emphasize your cheekbones, here . . . go with your new hairdo . . ." Yeah, he thought, that's what she would have seen with this Orphan Annie hair, these highlighted misty-rose cheekbones. And the teenagers now seemed to be wearing their eyelids blue . . . OK . . . He painted her eyelids blue. "Could stand some mascara." he said, "Your eyelashes are quite pale . . . But never use black. It doesn't go with your colouring . . ." And red red lips, that's what she'd want. "Finish with gloss," he said, "so your lips shine . . ."

"You make it seem so easy," she said. She was staring at herself. "Nobody is going to know me."

He was combing through her hair again, lifting it . . . almost dry. It makes her look like a Flemish painting, he thought. Not that they wore their hair like that then, but something about the way it changes her face . . . and the lights behind her . . . Like a halo. She could be a Flemish angel . . . a little boy angel . . . painted. "Oh," she was saying. "It's incredible! Just incredible. I don't even know *myself* . . . It's kind of scary, eh?"

"Don't wash your hair for a few days," he said, "for a week if you can stand it . . . It'd take some of the curl out. After that it's OK."

"I think I really like it . . . Oh, I do! It's beautiful." He smiled at her. But he had to go. He had another customer. "Alan," she called after him, "what time is it getting to be?" He told her. "Oh, I'm really late now. I'm super late! I've got to get out of here . . ."

Later in the morning, going for his third and last cup of coffee of the day, Alan passed the reception desk and saw Susan's red plastic purse resting there where she had left it. Oh, damn, he thought. He picked it up, looked inside. There was her B.C. Med card, her Social Insurance card, her driver's licence, her Eaton's charge card, her chequebook. Her wallet contained nearly a hundred dollars. He felt an angry buzz of personal, proprietorial annoyance with her, as though she were his daughter. Oh Susan, he thought, you little nit! He stood a moment with the purse in his hands and then carried it into the back and stashed it with his coat.

"BOYS AND GIRLS."

"Hello . . ." A nervous laugh over the phone; cut off, it sounded like a hiccup. "Is that the librarian named Leslie?"

"Yes, this is Leslie Fraser."

"Oh . . . Well, I don't know whether you remember me or not, Miss Fraser. This is Amy Wagner . . . ? Jeanie's mother . . . ?" A pause while Leslie was invited to remember.

"Yes, I remember *Jeanie*."

"Well, I don't know quite how to put this . . ."

Oh God, Leslie thought, not on Saturday. Don't do this to me on Saturday. She had grabbed the phone from her desk on passing, on her way to the shelves with a small boy. The small boy had now decided he wanted to hang on to her right hand. "Is there something you wanted Jeanie to read?" Leslie asked the phone, her voice crisp.

"Well. yes . . . ," Mrs. Wagner answered brightly, and then hesitated. Leslie waited. The woman said finally, "Well, it's fairly complicated, Miss Fraser. Do you mind if I . . . ah . . . We only live over on Twenty-eighth . . . Do you mind if I come in and talk to you for a minute or two?"

"No, of course not." The small boy was tugging.

"Oh, that's marvellous. I won't take much of your time." The connection was broken.

Oh God, Leslie thought, not on Saturday. She banged the phone back into its cradle, sank to her knees so that her eyes were level with the boy's, and asked him gently: "What do you want now?"

He pressed his lips into her ear and said, "Snakes."

"Snakes is it? All right." She stood, took his hand, and led him to the shelves. "You might like this one," she said, drawing out a book for him, "and the rest of the snakes are all in here."

Ted was waiting for her at her desk, that uneasy I-want-something smile fixed on his face. He was wearing his most natty of blue meet-the-public suits; it was well-cut, disguised his spreading mid-section. Until a few days ago he'd worn a neatly trimmed full beard which had lent him a limited ursine dignity, but some misguided stylist, she thought, in that glossy men's salon he frequented, must have talked him out of part of it; he'd come back from his lunch hour with upper lip and chin shaved naked, left with huge fuzzy pinkish sideburns. The scrubbed hairless flesh at the dead centre of his face gave him, she thought, the rotund banality of an Anglund drawing . . . as though a parody of a little boy were peeking out of this man's head, bag-eyed and bald on top. It annoyed her that she should have so much difficulty seeing the person inside (and he seemed a genuinely nice person) because of her distaste for his physical presence.

Ted was the head librarian at the Sherwood Branch. And he was "interested" in her. She seemed incapable of rejecting him firmly, although she knew that it wouldn't take much of a rejection to do it, that he wasn't the sort to persist if she made her feelings plain. And he was also the sort who was going to keep after her if she didn't. Oh God, she thought, why can't I ever do anything . . . just simply do it? Why did it seem so much easier to look for another job? And, of course, she hadn't begun to look for another job either. It was like every other damn thing, like retiring from swimming or getting her hair cut, remained in some shadowy realm of intention. "Busy day?" he was saying.

"It's always bad on Saturdays. The rain seems to have cut it down a bit though."

"I've finished the display," he announced, grinning. "Do you want to see it?"

"Oh, Ted, not on Saturday. I'll see it on Monday."

"It'll just take a minute, eh?"

She looked at his round waiting face. No matter what I've planned to do, she thought, I always end up feeling sorry for him. And then I do what *he* wants . . . But I'm not going to sleep with him. "All right," she said and followed him into the adult department.

"I never feel right now leaving the Children's," she said, "not since I caught that little Henley boy peeing in the corner of the shelves." He looked at her quickly, inquisitively, and then laughed. And she was already regretting her words, thinking, now he has another piece of evidence that I'm "charmingly direct."

Ted seemed to classify people into a formal system of his own devising, as elaborate as Dewey Decimals. So far he had classified Leslie as "moral . . . in the old sense," "conservative . . . but in a good way," and most recently, "charmingly direct." She could see him doing it, a kind of internal click: "Ah, I know why you said that . . . It's because you're . . ." And any protest on her part would only give rise to another classification; every book has its number, no matter how elusive or arbitrary that number might be. Ted categorized himself as well, had told her that he was "a student of human nature."

Passing the main desk, they caught Susan drinking surreptitiously from a cup of coffee. Susan was a "page," that is, the lowest item on the totem pole of the library hierarchy, of all the nonprofessional staff the least professional and the least paid. And she wasn't supposed to be at the main desk either, must have been standing in for Norma who almost certainly must have been hiding somewhere away from the public eye to smoke a cigarette. Ted wiggled his finger at the girl, clicked his tongue. And she blushed. She dropped her pale blue eyelids, and the hot colour began at her throat, mounted her neck, filled her cheeks and ears and forehead. That pretty child's face, chastened and scarlet, rasped against something inside Leslie, irritated her like a burr. Don't just stand there and blush like a schoolgirl, she thought. And was startled to find unpremeditated in her imagination the picture of herself taking the girl's pert little head between her hands and banging it sharply, once, against the wall.

But here was Norma back again, grinning, old enough to be Ted's mother, bouncing energetically, in her tweeds, back to place. "Sorry," she yelled at Ted. She didn't sound sorry. And Susan fled to dump her forbidden cup of coffee in the washroom. Ted watched, stood surveying the library, "his" library, a look of puzzlement on his face. He'd lamented once to Leslie that he presided over "a gaggle of hysterical women," and she'd lit instantly into internal fury, thinking, the only reason you're a head librarian, you asshole, is because you're a man. But had said nothing.

Ted sighed. He led her to a table at the front of the library where he'd built a "British Columbia display." Books by B.C. authors were arranged in a ring around a map of the province. The places the authors had written about were marked with coloured pins, the pins connected with ribbons to the books they'd written. The wall behind the table was hung with reproductions of Emily Carr paintings.

"You forgot something, Ted," Leslie said. "You should have a sprinkler system at the top to spray the whole thing with water."

His face went blank a moment; then he laughed. "Oh, you're having me on, aren't you . . . You mean . . . the rain . . .?"

"Yes. The rain."

He laughed again. "That's a good one, Leslie . . . it really is . . . Well, do you like it?"

"It's a beautiful display, Ted." He was a great one for displays. At times he changed them as often as once a week: part of his campaign to make the branch library "relevant to the community." But Leslie had never noticed more than the most perfunctory interest by the people of the community who actually used the library: the teenagers who came to do their homework and flirt with each other, the housewives looking for Gothic novels or self-help books, the young husbands wanting something on home carpentry, and of course the children who came attempting to wheedle Leslie into doing their school assignments for them. It's an abysmally middle-class neighborhood, she thought. ". . . lovely display," she was saying, "but I've got to get back. You know what happens on Saturdays, all these mothers who want to drop off Johnny . . . just for a while, you know . . . 'Oh, don't worry. I'll be back in six hours, dear.' It's like a bloody daycare centre."

"Yes, I know you, Leslie," he said, "you think a library is a book repository." Another piece of evidence that she was "conservative . . . but in a good way."

A woman had just rushed into the library out of the British Columbia rain, stood inside the door folding her clear plastic umbrella. She wore a vibrating and harassed look as though she were in pursuit of something . . . or something were in pursuit of her: a strikingly handsome woman, somewhere in her early thirties, Leslie thought, wearing gloves and an impeccable white raincoat. Leslie didn't know how she knew it, but this, almost certainly, was Jeanie's mother. "Leslie . . ." Ted was saying, "how about dinner?"

"Dinner?" Leslie said vacantly.

"Yes. You know, dinner. You were planning to eat tonight weren't you?"

"Oh, Ted, I was up this morning at five-thirty."

"I'm a responsible guy. I'll get you home early."

She looked at the round pink face. "All right, Ted. OK . . . But there's a mother looking for me."

"I know that woman from somewhere," he said, frowning. "Must have met her at a party . . ." But Leslie, with a vague placating gesture, had already turned away. The woman was coming to meet her.

"Yes, I remember you. You must be Miss Fraser."

"That's right. Leslie Fraser. And you're Mrs. . . ."

"Wagner. Amy Wagner." The woman followed Leslie down to the children's department; she talked the entire way: "I'm sorry to bother you. I know Saturday must be a hard day for you. But I did so want to talk to you about Jeanie . . . she spends so much time here . . ."

"I know. This summer she was almost a member of staff."

"Yes, that's right. She's a great reader, and I certainly wouldn't want to do anything to . . . stop that. We're lucky I know . . . We've been lucky. So many children don't read at all. And that's never been the problem with Jeanie. Right from the first, as soon as she could read at all, she was just . . ." The woman stopped and laughed tensely. They'd arrived at Leslie's desk.

"What's the problem, Mrs. Wagner?" Leslie said.

The woman was carrying a huge navy-blue purse. She set it down on Leslie's desk, opened it and drew out the double-volume set of *The Juniper Tree*.

"Leslie . . . Do you mind if I call you Leslie? That's how I think of you. That's what Jeanie calls you. You'd be surprised how much she talks about you. Little girls, you know . . . well, get crushes on older women. I suppose you run into that a lot . . ." She stood, holding the books in her hand, hesitating.

"You don't like what Jeanie reads?" asked Leslie carefully.

"I'd be the last person to interfere with what she reads. I think it's important that a child has the freedom to pick and choose. My

27

husband and I have talked it over quite a bit . . . and we don't want to interfere with Jeanie's reading. I'm sure it would backfire, that she'd just . . . well, keep on to spite us. I don't know how well you know her, Leslie, but she's an amazing child. There are times when she gives me a look of such maturity . . . such, I don't know . . . that it frightens me. But then other times she's just a very little girl. That's the age, you know . . . twelve. Right on the edge . . . puberty."

"But something's been bothering you about what she's been reading?" Leslie tried it again.

"Well, it's hard to sort out. There are a number of things . . ." Mrs. Wagner stopped, smiled. Then she drew out one of the books, turned to the end of it and read:

> "My mother she butchered me,
> My father he ate me,
> My sister, little Ann Marie,
> She gathered up the bones of me
> And tied them in a silken cloth
> To lay under the juniper . . ."

She looked up searchingly at Leslie. Leslie said nothing. "And a few weeks ago," Mrs. Wagner said, "it was some unbelievably weird Eskimo story about people being chased across the snow-drifts by a gigantic penis . . ."

"Mrs. Wagner," Leslie said slowly, "it's there with children already. It's worse if they don't have any way to formalize it, any structure to give it . . ."

"Oh, I'm sure you're right, dear. You know better than I do, it's your profession. And I wouldn't want to interfere with Jeanie's reading . . . But does she have to read *so much of it!*" Leslie didn't answer. "I don't know how well you know Jeanie . . . but she's a sensitive child . . . an unbelievably sensitive child. All of her life she's had . . . well, what my mother called them were 'night terrors' . . . nightmares I suppose. Night after night she'd wake up screaming. It's finally stopped, thank God . . . but she's so sensitive . . ."

"But if it's stopped . . .?"

"But children being butchered and eaten? Being chased by a penis as big as a polar bear? All these strange old fairy tales and legends and stories . . . I'm sure she must pick some of the oddest old books you have in the library. Oscar Wilde. I didn't even know Oscar Wilde wrote for children . . . And some of the pictures. It's not that I want to interfere with her reading . . . But don't you think a twelve-year-old girl should have outgrown all this fairy tale business by now?"

"Some people never outgrow it," Leslie said. "They grow up and become anthropologists or folklorists . . . or they write children's books."

"I know, dear . . . But it isn't just her reading. It's . . . well, it's almost like she's a little female Peter Pan. She just doesn't want to grow up. And . . . well, when I was twelve I'd at least noticed by then that the other half of the human race was male . . . but Jeanie . . . Oh, she plays with the boys. She's a great one for that . . . We sent her to this progressive school this year, she was doing so badly in public school that we thought it might help . . . And it's a very progressive school. And she seems to spend all of her time playing soccer. We went to open-house, and one of the teachers said, 'Mrs. Wagner, your daughter is an absolute wonder playing soccer. I've never seen feet like that on a kid her age . . . not even on boys . . .' And I didn't know quite what to think. It was a compliment, I suppose. But she still can't add two and two and get four . . ."

Leslie had become suddenly angry; she was afraid it showed in her voice: "Mrs. Wagner, athletics never hurt a girl. I was a competitive swimmer and it was the most important experience I've ever had in my life. I'm all for girls in athletics."

Mrs. Wagner spread her hands. "Oh, yes. Of course, I agree with you completely. I was raised to be so . . . well, prissy and dainty and all that . . . and I can appreciate that girls have to . . ." Her words seemed to have run out. Then she started again: "Leslie, I guess it's a matter of balance. She can play all the soccer she wants if only . . . Well, for instance, it's a major campaign to get her into a dress. I mean jeans are OK, but all the time? I mean liberation is all well and good. I'm glad she's not growing up the way I did. But eventually she's going to have to . . . well, live in the real world."

"She's only twelve, Mrs. Wagner."

"Yes, I know . . . but . . . Leslie, are there any books about modern little girls?"

"There are hundreds of them."

"I don't want to interfere with Jeanie's reading, but . . . well, she respects you. I mean . . . well, she has a real crush on you . . . and if you . . ."

"If I suggested . . ."

"That's right. Some things about ordinary modern little Canadian girls."

"Do you want me to stop giving her fairy tales?"

"Oh no. Of course not. But if *along with them* . . ."

"All right, Mrs. Wagner. I'll do the best I can."

"Oh, thank you so much. It's such a relief to me . . . so glad I talked to you."

Leslie watched the woman walking away, out of the children's department. Oh God, she thought, will I ever be a mother? Will I ever be a mother *like that*?

LESLIE SAT NUMBLY AT HER DESK. It was nearly closing time; all of the children had gone home, and Leslie was doing nothing. But no, she thought, that's not right; I'm watching Susan shelve the books (our little page Susan), and that's something. She's learning to be a girl, Leslie thought, and felt again the diffuse thorny annoyance that had been bothering her all day. Usually Susan came to work sensibly in pants and those funny mary-janes the kids were wearing now, but today she'd appeared . . . two hours late . . . in a mini-dress, her ruddy hair all done up into tight curls like a moppet, her face painted and walking awkwardly in little blue shoes with heels like stilts . . . And Leslie had been aware for some time now that what she felt for Susan was not quite proper. The very quality she found annoying in the girl also attracted her: something pubescent and undefined, an adolescent vagueness . . . yet at the same time a hauntingly sexual effect like a picture from some disturbing old out-of-print, pre-Raphaelite children's book. But today Susan's sudden change in appearance had upset Leslie profoundly. She thought that the girl looked absurd . . . and cute. Yes, she had to admit it to herself . . . cute. Oh, God help me! Leslie thought.

The worst part of it was that Leslie didn't particularly like Susan Mackenzie . . . this slender willow-wand kid who had been girlish enough in pants and who now seemed to have set herself to learn all of the cute little tricks that Leslie had never learned. The first year or two of the seventies, Leslie had been almost comfortable, as though the times finally had been coming along to meet her; but now girlishness was "in" again, and for a kid of Susan's age, of her background, it had never been "out," was just something you'd come to naturally . . . growing up. Looking at Susan's long white legs, Leslie felt an echo of what she herself had gone through at fourteen when her classmates had been climbing into cutsie-pie mini-dresses and going Beatle-crazy: she'd both envied them and found them unbearably silly. There had been a lack of something in them . . . call it spunk or backbone or force . . . and it had infuriated her; she saw this same lack in Susan. It made her want to take the girl over her knee and give her a good spanking. But at the same time (and this was maddening) she was attracted to the cuteness that went with the lack, imagined hugging Susan and stroking her, undressing her and petting her. And then what? She couldn't imagine a genuine act of sex with a girl.

Leslie was not exactly a virgin, that is she'd gone to bed in a desultory fashion with a few boys, but for all the pleasure she'd felt, she might as well not have bothered. One of the boys, a fellow swimmer, had said to her: "My, you're an energetic girl, aren't you . . . You're *so active*." It had not been a compliment. She hadn't liked him particularly, hadn't seen him after that, but still, years later, his comment rankled. What the hell had he expected . . . for her to lie there like Sleeping Beauty? The experience must have hurt her pretty badly; she'd fallen back onto the bed, cold and stiff and dry, let him do what he wanted . . . which had turned out to be not much of anything. And she'd thought that once again she'd stumbled upon the evidence of a secret knowledge that everyone else seemed to have absorbed naturally and she'd never learned. And so, after a series of stupid, fumbling, unpleasurable experiences, she'd stopped trying. That's what she seemed to have done, celibate now for over a year.

She had always thought that she had values. Her dad had been a big one for values: thriftiness, hard work, punctuality, responsibility, doing one's duty no matter how unpleasant. And athletics. What matters is how you play the game; no matter what you're doing, you do your very best. But now what was happening to her values? . . . We with our values collapsing . . . You let yourself slip into being a single middle-aged library lady, If that's what it takes to maintain your values. You drift into ordinariness. But if you have values, you don't entertain sexual fantasies about your pages.

Susan had made it to the far end of the shelves; Leslie pulled her focus back to the catalogue in front of her, found a presence out of the corner of her eye . . . and looked. Jeanie was sitting on the edge of her desk. She had no idea how long the little girl might have been there. "Hi, Leslie," Jeanie said.

"Hi, Jeanie," Leslie said. It was an effort to put her mind back in order.

There was nothing ambiguous in her liking for this child—straightforward and clean and simple—refreshing now when most things in Leslie's life seemed to have turned ambiguous, the most ordinary of her mental possessions grown double-headed, transfigured as though in a demonic fairy tale, for each familiar face another one beneath, snaky and sharp with an unpredictable bite. She'd liked Jeanie simply and unreservedly from the first time the child had walked into the library last summer . . . with her cut-off jeans and ratty sneakers, her short ragged blond hair, and small elf face like a Rackham child. Then, for nearly ten minutes, Leslie had taken her for a boy.

"My mom came to see you today, didn't she?" the girl said.

"Yes, she did."

"She thinks I'm reading too many fairy tales, doesn't she?"

"Yes, that's what she said." Leslie began to laugh. "How did you know?"

"Elementary," the little girl said gravely. "I heard her talking to Dad. Did she tell you to stop giving me fairy tales?"

"No, she just told me to try to get you to read some books about modern little girls."

Jeanie's face spread slowly into a small wicked smile. "OK," she said. "You can give me some to take home, but I don't have to read them, do I?"

Leslie laughed again. "No, you don't have to read them."

"I'll leave them around where she can see them. That'll take care of her . . . What did she tell you about me? Did she tell you I was sensitive?"

"Oh, Jeanie, you're incredible! Yes, she said you were sensitive."

"I'm not sensitive," the girl intoned slowly. "I'm a changeling."

And then she burst into a fit of giggles, jumped off the desk. "Come on, Leslie, find me something *good!*"

"It's two minutes to closing time. You know that?"

"I know that. That's why you've got to hurry! Come on . . . Come on, Leslie!"

"All right . . . Here we go, flat out." Leslie jumped up and ran to the shelves, the child laughing beside her. "OK, how about Lang's books, the coloured ones?"

"Read them."

"All of them?"

"Yeah . . . *all* of them."

"*The Hobbit?*"

"Read it."

"*The Golden Key?*"

"Read it."

"*At the Back of the North Wind?*"

"Read it."

"Come on, Jeanie, you're impossible."

"Find me some stories with poems in them."

"Poems?"

"Yeah poems. You know." The child began to recite:

"The Red Ettin of Ireland
Once lived in Ballygan,
And stole King Malcolm's daughter,
The king of fair Scotland.
He beats her, he binds her,
He lays her on a band;
And every day he dings her
With a bright silver wand . . ."

Leslie was stopped, unable to speak. Deep inside her there was something odd. Like a ghost of a memory . . . or a reflection of a memory. "Yeah," she said finally, "I know what you want . . . but I don't know exactly . . . Oh, Jeanie, can't you come in after school Monday?"

"Oh, all right."

"For now let me give you a Mother Goose . . . a good one, a big one . . ."

"Mother Goose! That's baby stuff . . ."

"No, really, Jeanie . . . There are some wonderful things in it." She'd found the book, begun to flip through it. "Like this:

Grey goose and gander,
Waft your wings together,
Carry the good king's daughter
Over the two-strand river."

Jeanie was looking up. Her grey-green eyes seemed amazed. "Read it again," she said. Leslie read it again. "OK, Leslie," she said, "I'll take it. And now you'd better give me some of those modern ones too." She giggled. "For . . . my mother."

"It's all right, Susan, I can take you all the way home."

"No, Leslie . . . No, really . . . Just here at the corner is fine."

Leslie pulled over and the girl began to climb out. "Thanks," Susan said, "see you Monday . . . Or is it Tuesday I come in again . . .?"

"You'd better find out, kid," Leslie said, laughing. Susan giggled and slammed the car door. Leslie made a U-turn at the end of the tree-lined street and began to drive home. That was my father's voice, she thought: "You'd better find out, kid." She was alarmed at herself; since when had she started calling people "kid"?

She threaded her way slowly back into the rush-hour traffic. Dark now going home, the turning of the year, she thought . . .

winter coming, the dark season. Susan had left a strong perfume that was lingering inside her little Datsun . . .

And she was passing that strange shop, the Page of Cups; there it was on the other side of the street. Here on her side, directly in front of her, was a parking space. She slid the car into it and sat there a moment looking across the street. Then she turned off the engine, slowly withdrew the key and held it in her hand. It's either blind sudden impulse, she thought, or it will never happen. She jumped out of the car, arrived in a rush at the door of the shop, nearly bumped into a boy who was leaving . . . caught only the most fleeting glimpse of his face . . . an astonishingly beautiful boy . . . but no, it was a girl: she was carrying a red plastic purse over her shoulder . . . And then Leslie, disoriented and somewhat frightened with herself, was inside.

"I'm sorry, dear," the man said, "we're closed." He was, obviously, on the point of leaving, pulling on a grey overcoat.

"I'll be glad to make you an appointment," said the woman. She had gypsy-dark hair, set into a rather elaborate arrangement resurrected from the thirties . . . a fashion-plate lady, painted, in a grey dress and shoes with heels that looked to Leslie painfully high.

The man kissed the woman languidly on the forehead, said, "Tara, love," and casually passed through the door. And the woman was looking at Leslie.

She's studying me, Leslie thought."What is it you wanted?" the woman said. And Leslie felt a sudden inexplicable panic. Her mouth had gone dry.

"I just . . ." She patted her head. "I just wanted a hair cut."

"Trim?" the woman said.

"No, a real haircut . . . nothing fancy. No set or anything. Just a haircut . . . short . . ."

"How short?"

"Oh, very short." And she laughed. She heard the laugh, detached, as though it were still there in the air, scratchy and tense.

"You don't mean a perm, do you, dear? One of those Little Orphan Annie things?"

"No. No, just a haircut."

It seemed to Leslie that the woman didn't speak for an interminably long time, stood tapping her pink painted fingernails on the open appointment book. Then the woman smiled. She seemed to have decided something. "Come on, love," she said, "I'll do you now. If you want what you say you want, it won't take me fifteen minutes."

But Leslie had decided that she didn't want her hair cut after all; she wanted to run out the door and drive away as fast as she could. She followed the woman through the open archway, allowed herself to be fitted with a pink plastic bib and tilted backwards in a chair, her head into a sink. "My name's Tricia," the woman said.

"Hi . . . I'm Leslie." Strong fingers were massaging her scalp.

And then she was in another chair, facing a disquietingly bright mirror, her hair hanging wetly. "I look like a drowned rat," she said. Her voice had come out tiny and girlish.

"Are you new in town, honey?" Tricia was saying.

"Oh, no. I've lived here all my life."

"Oh . . . Well, now let's see, love, let me make sure I've got it exactly right. You said you wanted it short . . . very short . . . not just a shorter shag. Is that right, love?"

"Yes. Very short."

"I want to make sure I know what you mean before I start to cut, love. Do you want it very short and *masculine*?"

Leslie felt her stomach contract. "Oh no, not masculine . . . I mean . . . well, maybe a bit boyish . . . tomboyish or something . . . but not masculine."

"I understand now, love. I know what you want . . . Yes, you're right, dear . . . get rid of that shag. Nobody wears a shag anymore. Yes, I see. How about bangs? Bangs are back . . . the old Beatle is coming back again . . . that could be quite elegant on you, love . . .

Oh, no . . . I know what you want." She had been combing while she'd been talking; now she began to cut. "Something like a little English school boy . . . a Prince Charlie we called it when I was a kid . . . That's going to suit your face . . . good bones, a bit like Audrey Hepburn, very lean . . . I suppose you've heard that before, love."

Leslie laughed. "Yeah, believe it or not, I have heard that before . . . but not since I was a girl." Leslie's hair was beginning to come off alarmingly fast. Some of it was falling onto her plastic-covered lap, long wet strands. They seemed like very long strands.

". . . layer it to make it fluff," Tricia was saying. "You're not much for fancy stuff are you, love . . . You seem a bit of a nature girl to me . . ."

"What?" Leslie said.

"Oh sets and perms, you know . . . I envy you a bit, you know, envy girls like you . . . but different strokes for different folks, as we say. Have you been down to the Clear Crystal?"

"To the what . . . ?"

"Oh, I thought maybe you had. It's just a bar. Maybe you'd enjoy it, I didn't know . . . down on Pender . . ."

"What are you doing?"

"Just shaving your neck, dear. Don't worry, love, you're going to come out just fine. I know what you want."

"OK," Leslie said, "I believe you."

Their eyes met in the mirror. "You really can trust me, love."

Leslie watched, fascinated, in the mirror as her wet hair began to rise around her face, into place, into "a style." "Don't suppose you're much for hair spray, are you, love?" Tricia was saying.

"No," Leslie answered automatically. But she'd stopped paying attention to the other woman's voice; she couldn't stop looking at herself.

"There, dear, isn't that what you wanted?" Tricia handed Leslie a mirror, spun the chair so that she could see the back, then the sides, then the front again. Tricia continued to fuss with her, brushing the small wisps at the side into place . . . like a little boy's sideburns.

Leslie was horrified. She didn't know what to say. But she kept looking, and gradually, in some highly peculiar way, she felt the horror fading away into delight. "I didn't realize how much it would change me," she said finally. She had straight bangs and little sideburns, a smooth fluff of hair at the crown of her head . . . sharp taper into the neck. It was both wonderfully bizarre and wonderfully beautiful. She looked like a young pretty boy. "It isn't what I imagined, but I think I like it," she said.

"It will take some getting used to, love," Tricia said. "But it suits you. Believe me. You're just too beautiful for words, dear." She whisked the plastic bib away, spilling hair. "Don't let it go so long next time. Make an appointment though. But come in again. I'll always take good care of you, love. I really will."

IT'S RIDICULOUS, SUSAN THOUGHT, ABSOLUTELY RIDICULOUS! Have to get people to drop you at the end of the block so they won't see your house. She stopped walking. There, parked in front, was her mother's camper. Perfect, absolutely perfect! She's back . . . back from wherever the hell it is she goes. Why couldn't she have waited until Monday! If she's going to be gone for days at a time, she could at least be gone when it'd be some help. That's not too much to ask, is it? She was tempted to turn around and walk away. She could call Bill from a restaurant downtown and tell him to meet her there. He wouldn't even think there was anything strange about it. But her feet hurt from wearing heels all day and she wanted to change. Oh, damn, she thought. Damn!

Susan knew every family on this block; this is where she'd grown up. Oh, what they must think of us now! Even strangers must know that weirdos live here . . . the lawn in front grown up waist-high like a bloody green Jungle, and mushrooms popping up along

39

the walk . . . does she expect *me* to cut it? Johnny always cut it. I never had to cut it . . . girls shouldn't have to cut grass. And then Daddy cut it. And now nobody cuts it. Does she expect me to cut it? Does she care? Well, I'd help her cut it, but I'm not going to cut it all by myself . . . grown all summer long. And the back yard was worse. The back yard looked like a bunch of drunken Indians had moved in. Not only gone to wilderness back there, the roses unpruned and unsprayed and thorny and ripped apart by rose rot, and no little flowers planted the way they had always been . . . but high swaying grass and strange weeds and vines, a haven for slugs and for forty-million neighbourhood cats who played tag with each other at night, yowling. And a dump for her mother. The old camper tires dumped. The big tent dumped. Boxes and cartons dumped and rotting in the rain.

She'd gone out with a beach towel one hot day at the height of summer and hadn't been able to find any place to spread it out. She'd stood and looked at the dump. Right there where they'd played croquet when she'd been a kid . . . now the dump. And Mr. Laing next door had leaned over the fence and said, "Bit of a mess, eh?" She'd been so embarrassed that she hadn't been able to answer, had only been able to bob her head up and down. "How's your mother?" he'd asked her. Everyone knew about Mother.

"Oh, she's still pretty broken up, eh?"

"Well, that's it." The sympathetic neighbours. They'd all come when Daddy had died. They'd brought food. They'd gathered in the living room and smiled kindly at her mother who'd sat there stiffly and stared straight ahead. But how long would they remain sympathetic as the grass grew higher and the mushrooms popped up by the hundred and the dump got dumpier?

She hesitated at the door. It was dark and blowing and cold and felt like rain again. And why couldn't everything be the way it used to be? Why couldn't she walk in and find her mother perfectly normal with a normal dinner cooking on the stove? Oh, damn! She folded her umbrella and pushed into the house. And right there, just in the hallway, things had been dumped. A heap of clothes, the small tent (all wet), and God knows what else. I'm going to come in here one day, she thought, and there's going to be a dead deer in the hallway. Just like the Eskimos up north when they started building houses for them and they didn't know any better and they'd just drag a dead deer into the hallway. Oh God! She dumped her umbrella on the dump, slid out of her raincoat, and hung it on the hook in the hall closet. She walked into the kitchen and there was her mother cooking something. It smelled like hell.

"Hello, Mom," she said.

"Oh . . . hello, Sue."

"What are you cooking, Mom?"

"Oolichans."

"Oolichans?"

"Yes . . . You know, dear . . . candlefish."

Fish, yes, that was the wretched smell. There were hundreds of the shiny little bastards lying in a heap, all silver and fishy and stinking, and her mother was throwing them into one of her huge heavy iron frying pans and frying them up, heads and eyes and tails and all. Her mother had thrown out all of the old cook-ware, all of the pots and pans they'd grown up with. She'd said that aluminum and stainless steel and teflon were poisonous . . . *poisonous* of all things! Now she'd only cook in iron or glass. The pots and pans she'd thrown away must have been worth hun-dreds of dollars.

"Well, Sue, how are you doing?" her mother said.

She never calls me Susie anymore . . . not even Susan. "Oh, just lovely, Mother." What does she care? I could have boys in here every night she was gone and sleep with them and she wouldn't care. I could have pot parties. I could sleep with hundreds of boys, one right after the other, and she wouldn't care.

Mrs. Mackenzie carried a heaped plate to the table—brown rice and strange pea-green greens and those awful little fish—pushed the bundle of leaves out of the way, and sat down. "Are you hungry, Sue?"

"No."

Once her mother had been like other mothers. Once her mother had worn nice dresses and nylons (and shaved her legs!). She used to go up to the corner and get her hair done. She used to keep her nails all nice. And now look at her, in those old sleazy jeans and Dad's smelly Cowichan sweater, her hair hanging down, and wearing gumboots in the house. Susan's eyes filled with tears.

"Sue, dear . . ." her mother said, and reached out to touch her hand. But Susan pulled away, stood up and leaned against the wall. She could feel the tears running down her cheeks; they gave her a strange satisfaction: Look, see what you're doing to me! This had happened before. "Sue, dear, it's never going to be the way it was."

"Oh, Mother . . . Mother, just look at you!"

Her mother shook her head and laughed. That crazy silly laugh. She never used to laugh like that. How can she laugh when I'm crying? "Sue . . . Oh, dear Sue . . . You're going to have to get used to me. Sit down, dear. Don't run away now. Sit down a minute, eh?" Susan sat down. "Tell me what you've been doing," her mother said.

"What do you think I've been doing? I've been going to school. I got a perm and you didn't even notice!"

"Of course I noticed."

"No, you didn't notice. You didn't say anything."

"I'd have to be blind, dear, not to notice. It's a pretty big change."

"Well, do you like it?"

"Of course I like it."

She doesn't care, Susan thought. She stood up again. "Are you going to be around for a while, Mother?"

"I don't know."

Susan stood a moment, looking. Somewhere inside this crazy old woman is my mother. But where? Susan turned and fled from the kitchen. She ran upstairs, shut herself in her room, unbuckled her shoes, kicked them into the closet, and threw herself onto the bed. She was crying again.

When she stopped crying, she was angry. I'll show her!, she thought. Looking in the mirror, she saw that her makeup was faded and smeared. But she didn't bother to take any off, just put on new over the top. Then she stripped off dress and bra, put on a sheer white blouse and the new jeans she hadn't worn out of the house yet . . . they were the smallest size she'd been able to get herself into. She grabbed the heels she'd just taken off, jammed her feet into them, and buckled the straps. She looked at herself in the full-length mirror. No, she thought. I look too trashy. I can't do it . . . Yes, I can . . . No, I can't. She frowned, unable to decide. But finally . . . No, I can't. She changed the heels for boots, put her bra on again, looked . . . OK, that's enough. Now I'll tell her I'm going out. That's all I'm going to say.

She was halfway down the stairs before she realized that she didn't have her purse. She hadn't brought it home with her. She hadn't had it all day. Oh damn, where is it? I can't ask her for money. She ran back upstairs and into her mother's room. Loose bills and change lay on the dresser the way they always did. She took a ten, pushed it into her jeans, and ran downstairs. Her mother was still eating. "I'm going out, Mom," she said, breathless.

"All right, Susan." Her mother was looking up at her; she didn't seem to have any expression at all.

"I . . . I don't know when I'll be in."

43

"All right."

And Susan was running up the street, crying. She doesn't care! she thought. She doesn't care if I stay out all night. She doesn't care who I'm going to see. She doesn't care what I'm wearing . . . how I do my hair. She stopped at the corner. It was raining. She didn't want to be going off into this cold night alone to eat in a restaurant.

What a terrible world it is, she thought, where things can change so fast . . . She wanted to bring back everything that had gone, her brother from Toronto, and her father from the grave and her mother back to what she'd been before . . . When she'd been normal, when she'd cared. It seemed impossible to Susan now that she'd once resented her mother for that very caring, that she'd once wanted her mother simply to let her alone. But now she'd gladly put up with it again . . . with having to keep her room neat, and twelve o'clock curfew, and silly rules about what she could or couldn't wear . . . if only things could be the way they were before.

THE OLD WOMAN OPENED THE DOOR AND STOOD, WAITING. She said nothing. On the walk over Alan had been rehearsing what would happen. Susan would open the door and be surprised to see him. He would hand her the purse and step back, careful not to give the impression he was paying her a visit. He would smile and say, "You should be careful where you leave this," or something similar, anything would do. And: "I was on my way home, thought you might be needing it." She would giggle, thank him. He'd ask her how she liked her hair . . . a further exchange of pleasantries, and he'd wave and walk away. But Susan hadn't answered the door. The old woman must be her mother. "Mrs. Mackenzie?" he said.

She didn't speak or nod or make any affirmative gesture, merely stepped back out of the doorway providing him the space to walk through. He hesitated. "Susan left her purse . . ." he said.

She didn't answer. And he was still wearing the purse over his shoulder, as he'd carried it. He felt, suddenly, that he'd done something unbearably foolish. He slid the purse off his shoulder and extended it to her in his hand. She did not move to take it. She gestured with her head: Come in. But he felt an inexplicable reluctance to step through the door. "I did Susan's hair this morning," he said. "She left her purse . . . Susan does live here, doesn't she?"

"Yes." She isn't staring, he thought, rather looking at me carefully and closely. Most of her hair had gone white, but her eyebrows were still black, black and bushy; they gave her face the tense air of menace that had been bothering him. He could see how they did it, knew exactly how they'd have to be plucked to destroy the effect; the discovery was a relief. He didn't know how long he'd been holding his breath, but he exhaled slowly, and stepped through the door. What she did next was so unexpected that it froze him: moving with uncanny speed for a woman of her age, she stepped past him and slammed the door in a single forceful movement. The sound of it was still in his ears, and he was pinned, not physically but by her proximity (he was drawing back) against the wall. She was staring directly into his face; her eyes in the half-light of the hall were so dark that they seemed all pupil. He gasped, pushed the purse at her as though it were a shield. She didn't take it, looked at him a moment longer and then turned and walked away down the hall. "You haven't eaten," she said matter-of-factly.

He waited a moment and then followed her into the kitchen. "Are you Mrs. Mackenzie?" he said. "Are you Susan's mother?"

"Yes," she said. "I'm Mildred Mackenzie." The kitchen was steamy and warm; the smells were strong and pungent, unfamiliar. He hadn't realized how hungry he was. "Mrs. Mackenzie," he said, "Susan left her purse this morning . . ."

And finally she acknowledged the purse. She took it from him, held it a moment, and then set it on the table. "Where do you live?" she said.

"In Kits."

"No, no . . . I mean exactly where." He told her. She nodded. "How did you get here?"

"I walked."

"Do you do a lot of walking?"

"Yes. The bus connections are so screwy it's almost quicker . . ."

"Good. Sit down. Here . . . I'll move this stuff . . . Sit down. So it was out of your way, was it?"

"Yes . . . it was . . ."

"Did you think Susan wouldn't remember?"

"Well, I thought she'd remember, but . . . Mrs. Mackenzie, there's nearly a hundred dollars in that purse."

She didn't answer. She looks puzzled, he thought. She was standing in front of the stove, poised as though she were waiting for something to happen. Her eyes had pulled away from him, had gone soft as though they'd lost focus. Her lips were moving. And now he had time to look at her. In the doorway she'd seemed eighty to him, but that was wrong, an illusion of the light. She must be in her sixties. Her hair was three distinct colours as carefully delineated as if it had been streaked: a few remaining strands of black, a dull pewter-grey, and white . . . an old person's white, turning pale srtaw-yellow like a spreading tobacco stain. And very long hair, worn like a young girl's, parted in the middle and hanging almost to her waist. He found something obscene in it: that ancient uncared-for hair hanging so freely.

She was not fat, but rather sturdy, as tall as he was and maybe forty pounds heavier. Her huge pendulous breasts hung without a bra inside an old dirty grey knit sweater She wore immense faded jeans and gumboots. The jeans were tucked into the top of one boot but had fallen out of the other and fell, wrinkled, to the floor. Her hands were broad, massively veined and spotted with age; the fingers were short and blunt, the nails cracked and dirty. And he'd begun to recover himself, be amused at the moment of terror he'd felt in the hallway. She's just an eccentric old lady, he thought, must be kind to her.

She looked at him again. She has a curious dignity, he thought. Her nose was huge, both broad and prominent, and her face was deeply wrinkled, but her eyes seemed alert and kindly now, even beneath the thick, unpleasantly furry eyebrows. And he was amazed at her ear. She'd pushed her hair back, shaking her head, and a single incredible ear had become visible. It was the largest ear Alan had ever seen in his life, the lobe as big as a thumb, the concentric whirls sculptured and solid. I'd love to paint her, he thought, seeing her as an early Van Gogh, a figure from "The Potato Eaters" . . . that aggressively substantial ear. "How far do you walk then?" she said.

"I don't know." He laughed. "I walk to work and I walk home."

"A couple of miles a day?"

"I suppose so."

"And what else do you do?"

"Do? . . . What do you mean?"

"To keep fit, eh?" She laughed, the wrinkles on her face spreading apart, showing momentarily, like flat dried beans, brown teeth, undoubtedly her own. He laughed with her, felt the last of that strange foreboding dissolve. She was turning out to be some dotty harmless grandmother.

"I take dance classes," he said.

And she was still laughing. Nothing that had happened was funny enough to merit that much laughter. She actually had tears in her eyes. She wiped them away. "How many?"

"Three a week."

"What kind?"

"Ballet."

"How long have you been doing that?"

"I started in college. It's been . . . oh, about six or seven years."

"And it's pretty strenuous, eh?"

"Oh yeah, pretty strenuous."

She was giggling, snorting and snuffling. She fished a man's handkerchief out of her jeans and blew her nose. "Oh my," she said.

He was fully relaxed now, leaning back in the kitchen chair, smiling sympathetically at her. And then he was crouched, halfway to his feet, hearing the chair bang as it fell behind him. She had crossed the floor so quickly it seemed as though the passage of time had been lost; he was still remembering her standing there blowing her nose, except that now she was leaning over him, her eyes a few inches from his face. She'd seized his hair, swept it back from his head and held it. With her other hand she framed his face, holding his jaws. "What are you?" she yelled at him.

"I don't know!" he said. She let go of him and he hung there, crouched, panting. His mind was totally void of any usable thought.

"Ah . . . ah . . ." she said, and began to stroke his shoulders as though gentling a horse. Still vibrating with shock, he straightened himself and stood. He could smell her: something sour like old mouldy bread.

Then she grabbed his stomach; her broad strong fingers digging into the muscles . . . a searing shock of pain. He doubled up. He yelled, or tried to.

And he was crouching on the floor under the end of the kitchen table. He didn't know how much time had passed. He seemed incapable of moving. He heard someone, a woman, humming. She was setting the table, bringing food. He could smell an unusual pungent spice. ". . . and what do they do?" the woman's voice said.

"They're both married," he said.

"I was married for almost forty years," she said. She picked up the chair where it had fallen, stood it upright, and invited him to sit. He climbed to his feet and sat down on it. "Did you get along with your sisters?" she said.

"Oh, yeah, I always liked my sisters. Especially Betty . . . the younger one . . ." Everything seemed perfectly ordinary to him except that everything wasn't perfectly ordinary. For one thing he didn't know where he was or who this old woman was. But it must be all right. It seemed as though he was about to have dinner. They must have been chatting. But why had he been crouched on the floor?

The old woman sat down on the other chair. She lifted the cover from an iron Dutch oven, with a wooden spoon dished a peculiar concoction of grains and vegetables onto his plate. "What happened to your husband?" he said.

"He had a heart attack and died," she said.

"I'm sorry."

She served herself, pushed a bread board to him . . . a half loaf of a dense blackish bread. He found that he was immensely hungry. "We loved each other very deeply," she said.

He began to eat. The food tasted good. He kept glancing up at the old woman, trying to remember who she was. There was a red plastic purse on the table; it irritated him. He seemed to remember carrying it somewhere, but he wouldn't do that, carry a purse around on the street. The old woman must have noticed the direction of his eyes. "Susan isn't here tonight," she said.

"Oh," he said. He could remember doing Susan's hair, could see her clearly the way she'd looked when he'd finished, her head framed in a mass of curls. He was becoming increasingly puzzled with his disorientation. His mind seemed perfectly clear, just that the important events of some important time sequence were gone. But it must be all right. He was eating dinner. And the old woman was Susan's mother, of course, Mrs. Mackenzie. "Did you like Susans hair?" he said.

She laughed. She seems like a kindly old lady, he thought, if a little bit eccentric. "Oh, I'm too far away from all that now," she said. "Susan was pleased . . . You enjoy your work, don't you?"

"Yes, I do."

"And you're good at it, eh?"

"Yes, I am."

"That's good," she said, and laughed again. "Alan," she said, "I want you to listen to me. You haven't known what you've been doing, but you've gone a certain way on your own . . . just by feeling your way along, eh? You've become much lighter. Do you understand me?"

He looked at her, puzzled. "I think so," he said.

"But you've got to stop eating animal fats. This is very important. You can eat fish. Particularly shellfish. If you can get fresh crab, that's good for you to eat. And clams. And you must eat grains, but not too much, do you understand? You must stop eating regular meals at regular times. You must eat only when you're hungry, and then only small amounts. Avoid things that were not grown here. Oranges . . . don't eat oranges. They belong in another place. They don't belong here. Do you understand me?"

"I think so."

"Clams . . . Clams are particularly important for you, I don't know why, but they are. I'll give you some jars I put up . . . And later you'll learn what you can eat in the bush. The plants will tell you about themselves. We're each different, and we have to learn different ways. I must eat thistles and stinging nettle. For you it will be something else . . ."

He was staring at her. And the lost events were suddenly there: her hand on his stomach, the shock of it. He jumped to his feet, heard himself screaming.

He stood, ready to run. He could feel the skin surface of his entire body tingling. "It's all right, Alan," she said. "Sit down."

He sat down very slowly. Her voice seemed dreamy. Somehow it calmed him. "I couldn't believe it either," she said, "when it happened to me. They were the things that happen in books, that happen to other people, eh? Or maybe they were all stories . . . myths. I came from the prairies, and B.C. never seemed right to me, it never seemed as though this is what things should look like. But it fascinated me. It drew me into it. And I was a great reader of the Indian stories . . . and then I found that they weren't stories . . ."

He stood again. "I think I've got to go," he said.

She pushed herself to her feet. She seemed ponderous and slow, an ancient stiff old woman. From the jumble on the shelves, she selected four jars of clams, set them into a paper bag, rolled the top down and handed it to him. "Come back when you're ready," she said.

"GOOD GOD, LESLIE!" Ted had sprung up so quickly that he'd almost dumped his chair; he caught it on the way down, slowly set it again on its feet.

"What's the matter?" she said.

He rushed around to help her off with her coat. "It's incredible, Leslie," he said. "I saw you come in . . . just glanced up and saw you, eh? . . . in the doorway. And I thought you were a boy. Isn't that funny?"

"That's ridiculous. I've got a skirt on." She felt prickly and defensive. After getting her hair cut, she should have driven directly to the restaurant. Instead she'd gone home, changed out of her working clothes (a bland conservative pantsuit), studied herself in the mirror, and then, for the first time in months, had put on a skirt and pantyhose and dress shoes.

"I know," he said. "It really is ridiculous. But I wasn't looking down . . . I was just . . . I saw your face on the other side of the room . . . and that long raincoat . . . and I didn't . . ." He shrugged. "What have you done to your hair?"

"I've had it cut," she said. Oh God, she thought, what *have* I done? Am I going to have to start wearing makeup and earrings until it grows in again? She felt an absurd mix of anger and self-pity, a kind of pouty heel-kicking petulance as though she were nine, had just done something daring and fun and naughty, and now were being punished for it. Leslie did not enjoy feeling like a child. "Will you stop staring at me!" she said.

Ted had been leaning out of his chair, craning around the end of the table. Now he snapped back as if he'd been stung. "Oh, sorry . . . It's just that . . . You know, Leslie, I've never seen your legs before."

And you're goddamned well never going to see them again, she thought. "I'm sorry I'm late," she said.

"Oh, that's all right . . . no harm done. I *did* order for us . . . but the service is very slow here . . . Food's excellent, though . . . It is silly, Leslie . . . must have been just a momentary illusion, the light or something. You're certainly every inch a woman."

Ted, stop it! she was screaming inside herself.

". . . haven't seen that hair style for a few years," he was saying, "but it suits you. Very elegant. I didn't realize what a fine long neck you have."

"Yeah," she said, "like Audrey Hepburn."

"Now that you mention it, the resemblance . . ."

"What did you order?"

"Crêpes . . . Is that all right? It might not be too late to change it." His worried pink face peering across the table. Oh God! she thought.

"No, that's fine."

"I thought, a bottle of wine . . ."

"You know I don't drink."

"Not at all?"

"Not at all."

"You're the last of the good strong old-fashioned women, Leslie . . . a really refreshing conservatism . . . Do you mind if I smoke?"

"Oh Christ, go ahead and smoke!"

"Are you all right? You seem a little upset . . ."

"I'm not upset!"

"Oh . . . sorry . . ."

"Well, I am a little upset."

He was sucking on the cigarette. That's what I've heard, she thought, why people smoke . . . something to do with their hands. She dropped *her* hands onto her lap. And she had a skirt on . . . was sitting upright with her knees together and her hands folded primly on her lap. She immediately rested her elbows on the table, folded her hands together, and rested her chin on them. That didn't help either.

"What's the matter?"

"Beauty salons upset me. It's like taking your life in your hands to go in there . . . don't know what they're going to do to you." He didn't say anything. Close your mouth, Ted, she thought, or something will fly into it . . . It was a remark of her father's. "I just wanted it cut short," she said, "for swimming . . ."

"Oh, you do that, don't you?"

"Yes, I do that."

The waiter brought their crêpes, laid the plates disdainfully down on the table. "This is an odd place, isn't it?" Ted said. "Have you noticed how they're all men . . . not a woman working here?" He leaned forward across the table, said conspiratorially, "I think they're all homosexuals."

"Oh?" she said, and began to eat.

Eventually Ted broke the silence, announced his intention to speak by a small clearing of the throat. "You don't smoke and you don't drink and you swim every day," he said, "and you go to bed early . . . How did . . . Well, how did you manage to live your twenty-four years so untouched?"

What on earth is that? she thought. How did he know I was twenty-four? Oh, it's on my job application. "I don't know what you mean," she said.

"Well, this crazy modern world . . . you know . . . and you seem so untouched by it."

"Yeah, I'm straight as a pin if that's what you mean. It wasn't until this year that I'd even been to a party where people were smoking marijuana, and I was so naive I didn't know what it was."

"What did you do?" His eyes were bright with curiosity.

"I went home . . . It wasn't just the marijuana . . . It was dark and smoky, and the music was too loud, and I was tired. And it just seemed so pointless."

"You know, I don't know much about you . . ."

Oh, Jesus! "There's not much to know, Ted. The only thing out of the ordinary about me is that I held a world record once."

"Oh, did you? I didn't know that."

"Yeah, for a little less than a week . . . And then the girl who'd held it all along broke it again. That's my only claim to fame. I didn't even make the Olympics that year . . ."

"I didn't know you were that good."

"I wasn't that good. I just told you. I didn't make the Olympics."

"No . . . I mean . . . well, most people don't even come close."

"Close only counts in horseshoes," she said. Her father's maxim. "I peaked too soon . . . The funny thing is that I went to Mexico City when I was eighteen . . ."

"What?"

"Mexico City's where the Olympics were in '68. And that one was just a lark. It was just another swim meet for me. I knew I didn't have a chance, so I just went and did the best I could . . . and it wasn't very good. I did my best times ever . . . but against world-class competition . . ." She made a gesture of throwing something away.

"Oh, so you did go to the Olympics? That's marvellous."

"Yeah, but not when it counted. I should have gone to Munich. I would have done something at Munich. But I peaked too soon, and then I blew the trials . . . not too good for somebody who's held a world record . . ."

Why am I telling him all this? she thought. "It was a funny year. I'd just graduated from U.B.C. . . . you know, with your standard useless Bachelor of Arts in English . . . And I didn't know what to do with myself. The Olympics was that summer . . . and . . . I don't know. I had all these crazy notions. I had a fling at modelling school that spring . . ."

"Modelling school?"

"Yeah, modelling school. I had an idea that I wanted to have a glamorous life . . . well, not glamorous, that's not right. I just didn't want to have an ordinary life. And I've always been built like a fashion model anyway, you know, no breasts or hips . . ."

"Oh, I wouldn't . . ."

"And so I thought, well, I'll become a model. And I'll make a name for myself at the Olympics. And I'll have some kind of a career. I guess I would have been something like Nancy Greene or Karen Magnussen if it had worked out. But it didn't. I thought modelling was just unbelievably dumb. And then I blew the

Olympic trials. And I went into . . . oh, I don't know . . . a kind of paralysis, or depression or something. And I thought, well, I guess I'll have to be an ordinary person after all. So I went to library school that fall . . ." She shrugged. "There it is in a nutshell."

He laughed. "It's more than I ever did . . . I just grew up in West Van, and went to U.B.C. and then to library school, and straight into the Vancouver library system, and been there ever since . . . Do you want coffee?"

"No, I don't drink it."

"You're amazing, you really are! I don't find you an ordinary person at all. And you're still in training, eh?"

"I don't know," she said.

"What do you mean?"

"Well, every morning, five days a week, I get up before work and go over to the Sherwood School where Dad's club works out, and all by myself I swim . . . oh, usually three thousand meters . . . as fast as I can." She shrugged. "And that's more than you do if you want to keep fit, and that's less than you do if you're really training. So I don't know what I'm doing. If I were really training, I'd start to work out with the club again, do intervals and all that stuff, enter some meets. But I haven't done any of that. I guess I know I'm over the hill."

"At twenty-four?"

"Swimmers mature fast. Most of the girls who hold the world records are in their teens . . . I don't know why that should be . . . no physical reason, especially in the longer events . . . *my* events . . . Maybe you've got to be a kid, you know, simple-minded and a little crazy the way kids are, to force yourself to do the work. I don't know what I'm doing. I think that I should quit it . . . It's been a year since I've pushed myself flat out . . . in competition or against a watch . . . I don't even know what I could do anymore."

"Maybe you should find out," he said. She didn't answer.

"Maybe you could make a comeback, eh?" he said.

"Not a chance."

"But do you know that?"

"Yeah, I suppose I do. But I don't really want to know it . . . kind of kidding myself or something. If I really pushed myself and the time was rotten, then I'd really know it . . ."

"It sounds to me, Leslie," he said, "like you don't have all the necessary information."

Everything's so simple for him, she thought. As wishy-washy as he is, as bland as he is, he doesn't have trouble making decisions. "Yeah," she said, "I could get my dad to time me."

"I'll time you," he said.

"At six in the morning?"

"At six in the morning. I've never seen a real swimmer in the water . . . except on television. It'd be a real treat for me. And . . . well, it's a part of your life I've never seen . . ." He was giving her a small tentative smile.

Why do I always feel sorry for him? she thought. Oh God, Ted, don't fall in love with me. You'd just break your heart. "OK," she said, "sometime . . ."

"Tomorrow?"

"Oh, that's a little . . ."

"Might as well do it soon, eh?"

"All right, all right," she said, feeling an elusive itching inside of herself; it was almost like anger. "Tomorrow you can watch me die."

THE WEATHER HAD TURNED WINTRY so abruptly that Alan had been unprepared, had worn only a light raincoat that morning. By the time he had walked home that night, he was chilled and shaking. The temperature must have dropped twenty degrees from the day before, and it was raining again. He pushed through the gate at the side of his sister's house, closed it behind him, and walked quickly down the narrow corridor where ferns grew on either side of the stone walk, passed the back of the house, the rosebushes, the yellow light from the kitchen pouring out over the lawn (a quick glimpse of Amy in the window; she held a milk carton in one hand, was reaching for the door of the fridge), and hurried down the steps to the door of the basement. God, I'm cold! he thought. And once inside, he unlocked the small separate door that led to his apartment.

He'd lived in the basement of Amy and Howard's house since he'd been in art school, for seven years now. When he'd moved in, the "apartment" had been merely a huge walled-off area, pipes at the ceiling and concrete on the floor. But over the years Alan had built his own world there, constructing it outward section by section, surprising himself both by his own developing skill and by the pleasure he took in the work. His brother-in-law had been dubious—"You want to do what?"—shaking his head at Alan's slow methodical work, at his daintiness (Alan would not pick up a hammer unless he were wearing gloves). But as the work progressed, Howard had become converted, not only to the grand plan of "decorating" the basement but to the possibility of liking his wife's odd little brother. After Alan had put in a floor and ceiling, had subdivided the space into bedroom, bathroom, sitting room and tiny kitchenette, Howard had looked at the work, run his fingers over it, and then announced: "All right, Alan . . . You've got a carte blanche with us. Plumbing fixtures, tiles, paint . . . anything. Go ahead and fix it up the way you want to."

The apartment by now was totally self-contained, had its own door just inside the basement door, leading to a short narrow hall. Alan flipped the switch, lit the bulbs behind the rice paper above his head, and the hallway filled with diffuse amber light. The walls were peach, hung with a few of his favourite drawings from art school, matted and framed. He slid back a section of the wall, revealed a row of brass fittings for coats, shed his raincoat and hung it, slipped off his boots and set them on the shoe rack, and closed the wall. In his stocking feet, he stepped onto the pile rugs of the sitting room, flipped another switch, and the hall behind him went dark, the lights of the sitting room came on.

This was as far as visitors ever came into Alan's private world. Muted and soft browns and beiges, leather chairs, walnut book shelves, asparagus ferns and miniature palms by the only window, small oriental rugs arranged on the brown wall-to-wall carpet, the room dampened sound. The kitchenette, visible through an alcove, held a pint-sized fridge and a two-burner electric stove fitted into a corner of shelves, copper-bottomed pans hanging above. Alan took the four jars of clams from the paper bag and lined them neatly on a shelf, folded the bag, and laid it away on the bag shelf. He switched on the cassette stereo, ran his hand down the stack of cassettes. Something gentle, he thought . . . chose Carole King, directed her into the bathroom speakers. And he unlocked the final door. He'd turned most of the available space into bathroom and bedroom, thinking, This is mine, I'll do what I damn well please with it. He had the only key, and no one had ever been allowed in.

The rug in the bedroom was a pale Wedgewood-blue; the walls were papered with tiny blue flowers except for the wall facing the end of the bed: it was panelled with mirrors. The bed was fitted with baby-blue silk sheets; the bedspread was dainty, fine-worked ivory lace. The curtains at the high window (he had replaced the clear glass with one of milky translucence) matched the bedspread. A girl's antique vanity table with mirror, refinished in ivory enamel, took up the space next to the closet. A matching bed table held a tiny television set, his telephone, jars of face and hand creams, recent fashion magazines, and a nacreous porcelain bowl filled with manicure tools. On a blue satin cushion, shelved into the juncture of two walls, sat his antique doll, a Victorian lady in full evening dress. She was a genuine museum piece, and he winced whenever he remembered how much he'd paid for her.

There were only a few pictures on the walls: a Gustav Klimt reproduction, two high-fashion photographs of the only girl he'd ever attempted to make love to, Sandy, now a model in Toronto . . . and a photograph of himself. At twelve, protesting loudly the entire way, he'd allowed himself to be coerced into doing exactly what he'd been hoping to do: be dressed as a girl for the Hallowe'en party at St. John's. He couldn't remember now exactly what he'd been supposed to be, Little Bo-Peep, one of Mistress Mary's pretty maids all in a row, or something like that . . . for the exact characterization had been lost in the game itself, the delight his sister had taken (and his delight as well, mixed with an acute squirming embarrassment) in turning him into the most feminine little piece of fluff imaginable. Their mother had photographed Betty and him before they'd gone to the party, and years later he'd found the prints and negatives at the back of a drawer, had chosen the best picture of himself to have enlarged into an eleven-by-fourteen print. He sat posed prettily in a chair the way Amy had arranged him, his hands in wrist-length white dress gloves folded in his lap, his knees together and legs tucked up to show off white stockings and black patent mary-janes borrowed from Betty, in pinafore and crinolines, be-ribboned, in a curly blond wig, his painted lips fixed into a frozen and somewhat frightened smile for the camera, his made-up eyes caught wide and amazed by the flash bulb. Alan stripped off his clothes and hung them carefully in the closet. He was so cold that his teeth were chattering. In the bathroom he began to run water in the huge peach-coloured tub, tossed in a sizable splash of bath oil. Naked and shivering, he ran back into the kitchenette, put on water to boil, dropped two sugar cubes into the bottom of a cup, added a double shot of rum and a squirt of lemon juice. Jesus, I'm cold, he thought, hugging himself. When the water came to a boil, he filled the cup, fled back to the bathroom, pulling the door to the outside world shut behind him, and listened carefully for the sound of the lock falling into place. He brushed back his hair, wound it up and held it with two clips, pulled on a blue plastic shower cap, and settled into the bath. The oil was bubbling up, filling the air with the scent of roses. Oh Jesus, that's nice, he thought, feeling the warmth of the water striking his numb toes.

The entire wall of the bathroom was mirrors; it was bisected by a tilted shelf. On the shelf sat gels, oils, mineral salts in glass jars, bubble baths, creams, powders and puffs, perfumes, an electric toothbrush, and a hand-held hair dryer. On the shelves above the sink were astringents, lotions, beauty masks, and a facial sauna. Huge fluffy towels hung from a glass rod. A thickly piled blue floral bathmat rested next to the tub. Alan swung a fluted glass shelf out over the tub, gulped from the cup of hot rum, and rested it on the shelf. He let himself sink down into the water, the heat moving up over his body, loosening it, warming away the tension and chill that had been knotting him. Tonight I'll be petted and pampered, he thought . . . me taking care of me, nobody else is going to. See what's on the telly. Have a few drinks. Oh God, this feels good!

The phone in his bedroom began to ring. Sorry, he thought, not at home. The water had risen to his neck. He turned off the taps. And walking home, he'd been going over those peculiar events, that strange sequence beginning with his knock at the door of Susan Mackenzie's house. He'd decided that there was no way he could understand it, that he might as well stop trying. It would drop away eventually; he would forget it. Now sunk into the hot water, the familiar fragrant steam rising around him, he could almost make himself believe it had never happened. He drank the rum, slowly, sip by sip, until he'd finished the cup. He was floating away into a languorous dreamy haze.

He climbed out of the tub and toweled himself. He cleaned the inside of his ears with Q-tips, massaged his entire body with avocado lotion, dusted himself with talcum powder. He creamed his face and neck, touched his wrists and ears with perfume. He parted his hair in the centre of his head, swept it forward over each shoulder, selected two baby-blue ribbons from a box and tied his hair with them on either side. He was warm now; he was almost happy. The cassette had finished; he decided to leave the silence. He floated into the bedroom, enjoying the feel of the rug under his toes, and passed his reflection in the wall mirror . . . a slender pale boy with ribbons in his hair.

He unlocked the ivory wardrobe that stood inside the closet. For years he'd played an insane game with himself, had bought girls' clothes, kept them a while, and then, in moments of guilt and self-loathing, had thrown them away. A few month later, he invariably found himself buying the same things all over again. Recently he'd ended that cycle by making a contract with himself: he could keep what he bought if he didn't buy very much, chose only things of "true beauty." Now he was looking in the drawers where this collection lay among tiny satin packages of sachet herbs. He selected a floor-length midnight-blue negligée complete with panties. And then he chose the silver bedroom slippers he'd ordered from an ad at the back of a magazine. They were a high-glamour item from another age: five-inch heels and black marabou feathers at the toe.

He watched himself walk, poised delicately in the slippers. He settled onto the bed and arranged himself, posing, studying the effect in the mirror. No longer was he a pale slender boy; now he was a pale slender person of somewhat indeterminate sex, a girl except for the lack of breasts and the shadow-line of a penis folded away inside the blue lace film of the panties. To hell with the world, to hell with everything, he thought. I will not think about anything serious. He began to clean his fingernails. And the phone rang again.

Eventually he answered it, his voice cut-off and unfriendly: "Yes?"

"Alan, you are home . . . thank God!"

It was his sister Amy speaking from less than twenty feet away, from a point somewhere above his head.

"Yes, I'm home," he said.

"This is terrible . . . really terrible. I know you're not going to like this . . . but . . . our sitter cancelled on us."

Years ago, Alan had told her, "Just because I live in the basement, please don't think that you have a built-in baby sitter." Since then, Amy had been very careful, only calling on him in emergencies. He sighed. "Jeanie's a big girl . . ." he said.

"Oh Alan, you know how she is. I wouldn't feel right leaving her alone. You know what happened that other time, how absolutely hysterical she got herself . . ."

"Yeah, I know . . ."

"Really, I wouldn't ask you . . . you know that . . . but we have tickets to the concert, and that little Michaels girl called up just forty minutes ago to say she had the flu. Oh, I could skin her alive! Were you going out? . . ."

"No, Amy. I'll be right up."

"You're a love."

He held the phone in his hand a moment; then he placed it carefully into its cradle. All right, he thought. He was fond of his niece, could even say to himself that he loved her, but in the last couple of years he hadn't seen much of her. Howard, he suspected, didn't want his daughter spending much time with crazy Uncle Alan. All right, he thought again. We'll have a good time together. But he regretted the breaking of the spell, the destruction of his planned dreamy evening.

He replaced the slippers and negligée in the wardrobe, but, smiling, left the panties on, slipped a pair of jeans over them. The contrast enchanted him: the worn floppy jeans with a thick brown belt, the delicate lace panties secret beneath. Filled with obscure paranoias about possible automobile accidents and other disasters, he would never have worn them if he'd been going out on the street, but just upstairs was OK. He pulled on a sweater, slipped his feet into moccasins, took the ribbons out of his hair and shook his head. Looking in the mirror, he thought, I'm a boy again. And found, to his surprise, that he was laughing out loud at himself.

LESLIE LET HERSELF INTO HER ROOM, lit the light, and kicked off her low-heeled dress shoes, kicked them so hard they shot across the floor and cracked against the far wall, one right after the other: bang, bang. She shed her coat onto the floor and fell face down onto the bed. She had allowed Ted to talk her into stopping in at his apartment after dinner, and there she had spent an hour sliding away from his oblique approaches. The effort had left her exhausted. The day had left her exhausted. Get up and take your clothes off, Leslie, she told herself, but instead she fell asleep.

She dreamed she was kissing Susan Mackenzie. The girl's lipstick was flavoured; it tasted like cherries. And then, under the sway of this compelling dream logic, Leslie was not in the least surprised when Susan turned out to have a penis. It happened easily and naturally: Leslie felt herself entered and sank down sweetly to pleasure, luxuriously abandoning herself to it, like sinking into warm water. And then she was awake. She was irritatingly alive between her legs; her nipples burned. She rolled over. Her alarm clock said that it was only a quarter-to-nine.

The ceiling above her head was perfectly white and blank. She was filled with such longing and despair that she couldn't imagine doing anything beyond lying there and suffering it. Masturbation had never come easily to Leslie; it happened to her rather than her choosing it, exactly at times like this, rising from dream to discover that she was touching herself. And whenever it had happened, she had always felt a terrible grief afterwards . . . not so much anymore from memory of childhood sin as from sheer loneliness. She stroked herself lightly now, running her hands over breasts and thighs. Then, abruptly, she stood up. She was momentarily faint; her muscles were aching.

She stood looking at her room as though it were a stranger's, thinking, Oh God, what can I ever do! She turned on her radio, tuned across the FM band until she found a station playing classical music. She retrieved her dress shoes, set them back where they belonged on the floor of her closet. She picked up her coat and hung that up. She undressed, put on her pink flannelette pajamas. (She'd worn pajamas just like that as long as she could remember.) She put a cup of milk on the hot plate to warm for cocoa. And she walked across the hall and into the bathroom to brush her teeth.

Leslie shared the bathroom with the girl across the hall, and the girl was out, of course; it was Saturday night. But had left the bathroom hung with mementos drying on towels: grey pantyhose, blue pantyhose, white pantyhose. Leslie could have afforded an apartment of her own, but a stubborn streak of thriftiness wouldn't allow her to pay the rents they were asking in Vancouver now. And it wasn't a bad room, actually; from her window she could see the mountains. She squeezed toothpaste onto the brush, and then she saw herself in the mirror. She'd forgotten.

That damned woman! she thought. But no. I said it.

Did I really say it? Yes, I really said it . . . boyish . . . tomboyish . . . Oh Christ! She began to brush her teeth. Why am I so upset? People get their hair cut all the time. People wear the damnedest things now, they wear their hair every imaginable way. I've seen girls with shorter hair than this. It's out of my eyes.

But it wasn't merely that her hair was short; it was boyish and short and *cute*. It suited her, and somehow that was frightening. She walked back into her room and found the box of earrings tucked away in a drawer, carried it back to the bathroom. She'd had her ears pierced in high school, but it had been years since she'd worn earrings. She chose a plain gold circle, lined up the wire with the trace of hole left in her earlobe, and pushed. She felt a sharp pain. The wire wasn't going in. The hole had closed long ago. She felt a sudden anger, pushed harder, inhaled sharply with the pain. Oh, I've hurt myself! she thought. But it wasn't the pain that had done it . . . it was the blood, a single bright drop on her fingertip like a jewel. She burst into tears.

She fled into her room leaving the earrings behind. She cried for a long time. She didn't know how long, but the milk on the stove had been ruined, had come to a boil and been scorched. She turned off the burner, set the cup aside. She turned off the radio and climbed into bed. She kept a stack of children's books on the night table; for the last year they were all that she had read. She selected one at random, opened it, and began to read:

"The Student and Fiona lived in a little grey house on the shores of a grey sea-loch in the Isle of Mist . . ."

Leslie yawned. She felt emptied. She felt numb. She was having trouble concentrating. She looked at the clock; it wasn't even ten.

" . . . Fiona, when she was doing nothing else, used to help Anne to keep house rather jerkily, in the way a learned man may be supposed to like. She was a long-legged creature of fifteen, who laughed when her father threatened her with school on the mainland, and she had a warm heart and a largish size in shoes . . ."

Leslie yawned again. She lay the book open on the bed. I'll just close my eyes for a moment, she thought. I like the sound of the rain. I grew up with the sound of the rain. And she saw for a moment the hazy northern forests in the rain. I should turn the light off, she thought. I can't read any more. But she didn't do it. She'd walked with her father and grandfather once up a steep trail in the rain . . . somewhere . . . oh, the lovely sound of the rain. And then Leslie was asleep.

"ALAN'S GOING TO COME UP," Amy said.

"That's good," Howard said dryly. "Now do you suppose you can pull yourself together?" His wife was wearing only slip and bra, pantyhose and shoes. She'd taken the rollers out of her hair but hadn't brushed it out; her head was set with oddly stiff shiny curls as though she were wearing a wig made of marzipan. Howard was fully dressed, sitting in the little blue chair in the corner of the bedroom.

He looked at his watch, then pulled out his pipe and tobacco pouch.

"You would have just left her alone, wouldn't you?" Amy said.

"Get dressed, Amy. We're going to be late, eh?"

She sat down at the antique vanity table, began to brush out her hair. He could see, in the mirror, that her eyes were on him. "But you were going to leave her alone, weren't you?" she said.

"This is not the time to have another Creative Fight," he said.

"Oh, Howard, I don't want to have a fight. I'm just asking."

"Yes, I would have left her alone. Goddamn it, of course I would have left her alone. She's twelve years old."

Amy said nothing. She'd begun to smooth some kind of cream into her face. For twelve years now Howard had sat, with varying degrees of impatience, and watched his wife "put her face on." It must be an arduous procedure, he thought, for all the time it takes. But for all his sitting and watching, he could not have explained to anyone exactly what she was doing any more than Amy could have told someone how he did a root canal. Now she was drawing lines on her eyelids. "Amy, my love," he said, "do you suppose you could allow yourself to be just a shade off perfection tonight? It's ten to."

"Shut up. You're slowing me down."

"Well, I certainly don't want to do that," he said. During the first years of their marriage he'd found these intimate domestic scenes immensely satisfying, as though he'd finally stepped into a life exactly as it should be: the husband waiting, the wife fluttering about, painting herself. When he had sexual fantasies now, they were always of those years: Amy half-dressed in 1962 spike heels, in stockings and garter belt. They'd had a long honeymoon, even after Jeanie had been born, and he'd taken his wife sometimes, in the middle of dressing, saying to hell with whatever they'd been preparing for, carrying her giggling and protesting to the bed. "Why do you always want to make love to me when we're getting ready to go out!" Years now since that happened. Years now since much of anything had happened. Amy was still a beautiful woman, but would he enjoy sitting and watching her paint herself at forty? At fifty? At sixty?

"She's not your son, you know," Amy said.

"Christ, I know that."

"I wonder if you do."

"Well, she's not the latest installment of the Lehman girls either. Three such lovely daughters your mother raised, eh?"

"Oh, that's not *nice!*" She was putting something on her lips now. "I thought you liked Alan," she said.

"I do like him . . . in a funny kind of way. But he's not exactly the picture of the All-Canadian Boy, now is he?"

"Don't be so old-fashioned. This is 1974."

"You're a great one to talk about being old-fashioned."

She turned around to face him. "Now what's *that* supposed to mean?"

"Come on, love. Put the rest of your war paint on, and let's get it on the road, eh?"

She turned back to the mirror. "I don't expect Jeanie to be the kind of girl I was."

"You don't?" he said. "Well, that's good."

"I mean it, Howard."

"Yeah, I know. OK. Come on, love, for God's sake!" It's like something out of a soap opera, he thought, or an old fifties Hollywood movie where the couples had separate beds. And he also had the ominous feeling that he'd planned things, somehow, exactly that way. Oh, Amy stayed on top of the times. Whatever "everybody" was reading, she was reading too. For a while she'd been the Sensuous Woman in a black nightie. Then it had been that raft of women's books, and lately *The Joy of Sex* and *Open Marriage*. But none of it ever meant anything, ever made a dent on that person inside, the same girl she'd been at nineteen when he'd met her. Open marriage? Yeah, sure. He could imagine her reaction if he came home and announced that he'd slept with his dental assistant. But of course he hadn't slept with his dental assistant.

". . . it didn't hurt me," she was saying.

"What didn't hurt you?"

"Going to a girls' school . . ."

"Oh, Jesus!"

Amy jumped to her feet and jerked open the door to the walk-in closet. He really would have left her alone, she was thinking. And she slipped the dress from its hanger. Such lovely soft styles coming in again, thank God, she thought. I never did have it for the tomboy in a mini-skirt look. But now clothes were coming back that flattered her. This ruffled top, plunging neckline. Clothes for a woman and not some gawky little kid. A woman with breasts. I'm not over the hill, she thought, not by a long shot. I can still turn a head or two. A gold-and-green floral pattern on ivory rayon. Can get really elegant clothes again. But Howard hadn't changed a bit since she'd met him. Still the same man inside, just older. And she was finally getting some insight into herself, about time . . . at thirty-two. Daddy had died when she was nine, and of course she'd been looking for a father.

Why was Howard so difficult lately? He was turning into an old man. What would he be like at fifty? At sixty? At seventy? It was her own fault; she'd somehow chosen it, marrying a man ten years older than herself. But so difficult, no insight into himself, couldn't see what he was doing to his daughter. They should have had another child, a boy . . . then maybe he would have let Jeanie alone. Have to do something about Jeanie. With ordinary little girls you could let them be just as boyish as they wanted, encourage them, because they were still *girls* inside, but Jeanie . . . I'm not going to raise a daughter with sex-identity problems, she thought. She can grow up and have a career or whatever, but she's got to be a girl. Must be some way to get Howard to agree to send her to Stafford House. I liked it. Would be good for Jeanie to have to wear a skirt to school every day.

"For God's sake," Howard said, "it's five after!"

"All right, all right. I'm ready!"

Alan had come up from the basement and was draped across the chesterfield in front of the television set. Jeanie was sitting near him on the floor. "Hi, Alan," Howard said. "How have you been? Haven't seen you in a while."

"I'm fine."

"In bed by ten, young lady," Amy said to her daughter.

"Right, Mom."

"See that she's in bed by ten, won't you, Alan?"

"Sure, Amy." Alan watched his sister walk from the room. She needs her hair done again, he thought, and she's wearing too much perfume. And then Howard was poking his head back through the door. He winked at his daughter, saying, "At least by eleven, eh?"

Jeanie giggled. "Bye, Dad," she said.

The front door slammed. "Are you watching that, Alan?" she said.

"No," he said.

She turned off the TV. "I don't need a sitter," she said. "Mom thinks I need a sitter, but I don't think I need a sitter. Do you think I need a sitter? Of course I'm glad you're here, Alan, because otherwise I never get a chance to see you. You could just come up and visit me, you know."

"You could come down and visit me, you know."

"Really? Could I?"

"Sure."

"I will then. I'll call you up and I'll say, 'Hello, Alan. This is Jeanie. May I come calling? Can I see the back of your apartment, Alan?'"

"No."

"Why not?"

"It's the only space I have that's mine."

"You can see my room if you want to. Do you want to? I'll let you see it."

"I've seen your room," he said, laughing.

"You can show me. I won't tell any of your secrets."

"What secrets do you think I have?"

"Deep dark secrets, just like me. I can turn a cartwheel, do you want to see me?" She turned a cartwheel. Sitting on the floor, she said, "I know why you don't come up to visit. It's because Daddy doesn't like you."

"Oh?"

"He says you're . . . effeminate."

"Oh, he does, does he?"

"I shouldn't have told you, should I? But you can't keep secrets from your friends. We are friends, aren't we? Mom says you're not effeminate, you're just sensitive. That's what she says about me

71

too. I think you're a changeling just like me. Do you want me to read you a poem?"

"Sure."

She pulled a big book out from under the chesterfield. She'd marked something in it with a scrap of paper.

"My mother said I never should
Play with the gypsies in the wood.
If I did, she would say,
Naughty girl to disobey.
Your hair shan't curl, Your shoes shan't shine,
You naughty girl, you shan't be mine.
The wood was dark; the grass was green;
Along came Sally with a tambourine.
I went to the sea—no way to get across;
I paid ten shillings for an old blind horse;
I jumped on his back and was off in a crack,
Sally tell my mother I shall never come back.

"I really like it," she said. "Don't you? Of course my hair doesn't curl and my shoes don't shine *anyway* . . . "You could curl my hair, couldn't you, Alan? There aren't any gypsies any more are there?"

"Yes, there are still gypsies."

"But there aren't any in Vancouver, are there? Did children really run away with the gypsies in the olden times? I wish there were still gypsies. I'd disguise myself as a boy and run away. I'd come down to you and say 'Alan . . . bake me a bannock, and roast me a collop, for I am going off to seek my fortune.'"

"Is that what you'd say?"

"Yes, that's exactly what I'd say. And you'd say, 'No, Jeanie, I'm going to go with you. We will both go off and seek our fortunes.' And we'd disguise ourselves in strange disguises so that no one would know us. We'd pass right by my mother and father and they wouldn't know us. And we'd set of to seek our fortunes . . ." The child was looking at him with a mature solemnity that didn't seem to match the fairy tale she was spinning. She's got Lehman eyes, he thought, grey-green like her mother's . . . like mine. "And long we'd travel and far we'd travel," she was saying. "Aye, farther than human tongue can tell . . . And then what?"

"I suppose we'd be to Calgary by then," he said.

"Oh, Alan, that's not fair!"

"OK. Sorry. What then?"

"You don't want to play, do you?"

"Sure, I'll play."

"No. You don't really want to."

"Yes, I do. I'll play with you."

"All right. Tell me the most secret thing you know." He hesitated. "Show me your room."

"No, Jeanie."

"Oh, Alan . . . All right then. If you had any wish in the world, what would it be?"

"You go first."

"If I had any wish in the world," she said, "I'd wish that I'd been born a thousand years ago in a strange country where there was still magic. Now it's your turn."

"If I had any wish in the world," he said slowly, "I'd wish . . . that I'd been born a girl."

They sat looking at each other silently. Finally she said, OK, Alan, here's the plan. We'll pick a time in the middle of the night. And every night at exactly that time we'll *concentrate* very hard . . . and you know what will happen? One morning we'll wake up and we'll have *changed bodies!* Your mind will be inside my body and my mind will be inside your body. And nobody will know. It will be a secret. And then you'll be a girl . . . and I'll be . . . free."

73

"Do you think it will work?"

"No," she said, "of course it won't work." She climbed onto the end of the couch, pulled her knees up and wrapped her arms around them. "We're stuck, aren't we?" she said.

"Yeah, I think we are."

"They must think I'm so stupid," the little girl said bitterly. "They think if they don't come right out and say what they're thinking, then I won't know what it is. But I know everything they're thinking. I can read their minds. I know what they want me to do. I just don't want to do it." Alan said nothing. "Not only do they think I'm stupid," Jeanie went on, "they think I'm deaf!" She imitated her mother's voice, "Jeanie's some kind of little female Peter Pan. She doesn't want to grow up." She looked up at Alan's face. "Well that's right. I don't want to grow up. I never want to grow up." You've grown up already, Jeanie, he thought. "Yeah, but the sooner you grow up, the sooner you can get away," he said.

"How soon is that? I'm just twelve . . . They want me to be like the other kids. But do you know what the other kids do? They go out in the middle of Sherwood Park and sniff nail polish remover. Is that what they want me to do? . . . We've got to plan something," she said darkly. "We've got to make a plot . . . I've made a plot. Do you want to hear it? I'm going to let mom buy me a little dress and I'm going to wear it every day, day after day, until it falls off me, that's what I'm going to do . . . She'd like that . . . Come on, Alan, do you want a piece of cake? . . . I'm going to hide out on the back of the garbage truck. They'll never find me. I'll live in the City Dump. I'll catch rats and eat them. I'll forget how to talk. I'll turn all wild!" She began to giggle. "I'll run away with the Man from Glad!"

He had followed her into the kitchen. She took plates out of the cupboard. "Do you want some milk?" she said.

"Sure."

"You never lie to me, do you, Alan?"

"No."

"Well, tell me then . . . please . . . Tell me how you know if you're crazy."

"Do you think you're crazy?"

"Yes, I think I'm crazy."

"I thought I was crazy too when I was a kid."

"Did you?"

"Yes."

"Because you wanted to be a girl?"

"Yes . . . I used to lock myself in the bathroom and put on Betty's clothes. And then afterwards I'd feel terrible . . . really guilty and terrible. I was sure I was crazy."

"Oh, that's really sad. I won't tell anyone."

"I know."

"You can show me your room now, can't you?" she said. He stood, holding the plate in his hand. She cut him a piece of cake, gestured with the cake knife. He lowered the plate, and she slid the cake onto it. "All right," he said. "Come on. Bring your cake down. I'll show you."

She sat on the edge of his bed holding the plate carefully on her lap. Alan stood tensely, thinking, maybe I'm making a horrible mistake. "It's so quiet," Jeanie said finally. "Is that you?"

"Yes."

"How old were you?"

"Your age. Twelve. Your mother dressed up Betty and me for a Hallowe'en party."

"Who's that?"

"She's a girl . . . I loved."

"She went away, didn't she?"

"Yes."

"Oh, I knew it." Jeanie began to cry. "It's all so sad." He took the plate from her, set it on the floor, and stroked her head. "Do you have a kleenex?" she said.

She blew her nose. "Did you ever think of having a sex change operation?" she said.

"Christ, Jeanie, how do you know about things like that?"

"You don't think I'm stupid too, do you? I heard about it on the CBC."

"Well, I thought about it, but it didn't seem right . . . I don't know. I guess something in me . . . wants to hang on to all my natural equipment."

She nodded as though she understood perfectly. Maybe she does, he thought. "I'll tell you my darkest secret now," she said. "Things come and visit me in the night."

"What kind of things?"

"I don't know." She began to cry again. "I don't think it's just a . . . I think I really am a changeling. I think they want to take me back."

"It's nightmares," he said.

"Is it?"

"Yes. It's got to be nightmares. I had them too, when I was a kid."

"Did you?"

"Yes."

"Did they go away?"

"Yes."

She blew her nose again and began to eat her cake. "We know each other's darkest secrets now," she said. "We have to be friends forever."

"Yes," he said. "We'll be friends forever."

"We have to swear an oath, Alan . . . in blood."

"Oh, Jeanie!"

"Is this for play or for real?" she said.

"It's for real."

"Then we have to swear in blood." Her eyes were wandering around the room, came to rest on the bowl on the bed table. She picked out of it a pair of manicure scissors. "Give me your hand," she said. He gave her his hand, open, palm up. He felt a small jab of pain . . . blood on his hand. He was dizzy. This can't be happening, he thought.

"Now you do it to me," she said. She handed him the scissors, held out her hand for him.

"We could pretend," he said.

"No. It has to be for real."

He took her hand in one of his, with the other laid the point of the scissors against her palm. I can't do this, he thought. And then he'd done it. A single drop of blood had appeared, like a jewel. She had neither winced nor cried out.

She took his hand in hers, pressed the small cuts together, and held him. "I swear by my heart's blood," she said, "that I will be your friend forever . . . that . . . whatever is mine is yours from this day forward . . . forever . . . I swear it by my life, my fortune, and my sacred honour. Do you swear it?"

"I swear it," he said.

ALAN FLOATED UPWARD IN THE CARPETED ELEVATOR; there was no sense of motion, only the muffled steady hum. A little voice in his head was singing:

And it's over the water and over the lea,

And over the water to Charlie . . .

It was because he'd just ridden the bus over the water to the West End, he thought. Amazing how those little verses stick in your mind. Howard and Amy had come home to find Alan and Jeanie back, innocently, in the TV room, reading nursery rhymes to each other—Oh, it's over the water and over the lea!—and Alan at least one-quarter drunk on rum. The elevator door opened; Alan stepped out, and it closed behind him. He was on the twelfth floor, could see the numbers, 1201, 1202 . . . and began following the carpeted hall.

Jeanie had been put to bed. Neither Howard nor Amy had said anything about the fact that she was still up at a quarter to twelve. And Alan had gone down to his apartment and called Tricia: "Hey, can I drop over?" He'd never visited her at home.

"Well . . . there's nobody here but . . . some girls."

Some gay girls. "That's all right."

She'd laughed. "Yes, that's all right, love. Come over."

And there it was. Over the water and over the lea.

Trish had found time, somehow, to change the colour of her nail polish since work; it was now blood scarlet. So were her toenails. She was barefoot, wore a white lace blouse, her dark hair was tousled, she had on a lot of makeup; she looked sultry and sexy and slightly Spanish and half asleep . . . something like the young Ava Gardner. And she had on a pair of absolutely astonishing pants; they were cut high and nipped her waist, were fitted tightly to her buttocks, in fact divided her bottom into two distinct semi-spheres. "My God, Trish," he said, "those pants are something else."

"Yeah," she said, "a little slutty aren't they? . . You've never met my friend, Donna, have you? . . . This is Alan."

Donna was a tall woman, not fat, but substantial. She was also barefoot, wore a blue workshirt and jeans. Her hair was short, cut into a competent but undistinguished style. Her only decoration was a string of turquoise beads on a leather thong around her neck. She smiled and her face was lit, entirely, by a broad beamish grin. She took Alan's hand. "Hi," she said. "You want to do some weed?" She's younger than Trish, he thought. Must be in her twenties.

"Isn't he pretty?" Tricia said.

"Sit down, man," Donna said. "We just wiped ourselves out. All fuzzy in the brain. Gone to mush." She laughed; her entire body shook with it.

What a jolly lady! he thought. "What are you drinking, love?" Trish was saying.

Donna had lit a small soapstone pipe. She dragged on it, passing it to him. They passed it back and forth until they'd smoked it down to the stone bottom. "Now isn't that dynamite weed?" Donna said.

"Yeah," he said. "It's dynamite weed."

Trish handed him a glass, sat down on the couch with Donna. "You should have come a little earlier. We had a real party going."

"Maybe he wouldn't have liked it," Donna said.

"Yes, he would have. He's crazy."

"You crazy, Alan?" Donna said.

"Yeah, I am," he said. The rum and the grass had set him fizzling; he felt like a bottle of champagne from which the cork had been suddenly drawn.

"How are you crazy?" Donna said.

"I don't even know!" and he began to laugh. Donna and Trish began to laugh. Soon the three of them were howling.

"See," Donna said. "Now isn't that dynamite weed?"

"Oh, my God!" Tricia said.

"I knew this was going to happen," Alan said. "I don't know how I knew it, but I did. I just needed to . . . I just had to get off somewhere with some good people . . . and laugh."

"I like you too," Trish said. "You know, it's funny the way things ended up. I don't even have any men friends anymore. Do you, Donna?"

"I like some of the guys I work with at the Post Office OK."

"Yeah, but are they friends?"

"Shit, no."

"We just go our own ways, make little boxes for ourselves. I don't have any men friends. I don't even have any straight friends."

"Well, the straight world's kind of fucked, eh?" Donna said.

"Yeah, and so's the gay world," said Tricia. "It just seems kind of sad to me. We shut ourselves up in all these little boxes and never look out."

"You can say all you want to about people in boxes," Alan said, "but straight people are really scared. They're *really* in boxes. All miserable and closed up and scared."

"Everybody's scared," said Tricia.

"Yeah, but he's got a point," Donna said. "You eat so much shit from the straight world, you get sick of eating it. You want to say, 'OK, *you* eat some shit now.' It all comes down to politics in the end."

"That scares me," Trish said. "You young people can have that. I'm too old for it." Then she laughed, gave her friend a small malicious smile. "But I don't notice you out on the battle lines there, sweetheart."

Donna laughed. "Yeah, but I got a big mouth."

Trish sighed. "Oh God, let's not get all gloomy. It's Saturday night. You want another drink, Alan?"

"OK."

When she handed his glass back to him, he found her looking at him with soft eyes full of sympathy. "How long's it been since you've been with anybody?" she asked him.

"A year. More like a year-and-a-half."

"That'll make you sad right there. You don't have to be alone, Alan."

"There was a girl," he said, "a year-and-a-half ago. Her name was Sandy. Before that I'd thought, well I am gay. It's just stupid of me to fight it. And I'd let myself get picked up by some men, but it was . . . I don't know. It wasn't right. And then I met Sandy.

She'd gone to modelling school with my sister Betty. She was
Betty's age, a year older than me . . . Do you want to hear this?"

"Of course, love," Tricia said.

"Well, Betty never really had much of a career. She was just
starting to get some jobs and met this guy and married him. But
Sandy was serious. She was a professional. And there isn't a whole
hell of a lot of work in Vancouver . . . just some catalogue work
and stuff like that . . . but she was breaking into it. And there was
something wrong. Her hair wasn't right or her face wasn't right,
and she knew it. Betty told her, 'Go see my brother. He'll know
what to do with you.' I was working over in that dumb salon in
Kerrisdale then.

"Well, Sandy was doing everything wrong. She had a lean narrow face, and she was wearing a kind of a pageboy with it, you
know . . . part . . ." He gestured, "flip down here. It cut her face
at the sides and just made her look longer and leaner. And her eyebrows were shaped wrong, arched up at the outer corners and gave
her a mean sort of femme fatale look, and that's not what you want
to see in a catalogue, not when you're trying to sell clothes to ladies
in Salmon Arm and Kamloops.

"So I changed her eyebrows, gave her a new hair style, great bil-
lowy waves out at the sides to broaden her face. And I showed her
how to use a light foundation along the jaw lines, emphasize her
lips, tone down her eyes. And she was really pleased.

"And . . . Well, this is funny. She started courting me. She'd call
me up and ask me if I'd want to go out. She even sent me flowers. I
thought maybe she just wanted a pretty guy to be seen with, eh? But
no, she really liked me. Sometimes she'd pick me up after work and
we'd go to her house and have dinner and watch television. And I
didn't know quite what to do, because I'd decided by then that I was
gay, and this was upsetting that whole . . . Well, she turned me on.
I'd look at her sometimes, and I'd get really . . . Especially when she

had pants on, eh? Or a short skirt and tights. She was a really thin girl, very boyish.

"She started buying me clothes, things I'd never have thought of buying. Lace shirts and velvet pants and things like that. She really was courting me. I liked it. I thought, well, maybe. And so one night we went to bed. And before, just watching her walk around the place, I'd got unbelievably turned on, but when we went to bed . . . nothing. She was very understanding and everything. Said she wasn't in any hurry. We talked, and it turned out that we were unbelievably similar, like we'd been through the same trips. She'd thought maybe she was gay because guys didn't turn her on much, and she'd gone to bed with another woman, some ladies, but it hadn't been exactly right, and . . . She said she was in love with me." He stopped, shrugged. "I've never told anybody this before."

"It's all right," said Tricia.

"Well, she was a virgin. I mean she'd never really made it with a man, and she didn't have any idea what to do. And I didn't either. And that really terrified me. We didn't seem to be able to do *anything*, and . . . This is hard to talk about. I'd told her that I'd always wanted to be a girl, that I used to play around in Betty's clothes, and she . . . she even liked that. She said, 'OK, Alan, we'll get you some dresses.'

"But it just seemed too weird. I just couldn't do it. She wanted me to go to Toronto with her. She thought we could get a place, and I could . . . well, keep house . . . Like a housewife, I guess. It wasn't at all hazy. It was really graphic the way we talked about it. I could just see myself there in a dress and stockings and high heels, washing the dishes, waiting for her to get home from work. It was so seductive, so incredibly seductive. But I couldn't do it.

"I think I was really in love with her, but I was also . . . just terrified. I started drawing back from her. We'd have these horrible scenes where she'd just sit and cry. She used to say, 'You know,

Alan . . . neither one of us will find anyone ever again so perfect.'"
He began to cry.

"Oh, love!" Tricia said.

"I failed her," he said. "I was too scared. I just let her go. She'd try to call me, and I wouldn't answer the phone." He pulled a handkerchief out of his pocket, blew his nose.

Donna handed him a shot of whiskey. "Bottoms up." He drank. "We've all been through so much shit," she said. "I'll tell you sometime about the first girl I fell in love with . . . back at good old Eric Hamber. Oh God, the pain!"

"You better believe it." Trish said. "I remember one night . . . this was back before I ever had any idea I was gay. I didn't even know things like that were possible, eh? And I was at this crazy party, and there was this girl there. She got me up against the wall in the bathroom, and Jesus, I started having orgasms, one right after the other, like I was wired to an electric circuit. And I went home and cried for days, I thought I was some kind of disgusting pervert."

"I'll put on some music," Donna said. "We need a little music." She walked to the stereo. The Pointer Sisters came over the speakers. "You know what the Buddha said, don't you?" Donna yelled over the music. "Life is suffering."

ALAN DRIFTED OUT OF THE TAXI, along the side of the house, and around to the back. It had stopped raining, turned cold; there was a star or two among scattered moving clouds. He let himself into the basement and into his apartment. Just drifting along like a bubble, he thought, humming to himself. Marijuana always sharpened his visual imagery, and he'd been seeing, all the way home, a huge canvas, narrow and long as a house, which had been slicked its entire length with a creamy pigment the colour of ivory (titanium white and Naples yellow well-mixed with stand oil);

across the canvas stretched a single broad dark line of burnt umber and Prussian blue. The line floated gently, bobbing . . . like Alan himself, humming, stripping off his clothes. (Oh, he thought, I've been wearing girls' panties all evening, and laughed.) . . . But then, near the end of the canvas—and this had been what had fascinated him—the line suddenly imploded, splashed itself into an angry violent knot. Heavy impasto, he thought, the paint put on with a palette knife, the contrast of the creamy texture of the rest of the canvas . . . like a facial gel . . . with the knot. Mix sand with the paint. Rough dense knot. Oh, I'm so goddamned stoned!

This planned painting (but he'd never do it, of course) had begun at Tricia's, somewhere back at the end of a drifting strip of time well mixed with stand oil, when he'd thought: today has been an interruption, a jagged violent interruption, in the smooth flow of my life. And now he was thinking, oh, but the canvas would have to be so long that you'd go mad before you came to the knot, you'd be nearly screaming at the sameness of the milk-smooth paint. It would have to be blocks long, miles long . . . He was in the bathroom working night cream into his face. Wear gloves to bed tonight, he thought, smiling dreamily at himself in the mirror. Can always tell a lady by her hands. He smoothed avocado lotion onto his hands, and arms, powdered them, and slipped into white nylon evening gloves. Wonder if I could get away with clear nail polish? he thought, a rhetorical question he'd asked before. He chose a fancy pink negligee, slipped it over his head, and sat down on the foot of the bed where he could see himself.

The knot had been Susan Mackenzie's mother; that's where it had started. Everything had been perfectly ordinary until then, and everything afterward had been absolutely crazy. He looked at Sandy in the photographs. Beautiful Sandy! I shouldn't have let you go. But he'd spent his grief earlier, at Tricia's, and now the thought was curiously drifting and abstract. Detached from pain, it was possible to go further: it's not good, this secret private solitary sexual life. It's killing something in me. Anything I might do with another person, no matter how kinky or messy, would be better than this. When Sandy went to Toronto, that's when I turned so far into myself. OK, let things go crazy, let it all turn into Dada. I should get out of here. But not tonight. (He might be alone in his self-created world, but he was comforted there.) No, thank God, not tonight.

He looked at the photograph of the little girl who was really a little boy, himself at twelve. No matter how often he'd stared at that picture, he'd never been able to make the jump back into that chair, posed in Betty's clothes; that little girl lost now back along the smooth canvas of time was somehow a separate person. And how curious, he thought, that on Hallowe'en night, I should have become a baby doll and Betty should have become a little sex kitten in black nylons. Well, Betty, at least you got to grow up into your dream, and that was something I never did. Dear Betty, we used to be so close.

He crawled into bed, pulled the covers over himself, and turned out the light. Don't need to set the alarm, don't have to get up tomorrow . . . "Come back when you're ready," what the hell had she meant by that? Ready for what? Ready for anything? Am I really ready for anything? The black interruption that might end the painting, begin another painting . . . another canvas (he began to see it), messy . . . he'd have to get paint on his hands to do it . . . but vivid and alive. His fingers had found himself. He'd been planning to masturbate, but he was limp. Need a fantasy, he thought, a vivid vivid fantasy. But it didn't seem worth the effort. Rum and grass. The feel of the shiny silk sheets. The nylon of the negligée. Very comforting. Without his knowing it, sleep had caught up with him.

Two flights above where Alan was asleep, Jeanie was wide awake. She'd been asleep, but they had come back again. They spoke in soft murmuring voices, in repetitious rhythms that sounded like nursery rhymes, but too low for her to understand them. At other times they buzzed harshly like insects. But tonight it was that soft terrifying murmur. She had turned on the light by her bed and sat now, the covers pulled up, her knees drawn up, her hands tightly clenched together, staring across her room toward her window. That was where they tried to come in.

I must not scream, she thought. If I scream, it will wake mother and she'll say I had a nightmare. She closed her eyes a moment, but the voices became louder, so she opened them again. There was never anything big to see, no scary faces or anything like that, just some terrible things like the way the light would somehow go yellow in the room or the tiny movements outside the window, like fireflies sometimes (although she'd never seen real fireflies, had only read about them), at other times like shadows.

I must not scream, she thought, Mom couldn't help me anyway. No one can help me. They'd just come back again. It's something I've got to do by myself, figure it out by myself. I must not scream. The voices were saying things that she could almost understand . . . almost almost. But she was afraid that if she began to understand, they would take her away. I have to say something, she thought. I have to make a spell. She began to whisper the words that she'd learned from Leslie that afternoon:

"Grey goose and gander,
Waft your wings together . . ."

The voices rose and fell in a steady drone. It was like her heart beat. They seemed to want her to give up. Then they could take her away.

"Carry the good king's daughter
Over the two-strand river."

This must be what evil means, she thought, when it comes like this in the night. I must not scream.

"Grey goose and gander . . ."

Sometimes they left after a few minutes. Other times they kept at her for hours. Tonight she was afraid they weren't going to leave at all.

". . . Over the two-strand river . . ."

She knew that it didn't do any good to pray. It had never done any good. The only thing that ever worked was a spell.

"Grey goose and gander . . ."

I must not scream.

"Carry the good king's daughter . . ."

Maybe Alan would understand it. Nobody else would understand it. I must not scream.

"Grey goose and gander
Waft your wings together.
Carry the good king's daughter
Over the two-strand river."

Part II

One misty, moisty morning,
When cloudy was the weather,
I chanced upon an old man
Clad all in leather;
He began to compliment,
And I began to grin.
How do you do, and how do you do,
And how do you do again?

Mother Goose

HERE IS WHERE THE WORD IS MADE FLESH, Leslie thought, and smiled at her memory. For a few months in her teens when she'd still been wondering if she should be "religious," she'd gone to the Anglican church with a classmate. And one Sunday morning after a particularly stiff workout, she'd sat there drowsing, slipping off into eddies inside herself, and had awakened with surprise to discover that all the talk of *word* and *flesh* had not been about swimming. But *here* is where it happens, she thought, no longer enough of a believer to find the notion even remotely blasphemous . . . and standing quietly, looking out over the pool, the water that was not yet dancing and rebounding from the gutters, her reflection just as still waiting for her . . . And the word is made flesh. The preconceived form is gradually approximated by the reluctant body.

"Leslie?" Ted said. And he was still wearing the clouded look, like a worried Winnie-the-Pooh, he'd brought to her door that morning at a quarter to six.

"Shhh," she said, pressing a finger to her lips, aware of the theatricality of the gesture, a mime's movement. "I'll be ready in a minute."

The conception exists first, and then you learn to match it. Did he grow into the kind of man he was because he was "Ted," and before that probably "Teddy," and so must turn round and winsome and a bit silly, or lose the magic of the name? And how much of her had grown to match "Leslie" (and the natural diminutive of her girlhood—"Les")? How different would she be now if she'd been called Sue Ellen, or Mimi, or Mary Jane, or Elizabeth Anne? . . . each name with its own magic and its own requirements. But her mother's only legacy (beyond a few faded pictures and some lovely antique jewellery Leslie never wore) was the name. It's always seemed like a benediction to me, she thought, as though Mother might have been able to read the future as she'd been dying . . . saying, "It's all right. Grow up and match the name. You can be the fourth . . . and the best . . . swimmer." She didn't call me Mary Jane, she called me Leslie Cameron.

I was born to be a swimmer. I was a swimmer before I was conceived. I was a swimmer when Dad was a little boy paddling around in the few warm bays off Johnston's Inlet. I was a swimmer when Granddad came from Scotland and headed straight for the sea. The form exists first, and later the body matches it . . . Leslie's muscles had hypertrophied into the long smooth swimmer's lines.

She could tense her arm, and beneath the soft sheath, the flesh was steel; relaxed, it was as tender as a baby's. Her arms and legs had been cut with additional blood vessels to meet the tremendous demand of her heart. And the heart itself had hypertrophied; resting, it beat less than fifty times a minute. She wore an extra thickness of fat, the smooth garment that a serious swimmer puts on gradually beneath the skin (masking the hard angularity of muscle): reaction to plunging one's body into cold water every day. And deep within, at the level of cell where she no longer had the knowledge to catalogue the changes, she had also been prepared. This body, not a machine but a live organism growing to match an idea, had learned to take oxygen into the lungs, move it swiftly to blood, and blood through heart to arms and legs, to move the whole through water, burning energy at a tremendous rate, for distances from 800 meters to well over a mile. And Leslie had grown so close to matching the form that had existed previous to her very flesh, that a few days in the spring of 1971 she had been able to swim through 800 meters of water faster than any other woman in the world.

She stretched, pushing her arms upward until her elbows clicked. In the water, her reflection stretched. She could see herself clearly there, in the tank suit she hadn't worn for nearly a year now. She had warmed up before; she wouldn't pull anything. She'd explained to Ted how to operate the stopwatch; she hoped he wouldn't forget, or screw it up. "I'm about ready," she said.

"What do I say again?" he asked her.

"You say, 'Swimmers take your marks. Get set. Go.' That's all."

If I can make the 1975 standard for the Nationals, she thought, or if I can come close, I'm in. If not, I'm out. It's that simple. Eight hundred meters: nine minutes, thirty-one point one seconds. That's not much to ask for someone who's broken nine, was one of the first girls in the world to break nine.

"All right," she said, "I'm ready."

He made a small tentative sound like a cough. "Swimmers take your marks."

"Speak up, Ted, for God's sake. Yell. Especially when you're giving me my splits. If you don't yell, I won't be able to hear you."

"All right, Good luck. Swimmers take your marks." Leslie curled her toes over the edge of the pool. "Get set." Leslie sank into the start position, knees bent tense, arms stretched behind, looking out, just at the edge of pushing. She inhaled. "Go!" She heard the watch click in his hand as she lay in the air flat out above the water. Late start, Ted, she thought . . . by a fraction.

Then she was swimming. She felt a rush of obscure fiery emotion she'd known before only in competition: as though she were an animal going after another, intending to bring it down and kill it. She was at the far wall and coming back . . . this annoying short-course pool that made her feel that she was going around on a wheel, hamster-like. She slapped the near wall for the turn, and Ted yelled her time, "Thirty-two. You're four ahead."

That morning, awake ahead of the alarm, she'd sat and waited for him and written out projected split times. Keeping it simple, letting Ted stay at one end of the pool, she'd allowed herself thirty-six seconds a fifty. That would give her a 9:36, just a bit over the standard for the Nationals. She'd told him to give her only the times at the hundreds, for the other laps just to tell her how far ahead or behind of the projection she was swimming. But he'd obviously forgotten. She was back again. "One ten. You're two ahead," he yelled.

It's not bad, she thought. And finally her mind was beginning to blank out as it had taken to doing at practice. The various images, fragments of memories of old meets—a rather high-flown metaphor of her body measuring water as the watch, held ominous and clicking in the hand, measures time—were fading out, and she was simply at work, pulling, "You're still two ahead!" No time. He remembered finally. Would he remember the two hundred split? "Two twenty-two. You're still two ahead!" Yes, he remembered. And it's not bad. *Good girl, Leslie*: her father's voice.

She'd swum for so many years that the motions of it were more than automatic; they were a comforting groove she slipped into effortlessly, like the moment of trough running by her head that she created to breathe. And like a musician must feel when he's so far advanced he no longer has to worry about where his fingers are going and can attend to the phrasing, she set her pace. "Bang on!" Ted yelled. Uh-oh, losing a bit. Pick it up. She regained her two seconds and carried through the fourth hundred, arriving at 4:46.

She began to hurt. It was not yet serious, not yet the nightmare of having pushed yourself too hard and suddenly swimming into a terrible wall inside of your own body. It was still a slight sinister hint of things to come. I haven't got it, she thought. Oh Christ! "Two behind," Ted yelled. And in that comparison of measured seconds against subjective sensation was the beginning of fear: she'd thought she'd been going faster. "Still two behind. Six oh two." Well, at least I'm keeping it. Can drift back, let it slide a bit more, and sprint at the end. Always had a good sprint at the end. "Four behind!"

Then Leslie knew that she couldn't stand the pain anymore. The memory of pain is elusive and ghost-like, reduced to mere words: "It was bad. I really hurt myself." But the words lose charge. Only pain is a genuine reminder of pain. And something must have happened in the last year or so, because she knew clearly now, once again, just how bad it would have to get before it would be over, and she knew she couldn't stand it. Here is where she always went dead anyway, here is where she used to lose races, in the seventh hundred. "Ten behind!" he yelled, his voice rising in pitch. "Seven twenty-two."

Oh God! It's not there any more, she thought. And was twelve seconds behind. Her arms and legs were tired and heavy. She was getting sick at her stomach. It's almost over. Sprint now, sprint! She pushed herself against the edge of the pain. She missed the seven hundred split. It doesn't matter. I can't go any faster. And racing back the last lap, she was also racing her stomach. Would she throw up? She hit the wall, heard the watch click. She looked up at Ted, gritting her teeth against the vomit in her throat. "Ten . . . It's ah . . . ten oh two."

The pool was moving, the concrete under her fingers was moving, the far wall was moving. "Help," she managed to say.

"What? . . . What, Leslie? . . . What?"

How do you clean a pool after you've thrown up in it? Do you have to drain all of the water out? She'd never thrown up after swimming in her life. Her father would be so upset with her. "You asshole!" she yelled at Ted. She was so angry she wanted to pull him into the water and drown him.

"What is it?" That stupid worried face.

She held up a hand. He took it and pulled. She scrambled and floundered out of the water, ran for the dressing room. Her stomach contracted and neatly deposited a cupful of brown vile liquid into the toilet bowl. She stretched out on the floor and held her stomach. She was still gasping, just beginning to pay back her oxygen debt. She couldn't imagine any position she could assume in which her body would be comfortable. She began to cry . . .

"Are you all right?"

"Let me alone!" She stopped crying, pulled herself to her feet, and walked around the pool breathing. I don't have it any more, she thought. She had the insane desire to swim another eight hundred just to punish herself.

Ted was hanging in the doorway. "Leslie?"

"I'm all right." She pushed past him into the dressing room. "Get out of here. I've got to take a shower and get dressed. Go over to the boys' side."

Now I know, she thought. I knew before, actually, but now I really know. So now what? Yoga classes? Ballet lessons? Oh God!

In the car, Ted said heartily, "How about a nice big breakfast? That would make you feel better, eh?"

"I want to go home and go to bed."

"Was it that bad?"

"It wasn't *that* bad. If I were fourteen, it would have been splendid."

"But it was still . . ."

"I'm not going to be one of the best anymore. No matter how hard I work, I just won't be. And if I can't be one of the best, there's no point. It's too much work to be . . . well, just mediocre. This is it. I'm done." I can't stand the sight of him, she thought. I can't stand him another minute.

"Well, I really enjoyed it," he was saying.

"Oh, you did, did you?"

"It was just . . . quite wonderful seeing you swimming so fast. That's just a layman's point of view of course. I enjoy seeing someone do something well like that . . . up close, eh? Like watching a good violinist. You may not know how to play, but you can tell when you're seeing a real pro."

"Yeah." He'd pulled up in front of her place. "Thanks, Ted."

"Hope you feel better, eh? Here's the watch. Oh . . .

"Would you like to go to a Hallowe'en party with me Thursday night?"

She was incredulous. How can he ask me that *now*? He's got as much sensitivity as a troll. "I'll think about it."

". . . an old classmate of mine from U.B.C.," he was saying, "Gary Kovarian. Should be quite fun . . ."

"All right," she said, opening the car door. "I'll go. All right."

"You're OK aren't you?"

"Yeah, I'm fine." She slammed the car door and walked quickly away.

"I KNOW EXACTLY WHAT THE SON-OF-A-BITCH IS GOING TO DO," Gary said, "He's going to take me aside in that discreet ramrod-up-his-asshole way of his, and ask me about every legal problem he's had since the last time I saw him."

"Well, send him a bill," his wife said.

"Christ, I wish the son-of-a-bitch carried his dental tools around with him. I could use a scaling." Gary and his wife were sitting, seat-belted, within the intimate space of their Mini-Minor; she held the sleeping baby on her lap; he was driving across the Lion's Gate Bridge. "Oh, your family," he said. "It's like a visit to the loony bin, eh? To the bloody loony bin."

"We don't spend that much time with them," she said.

"You can stand it."

"Your sister," he said, chuckling. "I always look forward to seeing her. Just love the look of exquisite pain that passes across her eyes . . . like an actress in a silent movie. It's like . . . yeah, it's like she's got a large invisible bull dog chewing away her ass at all times. I can just see the damn thing hanging on there, chewing away, chomp chomp chomp. While she sits and bravely sips her tea and tries to pretend she doesn't notice. Oh, it's a real show all right!"

Betty was laughing. "You just watch your mouth, boy," she said.

"Butter wouldn't melt in it, Miss Puss," he said.

Betty glanced at her husband, at his profile . . . great knife of a nose. Oh, You handsome asshole! she thought. His dark skin, his black curly hair, his lush moustache that made him look like a wild romantic bandit. Gary Kovarian, an Armenian, of all crazy things. His parents ran a pizza house in the East End, Aram's Pizza. Sometimes they'd go to visit, stand out on the street and watch through the window while Gary's father—that wonderful silver-haired old man—winked at them and spun the dough high in the air, swirling it, dancing it. Her own family seemed effete in comparison, third-generation British Gentry going to seed in West Vancouver. We'll have healthy kids, she thought. Crossbreeding. Little lively mongrel brats. Looking down fondly on her sleeping child.

But he's learned more from me than he knows, she thought. He learned to say "bloody" from me, instead of "fucking." He learned to dress from me. When I met him, he looked like a flashy young gangster. And what did I learn from him? Force, life. Thank God I didn't marry a man like Howard.

"You know the only one who knows which end's up, don't you?" he was saying. "It's your little faggot brother."

"He really does. He knows what's coming down, eh? I look over and catch him twinkling at me . . . this kind of mental telepathy. Alan's all right . . ."

"Well, that's big of you."

"Don't get me wrong, Puss. I respect the little bugger. I think he's done just fine, considering. You know, your mother could castrate an orangoutang."

"You watch your mouth, you bandit!" she said, laughing.

"I'll get it all out before I get there, and then I'll be nice as pie. Christ, I wish the Queen Mother could cut down her command performances to twice a year, maybe Christmas and Easter."

"She's lonely, Gary."

"Well, she deserves it. I'll bet she rode your old man right into his grave."

"That's enough, man. I mean it."

He looked over at her with his mouth drawn down into a comic mask; he raised his black eyebrows at her. "Well now, Miss Priss," he said. "Miss Pussy Cat. Miss Puss-in-Boots."

She couldn't hold back the laughter. "You asshole!"

He parked in front of the house, walked around the car to let his wife out. "Here, give me the little cretin." She handed him the baby, swung her long booted legs out of the car. Wine-coloured boots just off black, over her knees, hand-made, and like everything else in her wardrobe, in exquisite taste . . . and expensive. You sexy little thing, he thought, ninety bucks worth. "Come on, Puss-in-Boots," he said, taking her hand. "Am I glad I'm making money! Your requirements in clothes would break the Serian National Bank."

"I don't feel a bit sorry for you, Mr. Pig. You wanted a flashy lady to show off, and now you've got one."

He slapped her on the ass. "I'll take it out of your flesh. When we get home, I'll fuck you till your eyes cross."

"Promises, promises."

He followed her up the walk and into the house. "What a little dear!" said Betty's mother, taking the baby from him.

"How are you, Mrs. Lehman?" He'd steadfastly refused to pick up her hints that he should call her "Mother."

"I'm as well as can be expected, Gary, dear. . . Such a little mite. So sound asleep."

"Let's hope he stays that way," Gary said.

"Poor little toad," his wife said. "He's all tired out."

"He should be," Gary said. "Started yelling at four and didn't stop till seven."

"He's persistent," Betty said. "Like his father." Betty followed behind her mother; she was feeling an unusual sympathy. Poor brave lonely old lady, she thought. I hope someone shoots me when I'm fifty. So sad getting old. Mrs. Lehman was a short spare woman, carefully arrayed in a pale mauve dress, matching shoes in a darker mauve ("old lady shoes" Betty thought, lace-ups with a thick heel), a string of pearls, makeup on her face, and clear polish on her old nails. Old hands with veins standing up like wires, swollen at the joints. Her mother's hair had been styled and sprayed, sat upon her head like a crown of spun grey metal. Why do they bother? Betty thought. After a certain age, what point is there in it? When I get old, I'll wear long plain robes like a monk. "You look lovely today, Mother," Betty said.

Mrs. Lehman smiled, an involuntary expression of pleasure; she patted her hair. "Oh, how nice of you to say so, dear . . . Here, we'll just put a blanket over him."

"He'll be warm enough, Mother."

"Hey," Gary called in to them. "The rest of the clan's here."

"Oh!" said Mrs. Lehman. "Alan!" And hurried back to the living room. Howard was helping Amy off with her coat. Betty embraced her sister. "Oh, Betty!" Amy said, squeezing harder than the meeting warranted. What on earth is wrong with her? Betty thought. Is she having another one of her breakdowns or whatever they are?

Amy was astonished to find that her sister's touch had brought a prickle of tears to her eyes. Family, she was thinking, that's all that lasts. "Oh, Betty," she said, "why don't we ever see each other any more?"

The women stepped back to survey each other. Something's up, Betty thought, looking at her sister's clothes. Where in God's name did she find that dress? How can she go around with her tits sticking out like that? Look like they're laid out on a bread board. Howard's probably screwing his dental assistant. "What a lovely dress!" she said.

Poor Betty, Amy was thinking. Gary's really turning her into a little tramp. How can she go around on the street with a skirt like that? And those boots? "How cute you look, dear. What beautiful boots. How can you possibly walk in them?"

"Just one foot in front of the other."

"We must have a good talk," Amy said.

Howard had got his pipe going, and Gary had produced one of his wretched black cigars, was licking the end of it. Is he going to smoke that rope in here? Betty thought. At least it's not cigarettes any more. *I* did that!

"The bastards can't skate," Gary was saying angrily. "Nobody knows how to check anymore. The damn defencemen won't hit. They don't know how to set up their shots." Howard was nodding.

"How have you been, dear?" Mrs. Lehman was saying to her granddaughter. "How sweet you look!"

Amy's got the poor kid in her Sunday best, Betty thought. Poor little tomboy. Jeanie wore a very short dress of green tartan, white knee socks (one of them had fallen down to her ankle), and black patent mary-janes. She was standing up stiffly to her grandmother's touch. "I'm fine, Grandmother."

Mrs. Lehman surveyed the room. "Well, everybody here . . . Oh no, where's Alan? Didn't he come with you, Amy?"

"We called him, and he wasn't there. I don't know where he is, Mother."

"That's so like him, the naughty boy. I hope he doesn't forget. That would be so like him."

The company parted, the men to the TV room, the women to the kitchen. Jeanie remained indecisively in the living room. "Hey, Mom," she called. "I'm going outside, OK?"

"Pull up your socks, dear." Jeanie pulled up her socks. And then Amy looked back, sharply, as though she'd just come upon something she'd forgotten. "If you get those clothes dirty, there's going to be trouble, young lady."

"I won't, Mom."

"Don't go too far away."

"I won't, Mom."

In the kitchen, Amy said, "You'd think one day a week wouldn't be too much to ask, but no. It's a major campaign."

"She's just a kid," Betty said.

"She won't be just a kid in another year."

"Children shouldn't grow up too fast," her mother said.

Outside, Jeanie sat down under a tree (she was carrying a book with her), but then she saw that her uncle Alan had just turned the corner a block away and was walking slowly toward the house. She jumped up and began running to meet him, but stopped. He was hunched forward, his hands thrust into his suede jacket, and seemed lost in thought. She slowed down, imitated his walk, and paced forward to meet him. He'd almost bumped into her before he saw her. "Jeanie!"

Oh, he thought, they've got her in drag today. And, as though she'd read his mind, the child said, "I'm in disguise."

"What are you disguised as?"

"I'm disguised as Amy and Howard's daughter. Where have you been? We were going to give you a ride."

"Just been walking around . . . around and around Kits beach. And then I came over here on the bus, and I was too early, so I walked around the park."

"You've been plotting, haven't you?"

He smiled. "Yeah, I suppose I have."

"Don't go in the house yet. Stay out here with me for a little bit."

"OK."

She arranged herself carefully under the tree. "I must not get my clothes dirty, or there will be trouble." She giggled. "I'm tired of being a princess!" And then she imitated her mother's voice: "You'd think just one day a week wouldn't be too much to ask!"

He laughed. "Yeah, I know. What's this? What are you reading now?"

"*The Black Arrow.* It's pretty neat up until the middle, and then it isn't too good anymore . . . Hey, Alan, why is it a sin for a woman to put on men's clothes?"

"Is it?"

"Yeah. That's what the girl in the book says. It's a deadly sin."

"I think it's in the Bible."

"But is it really a sin?"

"No, of course not."

"That's good. You see, there's a girl in the book and she goes around disguised as a boy and has all kinds of adventures. That's the best part of the book. But after she had to go back to being a girl, it isn't so neat anymore. I think if I ever run away, that's what I'll do. I'll disguise myself as a boy. I'll tell everybody my name's John, and they'll never find me, because they'll be looking for Jeanie. Shall we run away together, Alan? . . . Oh!" she giggled, "and you could be a girl. They would *never* find us then."

"But when they did, they'd lock me up for about ninety years."

"Do you remember our oath, Alan?"

"Of course I remember it."

She held out her palm to him, showed him the closed cut. "I won't ever forget it."

"I won't either . . . Come on, Jeanie, I've got to go in and pay my respects." He began to laugh. "You look ridiculous."

"I know." She turned three cartwheels across the lawn, bare legs and skirt flying. She said to herself, "Pull up your socks, dear," and pulled up her socks. "Alan, have you been plotting?"

He stopped, his hand on the doorknob. "I don't know. I've just been walking up and down trying to figure things out."

"Don't go in yet. Tell me!"

He jumped down the three steps in one bound, landed on the lawn. "All right, I don't really want to go in there yet. I've been thinking that I should go to Toronto and find that girl. The one in the pictures on my wall."

"Oh, you'll go on a quest! Can I come with you? I'll be your page."

"Jeanie, you know damn well that Amy wouldn't let you go to Toronto with me. I'd love to take you to Toronto, but . . ."

"I know, I know, but at least you can tell me about it. What are you going to do? Carry her off?"

"I don't know. I've got to find her first." He sank down onto the moist lawn. Clouds were piling up in the sky again; it looked as though the lovely autumn day were going to turn back to standard Vancouver rain.

"I've been plotting too," she said, "but I can't think of anything. They really are going to send me to that girls' school. She's almost got him convinced. She says it will make a girl out of me, but what she tells *him* is that I'm not learning anything at Sherwood Free . . . And that's right. I'm *not* learning anything. And I don't care. What can I do, Alan? I don't want to go there.

I wouldn't like *any* school, but I really wouldn't like it there."

The front door was opening. Jeanie glanced up at it. "And they came for me again last night," the girl said breathlessly, watching Betty step through the door.

"Oh, there you are, Alan," Betty called and began to walk toward them.

"They did?" Alan said.

"Yes. I made them go away again. But I'm afraid that they're going to come one night and I won't be able to."

"Don't blame you for hiding out here," Betty was saying. "How are you, little brother?"

He stood and hugged her. "It's been awhile," he said. Jeanie was looking up into his eyes.

"Can you go play somewhere, darling?" Betty said absently, dropping a hand onto Jeanie's head.

Alan gave Jeanie a grimace of helplessness. She sighed, turned away toward the house. Betty slipped her arm through his and walked him away down the street.

He didn't know what to say to his sister. "You look gorgeous," he said.

"Thanks."

"You ought to wear heels all the time . . . give your legs a lovely long sleek line."

"They teach you that in beauty school, Alan?"

"No, just one of my personal neurotic obsessions."

She laughed shortly, stopped walking, and turned to face him. "What's the matter with Amy?" she said.

"Is there something the matter with Amy?"

"I thought you'd know."

"I hardly see Amy."

"Well, the minute we got into the kitchen, she promptly burst into tears. It was just too much, Mother patting her one hand and me patting the other. I just can't take these little family affairs. Too heavy for me."

"What did she say?"

"Something about how Howard wasn't going to take her to the Bahamas . . . again . . . after he'd promised her now for three years."

"Oh Christ . . . Well, they're probably going through one of those periods again," he said. "Remember the last time? . . . Maybe he's sleeping with his dental assistant."

She laughed. "I wouldn't put it past him, the randy old bugger . . . It's so dismal. I keep wondering if I'm going to end up that way. You can get really bored with someone in ten years, eh?"

"You bored?"

"Not a chance. Gary keeps me hopping."

"How's your kid?"

"Oh, the poor little termite. I love him . . . Come on, let's start back. I should have worn a coat."

"I wanted to ask you something too," Alan said. "Do you ever hear from Sandy?"

"Yeah, but not often. I got a card from her at Christmas."

"What did she say? How is she?"

"Well, she's married now and . . ." She must have seen the look on her brother's face. "You were really stuck on her, weren't you?"

"Yeah, I was. Did she sound happy?"

"How can you tell from a Christmas card? She married some kind of professional man. Can't remember now what he does. She's got a baby . . ."

"Oh, Jesus!"

"Alan, there are lots of skinny little fashion-plate ladies with no tits."

"Not like Sandy."

"Yeah, she was weird."

"She was special."

They'd walked back to the house, had arrived under the tree on the front lawn. "Hey, Alan," she said, "are you gay?"

"How many years have you wanted to ask me that? No, I'm not. Not really. I'm not exactly normal, but . . . I've slept with some men, but I'm not gay." He shrugged. "I think it would be easier if I were."

"The way you were as a little boy, I thought you were going to grow up to be the Queen of the Fairies."

He laughed. She must be getting frankness lessons from Gary, he thought. "I don't know what I am."

"Remember how you used to put on my clothes?" she said.

He stopped laughing. "Did you know about that?"

"Of course I did, you twit."

"Do you think . . . Did . . . Do you think that mother knew?"

"You know her. She only knows what she wants to know."

"Yeah."

"Oh, but you were an amazing kid. Do you remember that Hallowe'en party. You went around for weeks before practically begging me to dress you up like a girl."

"I did?"

"Sure you did."

"What did you think of that?"

"I thought it was cute. And used to get really pissed off at you. I used to think, 'It's not fair. He's prettier than I am!' You made a lovely little girl. You were the most feminine one of us all."

"You weren't exactly Miss Liberation, Betsie-poo."

"Oh, you little bitch," she said, laughing.

"Why haven't we ever talked?"

She looked at him closely. "Marriage takes up a lot of you."

"No. We were always friendly, but we never talked. Not since we were little."

"I thought you were weird," she said flatly. "There was a time in my life when I didn't even want to be *seen* with you." Then she said, "I'm sorry. I don't feel that way now." She reached to pat his shoulder, but he took her in his arms. They stood a moment holding each other.

Jeanie remained sitting motionless on the other side of the tree. Quiet as a mouse, she thought, holding her breath, all ears.

"My sweet sister," Alan said.

"Stop it, for Christsake! I can't stand it. The sentiment's flowing by the gallon today." They were both laughing. They walked up the steps.

The television set was showing a football game from somewhere in the States, but Howard and Gary were talking hockey over it, Howard saying, "Half the guys in the WHL are just wishy-washy rookies, eh? They shouldn't even be on the ice in major league hockey. And the Russians train twelve months out of the year, while our guys are out playing golf."

"That's right," Gary said. "We can't even pass . . . The Russians were playing hockey and the Canadians were playing tiddly winks . . . Oh, hi there, Alan."

Gary seized Alan by the hand and squeezed as hard as he could. Then he jerked Alan into the room. "How the hell are you?" he said, and hit Alan on the shoulders with his knuckles.

"I was doing fine until I came in here." He wants to sleep with me, Alan thought, and he doesn't even know it.

Gary was smoking his cigar with a grinning toothy flourish. He looked to Alan as though he were about to say, "They can all walk the plank." Howard sat perfectly erect on the couch, his tie and jacket still on, smoking his pipe.

The baby was crying. Betty stuck her head through the door. "Hey, Gary, change the monster will you? I'm making gravy."

"Me? You're not talking to me, are you, puss?"

"Off your backside, sweet," she said.

"Oh, mother of Jesus! The next thing, they're going to want the vote. Eh, kid?" And passing Alan, he gave him a rough quick pat that was almost an embrace.

Alan began to drift reluctantly toward the kitchen, found himself stopped by Amy who began to stroke him as though he were a large dog. "Oh, Alan, I wanted to talk to you, but you're so elusive lately. I know you're not going to like this . . ."

"Still haven't got a sitter?"

"You're so perceptive. It's Hallowe'en. We're going to Betty and Gary's. Could you pick up Jeanie and feed her . . . I'll give you some money . . . and then take her to the party at St. John's?"

"We could go to a masked ball," Jeanie said gravely and went off into a high strained laugh. Her mother jumped back. Neither she nor Alan had seen the little girl who, somehow, had been standing right next to them.

"My God!" Amy said. "You sneak around like . . . like a . . ."

"Like a mouse," Jeanie said.

"Oh, you've got mud on your good shoes, young lady! You come with me."

"Yeah, of course I'll do it," Alan said to his sister's retreating back.

Alan sighed and walked into the kitchen. His mother, aproned, looked up. "Alan, dear, I was afraid you'd forgotten us. I'm so glad you're here now. We can eat soon, love. Come and kiss me. Isn't your hair awfully long? I suppose it's the style . . . I do wish you'd call me now and then, love, I do worry about you so. You seem thinner . . . Did you see the front lawn? I have a new one now . . . Koko or Toko or something. I can't keep their names straight. He seems much better than the other one. I don't think you even noticed, did you, dear? Alan, I'm so glad you're here! Are you all right?"

"I'm fine, mother," he said, and found himself flooding with a familiar weariness.

"I JUST DON'T KNOW WHAT TO DO ABOUT JEANIE," Amy said. She was sitting on her mother's bed, smoking one of her infrequent cigarettes. She never looks right smoking, Betty thought, watching her sister's abrupt movements. She doesn't even inhale. The air between them was filling with a series of angry puffs.

"Why do you have to do anything?" Betty said. "Oh, give me one of those!"

"I thought you'd stopped."

"I did. Give me one anyway. Thanks . . . I had to quit or Gary never would have . . . OK, what's the matter with Jeanie."

"You know what's the matter with Jeanie."

"Well, she's a little tomboyish . . ."

"A little! Betty, my God! You know, she used to say to me, 'I'm not going to be a girl when I grow up, mummy. I'm going to be a boy.' I think she'd still say it if she hadn't learned that it drives me absolutely frantic."

"It's a different generation, you know. A lot of girls go through a tomboy phase."

"I don't think it's just a phase with Jeanie," Amy said. "I've read everything I can get my hands on, and it doesn't bode very well."

Poor Amy, Betty thought, she's always talked like a Victorian novel. "What doesn't bode very well?"

"I'm afraid she's going to grow up to be a lesbian," Amy said, depositing this piece of information as though unloading a huge weight at her sister's feet. "Why does it keep happening to us? First there's Alan . . ."

"Alan's fine!"

"Alan's made a very good adjustment to *his problem.*"

"Oh, Jesus!"

"Don't hide your head in the sand. That's what mother's done all these years. I started reading about . . . well, 'gender conflict' is what they call it . . . and it just made me sick. I could just see so clearly everything that happened to Alan. You know, I was the one who started putting dresses on him . . . I'll never forgive myself."

"Somehow it seemed so easy with him."

"I know it did. He was always playing with Mother's clothes. They just seemed to delight him . . . the colours and the textures, And I thought, oh, he'd make such a pretty little girl. He was always pretty, right from the first day they brought him back from the hospital . . . Those big eyes and long lashes . . . And you were unfortunately just the right size, and so . . ." She shrugged.

"If you want to have a guilt-sharing session," Betty said, "I can get in on it too. Alan always loved playing with me . . . playing *dolls* with me. And it just seemed perfectly natural to dress up Alan too. He and I were really close as kids. We did everything together. It was like having a little sister."

"But you see . . ." Amy said. "Well, what happened to Alan . . . I don't want the same thing to happen with Jeanie."

"Do you think it's that serious?"

"It just might be. I started reading, and everything fell into place. She was a prickly, kind of nasty little baby, and then a very active child. Always played with trucks and guns, always played with boys, and the rougher the better. She's fallen out of more trees than I even looked at as a girl. And no interest in dolls, no interest in pretty clothes. Try to put her into a dress and she throws a fit . . . Oh, I know what they think of me . . . old prissy Amy. But I'm not *that* old-fashioned. I know that the world's changing. But one thing . . . Well, all the reading I've been doing . . . You know there's a difference between what they call 'gender role preference' and 'gender identity.' It's like . . . 'gender role preference' is if a girl wants to be a truck driver or an engineer or something like that, but she still thinks of herself as a woman. But if her 'gender identity' isn't right, she doesn't just want to do the things a man does, she wants to *be a man*. Do you understand?"

"Yes."

"All right. So I know Jeanie's never going to be Miss Canada. But I just don't want her to grow up to be a lesbian. I don't want to make the kid miserable, but . . ." She pressed one of her long white hands over her eyes.

"Are you crying?"

"No, it's all right . . . And Howard just doesn't see any problem. He just says, 'She'll outgrow it.' But I'm afraid she isn't going to outgrow it. And I just don't know what to do . . . except send her to Stafford House. At least there she'd get approval for being feminine and disapproval for being masculine, and maybe she'd turn into a reasonable facsimile of a girl. That's all I want. Just a reasonable facsimile."

She can always get me to feel sorry for her, Betty thought. I don't know how she does it. God help me, I never want to turn into a lean and worried housewife living in the suburbs. Never never never.

HOWARD CLEARED HIS THROAT. "Do you think there's anything wrong with my daughter?" he asked Gary Kovarian.

"Hell no," Gary said. "What makes you think there is?"

"I don't think there is," Howard said, "but Amy does. She thinks Jeanie's too much of a tomboy."

"Oh, Christ, man, a girl can't be too much of a tomboy these days. It's the in thing to be. She'll start a Woman's Liberation group in her school. She'll be the hit of her class."

Howard laughed.

"She'll tone down a bit when she comes to dating age," Gary said.

"That's it. But Amy's a great one for making mountains out of molehills . . . Are you watching this?" Gary shook his head. Howard turned off the television. "Amy's got a great streak of drama in her. She's got to find problems where there aren't any problems."

"If she's anything like Betty, why don't you try a little force . . ." He laughed at the expression on Howard's face. "No, man, I don't mean take her over your knee. I mean *talk* forcefully. I know Betty was spoiled rotten. I bet Amy was too."

"My sister," Howard said through teeth clenched around the pipestem, "was a bloody roaring tomboy . . . Go out in the bush in the summer . . . could outrun me, outshoot me. Hell, she was better than all the boys. Now she's married and got three kids."

"There you are," Gary said. "We mollycoddle our kids today. If you give them a lot of good outdoor exercise, a firm direction . . ."

"Now you're onto it, eh? That's the only thing that's wrong with Jeanie. That goddamn free school. Why, Jesus, Gary, they don't have to do sweet buggerall."

"I'd yank her right out of there. The public schools are plenty good enough for kids. That's what we pay taxes for."

"I couldn't agree with you more. But now Amy's got another idea. It's that damn girls' school that she and your wife went to."

"Christ, you want to send her out there with that little bunch of snobby brats, bunch of little pseudo-debutantes for fuck's sake?"

"Maybe she'd learn how to add."

"She could learn how to add at Eric Hamber."

"That's it. But Amy doesn't agree, of course."

"Why'd you ever take her out of public school?"

"Jeanie got into some trouble." Howard began to chuckle. "They were playing a pickup game of soccer after school, and Jeanie was the only girl playing, in fact she was the best damn soccer player around the place. And there was one little boy . . . Oh, he wasn't so little either, eh? He said he wasn't going to play with a girl. He pushed Jeanie down, and Christ, she trounced him! Sent him crying home to his mommy with a bloody nose."

"Good for Jeanie," Gary said.

"Oh, it was priceless. And then Amy said . . . You won't believe this, Gary . . . Amy said, 'I'm going to take her right out of that school. I won't have my daughter around kids like *that*.' Eh? Just as though it was the boy who beat up Jeanie."

"That's fucking funny. I think it's good for a girl to have a bit of spunk in her."

"That's it," Howard said. "I think girls are better for it in the end, if they've done something besides sit around all their lives and paint their faces." Both men laughed.

MRS. LEHMAN, HER SON, AND HER GRANDDAUGHTER were huddled together peering into the bird cage. A small yellow bird, his head cocked to one side, was peering back at them. "Cheep, cheep, cheep!" The bird didn't answer.

"Maybe he doesn't have much to say today, Mother," Alan said.

"Oh, naughty dickie bird. Cheep cheep cheep!"

"Cheep cheep cheep," Jeanie said. She was grinning wickedly.

"Cheep cheep cheep," Mrs. Lehman said.

"Speak up, bird!" Alan said.

The bird said nothing. He cocked his head to the other side.

"Now what's the matter with you today, naughty little dickie? Mrs. Lehman said. "You were singing just like a nightingale before anybody came."

"He probably just sings in the shower," Alan said.

"Oh, no. He just sings like a little nightingale. Don't you dear? Sing for Mother now. Cheep cheep cheep."

"Cheep cheep cheep," said Jeanie.

"Cheep cheep cheep," said Alan. They exchanged amused glances. and Jeanie began to fly around the kitchen, flapping her arms and singing, "Cheep cheep cheep!" in a small treble voice.

Alan immediately took after her, flapping frantically, and booming a bass voice: "CHEEP CHEEP CHEEP!"

"Really, children!" Mrs. Lehman said. "Children, now really!"

Jeanie jumped onto a kitchen chair and preened herself. "What kind of a bird am I? Churp churp churp?"

"You're a robin," Alan said.

"No."

"You're a little parakeet?" her grandmother said.

"Goldfinch?"

"No."

"Nightingale?"

"No, Churp churp *churp*!"

"All right, dear, what are you?" said Mrs. Lehman.

"I'm a grackle!" Jeanie yelled and jumped off the chair.

"What am I?" Alan said. He rose on his toes, spread his arms out stiffly. "Awk!" he said.

"A puffin?" his mother said.

"I know," Jeanie yelled between spasms of laughter. "A buzzard!"

"Right," Alan said.

"Oh, really, Alan," Mrs. Lehman said. "A buzzard!"

"Now you be one, Grandmother," Jeanie said.

Mrs. Lehman smiled oddly, then extended stiff fingers and waddled up and down the kitchen splay-footed. "You're a penguin!" Jeanie yelled.

"That's right, dear."

Suddenly the bird in the cage fluffed out his feathers and began to sing. He produced a shower of small delicate notes like pinpricks. Alan was laughing so hard that he allowed himself to slide down the wall and collapse weakly onto the floor. "He thinks he's in an aviary!" he said.

"Such a little dear," his mother said to the bird. "Such a sweet little dickie. I knew you'd sing for Mother. I never doubted it for a minute."

"Cheep cheep cheep!" Jeanie yelled, jumping up and down.

"Cheep cheep cheep," Alan answered, and went off again into a fit of laughter.

"SOMETHING'S GOT TO HAPPEN," Alan said. He was sprawled, boots off and feet up on the coffee table, in Trish and Donna's apartment. And even though he hadn't eaten any of the turkey, he was still uncomfortably full from his mother's dinner. For the last few days, he'd been eating tiny meals, bits and bites throughout the day; he found now that he couldn't handle that much food at one sitting; he was suffering.

"Things are just too weird lately," he said. "I'd come out, if I knew what to come out into."

"Well, what do you want?" Donna said.

"The same thing I've always wanted," he said, shrugging, "I want to be a girl."

"Have you ever thought of having a sex change operation?" Tricia asked him.

"Of course I've thought of it. But there are a couple of things about it that bother me. One thing is . . . I really like my penis, eh? I'm kind of attached to it." He laughed without humour. "And there's something in me that . . . Well, it would be a kind of mutilation . . . would be unnatural . . . something like that. I just have the feeling that I should stick with the equipment that came with me. And the other thing . . . Well, you know what I'd be if I had a sex change operation? I'd be a lesbian."

There was a hesitation in the room as though someone were counting, one, two, three, and then the women laughed. "Whew," Donna said, "That's an interesting idea."

"You really don't like boys, eh?" Trish said.

"I can't say that absolutely. I don't like *men*, I know that. But sometimes boys will turn me on . . . once in a long time. Young, slender, kind of tough boys . . . pretty boys. They've got to have something feminine about them, but not like a drag queen. Just slender young boys with a kind of girlishness. The exact quality is very rare. I only see somebody like that maybe once a year . . . But basically I like girls."

Donna was chuckling. "A male lesbian," she said. "I never even thought of that."

"I used to sit over in the damn public library," Alan said, "and read my way through all those books on abnormal sexuality just trying to find out if there was anybody at all anywhere like me. I finally decided I must be what they call a "heterosexual transvestite" . . . And wow, was that a relief! You know, finally found a *name* for it. But that's as far as I got, because nobody seems to know a damn thing about it. All I could ever find was like maybe a paragraph . . . or a footnote."

He swirled the brandy in the glass, watching the smooth honey-like flow of the liquid up the sides of the glass; it spilled over the reflection in the crystal. He could see Tricia in the glass. He swirled her over with brandy. "Look," he said, "Do you mind . . . I mean . . . You know, I just come barging in here. I had to talk to somebody."

"No problem at all."

"You know, Alan," Trish said, (She had been studying him, resting her chin on her hand.) "there are some gay girls . . . sort of wishy-washy AC-DC girls . . . you know, kind of on the cusp . . . who would like you. Don't you think so, Donna?"

"Hummm," Donna said, "Not the real gay girls . . . But yeah . . . Somebody on the edge. That's what your friend sounded like. The one you told us about."

"Sandy," he said. "I just found out today she's married. She's got a kid."

"Well, she probably got scared," Donna said. "Do up everything straight as a pin, eh?"

"Alan," Trish said slowly, "Let me put a dress on you."

"What?"

"I just want to see . . . what happens."

His thickly weighted after-dinner lethargy was gone; he felt an electric tingle in his stomach. "Yeah, man," Donna said, "I'd like to see that too."

"All right," he said.

"That didn't take much argument," Donna said, laughing.

"Come on," Trish said. He followed her into the bedroom. "I don't want to do a big production number, eh love? Just want to see what happens with a minimal effort." She handed him a pair of black tights.

He stripped off his clothes, pulled the tights on over his jockey shorts. She fastened a bra around him, stuffed it with Kleenex. "OK, now let's see . . ." She gave him a black jersey. He slipped it over his head. "Oh, this ought to do it . . . no waistline at all.": a wine-coloured, corduroy mini-dress, now thoroughly out of fashion, cut straight down and flaring into a slight A-line skirt. "Christ," Tricia said.

"What?"

"I'm just amazed, that's all . . . Here, let me do something with your hair." She brushed his hair forward, fastened it on either side with a bobby pin; it now framed his face and hid his sideburns. "You wouldn't get into my shoes . . . Hey, Donna, do you have any femmy shoes?"

They heard Donna's throaty chuckle. "Yeah, in the closet . . . in the back. *Way* in the back." Trish found a pair of old low-heeled dress pumps. Alan slipped his feet into them. "Well, that was quick," Tricia said.

"What? What do I look like?"

"Come on, let's show Donna." They walked back into the living room. Alan stood stiffly in the middle of the floor.

"It's amazing, isn't it?" Trish said.

"It sure is. Christ, man, you look like a little conservative school teacher or something."

"You know, love," Trish said, "you really have missed your calling. There are so goddamned many female impersonators around who just don't make it, and you are just perfect. I mean perfect. What did it take . . . five minutes? What did we do? Hardly anything. And it isn't any question of you *passing*. We could walk into the Clear Crystal right now and nobody would think you were a gay boy. They'd think you were one of *us*. And those women have sharp eyes."

"You're kidding me," Alan said.

"No, love, look." Tricia pointed to the full-length mirror in the corner by the door. Alan stepped in front of it and looked. He saw an absolutely unremarkable girl. His legs began to shake.

"He doesn't even have any makeup on," Trish said.

"Why don't you go work in a club, Alan? . . . Toronto or California."

"That's not his trip, eh?" Donna said. "He's no drag queen. Those dudes are into glamour, man . . . tinsel and sequins, and that's not your trip, is it?"

"No," Alan said. He walked unsteadily back to the couch and sat down.

"He doesn't look a bit campy, eh?" Donna said.

"No," Trish said, "he looks real."

Alan stared down at the carpet; he was blushing. The women burst out laughing. "Christ, love," Tricia said. "You don't have a problem. If you looked like Gordie Howe, you'd have a problem. But you don't even have much of a beard, eh? But you could have electrolysis done . . . Hey, you don't believe me, do you?"

"I don't know."

"Well, come on," she said, standing.

"Let's go downtown. I'll *show* you. We'll go in a restaurant and have a cup of coffee. And you know who people will stare at, don't you? Not you. *Donna!*"

Donna laughed. "That's right, man."

"Come on, Alan. Let's do it."

His entire body began to shake. His hand was shaking so badly that he had to put down the brandy glass. "I . . . I can't," he said. His teeth were chattering. His mouth had gone dry. The idea of going out on the street was stark terror.

"Calm down,: Donna said, patting his shoulder. "You don't have to go anywhere."

"I'm going to change," he said and ran into the bedroom.

LESLIE WAS AWAKE. The moment before, she must have been soundly asleep because there was no memory of anything at all. But now she was awake, wondering why the alarm hadn't gone off. The dim yellow glow of the clock face was the only light in the room: five-thirty, precisely the time the alarm *should* have gone off. Then she remembered she hadn't set it for five-thirty, she'd set it for seven. She'd retired yesterday. I'll go back to sleep, she thought. But she was wide awake. She could hear the rain outside falling steadily.

She stretched her legs. They were sore: feet, calves, and thighs. She linked her fingers and reached out into the dark, pushing, and her arms and shoulders were sore. I've really done myself in, she thought. Going to hobble around today like I'm eighty. Athletics . . . it's crazy. You always have some part of you that's sore. No matter how good the shape you're in, you can always pull something, work out too hard. You are never allowed to forget that you have a body. Swimmers, the most amazing hypochondriacs, always worrying about their sleep, their diet, their muscles. Well, it's over.

She pulled the blanket up to her nose, cuddled down into the pillow. But she was wide awake.

What the hell are you doing to me? she addressed some part of herself. But the part that was doing it didn't answer. She turned on the light, sat up, swung her feet out of the bed. It was cold and moist in the room, the window standing wide open . . . What do I think I am, some kind of Spartan maiden? She hurried over, wincing from the ache of her stiffened legs, and slammed the window. She pushed her cold toes into the worn pair of pink bunny-fur slippers that someone—one of her aunts probably—had given her when she'd graduated from high school. And then she sat in the only chair and looked around her bare undecorated room. All that was on the walls was a framed certificate stating that she, Leslie Cameron Fraser, had once held a world record. And now what am I supposed to do? she thought, sit here until it's time to go to work? The back of her neck hurt, dully, as though it were pressed by a padded vice. She had a headache. And it was raining outside. This is the only part of me that's real, she thought. The library's not real, Susan Mackenzie's not real, cocoa and children's books at night aren't real. This is it, the only thing I've got. She stripped off her pajamas, pulled on panties and jeans, sweater and runners. She rolled a towel and stuffed it into the pocket of her oversized torn raincoat (another ancient gift or hand-me-down). She had located the bathing cap in the pocket of her jacket before she remembered that she didn't need it anymore. Good, she thought. She grabbed the red umbrella (someone had left it at the library and never returned for it), turned out the light, and hurried out of her room. It doesn't matter, she thought. Doesn't matter that I can't beat every girl in Canada anymore, that I can't even beat every girl in B.C. It just doesn't matter. It's all I've got.

The entrance to the rooms on Leslie's floor was at the side of the house; she had to walk down a narrow lane bounded by a hedge to get to the street. She stopped at the end of the lane to raise her umbrella, looked down the length of the walk, and saw her grandfather waiting for her under the streetlight. He wasn't as she remembered him from the rest home, rather more as when she'd been ten or twelve: a bald, energetic, old man with white eyebrows and a wry, somewhat frightening, smile. "Grandpaw!" she said out loud. The old man nodded to her. There was nothing the least bit ephemeral about him; she could see him clearly: the checked lumber jacket, baggy trousers, and gum boots. The old man had been dead now for six years.

Something—it felt like a lump of cotton—was stuck in Leslie's throat. She swallowed it and began to walk quickly down the lane, but when she reached the sidewalk, he was gone. But that gave me a scare, she thought. Must have been an old derelict, some funny old man out drinking all night and walking the streets. But Christ, he looked like Grandpaw!

The rain was blowing in her face. She walked more quickly than usual, past the Danish bakery and the record store, past the Page of Cups, now darkened . . . Good morning, Page . . . and she was halfway across Sherwood Park before she realized that someone was waiting for her on the steps of the school. Oh no, she thought, stopping. There wasn't enough light to tell, but it seemed as though an old man were lounging there.

She stood and listened to the rain tapping on her umbrella. He seemed to be hunched up with his hands in his pockets. But now he shifted, straightened up and waved at her . . . just the way, when he'd see her coming from a distance, he used to wave, when she'd gone to visit. Her teeth began to chatter. I will watch very carefully, she thought, and began to walk slowly toward the school. By the time she reached the foot of the concrete steps, she could see that it *was* her grandfather. He smiled and looked down at his feet, rubbed the back of his neck: gestures she'd seen him make hundreds of times.

And she didn't know how it had happened (although she'd been watching for it), but by the time she'd climbed the steps, he was gone.

She looked back across the park the way she'd come. Everything seemed perfectly ordinary. Her hand was shaking so badly she could scarcely get the key into the lock. Once inside, she found herself running down the hall past the lockers, banging through each of the doors as fast as she could, going down and around, through the gym, through the weight room, and finally into the dressing room off the pool. Breathless, with the sound of her heart in her ears, she pushed through this last door. And there was just enough light in the room, a grey chilly slant of it from the high dirty windows, to see that someone was waiting for her, sitting on the bench in front of the locker where she always stored her clothes.

Leslie began to cry. It wasn't a usual crying; there was no sobbing with it, no change in her breathing or slightest motion of her diaphragm, just a steady flow of tears down her cheeks. It was a detached way of crying, something she'd never experienced before, as though the tears were unrelated to any emotion . . . certainly not related to an emotion as ordinary as grief. When I turn the light on, she thought, he won't be there.

She turned the light on, and he was sitting on the bench not ten feet away. She could see the veins in his nose and cheeks, the dirt under his fingernails, his white eyebrows . . . even such details as the rust on the snaps of his jacket, the mud on his gumboots. He was smiling at her, that wicked old Scots grin that used to terrify her as a child. She was angry at him. What was he doing here? Why hadn't he stayed in his grave where he belonged? "What do you want, Grandpaw?" she said sharply. And he was gone.

She ran into one of the stalls, jerked down jeans and underpants. She'd made it just in time; her bowels had turned liquid, and now liquid was pouring out of her as forcefully as if someone had overturned a bucket of water. Her teeth had begun to chatter again; she seemed to be having a chill. She bent double and pressed her forehead into her fists. She was afraid for a moment that she might pass out, but then her head cleared. She sat up.

He'd gone quite mad in his last years, punching attendants, lurching through the halls, yelling in a thick Scots dialect recalled from his childhood . . . from the Glasgow of sixty or seventy years before. She remembered his glittering and terrified look as he'd pushed away the young men in their white coats and stumble toward her and her father, yelling, "Awa tae fuck, ye wretched Christian buggers . . . Ye bloudy wee men . . . Ye dinna ken wha I seen! . . . Awa tae fuck wi ye!" They'd had to strap him down. At the end, he'd refused to eat. She'd sat next to the bed, seeing him quiet finally, withered and small, with the tube running into his arm. The quietness had brought lucidity: he'd known his relatives again, had asked for Leslie, but by the time she'd come, he'd forgotten her. She'd sat and patted his hand while he'd muttered something about the drums and rattles . . . hearing the drums and the rattles in the night. When she'd risen to go, he'd turned clear eyes to her and said, "Aye, Leslie, ye're a guid lassie."

She began to cry again. This time it was the usual kind of crying. She pulled on her jeans, ran into the dressing room, and called out to the empty space: "It's all right, Grandpaw! You can come back. Come back, grandpaw!"

She sank to her knees on the cold concrete floor, then stretched out full length and hid her face in her hands. I am losing my mind, she thought. I am genuinely losing my mind.

Eventually she sat up. Well, I'm here, she thought. It's pointless not to do it. Usually she stood a moment looking across the pool, but today she merely stripped and dived in quickly. The swimming quieted her, as it always did now, but she didn't make her three thousand yards. Walking home afterward, she felt exhausted, as flat and grey as what the day had become: steady rain and grey sky, the ordinary world of people on their way to work, cars, shops opening. Back in her room, she made toast, scrambled four eggs on the hot plate. If I stopped swimming, I couldn't eat like this, she thought. She was yawning. Now I could go to sleep . . . now when I've got to go to work.

I must become perfectly ordinary, Leslie thought. Unless I do, I'll be lost. But lost into what? She didn't know . . . only that she was as terrified of it as she would have been to dive into the rough icy seas off the coast in winter. But even that terror seemed flattened now, pushed back. She was beginning to realize how completely she'd exhausted herself the day before; she yawned again. And she had never worn a dress to work, not once, but now she pulled one at random out of her closet. They were all out of fashion, old dresses, skirts too short, but it didn't matter. She slipped into the dress. It was blue; she'd never liked it. And pantyhose. And her one pair of good shoes. It doesn't matter, she thought, yawning. Fatigue was making her eyes water.

Her little car seemed perfectly ordinarily. Driving to work seemed a perfectly ordinary thing to do—through the usual British Columbia autumn rain and there would be nothing new or peculiar at the library. I'm going to have to have a cup of coffee to get through the morning, she thought. Going to forget my absurd athlete's ethics and drink a cup of coffee. Ordinary people drink coffee. I'll go out for a minute. Ted won't mind. I'll just flirt with him, and he won't mind. That's the ordinary thing that ladies do. She yawned again. It doesn't matter, she thought, and it won't matter. Ordinary people probably aren't very happy much of the time anyway.

FLAT AND BANAL, LESLIE THOUGHT, like one of these modern children's books in which all the magic turns at the end into a lecture on soil erosion and conservationism. She was sitting at her desk, a stack of books in front of her. She was supposed to be preparing a lecture for some damn mothers' group on children's literature. She was trying to make notes, but so far all she had written at the top of the page was "flat and banal." If I can manage to waste another ten minutes, she thought, the kids will start coming in from school and then I can put it off until tomorrow. That's it: put everything off until tomorrow. She was imagining the inevitable questions from the progressive young mothers who would say, "What is all this nonsense about kings and queens and princesses, goblins and fairies? We live in the Twentieth Century. Aren't there any books about *modern* children . . . with *active* little girls in them?" And yes, Leslie would say, there are hundreds of them. They come mass-produced on a conveyor belt straight from the States, books full of modern kids all of whom live within fifty miles of New York City . . . full of brash, flip, ironic, bright, neurotic modern kids all of whom could stand a good spanking. But she couldn't say that.

And the old-fashioned mothers were almost worse, the ones in love with Christopher Robin, the ones in love with some antique vision of childhood, golden and Wordsworthian. The kids are OK, Leslie thought, but it's the mothers. She yawned. Her strange experience of that morning had fallen away, now seemed impossibly remote. Flat and banal, that's what everything comes down to in the end. She couldn't imagine what had possessed her to wear a dress to work, particularly this absurdly short dress. Ted had gone practically crazy when he'd seen her; he'd followed her around all morning until she'd wanted to pull over the shelves on him, sink him under an avalanche of books. (I'll ask for a transfer, she thought, go to another branch.) What had she been thinking about? To be ordinary, perfectly ordinary. What a strange morning! Her life seemed to be coming apart into discrete sections, unrelated to each other. She was a different person at six o'clock in the morning than she was now in the late afternoon. Had she really seen her grandfather? And how could I hope to be ordinary anyway, she thought, in a children's department? Here, surrounded by fantasies.

She walked to the window. A steady sluice of rain was washing over it. If you can't make it in the adult world, if your fantasies aren't acceptable, then you write children's books. Is that what happens? Could she say that to the mothers? We take all of our impossible dreams and wishes and utopias and lay them on our kids. And oh, the incredible seductiveness of children's books! In her own childhood all she'd read had been boys' sports stories, but in library school she'd been drawn right in, caught in a world of enchantment. Magic! Maybe it's all for us, she thought. Maybe we should let the kids alone, let them watch television and read the backs of cereal boxes. And Susan Mackenzie was saying, "Hi, Leslie."

I've made it, Leslie thought. School's out. "Hi, Susan."

"Oh, Leslie, what a sweet dress!"

That's a compliment, I suppose. "Thanks." You look pretty good yourself, kid. "White and golden Lizzy stood . . ." Well, if not precisely white and golden, at least a good approximation . . . slender little girl in a shiny salmon-coloured dress, silly little shoes, salmon-coloured fingernails. White and salmon-coloured, Susan stood, waiting for instructions.

"You've got me today," Susan said.

"Oh, I do, eh?" The-half-remembered verse was appearing, unpleasantly, in Leslie's mind:

"Did you miss me!

Come and kiss me . . .

Eat me, drink me, love me;

. . . make much of me:

For your sake I braved the glen . . ."

Oh Christ! Leslie thought. "You can start shelving," she said. She turned back to the window, to the rain. I'd better take some time off, she thought. Something terrible's happening to me. And the fear of the morning was suddenly back, solid and real. It's no joke, she thought. No joke at all. She walked back to her desk and saw Jeanie trotting down the stairs: a small sturdy figure in khaki-green poncho, jeans, and small brown lace-up boots. She was curiously glad—even relieved—to see the child.

"Hi, Leslie. Here's *The Black Arrow* back. It's pretty neat up until the middle when Joan has to be a girl again, and then it's not so neat anymore. And here's a couple my mother had a chance to look at." She giggled. "She heartily approves. That's what she said. Did you find anything?"

"What was I supposed to find?"

"But you said to come back on Monday!"

"That's right. Stories with verses in them. Oh, Jeanie, I'm sorry. I just . . . Well, there must be something." She began to walk down the shelves. "The trouble with you is you've read half the library by now. Have you read *The Princess and the Goblin?*"

"No. What's it about?"

"There's a little princess, and the goblins are planning to steal her."

"Oh?" Jeanie said.

"And that's where the verses come in," Leslie said. "That's the way you scare away goblins, by saying verses to them."

"Oh, it is?" Jeanie said. Their eyes met. The little girl's face was thoughtful. What is she thinking about? Leslie wondered. Those cloudy grey eyes. "I knew that already," Jeanie said slowly. "OK, I'll take it." Then the grave face was transformed by the familiar elvish smile. "Hey, Leslie," she said, "you look really neat today. You look just like a pageboy."

"Thanks, Jeanie." Of all the comments she'd heard about her appearance that day, this had been the only one she'd liked.

"THE OTHER NIGHT . . ." ALAN SAID, "what did you do to me?" His voice sounded apologetic, not what he had intended at all. He had been planning to ask her the minute she opened the door, but when she had, something had stopped him: that she'd seemed such a perfectly ordinary old woman. She hadn't been surprised to see him, had invited him in, made him herb tea. And since, she'd been chatting with him about his life as though she'd known his family for years. It was as though he'd come to visit a grandmother or eccentric aunt, paying a duty call, sitting in her kitchen watching as she baked a pie. Except that she wasn't baking pie, she was selecting little bundles of dried leaves from the huge sheaves of plants hanging on the wall, dumping the bundles into a huge wooden mortar and grinding them.

"Oh my!" Mrs. Mackenzie said, laughing. "I didn't *do* anything to you." It was all so ordinary in the kitchen that he was ready to believe it. But then she said, "I just pushed on you in a certain way, and *you* did it. It's a trick, eh?"

"A trick?"

"It's not much of anything. Just a trick. You'll learn how to do it too." She had brought water to a boil in a black iron pot; she threw the contents of the mortar into it. The liquid bubbled up a moment and then subsided. She turned down the fire. "Come in the study, Alan," she said. "Susan may come back . . . Oh, in that broom closet right behind you . . . Get that big bucket. Yes, that one."

He followed her into the front room off the hall. It was paneled with dark wood, the walls lined with maps and bookshelves. There were racks of guns, huge leather chairs, a desk, a large world globe, and on the floor a bear pelt pretending to be a rug.

"This was my husband's study," she said. "He took wonderful journeys in here . . . with the National Geographic." Alan was embarrassed by the row of pipes over the fireplace, by the glass humidor still full of tobacco. He turned away, afraid of the old woman's pain. But she was laughing. "I'm afraid I've messed it up since he died," gesturing toward the heaps of books and papers, charts of the coastal waters, maps. "Just kick that stuff out of the way," she said, "and sit down."

Alan sat down, found himself facing a screaming distorted face, a stretched body squashed to the wall like a flattened insect. "What's that?"

"A wildcat. My husband shot him. We did a lot of hunting once, but I don't kill anything anymore . . . We were going to Alaska after he retired, going to . . ." She laughed again. "Oh well, but his heart stopped, poor old man." She saw Alan's look. "It's not bad for me anymore. He covered a lot of miles in here, Alan. He was a happy man . . . Well, let's see now. I was going to tell you about the trick."

"Yes?"

"It's like stringing beads, eh? I mean it isn't really, but we'll try it out that way. We all spend all of our time stringing beads, putting on one right after the other. We get so busy doing that, we forget that there are a lot of beads and a lot of strings lying around that we don't pick up. Well, the other night I saw that you were about to slip the next bead on your string, and I pushed it away so you couldn't get it. And your string broke for a little while."

Alan looked at her dumbly.

"Don't worry about it," she said. "It doesn't do much good to talk about it." She pushed herself up and left the room. He looked through the empty doorway, puzzled. He was still looking when she came back with a large mug and handed it to him. "It's not hot," she said. "I've cooled it with water. Just drink it right down now." Again he saw her as a kind, batty grandmother, prescribing sassafras tea or a similar ancient remedy for a cold. He took the mug and sipped. It didn't have a particularly unpleasant flavour. "Drink it right down now," she said, smiling, leaning over him.

He could see her dark furry eyebrows bobbing up and down; they seemed exquisitely funny. He drained the mug. She took it from his hands, pushed the bucket toward him with her foot. He smiled back at her.

The first spasm hit him, sharply, like an electric current in his stomach. She began to laugh. "Go ahead," she said, and kicked the bucket again.

"My God!" he yelled, suddenly terrified. "What the hell was that?" Then he was down on all fours, crouching over the bucket and throwing up.

"Don't fight it," she said. "You'll just hurt yourself."

As angry as he'd become, he abandoned himself to it. He vomited until there was nothing left. She handed him a rag to wipe his face, carried away the bucket, returned with a glass of water. "Go ahead," she said when he hesitated. "It's just water."

She sank down into the chair opposite him, laughing, her round heavy body shaking. She covered her eyes with her hands; she snorted and snuffled. She made a sound like a horse whinnying.

"You're doing it again!" he yelled, jumped up, ready to run.

"Sit down, Alan!" she said sharply. "Now tell me . . . when did you first know that there was something strange about you?"

"I don't know . . . When? . . . Christ . . ."

"You're a very little boy," she prompted him.

He sank back onto the chair. He was shaking and sweating. His stomach ached painfully. "Ah," he said. "I was in my crib, and I kept hearing things."

"What things?"

"I don't know . . . I'm very little . . . I can't talk yet, don't have any words yet. I can feel . . . the wood . . . the corner . . . a kind of post on the crib. I'm pressing my chin against it. And there are sounds out there somewhere. It's a kind of buzzing . . . and a light. I'm scared. I want to yell out, but I can't. I can remember the bars

. . . or rungs . . . or whatever . . . in the crib. The light's on in my room. I think my mother left the light on . . . Christ, I don't want to remember this!"

"So it was a buzzing and a yellow light, eh?"

"Yes."

"Was that the only time?"

"No. All the time I was little. Sometimes I scream, and my mother comes and takes me into bed with her. I remember my sister Amy . . . just a little girl . . . and they came and got me. And Amy kept saying, 'What's the matter with Alan? What's the matter with Alan? Mommy, look at his eyes!' Because I was peering all around. I could see it."

"What was it?"

"I don't know. A kind of pattern in the air. A yellow pattern . . . or like coloured rain falling. I'm so scared I can't make a sound. Just gasping."

"How old are you?"

"I don't know. Two or three I guess. Oh Jesus, and it used to try to come in the window!"

"Sit down. It's all right. What window?"

"In my room. It'd be there at the window! Oh God! . . . This is later on. I'm five or six . . . Oh God! . . . It's just outside the window. A dream . . . that I've got to get to the window and shut it . . . push it down. But I can't budge it . . . because I'm just a little boy . . . and I can't . . . But I wake up, and it's already in! Oh Jesus!"

"Shut up, now! You're just frightening yourself. All right. Take your time. What direction did the window face?"

"Direction?"

"Yes. The direction."

"I can't remember that."

"Don't you remember the house?"

"Oh, yes. My mother still lives there."

"All right then."

"Well, let's see . . . The room's up in the corner, and the mountains were over on the . . . Let's see. It was north. No, more northwest."

"Good. And how long did it keep coming back?"

"Until I was in grade school. I learned how to stop it."

"How did you do that?"

"I used to recite the multiplication tables until it went away. I used to go: two times two is four, two times three is six, two times four is eight. Like that. Until it stopped. Once it happened in school. Oh Christ, that was terrible! I didn't think it could happen in school. I was . . . It was a reading period or something, because everything was quiet, and I was getting a book at the back of the room, and it started. I thought, oh, this is just awful. What will I do? Because I couldn't make a fuss in school, eh? I stood there and recited the multiplication tables until it went away." He was becoming calmer. He opened his eyes. "What are you doing to me?" he said.

"You're split along a certain seam," she said, "and we have to break you there so you can open."

"Suppose I don't want to split?" he said, laughing harshly from the strain.

"You'd probably split there anyway . . . without me," she said. "But it might kill you . . . All right, was that the last of it? In grade school?"

"No. It happened just once more. When I was twelve or thirteen, I ah . . . I used to . . . well . . . I used to hide in the bathroom and put on my sister's clothes. And there was one day . . . Well, usually it was pretty quick because I didn't want anybody to catch me. But one day, there was nobody home, and I really did it right. I put on a whole outfit, and then I got scared and took it off . . ."

"Slow down. What did you put on?"

"You know this isn't easy to talk about."

"Stop trying to pull everything back together. You can do that later after you leave. You'll be able to protect yourself, but later. All right, what?"

"It was kind of funny. I made myself sort of half a little girl, half woman. Put on my sister's dress and shoes and stockings, but then I made myself up like a grown woman, and put on a wig of my mother's. I looked at myself in the mirror, walking up and down, trying to walk like a girl, move my hands like a girl. Then I got scared. I mean it didn't come back then. It was something else. I got scared because it seemed so absolutely natural. I mean, when I first started putting on the clothes, I got really turned on, had an erection, and I had to wait until it went down before I could put the panties on. But then, after I got dressed, I was still turned on, I guess, because I felt a great excitement, but it had all gone inside. It just felt natural, you know, perfectly ordinary. I remember thinking, I didn't do it right. I shouldn't have put on all this makeup. Betty wouldn't have done that. It was the Mod period, and girls were wearing eye makeup and very pale lipstick, but I'd put on bright scarlet lips . . . very old-fashioned, you know, like my mother. I thought, well, that's not right. But *I* know what's right. I could just slip into Betty's clothes very easily, could even go downtown, and everybody would think I was an ordinary girl. I had this little English schoolboy haircut then, and it was a lot like girls were wearing, and I could have . . . Well, I even thought of doing it. Taking all the heavy makeup off, and taking Mother's wig off, and leaving Betty's clothes on, and fluffing my hair up a bit, and going out and getting on the bus and going downtown. I knew nobody would notice me. How easy it would be. And then it started to happen again, the buzzing . . ."

"Yes?"

"So I took the clothes off and put on my ordinary clothes and went out and started walking. I walked around and around the block . . . oh, it must have been for over an hour, until it stopped. And it never came back after that."

"Did you always want to be a girl?"

"Yes, ever since I can remember. When I was really little, I asked my mother how you could tell whether someone was a boy or a girl. She said, 'Their bodies are different.' That didn't make any sense to me. I looked at my hand, and it just looked like one of my sister's hands. That's what an uptight family I had. I'd never seen my mother or my sisters naked. So I decided there had been a mistake, that I really *was* a girl and they weren't telling me. It seemed cruel to me. And then later when I realized that I really was a boy, I used to pray every night, oh God, please make me into a girl."

She gestured for him to continue. "And it was really confusing, eh? Because my mother would say, 'Alan, you're going to grow up into a fine strong young man.' But I used to put on her high heels, and she thought it was funny. When I was little, my sister used to dress me up in girls' clothes, and my mother . . . just seemed to think it was funny. She'd say, 'Oh, Alan's always been so pretty.' And . . . well, my father was dead, eh? So there wasn't anybody around to bring any other point of view into it. And later on, when I started school, I realized . . . Oh, they called me a sissy and used to push me around, and I realized that I'd have to hide it. So I became very secretive. I never played with the boys, only girls. The boys seemed cruel and . . . well dirty, like animals or something. But I always had little girl friends I played with, Betty's friends. When I was six or seven, I got my courage up . . . I mean it really took courage because I knew by then that it was wrong somehow, and asked for a doll for Christmas. My mother didn't seem to think that was the least bit strange. She just got me a doll.

"Later on, when I was a teenager, I learned how to pretend I was a boy, how to act like a boy. And I changed schools by then, so there was . . ."

Mrs. Mackenzie gestured impatiently. "This isn't important."

"Not important? It's my bloody life!"

"Yes, Alan, I know it's important for you. It's the beads on your string. You just keep going over them, but it's nothing useful." The old woman seemed lost in thought. She was staring away, frowning. "Did you want to go to bed with boys?"

"No. That's another thing that was confusing. I used to think that if I were a girl, then I'd have to sleep with a boy, and I didn't want to sleep with a boy. I wanted to sleep with a girl. I wanted to be a girl and be around girls and have girl friends and sleep with girls. Almost like I wanted to live in a totally feminine world. I used to imagine . . . like it was my favourite fantasy . . . being in a very strict old-fashioned girls' school where everyone had to dress just so all the time, and I'd learn only feminine things . . . manners and makeup and fashion and sewing . . . and how to walk in heels . . ." He laughed nervously. "And I used to imagine I was the only boy there, but I was so completely feminine that nobody knew it but the teachers . . ."

The old woman sighed, shifted her weight in the chair. She seemed to be growing impatient. "I used to imagine," Alan said, talking quickly, "that the head mistress would take me into her office and say, 'Alan, since you're really a boy in disguise, you must work very hard. You must become the most feminine little girl in the school. I want to be able to use you for a model, point you out to the other little girls and say, that's the way you should be. That's the ultimate . . .'

"Hold on, you're going off again. You know, there's a difference between following a course and becoming obsessed with it. If you get too fascinated with the details of where you're going, you can

136

be lured away by certain . . . well, you can be destroyed very easily." She sighed again, rubbed one of her broad hands over her face. "Well, you have worked on it, haven't you?"

"I suppose I have. For years I . . ."

She held up a hand and stopped him. "No, that's enough of that. All right, Alan, you're a girl."

"What?"

"When you come back again, you will come back as a girl."

He sat, unspeaking, and looked at her. "The line lies in that direction," she said. "Use it. The way I broke the string for you . . . You can break the string for everyone else. You could stand up right now, dressed as you are, and walk out the door, and everyone would take you for a woman. If you knew how to break the string, you could walk into your mother's house, and she wouldn't know you. Do you understand?"

"No."

"All right. You don't know how to do it that way, but you do know how to do it. Use whatever you have to. But you must not have the slightest doubt or fear or hesitation. Not the slightest, eh? And listen to me very carefully. This is very important. All you have to do is say, 'Now I am a girl.' And then you are. And you will go firmly ahead without the slightest hesitation. What are you called?"

"Ellen," he said. "My name's Ellen."

"All right. You dress. You say, 'Now I'm Ellen, and I'm a girl.' When you want to change back, you change your clothes and say, 'Now I'm Alan. Now I'm a boy.' Do you understand? There must be no confusion between the two. You're either one or the other. Do you understand?"

"I think so."

"All right. Do you have a day off this week?"

"Yes, I have Wednesdays off."

"Come back Tuesday evening. Come for dinner. We'll catch the last ferry for Bowen Tuesday night, spend the night there, and come back on the last ferry Wednesday."

"Bowen?"

"I have property there. . . . And when you come on Tuesday, you will come as Ellen. Whenever you see me after this, you will be Ellen. Do you understand?"

"Yes. But look, is it only when . . . ?"

"No. You can be Ellen anytime you want. Go home now. I'm tired. Don't do anything unusual tonight. Do everything in a perfectly ordinary way."

He stood. "But look, Mrs. Mackenzie. What if I come over here and run into Susan?"

"If you run into Susan all she'll see is a perfectly ordinary young woman. She certainly won't see Alan. Tell her you're a relative . . . Yes, a cousin. Tell her you're my cousin Ellen Wallace from Winnipeg."

HE'S GETTING OLD, LESLIE THOUGHT SADLY. Not ancient like Grandpaw, just ordinary, everyday run-of-the-mill old. But why hadn't she noticed it so strongly before? (After all, she did visit him every couple of weeks.) It had struck her when she'd watched him take her coat and fold it carefully, lay it with a pat over the back of the chair: those precise finicky gestures . . . and his careful upright back. He's turning into a stiff, round old bear, she thought. His hair had been white for years; now it was scattered and thin but still wound about in a habitual pattern that must have hidden the bald crown when he'd been forty. His translucent skin had never tanned (she remembered him in the summer going the colour of brick, his huge bulbous nose flaking away), and now it was pale and pinkish and deeply seamed. His eyes had always been an alarming pale blue, and still were, but that sharp cutting edge they'd had, that bright frightening glitter, seemed to have been dulled. He sat now upright in his chair, and his eyes were watery and bemused. Oh, she thought, in three years he'll be seventy.

"Well, you weren't exactly training, eh kid?" her father said.

"Three thousand meters a day is more than *not* training," she said.

"Depends," he said, laughing, "on how fast you do it. That's workhorse stuff, Les. That's just grind."

Their living room had taken on the look of a museum, everything in it commemorating events that had been over and done with years ago. The careers of four swimmers (her father, Martin, Ed, and herself) were documented with trophies and medals, framed photographs and newspaper clippings. Weddings seemed to be the other events of interest . . . her grandfather's, her father's, Martin's. Here in a large gilt frame was the entire family. Sixty-one or two. She'd been on that uneasy edge between twelve and thirteen, a whittled stick of a child, long-legged and undeveloped. Well, she thought wryly, I never was going to develop very much. She remembered picking out that absurd outfit, and nobody around to stop her. She stood stiff and earnest in the photograph, holding flowers, the white gloves on her hands too big, the flouncy dress too young, and the ridiculous high heels of the time too old—a gawky awkward child—and no woman around to say, "Leslie, it's not right." But why didn't one of my aunts? she thought. Oh, but I didn't pay any attention to them. And there was gentle Martin, already losing his hair on his wedding day. And rakish handsome Ed, scowling. And her father, hale and grinning as though he'd live forever.

"What do you do, Dad," she said, "when you quit?"

"You coach, that's what you do."

"I never thought I wanted to do that."

"Why?"

"It seemed . . . well . . ." she shrugged, "sort of an anticlimax."

"It can be very satisfying, especially if you get somebody who goes all the way. Like you did."

"Like I *didn't*."

"Oh, Leslie, what did you want?"

"Just to go to Munich, that's all. That would have been enough."

He shrugged. They looked at each other across the distance of the room. "You worry too much, eh? It's been gone for years, and you're still worrying about it."

"I was just afraid . . ." she said, looking away. "I was just afraid I let you down." It seemed that she'd never been able to say that to him before.

"You never let me down. You were the best of all." He was smiling. "I think you must have let yourself down. That's what hurt. By that time I didn't have much to do with it anymore. You were coaching yourself when you were fourteen."

She didn't answer. "Les," he said. "Forget it. It's over. How many people hold a world record?"

"For a week!"

"Sounds to me like you're still feeling sorry for yourself," he said sharply. And then in a softened tone, "You might like coaching, eh? You get to really like the little buggers . . . get to really care about how they're doing."

"If I felt finished with it, maybe then I could coach."

He doesn't leap to his feet anymore, she thought . . . He'd pushed himself slowly out of the chair. The man who used to pace up and down alongside the pool, stopwatch in his hand, yelling, his step springy, his body tense and coiled . . . That man is gone now.

"Have you had dinner?"

"No, Dad."

"I have some stew on. There's enough for both of us. No . . . sit still. I'll get it ready." He paused in the doorway to the kitchen. "*I was afraid* . . . When you were a kid, I was afraid that you weren't having any fun. I was afraid that swimming was never any fun for you."

"Oh, I had my share of fun. Besides, one of us had to be serious."

They both laughed.

Poor Edward, she thought. Her father had been practically a one-man swimming team for B.C. back in the twenties. And then the first son, old slow-but-steady Martin, had turned into one of the best freestylers in Canada in the fifties. And along comes Ed and has to try to live up to *that*, and not only that, but a little sister two years younger damn near pushing him out of the pool. The only thing that saved him, she thought, was that I was a girl and he didn't have to compete with me.

But there had been one day . . . She laughed, remembering it. She and Ed had gone through years of hating each other, and one day after practice, he'd said, "You think you're something, don't you? Do you think you can take me in the hundred?" Even at the time, she'd thought it cowardly of him: of course she couldn't have taken him in a hundred. He'd been sixteen and big and strong as a lumberman, a dazzling sprinter with a start like coiled steel unleashing. And she'd been fourteen, a girl, lanky and underweight and still built like a kid. And she'd never been much of a sprinter, and never would be. What had she been thinking about to race him? Her father hadn't been there to see it, must have been talking to someone in the dressing room or he never would have let it happen, but the other swimmers had crowded the edge of the pool.

Ed had beaten her by a couple of body lengths, and they'd hung on the gutter, panting. She'd been furious, thinking: You coward! She'd yelled at him, "You don't have the guts to try it over eight hundred meters, do you?" And he'd had the guts. Her friends had told her later that he'd looked as though he were dying near the end, that they'd seriously wondered if he were going to drown before he finished. She'd beaten him by over three lengths of the pool. For a month after that he hadn't come back to practice.

She stood and walked to the mantle to look at his graduation picture. He's always been too handsome for his own good. Looks more like Mother than like Dad, she thought, just like me. And he'd always been in trouble. Stolen cars, and whiskey, and girls. But a fine sprinter. An incredible start. Without training, on sheer guts and self-confidence, he'd always been able to beat everybody . . . until he'd gone to the Nationals. They'd killed him at the Nationals, and he'd never swum again. She hadn't seen him now for years, would hear occasionally that he'd called her father, collect, from Toronto. And each time he'd called, he'd have a new job, the one that was going to make him rich. But each time he'd call, he'd need a "loan." Only twenty-six now, but married for the second time, and the last they'd heard, selling used cars. When she'd broken the world record, he'd called to congratulate her, and for once he'd paid for the call himself. She'd taken it as a final offer of peace, a sign that he'd forgiven her after all these years. But he'd signed off by saying, "*I* could have been good, Leslie. I just never wanted to."

Maybe that's what I'm afraid of, she thought, turning out like Ed . . . another mediocrity, just another ordinary screwed-up person who could have been good. She looked at the pictures. Here she was with her brothers at her most tomboyish; in fact it was impossible to tell from the photograph that she wasn't a boy, the youngest brother. And here she was a couple of years later, when she'd broken her first age-group record, a thin, very serious girl standing by the edge of the pool. And here was her graduation picture; the combination of her own badly applied makeup and the efforts of the asshole photographer who'd wanted to make her look glamorous had produced a stiff mask that no one ever recognized.

Is this me when I broke the world record? she thought. Is it really? How could I have broken a world record and looked like *that*? It was a spread in the newspaper, one shot of her in the water, another of her in clothes: in a short slick dress, in stockings, her hair set and her face painted. Karen Magnussen, here I come! And reading down the article . . .

"Leslie Fraser does not fit the stereotype of the woman athlete. In fact she looks as though she might win a beauty contest as easily as a swimming meet. She is pert, perky and pretty, and distinctly feminine . . ." Oh God! She turned away and walked into the kitchen.

Her father had white bread on the table. "You know better than this, coach," she said, tapping the loaf.

"I know, Les, but it's all they carry down at the corner." He'd sold the car after he'd retired. He could no longer afford to run it.

He set out plates of watery stew. She'd forgotten how terrible his cooking was; when she'd been growing up, it had been merely "food." But when she began to eat, she found that she was immensely hungry.

"What do you think you'll do?" her father asked.

"I haven't a clue. Maybe I will help you coach the club. I don't know . . . Dad?" she said, and this was what she had come to ask. "Do you remember when Grandpaw was in the hospital? When he was dying?"

"Yes."

"What was he talking about?"

"What do you mean?"

"He kept saying something about the drums and the rattles."

"Oh. He was talking about the Indians up at the inlet. He told me once that you'd only hear the rattles when the medicine man was working."

"Do you remember it up there?"

"Not very well. I remember the Indians used to scare me though. They seemed very dignified. One old fellow used to come and see Dad. He was a great chief . . . or that's what the old man said anyway. They used to sit and talk. I used to peek out of my bunk and watch them. I was very little, and that's all I remember. Guess the old man's mind went back to all that when he was dying . . . because he'd lived up there so long . . . with the Indians all around him. It kind of touches me, you know . . . that he should be thinking about the Indians when he was dying."

"Where was his place? His cabin?"

"I don't even know any more. Up Johnston's Inlet somewhere. Martin might know. You remember, he went up to visit when he was in high school."

"No, I don't remember, Dad. When Martin was in high school, I was just a baby."

"That's right too. Yes, that's right."

"How is Martin?"

"He's all right. I think he's happy up there."

Martin had planned on being a coach with a big swimming club, planned to teach phys ed in a Vancouver high school, but his first job had been up at Port Albert, not more than sixty miles from the inlet where his grandfather had lived for years. Martin had come home the first Christmas and told them Port Albert was a dirty little nondescript town with nothing to recommend it. From September to May, he'd said, there was nothing but steady rain. But he'd been teaching there ever since, had married a local girl and now had two children.

I wonder if he regrets anything? Leslie thought. I wonder if he feels that he's wasted himself? "I think I might go visit him," she said.

"He'd like that, Les. I'm sure he would."

They carried their coffee into the living room. Leslie passed the photograph of her mother that had stood on the desk all the time she'd been growing up. She always thought it a lovely face, a beautiful and warm face, strangely antique, wearing the period makeup of the forties. Her mother had died when Leslie had been only a few days old.

Her father was lowering himself carefully into a chair. His back must be bothering him again. He raised his coffee cup and toasted her. "Stick with it, kid," he said.

She wasn't sure what it was she was supposed to stick with but knew the comment to be one of his gestures of affection. They'd never been much of a family for sentimental speeches. "I will, Dad."

ALAN STOOD, NAKED, IN FRONT OF THE MIRROR IN HIS BEDROOM and looked at himself critically. "Do everything tonight in an ordinary way," Mrs. Mackenzie had told him, but he'd found that he couldn't do that: his usual way of thinking had been profoundly interrupted. The knot! Now if he were to paint that canvas of his life—that single line stretching for miles—he would have to add several other lines, all of them converging at the knot. A line for environment, he thought, a line for physical inheritance, and a third line for training. Yeah, I have been training for it, he thought, and I didn't even know it. Not fully, not consciously.

Since childhood he'd avoided any exercise that might have built up his arms and shoulders. In his teens he'd taken to collecting girls' fitness publications, had gone through daily "beauty" routines: stomach tucks and leg raises, kicking and stretching exercises. He'd rotated his feet to keep his ankles trim, had risen on his toes in sets of hundreds to build shapely calves. And since leaving home at eighteen, he'd taken dance classes. Ellen won't have any problems with her legs, he thought, she's got beautiful legs.

The only problem that Ellen was going to have was with her hips. There are plenty of narrow-hipped girls in the world, he thought, but none of them quite this narrow-hipped. This small firm ass (turning to the side to look at it) is unmistakably a boy's, but everything else is fine. Barefoot, he stood five-feet seven. He didn't have a scale to check it, but he knew that his weight was under a hundred and thirty pounds. His waist, relaxed, was twenty-eight inches, but that could be taken in. From ordering his bedroom wear through the mail, he knew that he took an 8 in girls' shoes. In a dress, he'd take a Misses 10 . . . or even possibly an 8. Ellen would be a tall slender girl, small-breasted, a bit of the willowy angular Vogue-model type. She would, he thought, be damn impressive. Probably a lot more impressive than Alan's ever been.

The problem was that Ellen didn't have anything to wear. The items in Alan's personal collection were all on the flamboyant side, and Ellen had to be very careful not to overdress or she'd look like a drag queen and not like an ordinary girl. So until Ellen could shop for herself, Alan would have to shop for her . . . as reluctant as he was to do that. It's going to cost me a bloody fortune, he thought.

The tub had filled by now. He lowered himself into the hot scented water. Taking his time, he shaved his legs all the way up to the crotch, shaved his stomach and chest and underarms. He climbed out of the tub, looked at his face in the mirror. Eyebrows, he thought. Most girls don't do much with them these days, but just a touch. He plucked the stray hairs over the bridge of his nose, thinned the brows slightly at the far edges. That's enough, he thought, or it'll show on Alan.

Back in the bedroom he opened his locked chest and laid out all of his collection on the bed. Padded bras and panties and stockings. And here was a cute little item, a genuine corset from a shop in California; it was finished in peach-coloured satin, edged with lace, fitted with garters, and severely boned, cut to give a dramatic indentation, "wasp waist" the catalogue had said. There was nothing more that Ellen could use. She certainly wouldn't go out on the street in a Mae West sheath dress or fifties spike heels.

He put on the dance belt he wore under tights for ballet classes, put on one of the padded bras, fitted himself into the corset. By the time he'd finished lacing it up, he'd broken out into a sweat. No, he thought, Ellen couldn't last an hour, not even half an hour, and (looking in the mirror), it's too much anyway. He checked himself with a tape measure. His waist was now twenty-four inches. No, he thought, that's unnecessary. He loosened the laces, checked himself again. Twenty-five inches. That's more plausible, he thought, that's believable. But could she wear it all day? He walked around the room, sat down on the bed, stood up. Maybe she could get used to it. If she's going to get in a Misses 10, she's going to have to.

He put on stockings and panties, and, to check the effect, the fifties heels, stood for a long time in front of the mirror. Ellen's not going to have any problems, he thought. There was a girl looking back from the mirror. Even without makeup, even with his hair the way he always wore it, that was a girl in the mirror. In these heels, in this extravagant underwear, she looked a bit like a prostitute prepared for a customer, but there was no doubt about it . . . she was a girl. "Without the slightest doubt or hesitation," he thought. Yes. Of course I can. Of course *she* can. He undressed and climbed into bed. He didn't expect to be able to go to sleep, so he didn't know until the alarm woke him the next morning just how deep and peaceful his sleep had been.

ALAN WAS ALONE IN THE SHOP, BRUSHING OUT HIS HAIR. At closing time he'd left with Kurt and Tricia just as usual, had walked three times around the block to let them get well away, and then had let himself back in, locked the door behind him, left the lights off in the reception room, returned to his station, and had gone to work on himself. He'd cut bangs, set his hair on small rollers. While under the drier, he'd shaped his fingernails and painted them . . . a coat of frosted peach, a coat of supersealer. A good thing I've had years of practice at this, he thought. He stopped brushing a moment and looked at himself. He'd never set his hair before. He had a smooth crown on top, softly feathered bangs that covered his forehead, and huge masses of curls at the side. A rather finicky hairdo he'd given himself. Was it too much?

He'd shaved his face, patted his skin with astringent lotion; it was still tingling. Now he worked a pale translucent beige moisture foundation onto his face and neck. He touched a hint of brush-on blusher to his cheeks. Don't overdo it, he told himself. He painted his eyelids with a faint suggestion of smoky plum, lengthened and darkened his lashes with mascara, not black but a deep brunette. OK, sweetheart, he thought, let's see how Frosted Strawberry Supergloss suits you; he opened the small jar and, using a brush, coloured his lips. He went over them again with a clear gloss. Finally he dusted himself lightly with a misty powder. And he didn't know the face in the mirror. It was a stranger, it was Ellen. She was giving him a moist-eyed and somewhat trembly smile. Frightened, he turned away.

In the lavatory, he quickly stripped off his clothes. He'd begun to shake; he could feel his heart racing. Cleavage, he thought. Ellen may not have much in the way of tits, but she's got to have something. He pulled the roll of adhesive tape from one of the paper bags on the floor. How do drag queens do it? They simulate cleavage with tape somehow. He pushed the flesh over his pectorals together in the front and taped it in place. Perfect, he thought, like I've been doing it for years. He dressed quickly in dance belt, corset, stockings, and panties. He opened the other packages. On his lunch hour, he'd made a hurried run through Eaton's; he'd blown over two hundred dollars in forty minutes.

He slid the slip over his head, then put on the silk blouse and the rather severe, forties-style suit he'd chosen. The tailored jacket would show off his waistline and also disguise the boning beneath; the low neckline would show off that bit of cleavage. The skirt was the newly fashionable length, just below the knee. He opened the shoe box. He hadn't been able to resist the dainty brown-and-white oxfords; they had something of an extravagant heel. And that's putting it mildly, he thought, working his feet into them. He'd thought he'd been looking for sensible working-girl shoes, but he'd bought the highest heels in the store. He laced them up. And then he sat there a moment, dizzy and afraid of fainting. He inhaled deeply. He stood up. His entire body was trembling; his legs were shaking so badly he was afraid he wouldn't be able to walk. How can I go out on the street? he thought. And then he remembered the bracelet; he'd thought that Ellen should wear a touch of jewellery. He poured it out of its sack, snapped it onto his wrist: a delicate silver chain set with tiny lacquer flowers.

All right, he thought, now I'm a girl. Now I'm Ellen. The shaking stopped immediately. She walked quickly out of the lavatory to the full-length mirror. I didn't really know who I was, she thought, didn't know what I would look like. She knew it would take her a long time to get used to herself, get to know herself. She adjusted her skirt, rearranged her hair slightly. She turned for a side view. She walked away from the mirror, walked back again. I didn't know I'd look quite this mature, she thought . . . older than Alan, with more of a presence. She didn't know until then that Alan must have been expecting something different—a silly schoolgirl or dainty young miss but she wasn't like that at all. She looked like a very expensive and thoroughly competent secretary. No, more than that, like a clever young woman with her own business. She looked lean and fit; in heels she was quite tall. She wouldn't be able to hide in the background the way Alan had tried to do.

Alan had been so nervous that he'd been sick at his stomach, but Ellen felt fine. Not relaxed, she thought, but alive. She was tingling with excitement, smiling as though sharing a wonderful joke with her image in the mirror. She felt as though she were in the midst of a great adventure, something possibly dangerous and certainly frightening—but nothing that she couldn't cope with. Poor Alan! she thought, he's never felt this alive in his entire life.

But I've got to go, she thought. She emptied Alan's pockets into her purse: his wallet, his keys, his change. And then her cosmetics. She stuffed Alan's clothes into one of the paper bags and stashed them on the shelf in the lavatory. What if Kurt or Trish finds them? Well, tough. She tied a scarf over her head to protect her hair from the Vancouver drizzle, put on the beige raincoat Alan had bought for her; it had a wonderful swirling skirt like Tricia's. Alan's got good taste, she thought. She slipped on the short brown unlined gloves, settled the purse onto her shoulder, picked up the overnight bag, and looked at herself in the mirror for the last time. Have to get a dramatic rain hat, something with a wide brim.

She turned off the lights, walked through the waiting room past the Page in the window, let herself out and locked the door. That's good. I'd better take the bus, she thought. I'm probably late already. She couldn't walk as quickly as Alan, had to take shorter steps; the entire sense of balance was different. One thing to walk around a bedroom in heels, she thought, quite another to walk three or four blocks in them. By the time she reached the bus stop, her legs were aching. She could feel the sharp pull behind the knees. She'd have to build a whole new set of muscles.

The bus was crowded, and Ellen felt a moment of panic, not from any doubt about herself but from the looks of frank sexual interest she was getting from some of the men. Now she had an idea of what Tricia must feel like. How do you let them know that you like other girls? You don't. You just live with it. A teenage boy in a seat cleared his throat, said, "Excuse me, Miss. Would you like to sit down?"

"Well, thank you," Ellen said. He stood for her, and she sat down. She smiled at him, and he blushed; the young hairy thug in his levi jacket actually blushed! Ellen looked away, flustered. It was a lot stranger than Alan had thought it would be.

When she knocked on the door, Susan Mackenzie answered. "You must be my cousin, Ellen."

"Yes," Ellen said, "and you must be Susan. I'm so glad to meet you."

EVERYTHING'S THE SAME AND YET EVERYTHING'S DIFFERENT, Ellen thought. Alan remembered the shelves of jars, the dried plants hanging on the walls, the dirty stove top, the dishes piled in the rack on the sink, and Alan's memories were available to her, so the kitchen was familiar, yet they were not *her* memories. Ellen was seeing things for herself. The process was so compelling it took nearly all of her attention. Throughout dinner she'd spoken very little. She'd eaten, but not very much. And Susan had been staring across the table at her, her eyes avid and sparkling. She hasn't stopped looking at me since I walked through the door, Ellen thought. What does she want?

Mrs. Mackenzie had cleared the table, was now bringing a Chinese iron teapot and cups.

"Oh, mother," Susan said, "maybe Ellen wants coffee. Some people still drink coffee, you know." And turning to Ellen, "It's not even real tea. It's made out of herbs . . . Do you mind if I smoke, Mother?"

Mrs. Mackenzie shrugged. "If you want to smoke, dear, smoke; My telling you not to isn't going to change anything."

The old woman sat down stiffly and slowly as though unloading an immense sack onto the kitchen chair. She's playing at that,

Ellen thought, and she's good. Alan believed it, but I don't. The old girl can move like a whirlwind when she wants to.

"I didn't even know I had a cousin in Winnipeg," Susan said. Her hands were nervous on the table, patting, bouncing, tapping. She was picking off the salmon-coloured nail polish. She saw Ellen looking at her hands. "Oh, they're a mess, aren't they?" she said and glanced at Ellen's nails.

Mrs. Mackenzie laughed in her snorting horse-like way. Her daughter gave her a reproachful look, said, "You're not married, eh?" She was looking at Ellen's bare left hand.

"No, I'm not."

"What do you do?"

"I work for an insurance company," Ellen said, improvising.

"Do you like it?"

"It's a job . . . It's not particularly fascinating work. I thought if I found something here, I'd stay in B.C."

"Oh, everybody comes to B.C. eventually," Susan said. "Do you know what I thought you were going to say you were? . . . A model."

Ellen laughed. "In Winnipeg!"

"Well, *I* don't know, eh?" The girl gestured helplessly and smiled. Ellen smiled back.

"We should get going, dear," Mrs. Mackenzie said, "or we'll miss the last ferry."

"Oh, Mom, why do you want to take her to Bowen tonight? It's raining. I'm sure I don't know what the two of you are going to do on Bowen at night in the rain . . . It'll be rotten!"

Driving away in the camper, Ellen felt soothed. The rain was falling steadily, the windshield wipers cleared it with a rhythmical slap. She allowed herself to relax into the seat, no longer forced herself to sit with her knees together. "What *are* we going to do on Bowen in the rain?" she said.

"The rain's perfect."

"Perfect for what?"

"If you really want to see the coast the way it should be seen, you should see it in the rain."

The ferry ride was short, and the view was detail from a Turner or a Ryder, Ellen thought . . . slanting, uncommunicative brush-strokes. Mrs. Mackenzie drove them off, up from the dock, around winding roads up several hills, and into a driveway. Ellen could see the dark shape of the house.

The old woman led Ellen inside, lit kerosene lanterns. "We'll make a fire," she said, "take the chill off."

"I'm afraid I can't be much help," Ellen said. "Alan never learned how."

"Don't worry, dear. Sit down."

"Mildred . . ." Ellen said. Alan wouldn't have called her Mildred, she thought. "Do you remember the first time Alan met you? You said something about learning the plants. Is that what you're going to do over here, teach me the plants?"

The old woman made a wet, gurgling sound: another of her laughs. "Well, you could try reading *The Edible Plants of British Columbia*."

Ellen laughed too. "You're a hell of a . . . medicine woman . . . or whatever you are. Is that what you are?"

"I don't know what you could call me. There! That will warm things up a bit, eh? Now I'm going to make a special tea for us. Skullcap, valerian root, and gentian. Are you listening? There's some information." She chuckled. "It tastes foul, but it will relax us . . . Come out in the kitchen. Yes, it's a nice kitchen, old wood-burning stove. I've always loved this stove . . . You know, herbs work better if you're ready for them, if you're clean."

"Clean?"

"Have you been eating meat?"

"No. Alan hasn't."

"That's good. The cleaner you get, the more effect the herbs will have on you."

"Look, Mildred," Ellen said, "will you tell me something about yourself? Where you come from. How you got into all this. Just what it is you're doing."

"I don't know quite . . . Well, let's see. There was nothing out of the ordinary about me, eh? I grew up in Saskatoon. All my family's back in the prairies. But my husband was from here. We met during the war, and we got married right after the war was over. We didn't have much when we started out. Didn't even have any furniture for our place, slept on the floor for two months until we could afford to buy a bed. John was too proud to take one from his relatives. But we flourished, I guess you could say. Nothing out of the ordinary. John got a job at the Parks Board, and that's where he stayed. John Junior was born in '47, and we didn't plan to have any more, but then Susan came along. I thought I was too old. We were careless." She laughed. "But it was a good thing. She and her father were very close.

"We'd bought our house by then, and this place over here, and we had pretty much everything we'd ever wanted. We went camping and fishing a lot. Johnny was a sportsman like his dad, but Sue never took to it. She'd go along, but she never enjoyed it . . . I suppose we were a happy family. John Junior went to U.B.C., moved to Toronto, and then . . . Well, my husband died. All of a sudden, like that. One day he was there, and the next day he was gone. We didn't even know he was sick. He'd complained about being tired, about pains, but we thought it was heartburn. He was on his way to work one day, and someone hit him from the side, came through a stop sign and hit him, and he tried to get out of the car, and he fell down by the side of the road and died. His heart had stopped. He was dead when they got him to the hospital.

"There'd never been anything unusual about me . . . I mean my whole life had been just an ordinary life. But that stopped me. I hadn't thought it could happen that way, didn't think I'd be alone again. It's more than you just get used to someone. They become a part of you. You can't imagine your life without them. And there I was at sixty-four, and my husband was gone, and I didn't see any point in going on with life, eh? . . . Here . . . here's a cup. Let's take it back into the other room, sit by the fire. No, don't try to drink it yet. It's too hot."

They sat, side by side, on the couch. The fire was burning well now. "What did you do?" Ellen said.

"I'd come over and just sit in the rain all day. I didn't care if I lived or died. And one night there was a little owl, one of the little owls who live around here. I heard him outside, and I went out to listen. I always liked the sound they made. And I was just standing there listening to him, and he said, 'He didn't eat right.'

"I couldn't believe it, eh? I said. 'What?' And the owl said, just as plain as anything, 'He didn't eat right. That's why he died.' I listened some more, but all I could hear was just the ordinary owl sound. So I came back in here, right to this couch we're sitting on, and I lay down on it and cried. I must have cried all night. The next day I drove back to Vancouver, and I began to read everything I could about food."

"You really heard the owl say . . .?"

"Yes, I did. I decided I'd just imagined it, but I started reading about food, and that was the beginning of everything."

"What happened then?"

The old woman shrugged. "It doesn't matter. It isn't important . . . the details. For everybody who does it, it will be different. I started going farther and farther away, up the coast, into the interior. Everywhere I could drive and a lot of places I couldn't. I was walking again. I'd walk for miles. My health started to come back.

"And I started to learn things, a little piece at a time. I used to think that all the knowledge was gone, because all the old Indians were gone . . . or going. But that's not true. Because the things that taught the Indians are still here. But it's a dangerous way to do it, without any tradition behind you, because there are hundreds of things out there ready to catch you up if you're not careful. They can do more than kill you. They can steal your soul."

Ellen laughed nervously. She was shivering. "I can't . . . It's hard for me to believe this."

"I know. It was hard for me too."

"So what are we going to do over here?"

"Just make a beginning. Later on I'll take you up the coast. There are special places. I want to hear what the ravens will tell me about you."

Something in Ellen was drawn tight. She felt she had to release it or she'd burst. She laughed again and said, "The ravens are such gossips, eh?"

Mrs. Mackenzie turned abruptly to face her. "It's not a joke, you bloody fool!" she said. "Don't ever think it's a joke. We can be killed. We can be destroyed so that no one would ever remember our names." She seized Ellen's hand. Ellen drew back from the suddenness and the pain of the grip. Mrs. Mackenzie was staring directly into her face. "We work alone, but there are others of us, and we don't even know who they are. We're all connected. If we win, we form a bond stronger than death. But if we lose, then the world dies with us."

ELLEN AWOKE WITH DIFFICULTY. Mrs. Mackenzie was standing above her, prodding with a foot, holding high a kerosene lantern. It was still as dark as night. "Hurry!" the old woman was saying, "There's no time to lose."

The herbs Ellen had drunk the night before had put her to sleep early; now she was having difficulty fighting herself awake. "What time . . .?"

"Time doesn't matter now. It's not yet dawn. Hurry. Here are some old clothes of Susan's. Don't forget the work gloves."

Ellen wormed her way out of the sleeping bag. There were still a few coals at the back of the fire. The room was chilly. She grabbed the clothes and scurried to the fireplace.

What is the goddamned hurry? she wondered. Mrs. Mackenzie's impatience was infecting her: she was frightened. She saw the light returning from the kitchen. "Are you dressed? Come on."

"Coffee?" Ellen said.

"Nothing. Today we don't eat or drink. Come on, *move!* No, don't talk. Save your strength."

Ellen slogged along in the mud behind the old woman. It was raining steadily—and black—not a trace of dawn anywhere. She was led to a small wood building. It could have been anything, a chicken coop, a garage, a tool shed. Mrs. Mackenzie set the lamp on a shelf, and Ellen could see that the earth floor inside the shed had been dug into a deep pit full of wood ashes and stones. "Quick! Get the stones out. Come on, *move*. Pile them in the back there. Faster. We don't have any time to spare."

Ellen was in the pit heaving out the stones. Good Christ, she thought, they must weigh fifty pounds apiece. And hundreds of them! It seemed as though she'd only been at it a minute or two and already her heart was racing and sweat was rolling down her face. This is crazy, she thought. I can't do this. But "Hurry!" the old woman was yelling, so she kept at it. The stones were beginning to make an immense pile at the back of the shed.

Mrs. Mackenzie brought armloads of kindling, piled it to one side. She just keeps on going, Ellen thought, never slows down. And I'm doing harder physical labour than Alan's ever done. She lost all track of time. It could have taken her ten minutes or an hour. "There," she said, panting. "That's the last one."

"We've got to get the wood now. Come on, hurry!" They hauled logs from the side of the house. At the third trip, Ellen began to count to distract herself from the growing pain in her arms. She counted twenty-seven trips.

"All right," Mrs. Mackenzie said. "Now we build a fire. First the small kindling. Then the bigger kindling. Then the logs. We criss-cross them . . . Come on, girl, help me . . . That's right. Build it up."

When they'd finished, Ellen lay down on the floor by the side of the pit. "Oh Christ!" she said.

"Don't talk. All right, now the stones go back in."

"Oh no!"

"Yes. And don't just heave them in. They've got to be laid carefully or we'll smother the fire. Yes, like this . . . *lay* them in. If you drop them, it breaks the wood."

Ellen had passed beyond the point where her muscles ached; now she was operating on dogged plodding will power. Only her legs were standing up to it. It must be something like this in a concentration camp, she thought . . . just work until you fall over and die. But finally it was finished, and Mrs. Mackenzie lit it. Fire licked the kindling. "It's a good one," she said. "No. Don't say anything."

When the fire was burning well, Mrs. Mackenzie went outside and pulled ropes that opened two great trap doors in the roof. The rain fell through but it didn't seem to matter; the fire looked unstoppable. Ellen leaned against the wall, too tired to move. Already the inside of the shed was growing intolerably hot.

"We're just in time," Mrs. Mackenzie said. Ellen followed, stumbling in the dark and rain, sliding in the mud, up a trail back of the house to a cleared rise of ground that looked down toward what must obviously be the east, for there was the dawn like a spreading of milk on the horizon. "Look," Mrs. Mackenzie said.

"Look at what?"

"Shut up. Just look."

Ellen stood, the rain pouring over her. All she could see was the light spreading carefully; it was greyish-blue. And out of the corner of her eye saw a trail of sparks rising into the sky (still dark) from their fire. She must have been drowsing: Mrs. Mackenzie had just given her a sharp push. "Don't go to sleep. Look!"

Ellen could see nothing but the dawn coming through the monotonous rain. The colours were pearly now, translucent. Impossible to get them in oils, she thought. Take a master to create even the illusion of them. "There! Look!" Mrs. Mackenzie had just seized the back of her neck, jerked her head forward. For a moment, she saw something. A rolling motion, like a sheet on end, in the centre of the rain . . . as though the sky had been parted and something allowed through. She blinked and it was gone. "Look again."

It was there again, a wheel of rain, its edge toward them. It seemed to be turning slowly. She saw that the old woman had bent forward to peer into her face. The bushy black eyebrows seemed strangely comical; Ellen began to giggle. I'm so tired I'm silly, she thought.

"That's enough now." Mrs. Mackenzie walked away; Ellen stumbled behind her. "Here's our spruce." It looked like any other evergreen to Ellen. "She's a Sitka spruce," the old woman said. "You'll always know her by the way she likes to grow near water. You'll only find her on the coast. And she's sharp. Feel."

Ellen felt the needles. They were very sharp. "We're going to cut four of your branches now," Mrs. Mackenzie said to the tree. "Thank you for your branches. You must thank her too."

"Thank you for your branches," Ellen repeated. I can't be doing this, she thought. Mrs. Mackenzie cut the branches near the end, where the wood was pliable, each about two yards long.

When they returned to the shed, the fire had burned down. The stones were now resting in a bed of coals. "Good," Mrs. Mackenzie said. The fire had scorched the walls and ceiling. "Going to burn this place down someday," she muttered. She closed the trap doors in the roof. "Need water now, Ellen. Over there. You can see at the edge of the bush . . . the pool. There's a bucket by the side of the house."

Ellen couldn't tell if the pool were fed by a stream or a pipe. It was still too dark to make out anything but the dimmest outlines. The pool was a small deep hole dug into the soft clay bank; now, in the rain, it was overflowing. Ellen filled a bucket and carried it into the shed. Mrs. Mackenzie threw it onto the last of the fire, onto the hot stones, and a great billow of smoke and steam rose up. "That's it. Hurry. We need lots of water!"

As they continued to throw water into the pit, the shed, which had been tremendously hot to begin with, began to fill with steam. Each time that Ellen carried a bucket in, she felt close to fainting, as though she were being scalded by the moist heat. "Off with your clothes," Mrs. Mackenzie said. Ellen stripped to bra and panties. The old woman pushed her forward into the shed. Looking back, Ellen saw that Mrs. Mackenzie was naked. Huge hairy thighs, great pendulous breasts. She felt a spasm of revulsion; then she was inside in the dark. Sweat began to pour from her in torrents. She was panting; she couldn't breathe. "I'm going to strike you with the spruce now," Mrs. Mackenzie said. "Stand still and don't cry out. It won't do much damage to you, but it's painful."

Before Ellen could say anything, there was a cutting sound, and she felt a sudden hot pain across her shoulder blades. "Oh!"

"Quiet now. Don't hold your breath; you'll pass out. Let your body relax."

Relax! Ellen thought. The spruce was falling on her shoulders and back, on her legs. She could smell the sharp resinous odour of it, Christmasy. The pain, after the first shock, was not so bad that she couldn't stand it.

"Good girl. You're doing fine. Now you do it . . . Here, take the branch. Go over all of yourself. Chest, back, legs. Go on." Ellen, to her amazement, found she was striking herself with the spruce branch. She realized immediately how gentle Mrs. Mackenzie had been; she was sure that the first of her own blows must have cut her to the bone. "Good. Keep it up . . . All right, that's enough. We need water now." She was being pushed outside. Her body steamed in the rain. And she was being pushed along toward the pool. In the rapidly growing grey daylight, she could see that she had not been hurt badly, only a light tracery of marks on her skin.

The old woman pushed her into the pool. She was up to her waist in the water, could feel the ooze of mud beneath her toes. She gasped from surprise and anger. She'd cut her arm in falling.

"Dunk yourself. Come on. All the way." She lowered carefully down, immersed her head. The water felt pleasantly cool against her hot skin. She rose again, shook herself. "Keep dunking yourself. Stay in as long as you can.

Soon the water turned ominously cold. "My God, it's like ice!"

"Of course. It's a cold day. Dunk yourself again . . . No, don't get out yet. Stay as long as you can."

Ellen stayed until the pain in her toes was driving her nearly frantic. She was thrashing about from side to side in the water. The rain was pouring down on her bare shoulders. And it was full daylight now, ordinary British Columbia daylight. Some detached part of her mind was saying, God, she looks ridiculous. Naked fat old woman standing there. "I can't take any more," she said.

"Come on then."

Shivering, she ran barefoot through the mud back to the shed. The heat inside was relief for only a short while; soon she felt suffocated. "Here's the second spruce branch," Mrs. Mackenzie said.

"Oh no! Do I have to do it again?"

"Four times. We cut four branches."

"Oh God! I can't . . ."

"Goddamn it, get going. It's no joke, eh?" Ellen took the branch and began to slash at herself.

They went through the cycle three more times. Then Ellen was allowed to dress. She followed the old woman back to the rise where they'd watched the dawn come in. "Just sit," Mrs. Mackenzie said. She planted herself solidly in the mud. Ellen sank down next to her.

"What are we supposed to do?"

"Just sit and look."

"Look at what?"

"The rain."

Ellen sat and looked at the rain. Her teeth were chattering; she seemed to be running a fever. I don't think Alan could have done this, she thought. She began to fall asleep, but Mrs. Mackenzie cracked her sharply between the shoulder blades. She sat up straight again. The strange rainy wheel in the sky was gone; there was nothing to see now but steady ordinary rain. She watched the light change in the sky. It seemed that at least two hours must have passed. "All right," Mrs. Mackenzie said. "We're finished. We can go back."

"Go back?"

"To Vancouver."

"Thank God!"

Riding in the cab of the camper, Ellen was herself again, dressed in stockings and heels; but she was also wrapped in two sweaters and a blanket, shivering uncontrollably. "It's over," Mrs. Mackenzie said. "You can go to sleep now."

Ellen slept through the ferry ride and the drive back to the city. Then she was home. "Listen," Mrs. Mackenzie said. "Go in and eat something light and get some sleep. You'll be all right. You must turn back to Alan immediately, you must not become Ellen again until Sunday. Do you understand?" Ellen nodded dully. "Come back to me on Sunday morning. You did really well today."

"I did? Nothing happened."

"Oh, yes, plenty happened. Go on. Get some sleep."

"YOUR SISTER'S HERE," TRISH SAID. Alan opened his eyes; he'd been asleep. He saw Betty in the mirror, walking toward his station with that lean balanced stride of hers, purposefully.

"Glad you could fit me in," she said.

"I can always fit you in."

"Think you can make me look like Scarlett O'Hara?" she said in a wry flat voice.

"I could make you look like the Queen of Sheba . . . Scarlett O'Hara, eh?"

"Yeah. For the Hallowe'en party."

He fastened the shampoo cape around her neck, settled her into the basin. "Want me to do the makeup too?"

"Of course."

"You've got at least an hour, eh?"

"Got till five. What were you planning to do to me, cosmetic surgery?"

"When's the last time you had sausage curls put into your hair? Those southern belles had a lot of time on their hands."

"I can sympathize with that."

"Do you have the costume?"

"Sure," she said in the same dry ironic voice. "Gaiety Costume Rentals. Cost a bloody fortune. Both Amy and me. I'm Scarlett and she's Melanie."

Alan laughed. "I didn't think she had that much sense of humour."

"It is funny, isn't it? The four of us went to see it last week. We came out of that theatre, and she said, you know, with that perfectly serious way of hers, 'Now we know what to be for Hallowe'en. You be Scarlett and I'll be Melanie.' Then we looked at each other and both of us burst out laughing. And it kept on being funny until we found out how much it was going to cost . . . You'll have to see us, Alan. Corsets and all."

"Marvellous."

"Yeah, Gary thinks so too. He's really getting his rocks off. If I know him, he's going to want to screw me after everybody goes home. Christ, screwed in a corset. Well, a first time for everything."

"What's Gary going to be?"

"Some kind of Middle Eastern bandit. What else would he be?"

"If I didn't have Jeanie for the night, I'd come around to see you."

"Come around anyway. Amy won't mind if Jeanie pokes her nose in."

What if Ellen turned up as the third southern belle? Alan thought. But no, that joke would be too dangerous. He yawned. He'd drifted through the day in a fog, half asleep, his muscles sore and fluttery from that insanity on Bowen of the day before . . . and he'd been feeling oddly detached, as though he were floating several feet above himself. It's a drag being Alan, he thought: a kind of chant that had started in his head that morning when he'd crawled stiffly out of bed and pulled on his dull unpleasant clothes, continued as he'd limped to work . . . Oh, it's a drag being Alan, all day long! Transforming his sister into Scarlett was the first interesting piece of work he'd had that day, but even that wasn't delighting him as it usually would have done. I want to be Ellen all the time, he thought . . . and continued to wind Betty's dark hair onto rollers. ". . . getting to be a pain in the ass," Betty was saying.

"But who else does she have to talk to, eh?" he said.

"But why me?"

"Because you're her sister."

Betty sighed. "That's right. But she does grow tedious. There! I'm even sounding like her. I think she'd be better off, and Jeanie would be better off, if Amy would just . . . well, let go. You're doing all right with 'gender identity problems' aren't you?"

Alan stopped winding. I don't know what to say to that. I suppose I am."

"Besides, who cares these days if a kid's a tomboy? Nobody. Except Amy. I don't know what she expects from me. She's averaging a phone call a day now . . . Christ, I've got my own problems!"

Alan met his sister's eyes in the mirror.

"Oh, I *am* doing all right. I've got everything I ever wanted. Is there a cigarette in this damn place?"

"Yeah, I can get one from Tricia."

He brought her a cigarette, held the match for her while she lit it. She inhaled savagely, as though she were an invalid pulling on an oxygen tube. "Oh, it's all so crashingly banal," she said. "What do you do when you find that your life looks like a goddamned soap opera? I seem to have acquired all these young housewives for friends. We're all about the same age. We all have professional men for husbands. We all have babies from a few months to a couple of years old. And we were all sitting around just like on the goddamned telly, drinking coffee . . . and I looked around and . . . It was like I woke up all of a sudden and realized what we'd been talking about. And for about an hour, we'd been sounding like some kind of goddamn commercial . . . 'Oh, I think Ivory Snow is the best thing for diapers!' . . . And I said, 'Hey! My God, do you realize what's happening?' And there was this long guilty silence. Because there's not one of us who's stupid, eh? And then we all just sort of packed up our babies and fled home. Oh, Alan, it's ridiculous.

"You say to yourself *we're* different. We're not like all those other couples. Nobody has ever loved as much as we do. Nobody has as much fun screwing as we do. No other couple is as honest with each other as we are. We're going to do everything differently . . . going to be happy and fulfilled and creative . . . all that rot, eh? And then a couple years later you find you're just like everybody else, got exactly the same boring banal problems . . . You know what scares me, Alan? It's the thought that I'm going to be just like Amy."

She stubbed out her cigarette. "Sorry," she said. "I didn't mean to lay that on you."

"Nothing to be sorry about," he said. He lowered the dome of the dryer over her head. "Maybe you should have stayed with modeling," he said.

"It was just an excuse to wear the clothes. I love clothes, but put me in front of a camera, and I panic. It's a rat race too. Look at Sandy. She was *good*. And she's married."

"Yeah."

"Why don't you paint my nails while I'm sitting here?"

"Scarlett wouldn't have nail polish. It's out of period."

"Oh, screw the period. I'm not making a historical movie."

"OK, what colour?"

"Scarlet, of course," she said, laughing humourlessly.

"Shamefully scarlet?"

"That's it."

He filled the nail basin with soap and warm water, set her hands to soak in it. "Well, what do you want to do?" he said.

"Damned if I know. I should have been a designer, or a buyer in a department store, or a fashion writer, or run a little shop . . . something like that."

"Well?"

"Well, hell, man. Gary may be a crusading young lawyer, civil rights and all that. Loves defending Indians and pimply kids picked up with hashish in their pockets. But when it comes to his wife . . . Well, he's Armenian. In the home. *The home*, you know. Of course that's the way he's got to be. That's part of the soap opera too. He's a great admirer of *other* forceful ladies, but not *this* lady."

Alan was dabbing cuticle cream onto her fingers when he looked up and saw that Jeanie had arrived silently next to him.

"Hey, grab her quick," Betty said, "and give her a perm."

Jeanie skipped away, giggling. "No, you don't."

"What's in the bag?" Betty said.

"It's my costume."

"What are you going to be?"

"It's a secret . . . But you're Scarlett O'Hara, I know that. And Mom's Melanie. And Dad's going to be a Victorian gentleman. And Uncle Gary's going to be an Armenian bandit."

"My, aren't we well informed?"

"What are you going to be, Alan?" Jeanie said.

"I'm afraid I'm going to be plain old Alan."

"What can I do while I'm waiting?" Jeanie said.

"You can have a manicure," Betty said.

"I do not think that would amuse me," Jeanie said in a lofty voice. "I think I shall go to the library and read."

"Fine. I'll come by and get you. It'll be another hour."

"Take your time, dear," Jeanie said, striking a limp off-balance pose, one languid wrist in the air. "I'll be downstairs in the boys and girls. Tara." She tumbled out of the pose and trotted away.

"What was that all about?" Betty said.

"I don't know," Alan said, laughing. "I think she was imitating Kurt."

"What an incredible child," Betty said. "I don't think there's anything wrong with her that growing up won't cure."

LESLIE HAD ALWAYS IMAGINED that a genuine serious full-blown nervous breakdown, one worthy of the name, would be quite dramatic; storms of tears, tantrums, weird behaviour, screaming fits, and finally total incapacity. Some carefully drawn line would be crossed, the one side reading, "sane," the other "crazy." She was still swimming every day, although now she ran from the front door of the school all the way to the locker room, not really expecting to see her grandfather in a dark corner, but prepared in case she did. As I was walking down the stair, she found herself thinking (that silly little verse), I met a man who wasn't there. He wasn't there again today. But no, she thought, it's not funny. What's the matter with me? Why have I been staring at the card catalogue? It was as though it had mysteriously become quite frightening, all the demons and bogols and goblins and trolls of fairyland catalogued in alphabetical order. A is for Azazello, she thought, B is for Beelzebub . . . Leslie's new alphabet book, nothing for Kate Greenaway to illustrate.

It's probably not very dramatic at all going mad, she thought. The mistake I made was to think it would be a clear passage, like Alice through the looking glass. But it's not clear at all, probably just what's happening to me now, subtle, built of odd shifts in ordinary things. It's probably so subtle that you don't notice until it's too late, and then you're gone, sliding away.

She turned abruptly from the catalogue and began to walk upstairs to the adult library. I can't even decide what to wear anymore, she thought. That's probably how it starts, in something as banal as that. Each morning she had to figure out all over again who she was. On Monday a prim girl in dress and stockings. On Tuesday her usual librarian self in standard pantsuit. On Wednesday so casual—well, Susan's word "sleazy" might fit, in old baggy pants and cracked oxfords—that Ted had been silently upset with her. And today back to a skirt, one of those tartans her aunts had given her that made her feel as though she should be tramping across the moors. And here was Ted, coming down the stairs. They met in the middle. "Ted," her voice sounded too loud. "You know my two weeks I've got coming? Can I take them starting next week?"

"That's not much warning, is it?" He took her arm and led her back down the stairs. "Why don't we talk about it tonight, eh?"

"Tonight?"

"At the party."

"The party?"

"Leslie, you said you'd go."

She looked at his round face. His mouth was open. Oh God, she thought, I've hurt his feelings again. "If I said I'd go, of course I'll go . . . Ted, I've got two full weeks coming."

"I know you do. How about around Christmas time?"

"I can't wait until Christmas."

Jeanie walked past them and waved. "Hi, Leslie."

"Hi, Jeanie . . . Listen, Ted, it's really important."

He spread his hands in a helpless gesture. "I've got to have a bit of notice, you know. I can't just say to Personnel, 'One of my librarians has just decided to take off.' Why don't we talk about it tonight?"

She was silent with frustration. Then she said, "Where are we going?"

"I'm sure I asked you and you said yes. I'm sure I told you all about it."

"I'm sorry. You probably did. Tell me again."

"It's my friend Gary Kovarian . . . We were in school together. I'm sure I told you. A Hallowe'en party."

"Costumes?"

"Well . . . yes."

"Oh, I hate costume parties."

"Leslie, when I told you about it . . ."

What in God's name could she have been thinking about when he'd told her about it? "All you have to do is put a mask on and it's a costume. It doesn't have to be . . ."

"All right. All right," she said. "Now just how soon do you think . . . ?"

"Christmas?"

"I need some time off."

"What's the matter? Is there something I can help you with?"

"I need some bloody time off!"

"How about the last week in November? I could get Norma to come down and . . ."

"How about next week?"

He was fidgeting from foot to foot like a little boy. "I'd have to call Personnel and . . . Can't we talk about it tonight? I'll get you around eight, eh?"

She walked slowly back to her desk. She'd stopped saying to herself, I must be ordinary. Lately it had been, I must be careful, must be secretive. She didn't know why. A psychiatrist? Impossible. Only somebody close. Family. But tell Dad? Oh no. He'd hem and haw and look at the wall and talk about changing training routines. But there must be something I can do . . . So far, the only thing she'd been able to think of had been to swim harder.

Jeanie had waited until the sound of Ted's footsteps had died away. Then she'd walked to Leslie's desk and sat down on the edge. "That's my Uncle Gary's party you're going to," she said.

Leslie was startled. "You've got sharp ears, kid." She regretted the sound of irritation in her voice.

"That's what my mother says." Jeanie seemed in no way abashed. "Little pitchers . . . *I'm* going to a party at St. John's. But first I'm going out to dinner with my Uncle Alan. That's so

I'll be out of my mother's hair. Do you know what I'm going to be?"

"No, what?"

"I'm going to be a frog. A magic frog that changes into something. I'm just not sure what it is I'm going to change into." Her face was serious; she was looking into Leslie's eyes. "It's not much of a costume, but it was all I could think of. Do you think I'm young for my age?"

Leslie smiled. "Sometimes."

"I keep hearing that. 'Stop talking like a nine-year old, Jeanie!' Maybe I'll start being old for my age." She grinned, said in a lush voice, "What a lovely blouse you have, my dear! Did you get it at Fairweather's?"

Leslie laughed. "Is that what it takes?"

"I don't really know . . . What are *you* going to be, Leslie?"

"I hadn't even thought about it."

"You should be a pageboy," Jeanie said firmly.

"Oh, I should, eh?"

"Yes. Like Joanna Sedley when she's pretending to be John Matcham in *The Black Arrow*. I'll show you. Is it still here?"

Leslie found the book on the shelf, laid it on a table. Together they bent over it, looking down at the N.C. Wyeth illustration on the cover.

"See," Jeanie said, "your hair's even shorter than *that*." She flipped through to another illustration. "There she is again . . . You'd make a perfect page boy . . ."

The caption read: "'We must be in the dungeons,' Dick remarked." And Dick was crouched forward, descending a stone staircase alive with rats. He carried an arbalest in his left hand, raised high a torch in his right. Behind him, pale in the light of the fire, was Joanna dressed in her boys' clothes, steadying herself against the stone wall, and gripping a drawn dagger.

THE BOY WALKED OUT OF THE LIBRARY just as Alan was about to walk in. Alan stopped, caught by the face. Short dun-coloured hair with rumpled bangs like those of a schoolboy who's been playing in the wind, features that were both delicate and precise (clean to the point of hardness); prominent cheekbones, a narrow long nose finely drawn to flaring nostrils, thin lips now set firmly. Bone, Alan thought. The bone in that face shows, as though the skin were just thick enough to cover, and the only softness in eyebrows as gentle as velvet. The eyes were dark, concentrated, and fierce. The boy passed so close that Alan could see the scattering of freckles across the bridge of his nose. That, Alan thought, is the most beautiful face I've ever seen in my life.

Then, as the boy walked away and Alan stood watching, as the distance between them increased, there was a sudden perceptual shift that made Alan draw in his breath sharply, for the boy was a girl. First he saw the purse, then the plaid skirt, and suddenly the rest fell into place as in one of those test drawings in psychology books that are two images in one, but only one image at a time . . . Of course she's a girl, he thought. And why must I always suffer beauty, why must it hurt, as though something were lodged in me? Paintings too. In New York, turning the corner and seeing the El Greco at the end of the hall. Stabbed. Ah!

He stood and watched until the girl had become a tiny figure two blocks up the street; then he walked into the library, downstairs, and found Jeanie reading at a child-sized table. "You just missed my librarian friend," she whispered to him, gathering her books together. "Come on, Alan, I want to show you my costume. You'll be surprised." She gave him her wicked elvish smile. Out on the street, she took his hand.

"Do you want to eat now?" he said.

"No. I want to go back to where you work."

"What for?"

"To show you my costume, silly."

"All right." He was annoyed. Only for you, Jeanie, he thought, would I walk six blocks to get you and then six blocks back to where I started. He was walking quickly, but the child seemed to have no difficulty keeping up with him. The nights are turning cold, he thought, dark when I get off work. Hallowe'en, what does that mean? All Hallows . . . all saints . . . the eve . . . something. In the old days they must have used it to mark the coming of winter. He unlocked the door of the darkened shop. "No, don't turn the light on," Jeanie said.

"Why not?"

"It's a game. You've got to play by the rules."

"And where do the rules come from? You make them up, eh?"

"That's right. Now you must go in the other room . . . where you cut the hair . . . and wait until I'm ready."

"Jeanie, it's black as a coal bin in there."

"All right. You can turn the light on in there."

"That's a help."

"Oh, Alan, don't be so snarky. You'll be really surprised."

"OK, I'll try to get into it." He smiled at her, but she was waiting impatiently for him to leave.

In the other room he lit one set of fluorescent lights, sank down into the shampoo chair; he could stretch out nearly horizontal in it, his head above the dry shampoo basin. And once stretched out, he realized just how tired he was. All that insanity on Bowen yesterday, he thought. That crazy woman. What had she been trying to accomplish, just wanting to see how much Ellen could take? And nothing happened. She just got exhausted. He closed his eyes. And what had she been trying to get Ellen to do, have a vision or something?

He was falling asleep, or he had been asleep. He caught himself, sprung his mind back up to consciousness. Several minutes must have passed. What was Jeanie up to? He could hear her rustling about in the waiting room. Like a mouse; her own words. Well, maybe I'll just sleep a minute or two. He let himself drift down again. It was raining somewhere. Must be over on Bowen. Great stands of cedar. The smell of fir, resinous. He had to do something, but he couldn't remember what it was. He must be in his sleeping bag. He didn't want to get out of it. So warm. He just wanted to sleep. He was asleep.

Alan woke slowly, drifting upward from a long way down like a bubble rising to the surface of a jar of honey. For a moment he didn't know whether he was Alan or Ellen. Then he knew that he was Alan. His left leg jerked involuntarily. He stretched. He didn't know where he was, and something was wrong. Was he in bed? Was he over at Bowen? No, neither. But it was beginning to come back. He raised his head and opened his eyes. What he saw was so impossible—so frightening—that his mind was pierced, as though struck from above, forcefully, by a single dagger blow.

The Page of Cups from the window of the shop was sitting in the chair opposite him, chin resting on one gloved hand, regarding him with sombre eyes.

Alan could neither move nor speak. The Page said, "Are you awake now?"

Alan sat up very slowly. Very carefully he said, "Was I asleep a long time?"

"I don't know," the Page said. "I think so. It seems like a long time."

Alan began to laugh from sheer relief. "Jeanie!"

Jeanie laughed too. "I really surprised you, didn't I?"

"Surprised?" he said. "Oh Christ!" She'd put on the entire Page's outfit: wig and gloves and black velvet suit, even the black stockings and whorish six-inch heels. "You've stripped our poor mannequin . . . Oh Christ, Jeanie, you'll never know what you just did to my head!"

"What did I do?" she asked, giggling.

"I thought the goddamned Page had gotten up and walked out of the window."

She laughed, delighted. "Oh, good!" she said, and began to talk in a rush: "I had another costume, but I didn't like it. And I was sitting in the library, and it just came to me. I saw the Page in the window . . . in my mind . . . and I thought, oh, he's just my size. And then I thought I'd surprise you. I really did, didn't I? I just had a silly frog costume. Nobody would know it was a magical frog except me. This is much better."

"You mean you're going to *wear* it?"

"Sure. Can I, Alan? I won't get it dirty. I'll be really careful. I can be when I want to, you know."

"You're going to wear it to St. *John's?*"

"Sure."

"Even the shoes?"

"Sure."

"Jeanie, you couldn't walk across the room in those shoes."

"I walked in here, didn't I? Do you want to see me?" She stood, teetered dangerously a moment, then found her balance and walked to the far side of the room. "I have a mask too," she said. She'd been holding it, a plain black five-and-dime mask; she slid it on. And walked back. She was managing to achieve a certain tiny-stepped grace. She looks, he thought, unbearably sinister . . . like a Beardsley drawing brought to life. Change the shoes and it wouldn't be so bad.

"Why?" he asked her. "Why do you want to?"

"For fun."

He was feeling a growing panic. He knew he didn't have it in him to order her out of the costume. "At least change the shoes," he said.

"Why?"

"My God, Jeanie, you're practically on stilts!" He realized that she was now almost as tall as he was, and it was impossible to tell either her age or her sex. "Do you know what your mother would do to me?" he tried.

"No," she said. "She'd do it to *me*."

"Oh . . . You know she wouldn't like it then?"

"Of course she isn't going to like it. She's positively going to *hate* it."

So *that's* why, he thought. "Jeanie . . ." he began.

"Alan, aren't we friends?"

"You're going to wear it out to dinner, aren't you?" he said.

"Yes."

"And to the party at the church?"

"Yes."

"And then you're going to drop in on your mother at her party in it, aren't you?"

"Yes."

"Oh, good God!"

She took off the mask. "Alan, will you paint my lips like the Page?"

He looked at her. Something inside of him was shifting as though he'd begun to perceive, dimly, some peculiar version of divine retribution like a vast spiritual scale swinging into balance. He didn't know why, but he was feeling just as vindictive toward Amy as Jeanie must have been. What has Amy ever done to me? But there seemed a rightness about it. "Come here, Jeanie," he said, "and I'll paint your lips as red as cherries."

"MY GOD, LESLIE," TED SAID, "and I thought I was going to surprise *you*!" He was standing in her doorway, wearing his most formal of suits, an impeccable shirt, a muted tie, shined shoes. His hands and head were those of a gorilla.

"You look unbelievably funny," Leslie said, laughing.

"And you look . . . Well, my God, I don't know what you look like."

"I thought if we had to wear costumes, then I might as well really wear a costume."

Jeanie had given her the idea, and the idea had grown. She never would have allowed herself to spend money to do it, but all she'd had to buy was a plain black mask and the long grey feather she'd pinned into a brown velvet beret. She had always identified herself with the old Scots woman in the apocryphal anecdote (you told it about a maiden aunt if you had one, or about your grandmother if you didn't) who had died and left a house full of everything she'd ever owned in her life, including a large box with a neat label reading: BITS OF STRING TOO SMALL TO USE. And just as compulsively, Leslie had saved every article of clothing she'd ever owned, stored away in boxes at her father's house. There she'd found a brown leather dress she'd once been sent by a misguided relative. Not only had it been a size too big, but she never would have put herself into leather to start with, and so had never worn it. But now, simply cut off with scissors at mid-thigh, it made a perfect page's jerkin. Under it she wore a black silk blouse with puffed sleeves and black tights.

She'd found close-fitting brown leather boots with low walking heels, remnants of her Grade Eleven mini-skirt days; they laced up over her knees. The leather was badly scuffed and worn, but that was just fine, she'd thought. I'm not a flouncy court page, I'm a working page, seen some action. Finally she'd girded herself with a leather belt at the hips. And sheathed at her left side was a long sharp fishing knife of her father's.

The droll gorilla face was still staring at her. "What's the matter? I don't look that weird do I?"

"Oh no. You look . . . I mean . . . Well, you're a boy to your fingertips, eh? And a bit of a tough one too."

"You're damn right. I'm going to be knighted next week."

He shook his huge rubber head. "Well, Master Fraser, we'll show them a thing or two, eh? . . . Leslie, you know, you just never cease to amaze me. Maybe that's why you're so good with children . . . imagination."

"Come on, Ted."

In the car, she asked him, "What about my time off?"

"It's not really possible until after Remembrance Day."

"If it's possible after Remembrance Day, then why not next week?"

"You wouldn't believe the red tape."

"Yes I would. And you're a master of it. Why *not* Monday?"

"That's just not possible."

Riding up in the elevator in the high-rise apartment building, she asked again, "Why not Monday?" This outfit seems to be making me bolder than usual, she thought. Be bold!

He spread his black ape hands helplessly. "I'll see what I can do."

They were met at the door of the apartment by a woman dressed as a southern belle. The woman put her finger to her lips (her nails were lacquered a brilliant scarlet). "You must not unmask until midnight," she said. "Until then you must stay in character. These are the rules."

Ted nodded. He scratched himself and uttered a short chittering sound more like that of a chimpanzee than of a gorilla. A tall muscular man had seen them come in; now he yelled in a booming bass voice, "Ah ha, mates! I think I know that apey fellow." The man looked to Leslie like an athletic gypsy thief; he was masked, wore a silk scarf knotted loosely around his neck and a dashing white silk shirt open to the navel, showing thick black hair and the cleanly cut musculature of his stomach. Looks like an ex-football star, Leslie thought . . . just the first hint of pudge. His black pants were stuffed into giant black boots, he had a great rakish nose that the mask couldn't disguise, a magnificent waxed black moustache, and a gold loop on one ear. He strode across the room and seized Ted by the shoulders. The two of them danced a funny little circular jig away, laughing. Leslie was left with the woman.

Leslie made a deep formal bow. The woman smiled slightly and curtseyed. Her dark hair had been set into perfect tight curls, her lips were painted, and she wore a white slice of mask set with imitation pearls (it lifted at the corners giving her a perpetual cat-like expression). Her shoulders were bare and white, her dress cut low to show an alarming sweep of cleavage. She's lovely, Leslie thought. "Would you care for a drink, sir?" the woman said.

"Not sir," Leslie said. "I haven't been knighted yet."

Leslie could see the eyes behind the mask, liquid and bright. "You can call me Scarlett," the woman said. And then laughed. "For want of anything better."

"Master Fraser," said Leslie, bowing.

Scarlett curtseyed again, took Leslie's hand. "Let me get you a drink, Master Fraser," she said, and led her across the room.

The other guests seemed to Leslie stiff like waxwork figures, unsure of themselves and perhaps embarrassed. They stood or sat in clusters talking in abnormally hushed tones against the gentle music (a classical guitar) on the stereo. Here was a harem girl, blushing in veil and diaphanous nylon that showed the gold bikini beneath. She was being served by a Mandrake the Magician in formal tails. Ted was talking to the Gypsy bandit and to a stiff Victorian gentleman who looked like a shopkeeper. There was a chorus girl of some kind in short black silk pants and mesh stockings, another southern belle (an older one with her hair up in a chignon), a skinny bald man in a karate outfit, a dainty French maid perched on black patent heels, and a husband and wife team got up as Tweedle-Dum and Tweedle-Dee. But mostly recent period pieces: thirties and forties people, women in platform heels and tight skirts, men in ancient suits and Bogart hats. Everyone was masked.

"Champagne?" said Scarlett.

"Thank you," said Leslie, so caught up in the formal ritual she and this woman seemed to be acting that she'd forgotten she didn't drink.

Scarlett poured her a glass of champagne and handed it to her. Leslie raised it in a toast and drained it; that gesture too seemed to have been dictated by the costume and the game. Be bold, be bold! she found herself thinking again, the motif of the fairy tale, Mr. Fox. The woman was refilling her glass. "You've brought quite a thirst with you, Master Fraser . . . I'm not doing the southern accent because I can't. Forgive the lapse."

"I think I could play mine if I tried it," Leslie said. She deepened her voice. "It was a hard day's ride we had of it for the good King Harry, God bless him! And now I'll warrant you, we'll take our leisure." This is more fun than doing a puppet show, she thought. She'd drunk half the second glass of champagne. It seemed absolutely innocuous stuff, like bitter Seven-up.

Scarlett produced a tinkling coquettish giggle. (She may not have the accent, but she's got the laugh down, Leslie thought.) "Well, Master Fraser, you must mix with the other odd souls now . . . Yes, you can take your leisure. Here, let me fill your glass again . . . And this is little Mimi," she said, introducing Leslie to the French maid.

Betty lifted her skirts and drifted across the room in the direction of her husband. Now is that a boy or a girl? she thought. It's either a woman with a damn fine talent for acting or it's a boy about sixteen. But that couldn't be. What would he be doing here? Who are these people anyway? Did we invite them? Well, Gary seems to know the ape. Oh God, isn't this thing ever going to let me forget I'm wearing it; why doesn't my waist just go numb? Poor Scarlett, are you going to make it to midnight? She caught her husband's eye. "Who's that?" she said.

"Who's who?"

"That slender little pageboy thing talking to Bill Thompson's dizzy wife."

"Damned if I know," Gary said.

"Well, is it a boy or a girl?"

"It's a girl of course. Look at those legs. Boys don't have legs like that."

"Oh, come on, man, of course they do. You just never see boys in tights."

He continued to peer across the room. "You may be right," he said doubtfully. "I still think it's a girl. Who'd it come with?"

"With the ape you've been talking to."

"Oh. Ted. You remember Ted. He's been here for dinner."

"Good. I'm just glad they're people we invited. Why don't you ask him who it is?"

"That wouldn't be fair, Puss. You've got to wait for midnight like everybody else. It was your idea, remember?"

"Oh screw!"

"Right here in front of God and everybody?" He patted her stomach. "You ought to wear a corset all the time, Puss. You're the sexiest thing on two feet."

"You'd like that wouldn't you, you bloody sadist? Well, later, man. Just don't get too drunk. Christ, I hope the baby doesn't wake up."

Leslie had just disentangled herself from the French maid. Little scatterbrain, she thought. *She* has no trouble staying in character. And without planning it, Leslie found herself at the sideboard again, refilling her glass. She was feeling queerly light-headed. This must be what happens to people when they get drunk. That's it, I must be getting drunk. And rather than finding the sensation alarming, she was enjoying it. So this is why people do it, eh? She surveyed the room. Deep inside her, so deep she was sure that it didn't show, something was giggling. Bunch of silly fools, she thought. They can't even play-act very well. And her eyes rested, finally, on the Scarlett O'Hara lady. She's lovely. And I don't care. I'm not going to stand here and lacerate myself for enjoying her. I can look at her if I want to.

On the other side of the room, Gary was looking at Leslie. She's staring at my wife! he thought. Then he frowned. Maybe it is a boy, or maybe it's a goddamned lesbian. I'll ask Ted. No, I won't. I'll find out for myself. He walked toward her. "Come here, boy!"

"You 'boy' me again sir, and I'll call you out for it," Leslie said, the words tumbling easily out of her. I am drunk! she thought. She was feeling a mounting elation. Be bold, be bold.

"Oh, you will, will you?" said Gary, laughing.

"I will indeed sir, I warrant."

She was grinning. He was grinning back. She's a pretty little thing, he thought. Beautiful legs. Must be some crazy actress friend of Ted's. "Well, I meant no offence. Perhaps you'd care to join my merry little band. Little band of banditos you might say. Lots of sport in it for a strapping lad like yourself." He put his arm around Leslie's waist and led her back toward the sideboard. "We'll drink to it."

Betty stood, resting her back against the wall, and watched her husband chatting with that little page thing. Oh God! she thought. She lifted her skirts and drifted over to her sister. "Amy!" she said, "that goddamned little hermaphrodite is turning on my husband!"

"What little hermaphrodite?"

"The one that came in with the baboon . . . right over there."

"Oh."

"I swear to God, Amy . . . Men! They're such unmitigated ass-holes. Here I am trussed up like a chicken to look sexy for that son-of-a-bitch and he's off chasing some little . . . I don't know what. Jesus, I never would have believed it of him. He must have a gay streak in him a mile wide.'

"Calm down! He's just talking to her . . . him . . . whatever it is? What is it?"

"I don't know."

"I think you've had too much to drink, dear," Amy said, patting her sister's arm.

"I had too much to drink about an hour ago. Jesus Christ, costume parties! This is the last one, I swear to God it is. Look at the way he's looking at her. Look at that sappy smile on his face."

"Betty . . ."

"I know the bastard. I live with him. I know that look."

"Where are you going?"

"Just to see what I can see, dear."

Leslie felt a hand on her shoulder; it was the Scarlett woman. "You must be careful of bandits, dear," the woman said. "You can never tell what they're going to steal next." The gypsy fellow fell back a step with a stunned slackening of the mouth as though he'd been slapped. Leslie, quite dizzy now from the champagne, allowed the woman to lead her across the room and into the hall.

Once they were out of sight of the people, the woman turned to face her. She seemed to be furious about something. Her skin was so flushed that her makeup was superfluous. "Are you a boy or a girl?" she hissed.

The woman's skirt was so large that Leslie felt trapped by it in the hallway. The woman was just standing there, breathing hard, her lips parted. And the lips had been painted the same colour as her nails, that brilliant scarlet—and seemed to Leslie impossibly glossy, as though they'd been polished. Leslie didn't know what to say.

What on earth am I doing? Betty thought. Now I know why those Victorian ladies were fainting all the time! And she felt that, in some inexplicable fashion, her volition had melted, that something else was acting for her. Perhaps it was the costume or the role she'd taken on with it. It seemed impossible to stop playing now. She was being held firmly upright and breathless. And the pageboy person stood motionless, just looking at her, unspeaking, looking into her eyes. They were the same height; their eyes were level. Betty was delighted that their eyes were level. Oh God, I'm drunk! she thought. And felt herself moved by a spinning chaos of sensations; the balance of her heels, the brushing of the petticoats against her legs, the boning at her waist . . . and suddenly remembered, vividly, how she must look—an echo of some pleasurable childhood naughtiness—herself a fragile and delicious confection, offered on a plate. She closed her eyes and leaned forward.

The poor woman wants to be kissed! Leslie thought. Be bold, be bold, but not too bold. Out of a perverse sense of gallantry (surely that must be what it was), Leslie bent forward and kissed her. The lipstick didn't taste the least bit like cherries. It was sweetish and waxy. The kiss was going on somewhat longer than Leslie had anticipated. "Oh!" Betty said finally, opened her eyes and stepped back. It's a boy! she thought, and felt a momentary thrill of pleasure so intense it brought her close to tears. Leslie stepped back. Simultaneously they both turned to look down the hall to see if anyone had noticed. No one had been looking. Betty gathered her skirts and walked away, back to the party. Leslie as quickly walked the other way, down the hall, and found herself in a pale green bedroom. She shut the door, wedged it with a chair, and threw herself onto the bed. Am I going to cry? she thought. And discovered that amazingly she was not going to cry.

She found herself atop a dozen or so coats . . . fur coats, lumber jackets, raincoats. She lay on her back and stared at the ceiling. Be bold, be bold, she thought . . . but not too bold, lest that your heart's blood should run cold! What do you do when you get this drunk? Coffee? Is that what you need? Well, it's not as though I want to go to bed with her. Oh God, why can't men ever be as beautiful as women? Why do they have to be big and lumpy and out of shape and bland and silly like Ted? She sat up and looked around. It was just somebody's nice middle-class suburban bedroom. There was a vanity table with a mirror, and a closet where she could see mixed men's and women's clothing, and a small green bookcase with a copy of *The Joy of Sex* on top of it. She laughed. Next to the book was a green telephone.

She picked up the phone and dialed information. "In Port Albert, please," she said firmly, "I'd like the number of Martin Fraser." I don't sound drunk, she thought. She dialed her brother. "Hello Martin," she said when he answered.

"What a surprise eh? How are you?"

"Happy Hallowe'en, Martin. I'm drunk."

"Not you!" he said, laughing.

"Yes me. For the first time in my life. What are you doing, Martin?"

"We've just been sitting around with candy for the trick-or-treaters. Are you all right?"

"No, I'm not all right."

"That's what I thought. What's the matter?"

She hadn't seen him since July; they didn't get down to the city much anymore. But she remembered him clearly. He was the one of them who looked most like their father; the same pale blue eyes, ruddy skin, and bulbous nose. He was getting heavy now with no pool in Port Albert. Good Martin, she thought, gentle Martin. "I'm afraid I'm losing my mind."

"What makes you think that?" he said in his coach's voice.

"I don't know. Things are just . . . Can I come up and see you?"

"Of course you can."

"Can I come tomorrow? No, no, I can't . . . Friday or Saturday?"

"Of course you can. You know that. You can come any time you want. You can stay as long as you want. You know that, eh?"

"Thanks . . . I'll be up . . . I don't know . . . over the weekend."

She sat and listened to the phone line humming, stretched out three hundred miles up the coast of British Columbia. She imagined him on the other end, his face creased and worried, trying to think of something to say. I shouldn't have done this, she thought. He'll be upset now. "How's Dad?" her brother asked her.

"He's getting old, Martin," she said. A wave of dizziness was threatening to swamp her. "I'm going to go now, OK?" She hung up the phone. The room had begun to rotate slowly, then more quickly. She lay back on the bed.

GARY KOVARIAN JUMPED BACK from the end of the hallway so that his wife wouldn't see him. But *he'd* just seen *her* kissing that goddamned little pagegirl . . . or pageboy. Maybe it is a boy, he thought, or a dyke. He couldn't decide which was worse. He strode quickly to the sideboard and poured himself a straight Scotch into a water tumbler. I never would have believed it of her, he thought. She must have a gay streak in her somewhere. He gulped the Scotch. The heat of it was good, something to fight. Cool it, Kovarian, he told himself. Just keep it together now. But he was so angry he was shaking. And here was Betty sailing across the room to him just as brash as a nail. Well, that was quick. Just a little peck in the hallway, eh?

"What have you been up to, Puss?" he said.

"It's a boy," she said, triumphantly. She was flushed and panting.

"Oh, is it?" he said. A little titillation at the costume party, he thought. If we could go to bed now, we'd fuck our brains out. Except that she wouldn't be with me. "How do you know?"

"I asked him," she said, smiling grandly.

You lying little bitch, he thought. "Well, good for you. What else did you ask him?"

"Nothing else." They stared at each other. "There's someone at the door," Betty said.

"Why don't you answer it?" he snapped at her.

She looks beautiful, he thought as he watched her walk away. Just fucking beautiful! And it's a damn shame. The party's just getting going now, somebody's got some rock on, people loosening up. That's the trouble, people loosening up. There's Jill Thompson over there, got up like a little French whore, making a good solid pass at poor old Frank. What's happening to us? Are we turning into the sort of people who get drunk at parties and paw each other's husbands and wives? I never wanted that, just want a plain old-fashioned family. Why did I pick *her*? Why didn't I pick a nice Armenian girl? Because there weren't any nice Armenian girls, asshole! And she was so fucking classy. Goddamn little West Van wasp.

He took another hit of Scotch. The party was quite loud now. The steady buzz of voices, the music. And he was feeling increasingly choked, his stomach knotting. It's like grief, he thought, but I haven't lost anything . . . Or have I? Something parted in his mind and his entire life—his law practice, his wife, his family— seemed threatened, teetering at the edge of an unknown and hideous disaster. How can it happen so fast? In just one fucking wink of an eye? Just because she kissed a boy in the hallway? Is that all it takes? And he hated these people, hated all of them. He wanted to throw them out of his apartment. Fucking wasp bastards, he thought. All of them. These aren't my people.

Here was Alan, his usual sloppy self, blue jeans and hair hanging down, walking through the door with some incredible weirdo. Who is that? Gary thought. One of Alan's boy friends? How dare he bring him here? And he began to walk angrily toward the door . . . I'll just tell that little bastard . . . Then he began to laugh. By God, it's Jeanie! She looks absolutely absurd. "Hi there, kid," he yelled at her. "That's sure one hell of a . . . it's sure a fine costume."

"Thank you," Jeanie said primly and walked in carefully on those unbelievably high heels. Gary couldn't stop laughing.

Betty was heading off Amy. "Count to ten," she said. I've got to get her into the kitchen, she thought. Away from all these people. She's going to make a scene.

"Alan!" Amy yelled. Several people turned to look.

"Shhh, for God's sake!" Betty said.

"What's the matter?" Alan said. He's wearing his stupidest straight-man face, Gary thought. The little clown.

"You know goddamn well what's the matter," Amy shrieked. "Whose joke is this, yours or Jeanie's? Oh, you don't even have to answer. I know. That little bitch!"

"Amy!" Betty said. "Please come out in the kitchen. Come on now."

"I'm going to send her to a Swiss convent school," Amy said, snapping off her words. "You see if I don't! I'm going to find one where they dress the girls like Heidi and make them go to mass nine times a day."

"You've got half a cake," Betty said. Stop it, Betty, she told herself. But she couldn't stop it. "She looks like half a girl. Look at those shoes."

"Betty, you shut up," Amy said. "Alan, you get her out of here.

Do you hear me? Out. Right now. Get her home!"

He shrugged haplessly. "Of course."

"Hi, Mom," Jeanie said.

Amy turned away from her. "Go home, Jeanie," she said. "Go home with Alan now." Tears were running down from under her white mask.

"What's the matter, mom?"

"Please Jeanie, just go home." Amy allowed Betty to lead her toward the kitchen. Gary watched the sisters floating away in their vast rustling skirts. Amy's bare shoulders gave her away; she was sobbing. Going to be some tangled phone lines tomorrow, he thought.

Howard arrived, saying, "What's going on?" To his daughter, "My God, Jeanie!" To Alan, "What's going on, eh?" Alan couldn't find a thing to say. Howard gave him a single reproachful look and followed his wife into the kitchen.

"I really screwed it up, didn't I?" Jeanie said to Alan. "I didn't think she'd do *that*."

"Come on," Alan said gently. "Let's go home."

Gary held the door for them. "Don't worry," he said. "We've all just had too much to drink." He shut the door and tilted up the glass of Scotch, found that he must have drunk it some time ago. From where he was standing he could see down the entire length of the hallway to the bedroom. The bedroom door was opening, and the pageboy was coming out, walking unsteadily. What in God's name has he been doing in our bedroom? Gary thought. And his anger, which he'd forgotten for a moment, was choking him again. By God, I'll find out what sex it is! He began to walk quickly. When he reached the end of the hallway, he began to run. Leslie saw him coming, turned, and fled into the bedroom, slamming the door in his face. He crashed into the door, his full weight against it. She was sent lurching backward, stumbling. She caught herself on the edge of the bed. "Goddamn you!" he yelled at her. His anger was amazing: it seared him; it filled him completely.

Don't . . . lose . . . control! he told himself, and slowly shut the door behind him. And then he'd lost control, was after her, driven on the savage joy of release. He couldn't think of anything except hurting her. She was running away, but had nowhere to go. He trapped her in the corner, grabbed at her, knocked away her hands. He seized her between the legs with one hand, hard, squeezing. He'd found out what he wanted to know. He let go. "You goddamned little bitch," he yelled triumphantly. "You're a bloody girl!"

He laughed. His anger was far from spent. He reached for her again. He didn't know what he was going to do; he just wanted to get his hands on her.

Leslie drew her father's fishing knife. Gary froze. She jabbed the point lightly into his exposed stomach. "Hey!" he yelled and fell back a step. She jabbed him again, and he jumped back. He was astonished at how quickly she was after him. He felt his back slam into the wall. She ran the point of the knife lightly up against his bare skin above the solar plexus.

Her counter-attack had surprised him, but now he was thinking, she can't do this to me! No, not this bloody little girl! "Goddamn you!" he yelled. "What do you think you're doing?" He tried to step forward. The point of the knife went in, just breaking the skin, and immediately a drop of blood sprung up in the black hair. He winced. He was stopped. He closed his eyes a moment. He flattened himself against the wall and contracted his stomach muscles.

He opened his eyes and saw her shift her weight, take the handle of the knife in both hands and brace herself. He could feel the steady pressure of the point. As suddenly as if someone had

pressed a button to call it on, he began to sweat, felt the salt stinging his eyes under his mask, felt it running down his armpits. His
mouth had gone dry. "You mean it, don't you?" he said.

She nodded.

He was amazed at the various fragments of thought loose in
his mind. How the fuck do they do it on television? They just
knock the knife away, that's how they do it. But all she'd have to
do is lunge and she'd pin me to the wall like a fucking bug, solar
plexus, goddamned vital spot. How did she know? Does it kill
you dead, in an instant? Oh God! And he remembered being
chased by a gang in the East End when he'd been a kid. It had
been the most frightening experience of his life. He was more
frightened than that now. I've got to do something, he thought.
Come on, Kovarian! "Good Christ, girl," he said, "you can't
mean it."

He tried to reach for the knife. The blade went in. "Ah!" he
said, and flattened himself against the wall. That's my blood, he
thought, there . . . running down my belly in that steady trickle of
red. That's my goddamn blood! The point was in only a fraction
of an inch. Still just a scratch. But oh dear God, is she going to kill
me? Tears had begun to run down from the corners of his eyes. He
discovered that sometime without his knowing it—probably when
the blade had gone in that last time—he'd pissed himself. How
humiliating. Got to do something, say something. "I'm sorry if I
frightened you," he said carefully. She didn't answer. "Look.
Would you really do it?"

She nodded again, affirmative.

"Oh God! . . . Why?" She didn't answer.

He didn't know what was so frightening about her, whether it
was the mask or the costume or the way she was standing there,
unmoving, with her weight poised and not a ripple in her body.
There was not a doubt left in his mind that she could kill him.

191

"Please," he said. "Look . . . I'm sorry . . . Oh, my God . . . I've got a kid!" What am I saying? "Look, what do you want?"

She measured out her words one at a time. "Don't . . . ever . . . touch me . . . again."

"Oh, gladly!" he said. "Done."

He could see her dark eyes behind the mask. She looked at him for a long time. And then, slowly, she removed the knife. "Ah!" he said, letting his stomach muscles sag. He pressed the palms of his hands into the wall to keep himself from slipping to the floor.

She stepped back, hesitated, and then returned the knife to its sheath. She tore off her mask and threw it angrily to the floor. She shook her head. She was pale but seemingly unfrightened; her gaze was steady. "I'm sorry if I've hurt you," she said. He was surprised that he should find her so beautiful.

He jerked his own mask off and threw it down. "Oh Christ!" he said. He tried to laugh, but he couldn't do it. "I'm Gary Kovarian." And added, thinking even as it was coming out of his mouth how idiotic it must sound, "I'm a lawyer."

"I'm Leslie Fraser," she said. "I'm a librarian . . . of all things."

Simultaneously, they reached forward. They shook hands. She let go of his hand and stepped back, looking away. They both felt an immense confusion and embarrassment. He has a nice face, she thought. He's not a bad man. "Would you really have done it?" he asked.

"I don't know. I think so . . . Yes, I think I would have."

"Why?"

"I don't know." He was amazed that he didn't hate her now after what she'd done to him. He felt an odd comradeship with her as though they'd just gone through some terrible ordeal together and had survived. "I don't know why," she said. "Maybe I'm the kind of person who should never put on a costume."

"Have you ever thought of seeing a psychiatrist?"

She smiled. "It has occurred to me . . . Here, let me put something on that. You're bleeding all over yourself."

"OK . . . Yeah, thanks . . . That pillowcase there. Christ, do I need a drink!"

"I suppose I do too."

"Come on, Leslie Fraser, you can have the whole bar."

Betty met them at the sideboard. "What's this?" she said. Her voice was hard and bitter. "Shame on you. You're not supposed to take off your masks until midnight."

Part III

Chip, chip, my little horse.
Chip, chip, again sir.
How many miles to Babylon?
Three score and ten, sir.
Can I get there by candlelight?
Yes, and back again, sir.

Mother Goose

SHE HAD FORGOTTEN how gulls could hang motionless a moment, matching the ferry's movement, their bodies perfect speed forms like darts, legs tucked up and spread-eagle against the sky, held, like a swimmer in mid-dive. She leaned against the rail and looked up, the dawn wind icy against her face. And she had forgotten how fog, like cotton batting, could wrap itself low on the water, around the base of things (these mountains) while above, the sky would already be clearing amazingly fast, the slate grey turning to steel blue and that at the edges blowing clean. The day would be clear and sunny; she knew from having lived here all her life. Oh, but not here! she corrected herself. Too much inside of buildings—schools, libraries, indoor pools—and never enough out in the open air of the coast. It feels good, she thought. It feels right again: early, cold, windy, alone.

Training in an outdoor pool, as she had done for four summers, had felt good in just this way. She'd swum early and alone; by the time the first kids had begun to arrive with their beach towels, she'd already been finished and showered and on her way home. The sky had been clearing just like this on many of those mornings. Or it had been raining. But always cold, wretchedly, bone-achingly cold, even in the middle of July. The first shock of diving into the water is something you never get used to, she thought. It hurts every day. And she'd loved it, could remember standing looking out across the pool, holding for a moment (like the gull above the boat), surveying it . . . her world. The mountains, the slate blue light, the silence. Odd to swim thousands of meters outdoors in the summer and never get a tan. Early, cold, and alone.

I'm a different person here, she thought, and this is the person I was meant to be. I could leave it without a regret—my room, my library, my life—if I had a place to go, something to do. But would it be the same, living here? Fishermen get used to seeing killer whales. But that's right, a good thing to get used to, better than getting used to traffic and air pollution and a nine-to-five job. I should have been a boy, she thought, to go fishing or rambling up the coast with a pack on my back, to get lost in the bush, in mountain fog or up an inlet, and not mind; to dig clams and crabs, eat seaweed, salmon berries and salal berries, dig roots, thistles. I never wanted to have a penis (absurd theory, took a man to invent it); that isn't what you envy. You envy the freedom to take a pack and a sleeping bag and go.

There's nothing wrong with me. All I needed was to get out for a while . . . But even as she thought it, the tangle of her life rose up in her: it's a mess, a bloody mess! She hadn't been able to go to work Friday or Saturday, instead had lain about her room feeling like a leper, wondering if she should inflict herself on Martin, putting up with Ted's solicitous phone calls—and what she should have done was pack and get out as soon as possible. Here is where she should have been all along: out of the city, out of her ordinary life, riding a ferry up the coast to the north in the open air. The sun was appearing now, brilliantly, and reflecting back on the water. And the day was emerging as a bright cold Sunday morning in November. Her knuckles had turned pink with cold; the cutting wind was blowing back her short hair, and she felt good, thinking again, there's nothing wrong with me. Alone.

Something's killing me, she thought, eating out my centre like a worm. Not that any of the things I've been doing are wrong in themselves; they'd be all right for somebody else, but nothing has ever been perfectly right for me except swimming. The simplicity and cleanness of it: interval training, the timed waits, the split times, record times, your competitors' times. All simple numbers, could be written in black type on white paper. On this day, in this meet, Leslie Cameron Fraser did this time. And nobody would ever need to write down how she had felt about it.

In the spreading wake of the ferry, floating gulls above in their splendid isolation reflecting the absolute and inhospitable coldness of the water . . . there she wanted to dump some part of herself, had a sudden vision of doing it, a great lump cast overboard and left behind. It's as though I'm two separate people, she thought. And how did Leslie the swimmer manage to live in the same body with Leslie the fantasist, the wanderer in children's books, the sad girl in her rented room? "White and golden, Lizzie stood . . ." She saw, in memory, the Rackham illustration—the slender girl surrounded by the small pawing goblins and their seductively sweet fruit—and a hatred of herself stood out blackly a moment against the bright cold day. Throw that overboard, she thought. Leave it behind. Go far enough north, and it wouldn't matter. Images of the Canadian arctic, the austerity of tundra or the simplicity of winter. White, as she'd seen the pictures, and no sound, as she'd read, except the wind, and sometimes a loud crack as a tree, in the hideous cold, split itself end to end. But she wasn't going that far north, not on this trip.

Now she was alone, and everything was already becoming simple. In a few minutes she would have breakfast, would drive off the ferry at Nanaimo, drive up island, and get on another ferry. All she had to do was keep moving, and she'd be in Port Albert by ten or eleven that night.

SUBURBIA, ELLEN THOUGHT, MY GOD, IT'S QUIET. The bus that had dropped her at the corner had been the only moving thing in this bright cold Sunday morning, and now, empty but for the driver, it was vanishing up the hill, leaving her alone on the street. There wasn't a person to be seen anywhere; not a single automobile drove by. She stopped walking and listened. She could hear traffic, but so muffled and distant that even the discreet peeping of invisible birds was louder. She began walking again, thinking, well, there's one thing about high heels: it's impossible to be quiet in them. Each footstep banged unpleasantly on the pavement. And here were the houses, sleeping with their drapes drawn, the parked cars with their windows so steamed that anything at all could be inside and she wouldn't know. Christ, what a thought! I'm jumpy this morning. Frayed nerves. Maybe it's because I've never been out on the street in daylight before. But Mrs. Mackenzie's house, fronted by waist-high grass gone to seed and turned dun-coloured, stood out from the other silent houses in the nasty clarity of the early sun like one of Magritte's ominous effects. That's it, she thought. Every time I've been here, it's been weird. I don't know what to expect.

She wished that she could locate the birds. She'd thought she'd seen one hopping at the base of a hedge, but when she'd looked, there had been nothing but dew on the grass. She shivered, found herself tiptoeing up to the front steps of the house. Stop it! she told herself, and banged her heels down. The Sunday morning paper was lying innocuously on the doormat. She hesitated, looked down the length of the block the way she had come. Couldn't ask for a more sedate middle-class neighbourhood. Everything's perfectly ordinary. So why does it seem so sinister? She reached for the door knocker and stopped, the movement incomplete. She looked at her trim grey glove. Her hand was shaking. She grabbed the knocker and banged it several times. From inside, the house answered with a muted hollow echo.

Nothing happened. She shifted uneasily from foot to foot. She turned away from the door and saw that a small face was peeking at her from the long grass: a cat, black with an asymmetrical splash of white over half its nose and one eye. And it was gone, instantly, sleek shadow between the houses, leaving her recognition of it behind like an after-image. She gasped. Her freshly shaved underarms were stung, suddenly, with sweat. She knocked again, angrily. Then she realized she'd known all along that something hadn't been right. Now she knew what it was. Mildred's van wasn't parked in front. The tightly bunched muscles of her shoulders relaxed. She let her hand fall. She's not here, she thought, and I'm safe. The door swung inward.

Susan looked like a sleepy boy, barefoot in baggy blue flannelette pajamas, her short curly hair tousled. "Oh hi, Ellen." She yawned and bent to pick up the newspaper. "Come on in. Mom's not home." Dumbly, Ellen stepped through the door. "Hey, shut it, eh?" the girl said, grinning, "I'm freezing to death. What are you doing up so early? What time is it anyway? I was sound asleep."

"I'm sorry," Ellen said. "Oh, that's all right. Had to get up sometime. Oh wow, I'd better turn up the thermostat. It's really clammy in here . . . Yeah, just throw your coat anywhere. Want some breakfast? How about coffee? Mom doesn't allow coffee in the house, but I keep some hidden for when she's away. Don't tell her, eh? . . . Oh, yeah. She left a note for you."

The note was pinned down by a teapot in the centre of the kitchen table. Written with pencil in an old-fashioned loopy hand on the side of a brown paper bag it read:

Dear Ellen,
I'm sorry to miss you but I have to be out of town for
a few days. I've been thinking that there's no point in

spending good money to stay at a hotel when you can stay here. We have plenty of room and as far as I'm concerned you can stay as long as you want. I don't think Susan would mind either. Why don't you think about it? See you later in the week.

Mildred

"You have *my* vote," Susan said.

"What?"

"It's OK with me. I'd be glad to have you stay. I get tired of being in this big spooky house by myself anyway . . . Do you want some breakfast? I make really good porridge. I do it really fancy. Nuts and raisins."

"Oh, that's . . . That sounds just fine." Ellen read the note again. What is this, she thought, a trick? A test? *You can stay as long as you want.* What does she expect me to do?

"Did you say you wanted coffee?"

"What? . . . Oh yes, that would be lovely."

"I didn't know you were staying in a hotel. That's really a drag. We have so much room here, we could get twenty people in. I was hoping I'd see you again. Mom whisked you away so fast the other night that I didn't get a chance to talk to you . . . See, here's where I keep it." Susan was standing on a kitchen chair in front of one of the cupboards. Above her head she waved a jar of instant coffee. "Did you find a job yet?"

"A job? . . . No, not yet."

"You've got to keep looking. That's what everybody says . . . You know, there's something familiar about you. I kept thinking that the other night. Must be the Wallace look or something, some kind of family resemblance . . . How hungry are you? Should I make a lot?"

"No, not a lot." Now Susan was reaching up for a huge glass jar full of oats. She was standing on tiptoe, her pajamas riding up, and

Ellen found herself staring at the girl's ankles, at the smooth skin. Yes, she thought, she shaves her legs, and looked up to find that Susan had caught her, was staring directly back into her eyes.

Ellen felt an unpleasant prickling of the skin on her neck and shoulders. Susan was giving her a curious half-formed grin. After a moment, Ellen said, "Aren't your feet cold?"

"Oh," Susan said, laughing, "I couldn't imagine what you were looking at."

Ellen's mind seemed to have stopped. Nothing that was happening made any sense. If I stayed here, she thought, I'd be Ellen all the time. Slowly she drew off her grey gloves. Susan tossed a key down; it struck the table and rang like a harsh unmusical bell. "Front door. You've got to jiggle it a bit to get it to work. Come on, I'll show you the guest room. I think we have some clean towels."

Ellen looked at the key and then at her hands. Her nails were frosted pink. Not a good job, she thought. I was in too much of a hurry. She looked at Susan who was dumping oats, without measuring them, direct from the jar into the boiling water. "Thanks," Ellen said, "I think I will stay."

ELLEN WAS SITTING ON ALAN'S BED looking at herself in the mirror. Her hair had been set that morning on too many, too small rollers and now was over-abundant with curls; a viewer's eye would be distracted and wearied, as by the work of a bad pointillist. And she was wearing her only outfit. The skirt needed ironing, and the oxfords didn't go. They were too flashy, high-gloss, brown-and-white vinyl with extravagant heels, and needed to be worn with a touch of wit, with a very short skirt perhaps, as a parody on sex appeal, or with jeans as a throwaway effect. Paired with this skirt and jacket, they looked cheap, possibly gauche. I've got to be more careful, she thought, I know better than this.

The face, she supposed, could be called solemn or thoughtful, although surrounded by these busy-bee curls it might be taken just as easily for merely petulant. She'd packed everything she'd thought she might need, including clothes for Alan in case he should want to reappear suddenly, and then she'd paced up and down in Alan's apartment, looking at it. It's like a prison, she thought now. All these locks and doors. Underground. Why didn't Alan ever feel that? The sun was shining brightly outside, but in here no one would ever know it. Poor Alan, he's just been serving time.

Ellen had phoned Tricia and, imitating Alan's voice, had said that he had the flu and wouldn't be in. Now there was only one thing still left for her to do. She picked up the phone and dialed. Remotely, above her head, she heard it ring. Jeanie answered. "Hi," Ellen said carefully, "It's me. Can you come down a minute?"

Ellen walked into the living room and sat down slowly on the couch. I didn't expect to be this tense about it, she thought. Her legs were shaking. I hope this isn't a terrible mistake. She heard Jeanie's feet on the stairs, bang bang bang, jumping down two at a time. Before she was quite ready, Jeanie had arrived, running.

The girl stopped abruptly and stared. Her face was suspended, caught between expressions. She's all eyes, Ellen thought. Eyes like mine, the Lehman eyes, grey-green. Jeanie said, "Where's Alan?"

"I don't know," Ellen said.

Jeanie's upper lip was trembling. She stood, unmoving, on the spot where she'd stopped. "For a minute I thought you were Aunt Betty."

Quite deliberately, the girl took Ellen's hand and turned it over, palm up. The cut had almost healed, but there was still a trace of it, a pink triangle of new skin. Jeanie pressed her own palm into Ellen's and squeezed her hand. "So you have to be my friend too," she said.

"Yes," Ellen said, "I'm your friend too."

Jeanie sighed. "I was really afraid."

"What were you afraid of?"

"That Alan had gone. That he'd never come back."

"I don't know. My name's Ellen."

"Ellen," Jeanie said slowly, then again: "Ellen." Her expression was grave. "Do you know everything that Alan knew?"

"Yes, I know everything that Alan knew."

"It's magic, isn't it? It's real magic?"

"Yes, I guess it is."

Jeanie suddenly grinned. "Hey, that's really neat!" she said. "Can you teach me how to do it?"

"Jeanie, it's dangerous."

"You think I'm too young, don't you?"

"Yeah, I guess I think you're too young."

"Oh, I *know* I probably am. But maybe I'm not. In nine months I'll be thirteen. Then I won't be too young, will I? Thirteen's a magic number."

"I don't really understand much of anything. When I do, Jeanie, I'll tell you."

"Mom says that I've got to be a lady by the time I'm thirteen. A young lady. It sounds like some kind of a deadline. It's a witch's number," Jeanie was looking into Ellen's eyes. "I'm not really too young, and you know it, too!"

"Yes, I do know it. I just don't know what to do about it."

"Nobody knows what to do with me," she said with a trace of the wicked smile that Alan had seen on Hallowe'en.

"What's been going on . . . up there?" Ellen gestured with her head: the world above.

"Oh, it's been really neat! You should have been there. Mom said I should be punished. And Dad said he didn't know what I should be punished for because he didn't know what it was I had done. She said it was *obvious*. He said it wasn't obvious to him. She said I ought to get a good spanking. He said that he's never raised his hand to his child in his life and he wasn't going to start now. She said *she* would."

Ellen smiled. "How do you know all this?"

"I was listening outside the door . . . So she said she was going to give me a good spanking, but she couldn't do it either. I wish she had. It would have made her feel better. I was prepared. I would have been stoic. I wouldn't even have cried out. But she couldn't do it. She gave me a good talking to instead. I played dumb. I said, 'Oh, I was just dressing up for Hallowe'en. I didn't know I was doing anything bad!'" She gave Ellen the look of affronted innocence that she must have used on her mother: wide guileless eyes. Ellen laughed. "But it didn't work. They're going to send me to that girls' school in January."

"Oh, they are, are they?"

"Yeah. I've got an appointment with the head mistress. That's what they call her, the head mistress. And I'm going to start in January. Oh, it's going to be really neat. All I can think of to do is just to be as bad as I can so they'll flunk me out. Do you think that will work? But it isn't going to be very much fun. Maybe I could run away . . . You're going away, aren't you?"

"Yes."

"I thought so . . . You know," the girl burst out angrily, "you know sometime you're going to have to let me go with you!"

"Look, Jeanie, I'm not deserting you. I'm not. Really." She wrote Mildred Mackenzie's address and phone number on a piece of paper. "Here. This is where I'll be staying."

"Can I come to visit?"

"Yes, but I don't want your mother . . ."

"Of course not," Jeanie said, annoyed. She folded the paper and thrust it into her jeans. "So you're really doing it? For real."

"What?"

"Going on a quest, an adventure." The little girl looked at her sombrely and then intoned:

"How many miles to Babylon?
Three score and ten, sir.
Can I get there by candlelight?
Yes, and back again, sir."

"What's that?"

"It's a nursery rhyme," Jeanie said. "Or it's a spell. She smiled and then her face was grave again. Can *you* get back by candlelight?"

IT HAD BEEN YEARS SINCE LESLIE HAD BEEN IN PORT ALBERT, and Martin had moved since then. When she'd called to tell him that she'd definitely be coming, he'd given her directions. She sat now with the dome light on in her car looking at what she'd written on the back of an envelope. She had found the school all right, was parked directly in front of it. At least it *should* be the school, much too big a building to be the post office, and there was the Maple Leaf flying straight out in the high wind and rain. I screwed it up when I got lost downtown, she thought. I must have come up the hill from the wrong way, and now everything must be reversed, right to left. She turned the envelope upside down, and her markings on it suddenly made sense. There was Martin's house down the road to the left. She'd driven right past it. It's the rain too, she thought. Hard to see anything when it's coming down like this.

Martin had built a carport of sorts, a simple roof on six legs; she drove into it and parked behind his station wagon. He'd left a light burning for her, and he must have heard her drive in; he was already opening the door. She turned off the engine and jumped out of the car. For a moment he looked just like their father as she remembered him from years ago: balding but energetic, round pale face and bulbous nose. "My God, it's blowing!" he said. And she was inside, the door shut behind her, and he was Martin himself, not their father. Oh! she thought with sudden pain, he's getting older.

"Well, Les, you look fit. Got all your hair cut off, eh? I was worried about you. Gale warnings out."

"Yeah, and it started out as such a beautiful day too . . . Hello, Sylvia."

Martin's wife bent to hug her briefly and then retreated. "Did you have a good trip?" Sylvia's smile was tired and wary: she'd never been at ease with Leslie. Did Martin tell her about my crazy phone call? Leslie wondered.

"Don't like to do that much driving in one day," Leslie said, "but it was all right. Pretty uneventful until I got off the ferry at Bear Cove. Then I thought I was going to be blown off the road."

"We saved you some dinner," Martin said. "I was beginning to get worried."

"The boys wanted to wait up for you," Sylvia said, "but they got too tired."

"That's nice of them . . . to want to."

"Oh, they remember you," Martin said. "Don't worry about that. You had them spellbound at Dad's last summer. She can really tell a story, can't she Syl? I was spellbound too. Do you want a drink, Les?"

Their eyes met across the table. "No," she said, "no thanks."

"I don't know how you do it, you're slender as a whippet."

"Still swimming. Although I guess it's for fun now."

"There isn't even a pool up here. I try to play some basketball . . ." He shrugged.

Spaghetti and meatballs in a casserole dish hot from the oven, salad, milk, and bread. Leslie was immensely hungry. She heard rain pelting the windows; the small frame house shook and rattled with it. Food, shelter, Leslie thought. How simple. How good. "It's a little dried out," Sylvia was saying.

"Oh God, Sylvia, don't worry about that," Leslie said, "it's wonderful."

"I've got an early morning tomorrow," Sylvia said. "Martin will fix you up on the couch, eh?"

"Syl's working now," Martin said. "She's up at the school half days."

"Teacher's aid is what they call it," Sylvia said, "Actually I'm trying to get the books in the library straightened out." She bent and kissed Martin's cheek. "Goodnight, hon."

When she heard the bedroom door shut, Leslie said, "That was fast."

Martin shrugged. "She thought we'd want to talk, eh?" He got himself a beer. "You scared me. You know that, don't you?"

"I did?"

"Of course you did. That wasn't just your standard hi, how-are-you phone call, eh?"

"No, I suppose it wasn't. I'd been drinking."

"So you said. What's the trouble, Les?"

"Christ, Martin," she said, laughing, "can't you even let me finish eating?"

"Sorry," he said.

She looked at the brittle blue of his eyes. Like Dad's, she thought, that glittery edge. "I'll bet you're a scary coach," she said.

He laughed. "I've got a loud voice." He sat solidly in his chair. A huge powerful man, still looks strong as a horse, she thought, but soft now . . . in the gut. "It's funny working with Indian kids," he was saying. "You've got to revise your whole idea of what sports is all about. If they think they've got a chance, they damned near kill themselves, but if they can see they're losing, they just drop out. It used to infuriate me. But lately I've been thinking they may have something, and we're the ones who are crazy with our 'do your best at all times' business. Think it's that old British stiff upper lip. But they're very practical, these kids, and they only do it when it counts."

"If you don't do it when it doesn't count," Leslie said, "you won't be able to do it when it does."

"Hey, that's good. I'll put it up in the gym." He grinned.

She pushed her plate away. "Martin," she said, "do you ever feel like a failure?"

"No, not particularly. Should I?"

"I always thought you wanted more than . . . well, teaching socials and coaching in a little nondescript town."

He shrugged. "You get older and you adjust your sights down to something . . . well, what's possible. You find out that you're not going to be the best freestyler in the world . . . or marry Brigitte Bardot . . . or become the Canadian Olympic coach. And so you take the best job you can get, marry the nicest girl you can find, and . . . It happens to everybody, eh?"

"I suppose. What's bothering me is that I don't want it to happen to me."

"You might lose your . . . dreams or whatever you want to call them, but you settle down in the real world, and you get something else."

"What?"

He smiled uneasily. "Peace of mind. Something like that. Oh, I know it'll sound stupid, but you come to take such pleasure in your children, even in your job. I don't know. It's the little things. Sometimes just a damn fine day. And that's enough . . . How old are you now?"

"Twenty-four."

"You're just a baby."

"Yeah, I suppose I am."

"Don't look so down in the mouth, kid. Come on in the living room. Let me fix you a drink of something. Sit down and unwind a bit. Brandy? How's that?"

"That's just fine," she said, smiling at him. She sank down onto the couch. Her body was still driving, riding on the memory of the car and the road. He handed her a glass like a small fishbowl. She sipped. The liquid was pungent and fiery. "Maybe I'll be a drinker yet," she said, "doesn't seem any point anymore . . . to being so spartan."

"What's the matter, Les?" he said. "What's really the matter?"

Gentle Martin, she thought. Can I tell him about everything? No, of course, I can't. Well, what the hell am I doing here then? Maybe I just want to *see* him. "It's nothing simple," she said, "nothing I can put my finger on. It's . . . well, I just realized lately that I'm not a competitive swimmer anymore. And with that gone, it's left me . . . not very much. It's left me nothing, really."

"Do you like your job?"

"It's a job. I like the kids."

"Do you have a boyfriend?"

"There's a man I see, but . . . Martin, I've got to find something that means as much to me as swimming did."

"Have you tried coaching?"

"That's what Dad says too." She sighed. "I think the reason I came up . . . the main reason . . . I know this is going to sound strange to you. But I want to find the place where Grandfather used to live up Johnston's Inlet." He looked at her curiously. "I know it must sound funny. But I just want to find it . . . and look around . . . and imagine what it must have been like for him to live there."

He said nothing, walked into the kitchen and got himself another beer.

"You keep drinking beer that fast, Martin," she said, smiling, "and you're going to get as big as a house."

He laughed. "Do you want to stay around to remind me?" He sat down again. "Well," he said awkwardly. "I'm not very religious, so I'm not going to talk about God. But there's something good about going back into the bush. I'm glad I'm up here and I can take the boys out, eh? It's . . . I don't know. It's where we come from, and if we don't go back sometimes, I think we dry out. So . . . no, it doesn't sound funny to me, Leslie. Maybe it will give you something."

She didn't know what to say. She looked away. Then she said, "Can you show me where it is on a map?"

"I can show you roughly where it is. You're going to have to hire somebody at Huyatsi or Adagalis to take you up the Inlet, eh? The cabin's only a few miles from an Indian village . . . deserted now. Nobody's lived there since they moved all the bands down to the Reserve at Huyatsi. But if you find the village, you should be able to get some idea where the cabin is . . . or was. There's a trail to it. And it looks down over a cove . . . There aren't many places over there to tie up a boat. The rocks just rise up straight from the water." He grinned. "If I didn't have to work, I'd go with you."

Leslie didn't answer. She sipped at the brandy. She had just discovered, to her surprise, that she didn't feel like talking anymore. "I must be exhausted," she said finally.

"Bring your things in, eh? I'll make up the couch for you." When she came back in out of the rain, carrying her knapsack and sleeping bag, she found Martin spreading the couch with sheets and blankets. "You don't have to do that."

"Oh, no trouble."

"Martin . . . I wish I'd gotten to know you better. You were always so much older. And . . . well, Ed and I fought so much. It was nice to have a brother I liked."

He patted her shoulder without looking at her. "I'll get you a pillow."

"Will you tell me something straight?" she said. "I've wanted to ask Dad for years and I've never had the guts so I'll ask you." He's got that alarmed look on his face, she thought, just like Dad would

have. "Martin," she said quickly, "when I was a kid, I used to wonder if Dad hated me . . . or wonder why he didn't hate me, because
I *knew* he didn't . . . because I thought that I'd killed mother. She
never left the hospital. She went in to have me, and she never left
the hospital. And if she hadn't had me . . ." Martin was silent for a
while. Then he said. "She named you. You know that, eh?"

"Yes."

"I was just a kid, but I remember . . . I think I remember it so
clearly because I knew she was dying. Nobody told me. I just knew
it, so I paid attention. She kept asking about you. 'How's my
daughter?' She was glad about you, Les. She said, 'I have two good
sons. I'm glad she's a girl.'"

Tears stung Leslie's eyes. She blinked them away. "Oh, Martin,"
she said. "I feel like such a failure sometimes." When she could
look at him, she saw that he was wearing an odd lop-sided smile.
"Leslie," he said, "you were the best of us. You were the best of all."

OH, SO THEY'RE PUTTING US BACK IN PETTICOATS, ARE THEY? Ellen
thought. She was looking at the peasant-style dresses on the rack
in the Jeune Fille Boutique: minute floral prints closely fitted at
the waist, full skirts that hung just below the knee, the skirts lined
with petticoats from attached camisoles. Somebody could write a
complete analysis of the changing currents of North American
society, she thought, based completely upon women's fashions.
Back to petticoats, and high visibility too, an inch below the skirts,
dramatic white lace. Well, all the magazines have been saying that
ultrafem is in again, but is anybody buying? She looked at the
price tag. Ouch! Not at these prices. But the secretaries maybe;
they've got it to spend. How about me? Get one of those wide
peasant-look cinch belt with laces, nip my waist for dear life, wear
it with high boots. Might get into an 8. And she moved around
the rack from the 10s to the 8s. A woman was coming around

from the other side. For a moment both she and Ellen had their hands on the same dress. "Excuse me," the woman said.

"That's all right," Ellen murmured and stepped back. The woman was Betty.

Betty glanced at her, a distant abstracted look on her face, and then down again at the dress. Walk away, you damn fool! Ellen told herself. Do it now! But she couldn't move. Her mouth had gone dry; her heart was racing. She reached out to steady herself on the dress rack. A rolling wave of nausea was blotting her out. Her knees began to fold. She gripped the rack, felt the cold unresponsive metal hard in her hand. Oh, please, she thought, don't let me faint! She closed her eyes.

When she looked again, Betty was staring at her open-mouthed. Ellen began to count: one, two, three, four . . . When she reached twenty-seven, Betty said, "Are you going to be all right?"

"No," Ellen said in a tiny voice. She began to fall.

"Yes, you are," Betty said. She stepped forward and slid under Ellen's arm. "Let go of the rack, dear," she said. "You're going to pull it over." Ellen wrapped her arms around her sister. The light was turning black. "Don't faint here in the middle of the store," Betty was saying into Ellen's ear. "Nothing terrible is happening . . . Try to stand up now . . . Oh Alan, come on, please try! You're going to pull me over. Breathe. That's it. Come on, walk . . . Oh, what heels you have, dear. You're as bad as I am! Come on, can't have two wobbly ladies falling over in the Jeune Fille."

"Have . . . to sit . . . down," Ellen said.

"That's right. Here you go." Betty unfolded Ellen into one of the chairs by the mirror.

"Is anything the matter?" the salesgirl said.

You have too much makeup on, Ellen wanted to say, looking up at the little painted face. "I'm all right," she said.

"My sister just feels a little faint," Betty said.

The salesgirl withdrew to the far side of the shop but continued to glance toward them apprehensively.

"She has on too much makeup," Ellen said. Stop it! she told herself.

"She certainly does," Betty said. "Are you all right now?"

"Yeah, I suppose."

"Oh, Alan! Don't look so worried. I'm not going to give you away . . . You know, I must have been watching you off and on for five minutes. You were studying the clothes so carefully, and you looked so absolutely elegant, and I didn't know it was you. I really didn't . . . Until you practically fell over on top of me."

"It was like a childhood nightmare come true," Ellen said. "That dream used to really bother me . . . bother Alan . . . that . . . ah . . . he'd be out on the street in a dress, and he's run into you or Amy or mother. And all of a sudden, there it was, happening."

"Your colour's coming back. You must be feeling better . . . Look, Alan, if you run into Amy or mother, just walk on by. They wouldn't know you. They really wouldn't."

"I'm Ellen."

"Ellen?"

"That's my name. Ellen."

"Well, hello Ellen," Betty said with a slow smile. "Come on, you should get outside and get some air."

Ellen stood up; the world was firm around her again. "Do you fancy me in petticoats?" she said, gesturing toward the dress rack.

"I was wondering the same thing about myself . . . not sure I do at those prices." And Betty began to laugh. "If you're getting into an 8, we could go halves and share it."

Out on the street, Ellen was thinking of what Mrs. Mackenzie had said. "You're either Alan or Ellen. There must be no confusion between the two." But that's what had happened; when she'd seen Betty, Alan had started to come back. For a moment everything had been confused; she'd stopped being Ellen and had been Alan in girls' clothes. The danger of it had felt powerful and raw. But it was over. She was Ellen again.

"Is that your real hair?" Betty said.

"Yes, it's my real hair," Ellen laughed. "I got a chance to see the beauty business from the other side today. Went into one of those flossy shops on Robson Street and had it done."

"Streaked, eh? Whew do you look slick! You look so slick you actually annoyed me when I first saw you. I thought, oh, look at that hair . . . and that perfect nail polish. Some damn executive secretary, probably making eight hundred a month . . ." She stopped walking. "Look, Alan," she said, "I mean Ellen . . . come back to the apartment with me. Come back and have some coffee with me."

"What if Gary . . ."

"Oh, in our entire married life, Gary's never once come home early. He's an absolute fanatic about his work. You won't run into anybody."

And driving back to Kitsilano, Betty said, "You're doing this full time, eh?"

"Yeah, I suppose I am."

"I've got another sister," Betty said. "An ash blonde. Oh, incredible!"

She parked in the garage beneath the apartment; they took the elevator up. "Where's the kid?" Ellen said.

"The lady in the apartment a floor down has him. It's funny in these damn places. We'd both lived here for over a year before we met each other. We were down in the laundry one day, and we both had a load of baby clothes, and we looked at each other . . . and flash! Connection, eh? . . . I guess we both feel a little less like prisoners now . . . Here, just put your coat over a chair. Coffee? Or do you want a drink?"

"No, coffee's fine."

Ellen had not yet found a way to be at ease with her sister; she needed a moment of escape, turned away from Betty's dark eyes and walked to the sliding glass doors, stood looking out at the panorama of Vancouver which seemed from this height and distance as remotely attractive as a picture postcard: the buildings of the West End, English Bay, the mountains. Betty kept the glass doors perfectly polished.

"Yeah, we've got a hell of a view, don't we?" Betty said. Ellen turned away slowly. Her sister was still watching her. The apartment was white, clean, and modern. Tiny gold flecks sparkled from the plastered ceiling. "That's what I keep telling myself, eh?" Betty said. "Great view. And a garage, a laundry, a sauna." She shrugged. "I guess it was some kind of ultimate for Gary, coming from the East End. I would have preferred some funky old place, but . . ." She shrugged again. "Well, he's paying for it."

She set the lid onto the percolator, twisted it: sharp clink of glass on glass. Then, smiling slightly, her face still unreadable, she walked to the table, pulled out a chair for herself. "Sit down, little sister . . . I better teach you how to wear a skirt. You keep pulling at it all the time."

"I do?"

"Yeah. And that's a no-no. Ladies don't pull at their skirts. They slide into a chair ever so gracefully and the skirt falls into place of its own accord. And you don't have to sit there so primly with your knees together like that. You look like a prissy little schoolgirl. Try crossing your legs . . . Yeah, that's better . . . If you come over in the afternoons, I'll give you lessons."

"You're so goddamned deadpan, I can't tell if you're having me on."

"Oh, I'm half having you on . . . You've got most of it down really well, but you could stand a lesson or two. Like the way you got out of the car . . ."

"How did I get out of the car?"

"Like you had pants on . . . first one leg and then the other and the skirt every which way. Well, you might do that if there was a man holding the door for you and you wanted to get him going. But ordinarily you keep your feet and legs together and just swing around." She demonstrated on the chair.

"But, I'll bet you learn fast," Betty said. She brought the coffee and cups to the table. "When did you start?"

"Alan had been playing at it . . . privately . . . all of his life. But *I* appeared . . . well, less than a week ago."

"You're doing really well then . . . You know, it's funny. It's not that I'm getting used to you. It's almost as though you're a different person. I think you make a hell of a lot more plausible woman than you did a man. I mean it. Even with that kind of funny awkwardness you have about you now . . . You look like a girl who's been used to wearing jeans and has got herself all dressed up for some occasion."

Ellen still couldn't stand up to her sister's scrutiny; she lowered her eyes. "Something clicked when we were walking up the street," Betty went on, "and I thought it was really silly for Alan to try to be male all these years. He should have been a girl all along, and I think we all knew it. But there just wasn't anything . . . to do about it. You don't just take a little boy and say, 'OK, you wear dresses from now on and go to Stafford House with your sisters.'" She laughed. "Cream and sugar?"

"No, black."

"Oh, watching your figure, eh?"

Ellen sipped the coffee. "Are they really going to send Jeanie there?"

"I'm afraid so. Amy really has her back up this time."

"It's ridiculous. *I* should have been the one to go, not Jeanie. I've thought lately . . . This is crazy, I know . . . But that somehow Alan and Jeanie got reversed."

"Oh, it's not just you and Jeanie. It's the whole bloody family. Transplanted British gentry going to seed in the colonies, all of us loony as hatters." She laughed without humour. "When I married Gary, I thought I was escaping."

"Didn't you?"

She didn't answer for a moment, looked away through the polished glass doors. "I don't know."

Ellen sipped her coffee. She was searching for something to say to end the silence. She saw that Betty was still watching her. "Jeanie shouldn't go to Stafford House."

"No, of course not."

"We should do something."

"Now, Alan, just what the hell could we do?"

"Ellen."

"I'm sorry. Ellen. It's none of our business . . . Well, maybe Jeanie will like the horses."

"Maybe," Ellen said doubtfully. "You know, I used to envy you and Amy. I wanted to go there and learn how to be a girl."

"Yeah, you would have loved it. Walking around with beanbags on your head . . . Oh, Christ, it was all so veddy British. Yeah, they would have made a lady out of you." She was sloshing coffee around in the bottom of her cup. "Do you think it would have made any difference . . . if Father had lived?"

"Yeah, I suppose so. I used to hate him. Did you know that?"

Betty looked up. "Did you? Why?"

"Because he died."

"Oh."

"Kids aren't reasonable," Ellen said.

"Yeah," Betty said. "That's right. Kids aren't reasonable . . . Do you want more coffee?"

"No, I don't think so."

"Oh, Christ!" Betty stood in a single explosive motion, pushing back the chair. "Well, you can't be staying in Amy's basement . . . like that?"

"No, I'm staying . . . with friends."

"Have enough room for me?"

Their eyes met. "Are you serious?"

"No, of course not."

"What's the matter?"

"Oh, Gary and I haven't been speaking since that bloody party. Think the extent of our conversation has been: 'Pass the salt.' Gary got drunk, made a pass at some insane little girl who turned up here. Christ, I don't even want to talk about it." She jerked a dishpan out from under the sink.

"Look," Ellen said, "I'll give you the address where I'm staying, but I don't think . . ."

"Don't worry. I didn't mean it."

"I should probably go," Ellen said awkwardly.

"I'll drive you."

"All right . . . Betty, this is going to sound . . . Look, do you have any short dresses or skirts? Nobody in town has anything short now, and I want to show off my legs."

Betty leaned against the sink and laughed. "What do you want, a real mini? Oh, I have the perfect thing for you. Couple years old, white wet-look, absolute dynamite with your ash-blond hair . . . Can you wear my shoes? I have some white boots that go with it. Come on, we'll go through the closet."

LESLIE WALKED OUT TO THE END OF THE DOCK to watch the last of the daylight fading through the grey slanting rain. It was not the blowing gale of the night before; now it was a pervasive steady flow, airy, more mist than downpour. It blotted out the mountains across the water, hazed over everything, made the edges indistinct. She looked back to the great shed-like building where she'd

climbed out of the water taxi. WELCOME TO HUYATSI VIL-
LAGE was painted on the wall, the words encircled by the
Kwakiutl double-headed sea serpent, the Sisiutl. She knew him
from children's books: You were out fishing one day, drew up your
net and found an unusual snakelike fish; you continued to pull the
long body into your boat until you came to the end, where the tail
should be, and found the second head. Then you knew that you'd
caught dangerous and powerful magic.

Early that morning Leslie had waved good-bye to her brother
on the dock in Port Albert, climbed down into the silvery all-
metal water taxi, and been piloted through a long winding passage of lucent grey rain. It was like a blurred Chinese scroll
unrolling endlessly, she thought. Couldn't tell island from mainland, at times couldn't tell sky from water, past ghostly green
landscapes, past mountains that were shrouded and hidden, to
arrive here at Huyatsi Village to be greeted appropriately by the
guardian spirit of this hazy watery world, the Sisiutl, his paint
fading in the continuous rain.

Boats were bobbing on both sides of her, seine boats and gill-
netters; they seemed to be chatting to themselves in small, muted,
metallic voices. She turned to look back out over the water. She was
trying to remember what her grandfather had said about Huyatsi.
When he'd broken his leg, they'd brought him here to the only hospital for miles. And she'd heard from someone, not from the old
man himself surely, that Huyatsi was where he used to go on the
wild drinking sprees that eventually drove her grandmother into
Vancouver. But why should anyone want to come *here* to drink, to
this strangely muted village? The main street, slippery with mud,
curved along the water—to the left into the Reserve where (as
Martin had told her) several bands, not particularly friendly toward
each other, had been packed in by an edict of the Department of
Indian Affairs—to the right, as Leslie had discovered for herself,

going precisely nowhere, petering out into logged-off bush. "You'll just have to ask around," Martin had said, so she'd asked around. She'd been in the general store, the post office, the Department of Fisheries, the marine outfitters, and the Chinese cafe. Everywhere she'd gone she'd been stared at, not by white people (they'd averted their eyes), but by the Indians. The children and old people had been the most blatant, but everyone had done it, as though she'd been surrounded by questions that no one had wanted to ask directly. Self-conscious in her bright yellow rain poncho, she'd felt these people slip by her; bundled up in khaki coats, hats pulled down to their watchful eyes, they blended into the rain, into this indirect, blurred landscape. And everyone she'd talked to had said, "Oh, yeah, somebody can take you up the Inlet." But nobody had been quite sure who. Finally she'd given it up and booked a room for the night at the hotel called "The Mamalilikulla."

Now there was nothing for Leslie to see but the tail end of the daylight filtered through this monotonous rain, a pearly translucent haze in the direction she knew the sun must be setting. For a moment, she saw something—a rolling motion, like a sheet on end, in the centre of the rain—as though the sky had been parted and something allowed through. But she blinked and it was gone. Must be some kind of optical effect, she thought. She closed her eyes for several seconds and then looked again. There it was: a wheel of rain, its edge toward her. It seemed to be turning slowly. Leslie was suddenly afraid. She looked behind her at the dock. There was not a sign of a person anywhere. I'm the only damn fool crazy enough to stand out in the rain, she thought, and she began to walk quickly back to the village.

The Mamalilikulla was supposed to have a restaurant, and she supposed this was it: a large bare room with wooden tables and chairs, the "kitchen" in plain view: a refrigerator, coffee machine, and grill. Two men, white, were sitting at one of the tables. They

looked up at Leslie curiously when she walked in and then immediately looked away. She walked to the opposite side of the room,
shed her wet poncho onto a chair, and sat down. After a moment,
a young Indian girl walked to her table and said, "Did you want
something to eat?"

"Yes. Do you have a menu?"

"No." The girl smiled. "I can fry you up somethin."

"How about some sausages, a couple of eggs over easy, toast, a
large orange juice, and a pot of tea?"

Leslie smiled. Breakfast three times a day. And the two men at
the other table kept glancing at her and then looking away. I
should have brought something to read, she thought. And somewhere, there was a terrific din, shouting voices. Must be the beer
parlour at the end of the hall. She looked over to check on the
progress of her food and saw that an Indian man had come in and
was talking to the girl. The girl nodded in Leslie's direction. Leslie
felt her stomach tighten. The man walked toward her. He was in
his forties, wearing a khaki coat and khaki rain hat. His eyes were
quite black. He smiled at her shyly. "You're the one that's wantin
to go up the Inlet, hey?" he said.

"Yeah, I'm the one."

The Indian sat down at her table. He didn't take off his hat.
"You want coffee, Randy?" the girl called to him. He nodded. She
brought him a cup.

Leslie waited tensely. Christ, she thought, how long can he sit
there without speaking? Finally he said, "I live over at Adagalis,
hey?" He was looking at his hands. "I'm goin back tomorrow.
Maybe I could take you up the Inlet."

"Well, that's . . . that's really nice," Leslie said. "I'm Leslie
Fraser." She offered her hand.

He rose a few inches from the chair, touched her hand a
moment, and sat down again. "Randolph Paul," he said. Her food

223

was arriving. The girl must have thought she was cooking for a lumberjack: four pieces of toast, five sausages. "Lots of strange people comin up to the Village now, hey?" Randolph Paul said to the girl. She laughed. Leslie felt the back of her neck prickle.

Leslie began to eat. The Indian was staring into his coffee cup. Say something! she told herself. Anything at all. "There's a deserted Indian village up at Johnston's Inlet?" she said.

"Yeah, there might be," he said without looking up.

"My . . . ah . . . grandfather used to live up around there."

"A white man, hey?"

"Yes." He didn't seem ready to say anything more. "Look," she said. "I want to find his cabin. It's supposed to be very close to the deserted village."

He nodded. "*My* grandfather come from up there." She leaned closer. He spoke so softly she had trouble hearing him; and he had a blurry accent as soft as the rain outside. ". . . moved all the bands down to Huyatsi," he was saying, "long time now, hey? Nobody lives up there anymore. *We* go up there. Go huntin." He stopped speaking and showed no sign of beginning again.

Leslie ate slowly, looking into her plate. "Yeah," he said eventually, "lot of you people comin up here now. Don't know what you people doin comin up here." His voice was so soft that she couldn't tell if he was intentionally trying to annoy her.

"I just want to see where my grandfather used to live," she said. "That's all I want."

He set the coffee cup down on the table. "Maybe I could take you right there," he said, "to that village up there, hey? Maybe I could take you to the cove and you could walk right up to it."

"Could you?" she said.

"I'm goin real early tomorrow, soon as I get up."

"That's fine with me." He didn't speak. "I'd want to stay up there . . . Oh, maybe two days," she said. Now he's got me saying "maybe," she thought. "Could you come back for me . . . Say on Thursday morning?"

"I guess I could do that. But you'd have to be there, hey? I couldn't be goin around looking for you."

"Hi, Ellen," Susan said. She'd just walked in and found her cousin standing on a kitchen chair reaching up onto a shelf. The radio was playing, and Ellen must not have heard her coming; she seemed startled, was staring back over her shoulder. I wonder if *I* could ever look like that? Susan thought. Tall and thin as a model.

Ellen had a funny look on her face, then she smiled, said, "Hi," continued to hang, interrupted, poised on the chair. All of her clothes looked brand new, right off the rack. New jeans, quite high-waisted, and new blouse, new boots with slender heels. She's been shopping, Susan thought. Ellen had been on tiptoe, even those very high heels had been an inch in the air; now she lowered her weight onto the chair. Her hair was tied back with a scarf; she wore rubber gloves and a plastic apron. She had been washing the shelves. "You've been cleaning up," Susan said.

Ellen stepped carefully down off the kitchen chair. She's uptight, Susan thought. What's the matter? Ellen stripped off the rubber gloves and threw them into the sink. She pulled off the scarf and shook her head. Her hair had been streaked ash blond and permed. It fell in a tumble of ginger ale-coloured curls around her shoulders. "Hi," she said again.

Susan was tongue-tied. She hated it when she blushed. She didn't know why she should be blushing. "You've really cleaned it up!" she tried, hearing her voice coming out too loud. "It must have taken you hours."

"Not that long. I hope you don't mind."

"Of course not. How could I mind?"

"Well, it's your house, eh?"

Ellen hadn't heard the girl come in. She'd been lost in a soft-focus dream which she realized now had been a sexual fantasy; she'd been startled in the middle of it, and now felt a terrible tension, for she was sure that her spontaneous reaction to Susan must have given her away; she'd stripped off her scarf and rubber gloves, as embarrassed to be found dressed that way as any young housewife surprised by her husband; and she had turned to present herself to Susan. Look at me, my beautiful hair, my beautiful clothes! To this teen-age *girl*. "I think I must have the heat up too high," Ellen said.

"Oh?" Susan sai., "It is hot." Suddenly the girls were moving away from each other as quickly as if a director had shouted through a megaphone: Move! Susan to the thermostat and Ellen to the stove. "You're cooking too," Susan said. "The kitchen's all hot and steamy."

"Yeah, that's it."

Susan hung up her coat. She didn't know why she should be so reluctant to walk back into the kitchen. What's happening? she thought. What's the matter with me? Her father used to tell her that if she were nervous she should inhale deeply. She inhaled deeply and walked into the kitchen.

I can't stand it! Ellen was thinking. Downtown she'd found an improbable lingerie shop selling cute little items imported from France, and one particularly improbable item, something she'd thought only a French girl would have bought: a padded panty girdle, falsies for the bottom. It lifted and divided her buttocks, swelled them out a couple inches, and was cut high into a lightly-boned waist cincher, precisely what she'd needed to wear under jeans. When she'd put it on, the physical sensation had been teasing and provocative. But she'd been cleaning the kitchen, and the panty girdle was now too hot, torturously uncomfortable. She felt sweat running down her thighs; she was aching between her legs.

And here was Susan back again, looking at her curiously. The girl's eyes seemed to be drawing her to the edge of explosion.

Susan was looking at the stack of her mother's vegetarian cookbooks that Ellen had spread out on the table.

"You're not one too, are you?" she said.

"What?"

"A vegeterrible?"

Ellen tried to laugh. "Yeah, I suppose I am," she said.

"Well, *I'm* not. I'm a pure carnivore. Meat. Give me red-blooded meat." She gnashed her teeth and giggled.

Something inside Ellen contracted at the sight of the girl's teeth grinding together. She could be a boy, Ellen thought. Short hair, plain blouse, ratty jeans frayed at the hem, scuffed mary-janes set on wedges of cork. Except that she's painted her face, badly. Boy with makeup. Girlish boy, boyish girl. Oh, God! I should have known it would be like this . . . For if Ellen had gone out on the street dressed as she was, she would have turned on men, and she didn't want to turn on men. But she would have been delighted to turn on Susan.

Susan suddenly understood everything. She was surprised that she hadn't seen it before. She knew why Ellen was in Vancouver, why she'd spent the day shopping, why she seemed so strange and sad now. She must have broken up with her boyfriend in Winnipeg. She must have come out here to forget. She must miss him terribly. Oh, Susan thought, of course! I should try to cheer her up.

SUSAN WAS PAINTING HER NAILS; Ellen was acutely aware of the smell of the polish, persistent as the note of a small bell. That salmon shade is a good colour for her, she thought, goes with her skin. I'm surprised she had the taste to pick it. I would have expected midnight blue from her.

The terrible discomfort Ellen had been suffering earlier had trickled away during dinner. But no, she thought, not exactly gone, more that it's pulled back inside me: heat at the centre, but outside cool. She imagined a huge blue sphere with a single red dot in the centre. She imagined the excitement persisting as clearly as the smell of the nail polish, small bright stripe through beiges and browns, glowing alien odour through the smell of cooked vegetables and the spicy drying leaves on the walls. Or it was as though her entire surface had been shaved and then mentholated. Her thoughts were out of control, linking into the most extravagant of patterns, but outside cool. It was terrible and dangerous where she was, and although the strain was making her giddy, she wasn't afraid of it.

"Dad was real strict," Susan was saying. "Old-fashioned . . . Did you know him?"

"Ah . . . No, I never met your dad."

"Yeah. Well, mom was too . . . *then*." She laughed. "I can remember . . . I'd just turned thirteen, and hot pants were in then. I just had to have a pair, eh? They said absolutely no. So of course I bought a pair anyway, kept them hidden in the back of the closet. Oh wow, they were really trashy. White plastic." She giggled. "The way I picked the size . . . I just tried them on smaller and smaller until I got to the smallest pair I could get on. Oh, you can imagine what I must have looked like!" She was blushing. "I didn't even wear panties with them. Can you believe it?" Both she and Ellen were giggling. "And I'd put them under jeans and go downtown and take off the jeans in the ladies' room at the library and walk around town all day like that. And then when I'd have to go home, I'd put my jeans back on, just walk in, eh? Hi, Mom. Hi, Dad. Oh, it was a real howl. I can't believe I did that."

"I'll bet you were popular."

"Well, no. The boys were scared of me, actually. You know, *thirteen* . . . Oh, but a man tried to pick me up once! I mean a real man. He must have been thirty. He came up to me at the bus stop, and I thought, far out! He really wants to pick me up. And I told him, 'Hey; mister, I'm only thirteen!'"

"What did he do?"

"He walked away as fast as he could. Oh, it was funny, a real howl." Ellen was laughing so hard she had tears in her eyes. "Did you ever do anything like that?" Susan said.

Ellen paused. "No. I guess I was always too shy."

"You don't seem shy now."

Ellen didn't answer. She poured the tea. "Ellen," the girl said. Susan's face had gone thoughtful. "Do you know my mother very well?"

"Yes, I suppose I do."

"Do you think . . . Well . . . Do you think she's crazy?"

"No," Ellen said slowly, "I think she's strange, but I don't think she's crazy."

"Sometimes *I* do. She just doesn't seem to care about me anymore."

"I'm sure she cares about you, Susan."

"She sure doesn't show it. Some of the things I wear now . . . two years ago, she would have dropped dead."

"Maybe she thinks you're old enough to run your own life."

"Yes, but . . . It's like I don't have a mother anymore." She began to put on the next coat of nail polish.

"Your tea's getting cold," Ellen said.

"Ellen, could you . . .? I bet you could show me how to put on makeup. I never get it right."

"I'd be glad to," Ellen said. She stood, walked to the sink.

"Oh, don't do them yet," Susan said. "You made dinner. I'll do them later."

Ellen hesitated. There was a knock on the door. "Could you get that?" Susan said, waving her hands in the air. The fresh nail polish.

Have to lie down a while, Ellen thought, I feel really strange. She opened the door. There was Betty, holding her baby in her arms. The baby was crying. Ellen couldn't speak.

"You certainly make a sweet little housewife, dear," Betty said. "Aren't you going to ask me in?"

"Christ, Betty, " she said, "I thought you were kidding."

"Yeah, I thought I was too, but we just had the fight to end all fights. I've got a migraine that just won't quit." To the baby, "Come on, Lizard, shut up, won't you!"

"What . . .? What am I going to tell . . .? Oh God!" Ellen said.

"Tell them anything you want, I don't care . . . I didn't know where else to go. If I'd gone to mother's, he would have come crashing in at one in the morning . . . dead drunk. He's over at the bloody Cecil. He walked out, so I thought, OK, my turn."

"LESLIE! LESLIE!" THEY SCREAMED IN THEIR HARSH VOICES. She stopped and shivered in the bright morning sunlight. But of course they hadn't been saying "Leslie, Leslie" at all; they'd merely been calling to each other . . . the great northern ravens. She could see their black wings skimming into the dense evergreen forest. And she began walking again toward the totem poles. Well, this is certainly simple, she thought. The village lay not far above the high-tide line; it had been easily visible from the water. If she'd had her own boat, she might have found it herself merely by cruising the margin of the Inlet and looking at every likely spot to land. This was a fiord, and for miles rock rose straight up from the water, not high but sheer, and pleasant coves would be few; this one would have stood out, certainly: a half-moon crescent of rough beach with the tall poles strung along above it. She was close enough now to see the detail in the faces. There a carved raven, there a bear with lolling tongue, and there mysterious human figures, myth people. She supposed the one with the round protruding mouth was the Tsoonoqua, the wild old woman of the woods who ate small children. Their paint was fading. They were staring out to sea.

She had thought she would sit a moment and lean her back against the base of one of the poles, but as she approached, she felt a curious apprehension, hesitated. She shed her knapsack, used it for a pillow, and stretched out on the ground. She could see Randolph Paul's gillnetter; on the bright water it was a distant dark spot, moving away. "Leslie!" Her muscles contracted involuntarily. One of the ravens had come back. She could see it, black, in a nearby tree. "You're here! You're here!" it called to her. It's amazing how evocative their voices are, she thought. You could imagine they were saying anything. "Tok," the raven said flatly. And then again "Leslie!"

"What?" she called back, laughing.

It flew away, black wings a moment against the sky. "Leslie!" it called. From deeper in the bush, its friend answered, "Here! here!" Leslie stopped smiling. She looked thoughtfully at the quiet green landscape. Yes, I'm here, she thought. Tuesday morning, and I have two days. She was certain she'd find her grandfather's place that afternoon, and then what? She took the folded paper out of her skirt pocket and spread it out on her knee. Martin had sketched the cove, a semi-circle, and drawn a jagged line off to the left, labeled it "ragged trail." At the end of it he'd made an X. "It's about a forty-minute walk, or used to be," he'd said. "If it's all grown up now, it'll take you longer." Shouldn't take me that much longer, she thought. Well, I'd better make some kind of a camp.

She stood and hesitated again, looking. It was as though she'd walked into an old photograph in the Provincial Museum. Except that there were no people here. Find almost any pleasant spot near water up the coast of B.C., the juncture of two rivers or a sheltered cove like this one, and there you might find a town site where people had lived continuously for thousands of years. She turned slowly, scanning the forest behind the longhouse: immensely tall cedars in a line that ended abruptly, as though sheared off. Loggers who can go anywhere had been here, left behind well-developed secondary growth stretching away as far as she could see. If this place were not so remote from highways, tourists would have been here too, might have chopped up the longhouse for souvenirs, carried the pieces back to Vancouver, Seattle, or California.

But the longhouse was untouched except by weather; in fact it looked in good enough shape for the band to move back into it tomorrow. If I could get in, she thought, I wouldn't even have to put up the tent. But she found herself reluctant to approach it. Instead she picked a spot in the shelter of trees and set up her tiny mountaineering tent. It weighed less than eight pounds; rolled up, it was no larger than a loaf of French bread. She studied it a moment after she'd staked it out. A small, brave shelter, she thought. She walked toward the longhouse. Again she felt uncomfortable approaching too close, as though the Indians might have returned. But it was the bush that had come back, these primitive plants everywhere, horsetails and ferns. Eventually, she thought, the poles will fall, be blown down in a gale, turn back to logs, be covered with moss. The carved images of the spirits of the coast would return to the spirits of the coast.

It's so quiet here, she thought. She tried to imagine when it had been different, when there had been old people resting in the sun, telling stories, when there had been children playing and the beach had been lined with dugout canoes. Why did they ever leave? Because the white man had come and built his school and hospital in Huyatsi. Because the Indian agent in Huyatsi had administrative problems, couldn't manage bands scattered, star-like, up the coast through islands and inlets.

And now who remembers? Strangely, she found a verse jingling in her mind, a children's question and answer rhyme:

How many miles to Babylon?

Three score and ten, sir.

Can I get there by candlelight?

Yes, and back again, sir.

"Three score and ten," the span of a human life, that strange journey, she thought, so short it could be over in a night. But can you get there by candlelight? Yes, and back again. Back to what? Before the span of that single life, the thread flowing back . . . There was an evocative resonance in her mind: something that's always there, like a reflection at the edge of a dream—memory— of where we've been together, where we've come from. For whether we walked or came by boat, we came from the same place. That's what the oral tradition is, she thought. Memory. And for us, it's the Indians who stand at the edge of the dream, behind them, the bush, where we all began. My people lived in the misty north too; they lived in clans. They hunted and told stories. Memory. Where we keep it now is in the children's libraries. But if the modernists have their way, it won't even be kept there much longer.

She began to walk away from the village, looking for Martin's "ragged trail." Then she knew (had been gradually coming to know it) that she was not two people at odds with each other— Leslie the swimmer and Leslie the fantasist—they were the same person moving from the same centre. In order to do the deed, she thought, you must first tell the story, how it was done before, and will be done again. No, we must never stop reciting the old verses, telling the old stories, the ones that begin, "Once there was a king, and he had three sons." We must always be able to reach back for that thread running thousands of years. And already the forest was closing in around her, these immensely tall cedars. We must never lose this either, she thought. But no, not "either," for it's part of the same thing. If we forget the words, if we log off the forests, carry away the images, where will we go to get back again? Then we'd be truly alone here, and lost. Suddenly, the full awesomeness of these surroundings struck her, and she stopped, poised and watchful. It's right, she thought, it's genuinely wild. It's not a campground. Can I get there by candlelight? Her mind stopped as it did when she was swimming. And she didn't know how long she'd been standing there when she awoke again to find that she'd discovered the remains of a trail leading off further into the bush.

"I DON'T EVEN LIKE HIM HALF THE TIME," Betty said. "But I suppose I love him."

Ellen couldn't see her sister's face; Betty had fallen into an odd pose: elbows on the sewing table facing the window, arms pressed together elbow to wrist, and chin resting on her hands, fingers framing her face. Her nails were frosted the colour of winesap apples. Ellen felt an obscure emotion at the sight of her sister's profile, in the morning light as perfect as if newly struck in silver. "What are you going to do?" she said.

"Damned if I know," Betty said.

"I don't know what to say."

"Yeah," Betty said. "I don't know. Something about waking up in somebody else's house . . . The little cockroach started crying at his usual time, and I reached out for Gary, and he wasn't there. It took me the damn longest time to remember where I was. And then I thought, oh, this is silly. I should be at home with my husband. What time is it?"

"Must be nine."

"You didn't have to get up with me."

"I know."

"Maybe we should have breakfast."

"Yeah, maybe."

Betty straightened up, turned away from the window, and located her purse. She pounded a cigarette out of the pack, lit it. "Christ," she said, "just look at us!"

"What?"

Betty swung open the closet door. There was a full-length mirror behind it. "Look."

Ellen walked to her sister's side. In the mirror, she saw two young women with remarkably similar faces and figures. They were both wearing jackets and skirts over the knee, high boots, makeup and nail polish. "It's amazing," Ellen said. "We really are quite alike . . . except I'm taller and blond."

"Yeah, even the same goddamned *taste*. That's what blew my mind when I realized it. Were you consciously modeling yourself on me?"

"Not consciously . . . Maybe it *was* there in my head somewhere. I guess I always wanted to be like you."

"You know," Betty said, "I can't think of you as Alan anymore. You're familiar to me, but you really are another person. Ellen. I think I like you better as a sister."

Betty turned back to the window to look out at the rain. "He's such a lovable guy sometimes," she said.

Ellen could tell by the movement of her sister's back that she'd begun to cry. She hesitated a moment and then walked to her side, put her arm around her shoulder.

Betty turned around with an angry jerk, stubbed out the cigarette. "Oh, Christ!" she said. She took Ellen into her arms.

Ellen had planned to give her sister a nice hug. Instead she kissed Betty's cheeks and eyelids. And Betty kissed her on the mouth.

Ellen felt her entire body stiffen as though she'd just been stung on the lips by a wasp. Betty's eyes seemed too large at that distance, luminous and unreadable. For a moment Ellen had the sensation that she was looking at herself; the fear of it was a sudden dizzying rush, like falling down a well.

Then Betty stepped back. "It's confusing enough," she said, "that you're really my *brother.*"

A sudden sound throughout the house, a dull thump. "Jesus!" Betty said, jumping away. The bedroom door was standing open. Ellen ran for it, closed it, flattened her back against it as though she were trying to keep something out.

"What was that?" Betty hissed. She had retreated to the far corner of the room. She looked as though she were ready to spring through the wall.

Ellen laughed. "That was the furnace," she said. "The furnace going on."

"Oh Christ, I thought it was that little girl!"

"No. Susan's in school. It was the bloody furnace!" Ellen was giggling. "What the hell were you thinking about, Betty?"

"I don't know. What were you thinking about?"

Ellen didn't answer. She threw herself onto the bed. After a while she said, "I was always in love with you."

"I know." Betty picked up the ash tray and stretched out on the bed next to Ellen, careful not to touch her. "I'm sorry. I really am. It's like everything's collapsed and . . . I could do anything. Do you ever get the feeling that you're walking along on the edge of a pit or something? . . . Christ, it's like your life is this big," she measured out an inch between her thumb and index finger, "and all around you there's all the rest of this crazy stuff that you never look at. But it's there. It's always there."

"Yeah," Ellen said.

"And you know you'll never get to see any of it. And sometimes that gets to be so sad you don't think you can stand it, eh?"

"Yeah, that's right."

"And even if it's going to scare the piss out of you, you've still got to look . . . or just explode. I know you know. If it hadn't been for you somehow . . . You know, I slept with another woman once? . . . Sandy."

"What?"

"Yeah, I knew that would upset you. But I wanted to tell you anyway."

"She said she'd been with . . . but not . . ."

"She promised she wouldn't tell anybody. You know, Alan, there's something you get with a man, a kind of rightness about it. There is for me, anyway. And that wasn't there. But with Sandy . . . Hey, are you upset? Are you hurt? What's the matter? Alan?"

He stood and walked to the window. Since he'd kissed his sister, he'd been phasing back and forth between Alan and Ellen; it was making him sick at his stomach. Now he'd slipped altogether; he was a boy in girls' clothes. He was painfully aware of his penis. He inhaled deeply and closed his eyes. I'm Ellen, he thought. I'm a girl. Now I'm a girl. I'm Ellen. She opened her eyes and she was Ellen.

"Are you all right?" Betty said.

"Yes. I'm all right. So what happened with Sandy?"

"We were friends, and we were attracted to each other, and we both knew it, and one night . . . It really scared me, because it was so goddamned easy. I knew exactly how her body worked because it was just like mine . . . And it wasn't too long after that . . . I met Gary. And everything was in place for him, very firmly. He says all the time, 'You've got to live in the real world.' One of his pet expressions. And it was almost as though I said, OK, I'll take your real world and I'll make it my real world. Do you know what I'm talking about?"

"Of course I do."

"You know, Alan . . . Oh, goddamn it, I'm sorry. It's so hard to say 'Ellen' and then talk about you when you were a little boy."

"What about Alan when he was a little boy?"

"So that's how you do it, eh? He's a separate person. OK . . .
Well, Alan wasn't the only one who was fucked up. We all were.
And it's hard to figure out how much is *you* and how much is
everybody. Does everybody choose who to be? From just a hand-
ful of choices? I think some people don't choose. I don't think
Gary chose. I think he just grew up to be exactly who he was supposed to be. I think that's why I married him. Am I making any
sense?"

"Yes."

"And Alan should have been a girl right from the beginning?"

"Yes."

They stared at each other across the room. "Goddamn it, why
don't you have a sex change operation? You're such a goddamned
plausible woman, but I keep thinking that there's a cock and balls
under those clothes."

Ellen closed her eyes and pressed her fingers hard against them.
After a moment she looked at her sister again. "Here's Alan." She
tapped one arm of the chair. "And he's a strange boy, makes people uncomfortable, doesn't fit. But at least the polarity's right. He
likes girls." She tapped the other arm of the chair. "And here's
Ellen. She's had a sex change operation so she's a woman. And she's
a lesbian."

"Aren't there any happy lesbians?"

"It's not the easiest thing in the world, but yeah, there are happy
lesbians. I know happy lesbians."

"What happens," Betty said, "if you want to go to bed with
somebody and you have to take your clothes off?"

"I don't know." Ellen did not want to think about any of this.
She was getting sick at her stomach again. She stood and walked
to the window.

I wonder if I can lean on the sewing table exactly the way Betty
did? she thought. She tried it, sank forward, rested her elbows,

took her chin in her hands. Outside, the rain was falling steadily. I wish to hell Mildred would come back, she thought.

HE'D BUILT THE CABIN WELL. It was weathered but still standing, firmly overlooking a tiny cove where he must have tied up his boat. People had been here recently, had left behind empty cans and wine bottles. The door had been forced and now swung askew, and someone had carried away the stove; she could see the marks on the floor where it had stood, the hole in the roof for the chimney. But the bunks were still there; the old man must have slept in the lower one, her father (when he'd been visiting as a boy), the upper. She ran her hands over the rough wood of the walls. She didn't know enough about building cabins to have a name for it, but the construction was simple and solid and beautiful. Cedar. She stepped outside into the afternoon sunlight. Her two-hour walk through the bush, following the overgrown trail, losing it, finding it again, had been deceptive. As the crow flies . . . no, she thought, as the raven flies, she couldn't be more than a mile from the deserted village. She could see several of the totem poles quite clearly around the curve of the coastline. She sat down, looking seaward, and leaned her back against the cabin. She'd passed the stream Martin had told her about; she'd have no problems with water. She drew a canteen out of her jacket, and a plastic bag with hard sausage, bread, and cheese. It must have been strange for him, she thought, after his wife left and took their son to Vancouver. He must have been following some crazy Scots hermit impulse to come to this inaccessible place and build a cabin and live here for nearly thirty years with only the Indians for neighbours. And then, for the last years after the Indians had left, alone. But it wasn't as though he'd been totally isolated; he'd owned a boat, fished every summer, been able to take off for the beer parlour in Huyatsi whenever he'd wanted to. She smiled. It had probably been a good life for him.

Yes, and he probably had heard the drums from here, she thought, the "drums and rattles" as he'd said. The sound would have carried easily across the water. I wonder if they ever invited him to a potlatch. She looked down at the food in her lap. She'd missed breakfast that morning and now was ravenously hungry, but she felt, somehow, that she shouldn't eat. I'll save it for later, she thought, and repacked it. She stood and began to pace up and down in front of the cabin. She was remembering how her grandfather had looked waiting for her in the basement of the school. Her skin was prickling. It was hard to think of him as a ghost; he'd seemed so solid and real. "Grandpaw," she said out loud, "is this what you wanted? Did you want me to come and see it? . . . I'm here."

She looked down over the small beach strewn with rocks and logs. The sun would be setting soon; already its light was oblique and red. She'd spent the entire afternoon there, first inside the cabin, then walking up and down outside it, trying to feel something, to understand why she had come, what had brought her. And now she began to feel a great welling up of sadness. "I can't blame it on anybody but myself," she said out loud. She wasn't talking to her grandfather now, but she felt she was talking to something. "I suppose that's the way I would have wanted it too . . . You're alone. You do what you can. And if you fail, then it's nobody's fault but your own. That's what's so good about swimming. You're on a team . . . there's the club . . . but that doesn't mean much when you're in a race. Then you're alone. And . . . I don't know. Maybe I took it too lightly . . .

"They were always just meets to me . . . just more swimming meets. That's even the way I felt at Mexico City. It was just a lark. But the night before the Olympic trials, I couldn't sleep. I got out of bed and I began to get scared. I was swimming the race over and over in my head, and that had never happened to me before. I couldn't understand it. I went through all these things about my future . . . what I was going to do. I didn't get to sleep until dawn, and the next day I was exhausted. I just blew it. I didn't have it."

She began to cry. "I never thought it could happen to me," she said. "I'd always had steel nerves. I'd always fall into bed and be gone, dead to the world. But then when it mattered . . . I did it to myself!" She heard her voice, strangely loud, in this green deserted world. Who am I talking to? she thought. But she went on: "It changed my whole idea of myself. I never trusted myself after that." She was crying harder now. "I don't understand. I don't know what I should be doing. I feel like my life's coming apart . . . like a loose bunch of threads and I've got to . . . reach out and grab them, put them in some kind of order but I don't know how." She covered her face with her hands and sobbed. Then she inhaled several times as though she were hyperventilating for a race. She found a handkerchief in her jacket and blew her nose.

"I believe in my work," she said. "In a way I do. I believe in some of the children, and I try to keep books in my library that really matter . . . Oh, but I want more than that! I don't know what to do now." Tears were running down her cheeks again. She didn't seem to be able to stop them.

"Help me!" she cried out. "I've swum every morning. I've swum alone. I've done it every day when I didn't know why I was doing it. Show me the right way. Show me how to live! I want to live honourably." She sank, crying, to the ground. She cried until there were no tears left. When she stood again, she felt peaceful, as though something had been listening. "Help me," she said quietly to the growing darkness. "Make me strong."

IT'S STRANGE TO RETURN TO THE WORLD after three days absence, Alan thought, and the strangest thing is that it's fun. He hadn't expected it to be. The first few blocks in his own low-heeled boots had been awkward, unbalanced, as though he might tip over backwards with every step. But now, having covered a good two miles, he was swinging along in that old familiar distance-walker's rhythm, enjoying the movement of his body, the deep tides of his breathing. His pink bathroom scales had told him that Ellen had lost four pounds while he had been gone; he could feel the difference, the lightness. It was a crisp windy night with stars between scudding clouds. I can move easily through these streets, he thought, and no one will bother me, but Ellen was always on display, and she couldn't have walked this far in her heels. She doesn't get enough exercise. She'd better keep me around to take dance classes for her, to take these long walks. If she doesn't, she'll get flabby.

He'd reached Betty and Gary's high-rise. He pressed the button marked "Kovarian," heard Gary's voice metallic through the tiny speaker: "Yeah!"

"It's me. Alan."

The front door buzzed, and he pushed through it. Riding up in the elevator, he began to worry again about what Ellen had left him of herself: her fingernails and her styled hair. He'd stripped the nails of colour, of course, but they were still longer than a boy would have worn them, and filed too perfectly into feminine ovals. He'd brushed the hair straight back into a pony tail, hidden the curls inside his shirt, but it was still streaked ash blond. So what? he thought. Gary thinks I'm a faggot anyway.

But after five minutes with his brother-in-law, Alan realized he needn't have worried; Gary wasn't noticing much of anything outside of himself. "I take it this isn't just a pleasant social call," he said. His speech was just beginning to slur. He's good, Alan thought. He hardly shows a thing. But if that bottle of Scotch started out the night as a full one, he's loaded.

"No, it's not exactly a social call."

"Well, counselor," Gary said, his voice ironic, "what terms does your client want?"

"My client doesn't even know I'm here."

Alan saw Gary's focus shift outward, assessing. "What do *you* want then?"

"I'm not sure." I've got to be careful, Alan thought. He looks like he could explode. "My family has a certain taste for melodrama . . ." He shrugged.

"Yeah," Gary said flatly. "Drink?"

"I don't think so."

"I like you, you little prick. You know that? You're the only straight one in the bunch. I always felt we had a kind of understanding. Is that wrong?"

"No, I don't think so."

"Taste for melodrama." Gary laughed. "Yeah, that's a good way to put it. Christ, I didn't realize I was marrying your whole fucking family. I feel like I'm in a fucking masquerade half the time. Betty buys all my goddamned clothes, you know that? So I'll *look right!*"

"And you married her because she looked right," Alan said softly.

Gary stared at him. "Yeah, you're right. I did. And I'm right about *you* too, aren't I? You don't miss a thing, just sit there with that silly smile on your face, and nobody pays any attention to you, and you take it all in. OK, just what the hell is going on?"

"I don't know, but . . . Well, what she *says* . . . something about a girl at the Hallowe'en party. She says you made a pass at her."

Gary stood abruptly, cast his eyes toward the ceiling as though invoking heavenly aid. "Oh, sweet Mother of Jesus! *I* made a pass, did I. That's good. That's really good. Yeah, there was a pass being made, but I didn't make it."

Gary walked to the glass doors, drew back the curtains. The night was clouding over; the mountains were invisible, but the buildings of the West End were lit, their lights flickering through the distance. With his back to Alan, Gary said, "What the hell's she doing taking off like this?"

"I think she wants a little time off to be crazy."

"Crazy?" Gary said as though he'd never heard the word before. He looked out over the city. Then he turned back into the room, picked up his bottle of Scotch, sank into the chair opposite Alan. "My solution to things," he said, "get plastered." His eyes were bleak and distant. "All you people with your education. You make me feel like such a fucking dumb ass."

"Our education? Jesus, Gary, you went through university and law school too. I'm an art school drop-out."

"I guess I don't mean education like that. It's in the family, fucking novels or something. Betty reads all these fucking novels." He laughed. "Shit, I sound ridiculous. What the hell do you mean she wants time off to be crazy?"

"I don't know exactly."

"Christ, I've given her everything she ever wanted." When I met Betty, I thought, Kovarian, you'd better know what you're doing, because if you take on this one, you take on her world too. She'll make it all simple for you . . . She's a simple girl. She knows what she wants. And you'd better want that too."

Alan felt an intense rushing sensation inside himself, as though his centre were a tall vase of water into which a white-hot iron rod had just been plunged. He could see the water instantly vaporized, a rush to steam, and himself left as light and clear as an empty eggshell. He couldn't speak.

"Drink?" Gary asked again.

"All right. OK." Alan held out his glass. Gary poured.

"You must have had a hard life," Gary said.

"It's been hard at times."

Gary had refilled his own glass halfway up with Scotch. He looked at the glass sourly and shook it as though trying to cool the liquid. "Christ, Alan," he said, "it's fucking weird how much you look like her."

"Yeah. I know."

"All right, counselor," Gary said. "If you want to understand this case, you'd better ask your client what the hell she was doing kissing that girl in the hallway."

"What?"

"You heard me." Gary laughed harshly. "Oh, Christ, no. Don't say that. Just tell her . . . Well, shit, just tell her to get her ass back here and we'll straighten things out."

"ALAN! . . . OH, I'M SORRY. ELLEN."

"What?" Ellen said. Betty had stopped her just inside the door of Mrs. Mackenzie's house; now she was bending close with her finger to her lips. The long walk that Alan had taken and the Scotch he'd drunk at Gary's had blurred Ellen. She was tired; she wanted to go to bed. Oh Betty, don't be so theatrical! she thought. My crazy family, actresses every one.

"Jeanie's here," Betty said.

"What?"

"Shhh. She's in the living room."

"Christ! What the hell did you tell Susan?"

"I told her the first thing that came into my head . . . which happened to be the truth . . . that Jeanie was my niece." Betty laughed. "The only thing that surprised Susan was that up until then, she'd thought that Jeanie was a little boy."

Ellen couldn't laugh. She leaned against the wall and closed her eyes. "First I arrive as some unknown relative of her mother's, and I'm not supposed to know a soul in Vancouver. And then you turn up and we pass you off as an old girl friend from college . . . and now Jeanie."

"Susan's fine," Betty said in an insistent whisper. "We've been getting along famously. She loves the termite. She even liked changing him. *We're* the adults, remember? That's how she sees us. And she's enjoying the novelty. Don't worry about Susan. It's Jeanie."

"What about Jeanie?"

"I don't know what to say, actually. She's in a bad way."

"Oh Christ!"

"Well, Oh Christ, yourself. You had to vanish for the whole bloody evening! I didn't even know where to call you."

Ellen didn't answer. She walked to the hall closet with her coat. "She knows you're Ellen, eh?" Betty was whispering.

"Yes."

"Do you think that was wise?"

"I haven't a clue."

"She's just a kid."

"Goddamn it, I know that. Don't go all conservative on me, please . . . Sorry, I'm tired . . . What are we going to do?"

"We've got to call Amy, of course. But I think Jeanie ought to stay here tonight. She doesn't need to go home and get picked apart."

"God, I'm tired!" Ellen said. "My calves ache like teeth."

"Wear lower heels, silly." Ellen took Betty's hand and squeezed it. They walked into the living room.

Susan and Jeanie were sitting on the chesterfield together in front of the television set, Susan in pajamas with school books spread in front of her, Jeanie wrapped in a blanket. Jeanie was staring at the archway through which they were coming with a peculiar set to the eyes: a look both vacant and concentrated. Ellen knew at once that Jeanie was dangerously divided inside herself, fractured like a cubist painting, that a crucial part of her was absent on some business of its own; she didn't understand how she could have known it like that, suddenly, without a word being

246

spoken. She hesitated in the archway, appalled both at what was happening to Jeanie and at her own unexpected ability to assess it.

Susan looked up, grinning, and then looked down again at the book in front of her. The television set was loudly declaring the eleven o'clock news.

Ellen sat on the arm of the chesterfield next to Jeanie and dropped her hand onto the girl's head. "How are you?" she said.

"I ran away." Jeanie tilted her head upward. Her eyes were rolling about as though she were watching the slow passage of an invisible ball in the air. Oh, Ellen thought. It's what used to happen to Alan. She and Betty exchanged looks.

"You're going to stay here," Ellen said.

"Good," the girl said in a small expressionless voice.

AMY'S VOICE CAME CRACKLING THROUGH THE TELEPHONE so loudly that Ellen, sitting on the other side of the bedroom, could hear the anxiety in it, although not the words.

"Jeanie's here with me," Betty said. "I'm staying . . . with a girl friend." She smiled at Ellen.

"No, I don't think I can do that," Betty said. "I think she should stay here tonight, Amy . . . Well, she *is* staying here tonight. I'll bring her back tomorrow . . . She's tired and scared, and I don't see any point in . . . No . . . I said no."

There was a long pause. Betty pointed at her pack of cigarettes lying on the bed. Ellen handed it to her. "Oh, the police? That would be interesting. Where would you tell them to go?"

Betty jerked the phone away from her ear, held it at arm's length. Amy's voice, tiny and distorted, spattered into the room in an angry and unintelligible burst. Ellen bit the back of her hand to keep from laughing.

"Can you give me a light?" Betty said to Ellen under her breath. "What's that you're saying, dear? . . . I rather doubt that . . . Look,

Amy, slow down a minute, will you? Jeanie's had enough for the day. She's one scared little kid. I gave her some cocoa. And she's watching television now. And in a little while I'll put her to bed. She'll be perfectly all right. She'll be back in the morning . . . safe, sound, and repentant. And by then you won't be quite so frantic, eh? So maybe . . .''

Another long pause.

"That's right," Betty said flatly, "family's the only thing that lasts . . . Why don't you take one of your pills and we'll see you in the morning? . . . For Christ's sake, don't be so melodramatic. Try to step back a few feet and see the humour in it . . . That's right. I'm not giving you any choice . . . Look, Amy, it's not going to be . . ." Betty winced. "Christ," she said to Ellen, "she hung up on me."

"Family's the only thing that lasts, eh?" Ellen said, laughing.

"Right. It lasts and lasts . . . Wheww, sweet revenge. I've wanted to say no to her since I was three years old. God, was she bossy!"

"Yeah, I know."

"All right, so what *are* we going to do with Jeanie?"

"I'll talk to her." Ellen hesitated. "Betty," she said, "while we're closeted in here, I wanted to tell you. . . Well, Alan went to see Gary tonight."

"Oh, he did, did he?" Her face was expressionless. She inhaled on her cigarette, let the smoke rise slowly toward the ceiling. "You really *are* Little Miss Fix-it, aren't you?"

"There was something you didn't tell me . . . about the girl . . .''

"He saw it, did he?" Betty said.

"Yeah. He saw it."

"Oh. I thought she was a boy. Or at least . . . I thought that I thought I did. How the hell did you get Gary to talk to you?"

"Alan," Ellen said. "He just sat there and waited. Gary was drinking."

"Oh, goddamn it, I don't think I appreciate this, you know that?"

"It's all right to play with Amy's head, but . . ."

Betty laughed bitterly. "Just what the hell kind of game *are* you playing, little sister?"

"I don't know. I'm just feeling my way."

"Oh, yeah. You're sure doing that all right. What else did he say?"

"He thinks . . . The downtown law firm. The high-rise . . . He thinks . . . Well, look, Betty. You told me that you took *his* world. He thinks he took *yours*."

"Christ, Alan, you can't just . . . I mean Ellen . . . you can't just come in from the outside for five minutes and understand what's going on with a couple."

"Yes, I can."

Betty stared at her sister a moment. "You know, I almost believe you."

"What do you want, Betty?"

"Jesus!" she burst out. "Like a goddamned stale soap opera! Will Betty return to her husband? Tune in tomorrow for the next exciting saga of The Lehmans in Love and War . . . Oh, Jesus, Alan, I just feel . . . It's like I can't do anything that isn't a reflection of something. And it's my life!"

"Start somewhere," Ellen said. "What would make a beginning?"

"A job? Yeah, I guess that's where I'd start . . . a job." Then she said angrily, "But Jesus, it's not anything that simple. There's always so much more, just . . . somewhere. I can *feel* it . . . And it's not just getting a job. Or having affairs. Or leaving my husband. Or going back to him. It all seems beside the point. There doesn't seem to be any solution."

She stopped talking and blinked rapidly. "Christ," she said. "Look at you! You're my goddamned little brother, and here you are dressed up like a woman. And you're so goddamned plausible that at least three-quarters of the time I believe you are one . . .

even though I've known you all my life. And then I don't know who the hell you are, and . . . Well, I haven't got that kind of guts. Is that what it takes?"

"I haven't got that kind of guts either. There are forces . . . I don't understand it, but we're in love with magic just like Jeanie, and that's not . . . It doesn't seem like something you can reach out and grab. But in the meantime, we've got to live somehow. What would make a beginning? A job?"

"Oh, Jesus. Yeah, a job. Even if I was just a clerk in a boutique. But Gary . . ."

"He'd probably be relieved," Ellen said.

"Are you kidding?"

"I don't think you know him."

"I thought I did, but . . . I didn't think he knew me very well. Does anybody ever know anybody? Look, I don't even know you."

"Yes you do."

"I GOT LOST," JEANIE SAID. She was propped up on pillows in the bed. Her eyes were focusing normally now.

"Not just ordinary lost."

Ellen was standing stiffly in front of the partially open window. Unless she wanted to sleep in her clothes, she would have to get undressed eventually. Don't make a big deal out of it, she told herself. Not with Jeanie. She turned out the light, walked quickly to the closet, and stripped. She left on her bra, slipped into negligee and panties and quickly under the covers. Her side of the bed was cold. She was, for a moment, dizzy and breathless. Then she said, "Are you all right? Should I turn the light on again?"

"No," Jeanie said. "I'm all right."

"Tell me what happened."

"Oh, we went to visit that girls' school yesterday. They said they'd let me in."

Ellen reached out and touched the girl's hand. It was closed into a fist. Ellen patted it. Jeanie took her hand. "Maybe we should turn the light on," Ellen said.

"No, you don't have to. I'm all right now. I really am." She sighed. "I was going to run away. Right after dinner. I just walked out of the house. I knew exactly where I was going. I'd looked on the map to make sure. It isn't even that far . . . I got lost."

"The city changed. I wasn't in Vancouver anymore."

"Where were you?"

"I don't know. I walked and walked and walked. And nothing looked right. The houses didn't look right. And I'd pass people on the street and they didn't look right. The street names weren't right."

Ellen let go of the girl's hand, sat up, and switched on the lamp by the bed. Jeanie was looking at her, unsmiling. She's really scared, Ellen thought. I've never seen her like this. Not a single giggle. Christ, I'm scared too! "What do you mean . . . it didn't look right?"

The girl shrugged. "It wasn't Vancouver."

"Where do you think it was?"

"I don't know. I passed some people, and they weren't speaking English. Anyway, I couldn't understand them."

"Were they East Indians . . . Chinese . . .?"

"No, they were white people. Just ordinary people."

"Was it French . . . Italian?"

"I don't know, Ellen. I don't know what French or Italian sounds like. You were right. I'm too young . Oh, it was really neat for a while. When it first started to happen. But I walked and walked and walked, and then I didn't think it was so neat anymore. I didn't know what I was going to *do*. I thought eventually I was going to have to knock on a door or something and try to tell them I was lost. And I kept thinking how neat it would be if it was a story . . . But it wasn't a story."

"What happened?"

"Well, finally I just looked up and saw the street sign, and it was the name of the street you'd written down, and I knew that I was in Vancouver again. I walked along the street until I saw the house number that you'd written down. And then here I was. But you weren't here. Aunt Betty was here. I didn't tell her about it. I just told her I ran away. Ellen, what am I going to do? I thought if they came for me, they'd be like monsters or something . . . coming through the window. But it wasn't like that. I don't even know when it happened. I was just walking along, and it happened. What if I get lost sometime . . . and I can't get back?"

Ellen stared at the girl. Jeanie was not crying, and her expression said quite emphatically that she was not going to cry. Ellen looked away. "I don't know," she said.

"It could happen any time, couldn't it?"

"I don't know. Do you want a cup of cocoa?"

"No, that's all right."

"Well *I* do."

For the first time, Jeanie smiled. Ellen slid out of bed and into her peignoir and silly high-heeled bedroom slippers. "It would have been all right if I'd been with you," Jeanie said. "We could have had an adventure. But I didn't like it being alone."

Ellen was shivering. "Put something on your feet," she said. "You'll catch a cold."

They walked downstairs, Ellen clattering in her heels and Jeanie padding behind in her yellow boots, the laces trailing. Ellen put on milk to heat. "Do you think," she said, "that what set it off was this girls' school business?"

"I don't know."

Ellen felt that something inside her knew what to do, and once again she didn't know where the knowledge had come from, but she was beginning to trust it. "Look," she said, "I think we can do something about the girls' school. But about the other . . . Well, I think you should meet a friend of mine."

"What friend?"

"An old woman."

"Oh," Jeanie said, smiling slightly. "Is she a witch?"

Ellen paused. She laughed. "Yes, I guess so . . . Yes, I guess she is."

"Will she know what to do?"

"I think she will." Ellen sat down at the kitchen table with the girl. "Jeanie, you've got to protect yourself for now. And the way you do it . . . You've got to become very ordinary for a while."

"Ordinary?"

"For a while . . . until we know what to do. You've got to disguise yourself. So they won't know how to come for you. So they won't see you. Do you understand?"

"I think so. Like the princess is disguised as a beggar girl . . . or a pageboy . . . so the soldiers won't find her."

"That's right. And that will protect you. And it's just something you've got to do for now. Do you understand me?"

The girl's face was grave, but calm. "Yes," she said, "I understand."

"Hi Mom, I'm home," Jeanie called. She'd done her best to sound cheery, but she hadn't quite made it. And Amy did not come immediately rushing into the front hall to meet them. They heard noises from the kitchen: a metallic banging, the radio, the roar of the dishwasher. Alan and Betty exchanged looks. Betty shrugged.

Amy still hadn't appeared by the time they'd hung up their coats, and they all seemed oddly reluctant to walk on into the house. Alan saw, rather than heard, Jeanie's sigh: the movement of her chest. He patted her shoulder. It feels vaguely sacrosanct, he thought. It's that wretched childhood Anglican feeling. Maybe it's that Jeanie's dressed as though she's on her way to Sunday school. He'd evened her bangs, trimmed her ragged hair into a short girlish style like a twenties bob. She wore the clothes they'd bought for her that morning: a short navy-blue dress, white tights, and navy-blue mary-janes. She was posed, her feet placed carefully together, as though she'd stood to wait for the hymn. She looked up at Alan. Her mouth was set. "It's going to be all right," he said to her.

Amy walked toward them, drying her hands on a dish towel. Her face looked sallow and tired. "I've made some coffee," she said as formally as if these were not her relatives. "Won't you come into the living room?"

They sat at four distant corners. "Come on, mite!" Betty said to her son, "don't fuss so." The baby had grabbed one of Betty's curls and was tugging. She disengaged the small hand. Amy said nothing.

"Hey, Mom," Jeanie said, "I give up."

An expression that could have been anything passed fleetingly over Amy's face. Betty set the baby on the floor, and he immediately began crawling straight for the electrical cord of a huge white lamp. "Gary!" Betty called after him. He turned to look at her, laughed, and reached for the cord.

Betty jumped up and grabbed the baby. "Come on, Lizard, you can't be pulling the lamp down on your head. You wouldn't like it at all." He gave his mother a reproachful look, took a deep breath, and began to wail. "Oh, God!" Betty said.

Amy stood. "I'll get the coffee," she said. "Would everyone like that?" She put a smile on for a moment and then took if off again. She walked out of the room.

Betty stared after her sister, sent Alan an exasperated look, and then laid the baby on his lap. "It helps sometimes if you bounce him up and down." She followed Amy.

"Alan?" Jeanie said quietly. "She'll think it's because I want to stay at Sherwood Free. That's what she'll think, isn't it?"

"Yes," he said. He was bouncing the baby up and down. It didn't seem to help.

Betty found her sister clutching the edge of the kitchen sink and leaning forward. Her shoulders were shaking. "Oh, for God's sake, Amy!" Betty said. She paced frantically around the kitchen, located her sister's cigarettes on the table next to the toaster, grabbed one, and lit it. "Amy," she said, "can you try to get a grip on yourself? I know it must seem really obnoxious of Alan and me . . . keeping Jeanie last night . . . barging in here like this . . ." In the living room, the baby was winding up to full force: an unabashed, intemperate howl. Betty grimaced. "Amy?" she said.

Amy turned to face her, and Betty was astounded to see that her sister was not crying. She was laughing. The laughter seemed a bit out of control. "Oh, give up, does she?" Amy said. "Give up, my sweet ass!"

"Amy!" Betty said. She was genuinely shocked. "Listen, she's willing to meet you halfway. She really is, and it's probably not going to be as much as you'd like . . . But she wants to stay at the free school, and I think . . ."

"Shut up," Amy said. "For God's sake, Betty, stop nattering at me. Go take care of your own child."

Betty blinked. She walked back into the living room and scooped her son out of Alan's lap. The baby stopped crying at once. "Is she mad?" Jeanie said.

"I can't tell," Betty said.

Amy carried in a coffee pot and three cups on a silver tea tray. She set it on the coffee table. She lit a cigarette, inhaled. It was so quiet in the room that Alan could hear the sound of the burning tobacco. "Please help yourselves."

No one poured any coffee. "Oh, Jeanie," Amy said, "I give up too!"

Betty said, "Perhaps this is the time for us to make our exit."

"Perhaps it is, dear," Amy said.

Jeanie followed them to the door. "Alan," she whispered, "are you sure it's going to be all right?"

"Yes it is," he said. "And I won't leave you stuck. I'll come back as soon as I can."

Outside, Betty handed Alan the baby. "Or do you want to drive?"

"I don't have a licence." They climbed into the car, turned to look at each other.

"Whew," Betty said, "was that ever heavy! I'm not sure she's ever going to speak to us again."

"Yes, she will. Family's the only thing that lasts, eh?"

Betty put the car into gear and pulled away. "I think it's about time for all these little charades to end," she said. "I'm going home."

"Oh, are you?"

"Yes. I think we've had enough drama to last us for a while. Maybe that's what's wrong with us, Alan . . . the whole lot of us. We want our lives to look like something written by Dostoyevsky, and the best we can expect is *As The World Turns*."

"No, we can expect more than that."

"Well, maybe you can. But I think I'm ready for a little bit of the soaps again."

She pulled up in front of Mrs. Mackenzie's house. They climbed out of the car. He handed her the baby, and they walked into the house. "What are you going to do?" she said. "How long are you going to stay here?"

"I don't know."

Susan was standing in the hallway, wearing her pajamas and brown moccasins. She was holding a cup of coffee in one hand. She was staring at Alan.

Betty froze. She inhaled sharply. "Why aren't you in school?"

"I. . . felt . . . sick," Susan said, forcing the words out, one at a time. The coffee cup slid out of her hand, struck the floor, and exploded, throwing hot liquid onto Betty's dress.

"Christ!" Betty said, jumping back. The baby began to cry. Susan folded at the knees, swayed, and collapsed to the floor. "My God!" Betty said. "She's fainted. Alan!"

But Alan had pushed past her and was running up the stairs, taking them two at a time. He stumbled into the bathroom, fell, and slid on his knees to the toilet bowl. He jerked up the seat, pushed his head down, and vomited. He was losing light fast, a swirling blackness pressing in on him. He sat up, his head clearing. He shut his eyes tight. He couldn't stand the sight of the simple white tiles on the walls.

"Alan!" Betty yelled at her brother as he ran toward her down the hall. "Alan!" she yelled again after he had pushed past her and run through the door, leaving it open behind him. "Come back!" she yelled after him. "What am I supposed to do with her?" But Alan was already halfway up the block, running.

WEDNESDAY AFTERNOON, LESLIE THOUGHT. This is my last day. She had been walking back from her grandfather's cabin to her campsite in the village, had stopped here where the trail opened out above the inlet. She stood, looking seaward; below her the rock face fell sheerly down to the water. The sun was a sinking red ball, spotting the sea before it with fiery drops. It will be gone soon, she thought, and then it will be evening.

She breathed deeply. She couldn't remember the last time she'd felt this strong and rested. She'd spent the day looking carefully at each of the totem poles, walking in the bush, sitting by the cabin; she would have said that she hadn't been doing much of anything. She'd felt peaceful and untroubled, but also that there was something more for her here: a kind of waiting. Now she was not aware of waiting, only of a certain tension between day and night as she watched the sinking sun. She felt a distinct pause—or hesitation—in the atmosphere, as though the outcome might genuinely be in doubt, that the sun might reverse itself and rise again, refuse to allow the night in.

But the sun set. It left behind it a red light; eventually that too was lost, and the sky turned a sombre translucent grey. She began to feel a melancholy detachment as though she were now more alone than she'd ever thought possible, as though she were completely cut off from ordinary people living ordinary routines, as though she might have lost the way to get back to them. And then, from high overhead, she heard a single mournful cry; she felt the thrill of it in her stomach, and her sadness was gone immediately, leaving only the detachment. She now knew that she was waiting. She looked up and saw two geese flying far above her.

Her first thought was that she'd seen geese in formation before, but never just two of them like that. The cry was repeated, that single, painfully beautiful note. And for the brief time that the cry lasted, the geese were closer. She was aware that she was standing where she had been, firmly on the ground, that they were where they had been, high above her, but superimposed a moment on that awareness was another one, that they had been much closer, as though seen through a telescope. How odd, she thought. One of them cried out again, and this time they were so close that she could see the feathers on their long outstretched necks. Unbidden, her mind began to recite:

Grey goose and gander,
Waft your wings together,
Carry the good king's daughter,
Over the two-strand river.

And she would not have believed that anything could have

taken her with so much force. She was spun out, tearing, riding high upon her own scream. Below, the trees were falling away fast. She struck and hung a moment on a curtain of hideous pain; then she was through it, she was torn apart. The incredible high wind was rushing over her feathers. She could see all of Johnston's Inlet below, as small as if it were on a map. Above, the stars glittered insanely in a sky that was perfectly black. She could not comprehend this speed; already they had chased down the sun over the bright curve of the earth And then below was a wet blue ball, half in shadow, split night from day. And it was even colder where they were going, riding this expanding sky, even faster. She stretched her long neck and cried out. She was flying. Or she was falling.

ALAN HAD SPENT THE AFTERNOON WALKING up and down Kitsilano Beach, from the Showboat to the Planetarium and back, four times. He'd stood and watched the sunset, feeling an odd tension between night and day, as though he were waiting for something; he'd watched the red light in the west turn a sombre translucent grey, and he'd begun to feel a melancholy detachment, as though he were more alone than he'd ever thought possible And now it was night, a crisp clear night. It's like a bell, he thought. He was surprised at this idea appearing for no reason. Like a bell? Why is it like a bell? How can night be like a bell? He didn't know, but it seemed right to him.

He'd walked all the way back to the house. Ellen had been living here since Sunday; it had been her house, she'd walked in and out easily, but now he felt that he had to knock. He knocked. He knew he would have to talk to Susan, try to explain things in a way she would understand, and he was dreading it. He was waiting for Susan to open the door. Mildred Mackenzie opened the door. It wasn't that he hadn't expected her. It was more profound than that; he'd almost forgotten her. He stood paralysed on the threshold. "Come in," she said.

"Where's Susan?"

"She's at work. Come in."

He stepped inside, and she shut the door behind him. The memory of the first night he'd walked into this house was suddenly vivid; he felt his muscles contract with fear. "I didn't expect you," he said, hearing his own voice sound flat and stupid.

"Oh," she said, laughing, "I come and go, eh?" She smells rank, he thought, like dirt and sweat and fish. He followed her into the kitchen, and saw the origin of the fish odour: a huge one, silver, lying on newspapers in the centre of the kitchen table. That round dead eye. "Salmon," she said. "I'm going to stuff him and bake him. Are you hungry?"

He realized that he was hungry. "Yes," he said. He was feeling grey and gritty and bleak, like a jagged beach with the cold tide coming in. "Did you talk to Susan?"

"Oh, my," she said, and began to laugh. That great round pillar of a woman, her hair hanging down, in dirty sweater and gumboots, shaking and laughing; he was furious with her. "She hasn't been *that* glad to see me come home in years," she said, and wiped her eyes.

"I don't think it's funny," he said. His voice sounded petulant. His anger was growing. "It was really . . . What the hell did she *think*?"

"Alan," she said, and her voice was serious now, "remember when I told you about the beads we all string on threads to make our lives continue? Well, you broke the thread for her. All the beads rolled out of her hand for a moment. I couldn't do it because she thinks she knows me, eh? And she'd never let it happen. But you could do it. You did do it."

He thought that he was beginning to understand. "Goddamn it!" he said angrily. "You set it up, didn't you? Goddamn it, I feel used!"

"No, I didn't set it up. Not that way. Not the way you think. I just prepared things . . . and then got out of the way."

"Christ!" he yelled. "You got out of the way! That's beautiful. You know what happened when she saw me? She fainted on the floor. She fell over on the goddamned floor."

She spread her hands, palms upward. "Her life will never be the same. We've torn her open. Now she has to look for herself."

"Good God! And you think that's a favour? Jesus you're cold-blooded . . . I'm beginning to see it. I really am. And just what the hell did you have planned for *me*?"

"I planned nothing," she said, the words separate and forceful. Then, gently, "Sit down, Alan."

He continued to stand. "You really are crazy. You ought to be locked up. You're goddamned dangerous."

"Sit down."

"I will not sit down. I thought you were helping people, I really did. Jesus! And you're just playing with them. With me. With your *own daughter*."

"You're much stronger now." She laughed. "Got some fire in your belly now."

He was confused, felt outflanked. He sat down. She took up the fish and carried it to the cutting board. "Poor Susan," he said. "Poor me too. *My* life is never going to be the same. It was like . . . I can't find any word strong enough. It was like everything was just . . . shredded. I'm going home. I've had enough. I don't trust you anymore. I'm going home and . . ."

"No, you're not," she said. "Ellen's going up-island with me tomorrow."

"You think so, eh? Ellen's not going anywhere with you. And I'm not either."

"I'd like to ask Ellen," Mrs. Mackenzie said. "She can make up her own mind."

"Oh, I've got to admit that it's been exciting. Really exciting. Thanks a lot! But I've got to live in the real world."

"Which one?" she said, laughing. "I'd like to talk to Ellen."

"You crazy old bitch," he said, but his heart wasn't in it. She brought Ellen into the world, he thought. She has a right to see her again. "All right," he said. "But it's the last time."

When Ellen came down a half-hour later, Mrs. Mackenzie had put the fish in to bake and was washing up the dishes.

Ellen was feeling nervous and sullen. She sat down and stared at the table top. "I feel like I've been living in a bad romantic painting," she said. "You know, all fire and hot colours. Chiaroscuro. Impasto. Bad taste."

"What happened?"

Ellen frowned, trying to find the best way to put it. "I guess I learned that . . . well . . . just being me, being Ellen, didn't automatically make everything wonderful."

"I'm not interested in how you *felt*. I'm interested in what you *did*."

Ellen stared at her, confused and distrustful. "I got my hair done," she said finally. "What *did* I do? I talked to my sister. And I . . . Alan . . . talked to her husband. And I tried to show my niece how she could . . . well, get along for a while."

"These were good things, eh?"

What is she getting at? Ellen thought. "Yes, I suppose so."

"Would you say you were *helping* them?"

"No . . . No, I don't think I'd say it like that."

Mrs. Mackenzie laughed. "You understand, Ellen. And I don't *help* people either."

Ellen nodded. She was intrigued now, in spite of herself. "Once you begin to act, you begin to move along a certain line." Mrs. Mackenzie drew a line on the table top. "And you have to move along it until it ends. That's all. That's all there is."

Ellen didn't speak.

"That's why you have to come up the coast with me now."

"Mildred, I don't trust you anymore. I don't want to hurt you by saying that, but it's true. I'm not sure that you're completely sane."

"It doesn't matter. But what matters is that you finish what you've begun."

Ellen looked away. "Where?"

"We'd be in Huyatsi by tomorrow night. We'd spend the night in the hotel. And the next day we'd hire a boat to take us up Johnston's Inlet."

"Why?"

"I've told you . . . told both you and Alan. There are certain places where you should go. Special places."

"I don't think I want to get any farther into this. I think you're living in some kind of strange dream world, think you've read too many books. I'm not cut out to be an Indian brave." She tapped her fingers on the table top. "What has all this to do with me anyway? Going back and forth between Alan and Ellen has been driving me crazy! It'd be all right if I could be one or the other and stay that way for a reasonably long time, but this switching back and forth . . . My God, the strain is terrible!"

"Would you pick one or the other?"

She hesitated. "I think I would pick Ellen. I think I should have a sex change operation."

"Would you feel you'd lost anything?"

"Yes, but goddamn it . . . however I do it, I'm going to lose something!" The old woman didn't speak. "Well, aren't I? And Ellen's closer to what I want. Not perfect, but Christ, what's perfect in this world?"

"Ellen," Mrs. Mackenzie said very deliberately. "You have to finish what you started. If you don't finish it now, it will always be around waiting for you. It would come for you when you're not ready and kill you, destroy your soul."

Ellen was terrified. She picked up her purse, set it on the table, and took out the bottles of nail polish. She thought: one undercoat, two colour, two super-sealer. "Well," she said, attempting a smile, "if I'm going to be me for a while, I might as well enjoy it, eh?"

"IT'S REALLY BLOWING, EH?" the Indian girl said. "Sure is," Mrs. Mackenzie said. "Must be gale force . . . Could you make us some eggs?"

Ellen glanced up shyly at the Indian girl and then down again at the bare wooden table top. She didn't know quite what she'd been expecting, but certainly not blue eyelids and red fingernails and high-heeled oxfords much like her own. It helped, somehow, that she should find an Indian girl so prettily and conventionally dressed. And the tension seemed to be easing slowly, the terrible constraint inside her that had seemed, for the last several hours, to have robbed her completely of speech. ". . . some tea?" Mildred was saying. Ellen nodded. She could almost speak. She could almost tell Mildred that she didn't think she could eat.

It had started on the ferry ride to Nanaimo when she had seemed to be the centre of attention for every male on board. She hadn't known how protected she'd felt by the city, how terrified she'd be to leave it, journeying out into a world she imagined to be pervasively male, dominated by loggers and fishermen—the bush, the wild Canadian bush—where she'd never been, where Alan had never been. She had huddled in a corner by the window, wishing her heels weren't so high or her jeans so tight, tried to read *Vogue*, felt a compulsion that was new to her (although perfectly familiar to Alan): to hide. She hadn't been able to force herself down to the car deck to change into Susan's gumboots, but she had gone into the ladies' room and stripped off every bit of makeup she'd put on so carefully before leaving the house.

It didn't help, she was thinking now. Just made me look young and vulnerable. On the second ferry ride she hadn't been the centre of attention of all the males on board. Only of the teenage ones.

She made an apologetic gesture toward Mildred and walked to the ladies' room. She looked at herself in the mirror. I want to be beautiful, she thought. I do not want to attract male attention. The two desires seemed to be absolutely incompatible. The face looking back at her was pale and tense. What am I doing here? she thought. In a hotel in a place called Huyatsi Village. On an Indian reserve. With a woman who's probably crazy. She put on mascara, lipstick, and blusher. That's better. Don't look so much as though I've just been dug up.

Four slices of toast and an enormous mound of scrambled eggs were waiting for her. "I'm not sure I can eat."

"Well, don't. Drink some tea."

An Indian man had just come in out of the wind and driving rain. He was walking toward them. Ellen felt her stomach tighten. She immediately looked down at the table top, at her hands, at her frosted pink fingernails. "Heard you was lookin for me, hey?" he said to Mrs. Mackenzie.

Ellen glanced up and tried to smile. His smile was just as shy as hers. He was in his forties, wearing a khaki coat and khaki rain hat. His eyes were quite black. "This is my old friend, Randolph Paul," Mildred said. He sat down at their table. He didn't take off his hat.

"Guess you want to go up the Inlet, hey?" Mildred nodded. "Lot of strange people comin up here now." He spoke slowly and softly. "Took a girl up there Tuesday."

"Oh?" Mildred said.

"Yeah. She's still up there, hey? She was gonna meet me this morning and she wasn't there. I told her I couldn't be goin around lookin for her. Now I've got to go talk to the RCMP, I guess." He looked away. He didn't speak for a long time. Then he said, "Guess she's wishin she stayed in Vancouver, hey?"

"Yeah, it's really blowing," Mildred said.

Ellen drank tea and ate a little of the toast with marmalade. They make a fine pair, she thought. Both of them seem to be able to sit forever without saying a word. "Don't want to be botherin the RCMP," Randolph Paul said in his quiet voice.

"We'll look for her, Randy. Maybe we'll see her."

"Yeah. I told her I couldn't be goin around lookin for her." He stared at Mildred for a moment with an enigmatic quizzical expression. Not exactly hostile, Ellen thought. But it's not exactly friendly either. "You been comin up here a long time. We got kinda used to you. But a lot of strange people comin up here now. What do you guys want, comin up here?"

"I don't know, Randy," Mildred said. "Different people come for different reasons."

"Yeah," he said thoughtfully. And then he repeated, "Yeah." Eventually he said, "That land up there was sacred to my people years back, hey? I think maybe you guys ought to let us alone."

"It's sacred to me too, Randy," Mildred said.

"Yeah," he said slowly, "but you're not an Indian." He sighed. "I guess if she doesn't come back in a couple days, I'm gonna have to go lookin for her."

SHE WAS BEING POUNDED BY RAIN. Oh, this is awful, awful! She must have been thinking that to herself over and over for a long time: this is awful! Something in her mouth. Salty. Her face was pressed into mud. She raised her head and spat. Her stomach contracted. She had mud in her mouth. And something salty. Get up, Leslie, she told herself. But her head had already fallen back onto the ground. She tried to sort through the savage edges of nightmare to place herself in this whistling chaos: the rain that beat at her in spasmodic waves, the total absence of light, her memories flung apart and scattered. She needed to feel her body moving. She tried to roll over. Then she knew that her feet were sticking out over absolutely nothing. Panic knotted her muscles, sent her scrambling forward on her belly, crawling, clawing into the mud, digging with elbows and fingers, until she'd dragged her feet back over the edge. Below, she could hear a vast surf pounding against the rocks.

She clung to the ground in a mindless animal fear. Although her eyes were wide open, staring, there was nothing to see. The first thought she could construct was: have I gone blind? But then, no, it's night. And she'd been standing on the trail looking out to sea; that memory was clear and simple. Just as the sun had been setting. And now it must be night. Fainted, she thought. It was a comforting concept. Didn't eat for two days. Fainted. That makes sense. She arched her body, worked herself up to her knees, tried to stand. But her legs buckled. She lay again, belly down in the mud. It was becoming easier to think. She began to name the incredibly noisy racket of the darkness, calling it night, calling it rain, calling it gale force wind. I've got to get back to my tent, she thought, arriving finally at a purpose. She began to crawl.

"Oh, this is awful, awful!" she kept mumbling to herself as she thrashed about through the bush, stumbling, crawling on her hands and knees, finding the trail with her fingers. The rain sizzled around her. The trees bent and groaned and keened in the high wind. And she'd worked her way out of the bush, into a cleared area. She crouched, trying to remember. She could see something now, a barely perceptible form. As long as she didn't try to look at it directly, she could sense it off to the left.

She edged toward it. Reached out and touched it. Wood. One of the totem poles. She clung to it, panting. In her mind, painfully, she mapped the cove, the beach, the long house. Her tent had to be over there, in that direction. She began to crawl, feeling in front of her. When her hand brushed against one of the nylon cords that anchored her tent to the ground, she sobbed with relief. She unzipped the tent, unlaced her hiking boots and threw them inside to dry. Her jeans had been soaked through; she stripped them off, and then she smelled herself, rank and unpleasant. Her bowels must have emptied when she'd fainted. I'm foul! she thought. She threw her jeans and underpants away into the dark and let the rain wash over her bare skin. Then she scrambled into the tent. There was her knapsack, blessedly familiar, everything in its place. She dried herself with a towel. She drank from her canteen. She zipped the tent shut, crawled into her sleeping bag and gathered it tightly around her. Am I too cold? she thought, suddenly terrified again. Was her body too chilled to warm itself even with the sleeping bag? But no, she was shaking, her teeth were chattering, her hands and feet were full of fiery prickles. Eventually she began to feel the warmth filling in softly around her.

It was all right now that the wind was howling in from the sea. Her tent was low to the ground. It was all right that the rain was pounding her shelter, turning it into a taut drum. She was warm and dry. In spite of the noisy chaos outside, she was loosening, her muscles going soft, her mind unfocusing dreamily. She thought of the carved poles out there, of the Tsoonoqua with her round protruding mouth, hooting and whiffling through the bush on nights exactly like this one, searching for little children to carry away in her basket. Leslie thought she understood about the Tsoonoqua now: the immensely strong monster-woman of the woods who crashed about, knocked over trees, but who was so clumsy that any clever child could run away. Leslie was warm now. Her tent would have been a mere speck—no, would have been invisible—from high in the air. She slept.

WHEN LESLIE WOKE THE NEXT MORNING, her first thought was: I feel fine. Sunlight through the nylon turned the inside of her tent into a green glowing bower. She unzipped the flaps, crawled outside, and saw that the sun was shining benignly on a peaceful wet green world. Everything around her—plants, grasses, even her tent—was steaming. Birds were singing. And the hunger in her stomach was like a fierce fire. She hauled out her knapsack, unwrapped her food, and began eating fast, tearing with her teeth, hardly bothering to chew. She ate half the bread and cheese and all of the sausage. She forced herself to slow down, ate two cans of sardines, drank all of the water in her canteen. She looked around her at the sparkling day, puzzled. I feel fine! she thought again.

She dressed, packed everything back into her knapsack, leaving the tent until last to give it a chance to dry, and then walked down to the beach to wait for Randolph Paul to come for her. She settled onto a log. Surf was rolling in gently to break on the sand. Debris, driftwood, several logs had been piled up by the storm the night before, and seaweed, long stringy dark kelp and those odd sea plants that always looked to her like immensely enlarged sperm cells. Absently she gathered shells from around her feet and arranged them in a line on the log. The sun on the water was so bright it hurt her eyes. Something wrong here. Not a sign of a boat anywhere.

She'd been picking at her face. Now she realized that the skin itched. She looked down and saw the dry brown flakes under her fingernails. She found the small dusty hand mirror at the bottom of her knapsack and looked at herself. There was dried blood all down the side of her face and neck. She must have bled from the mouth. But that's crazy! she thought. I feel fine.

She picked her way down to the edge of the surf, knelt, and washed the blood away. She stood, turned, and stared back at the totem poles, the rotting house frames, the long house, the forest.

There was not a clue anywhere. Sun shining. Birds singing. But she felt an ominous puzzlement growing inside her. A raven called somewhere far away, and a shiver ran down her back. A skein of memory was blowing loose in her mind; it dizzied her, the ground turning momentarily under her, as though she were hurtling away. She breathed deeply several times, hyperventilating. Her sight cleared. She walked back to the log. The calendar watch her father had given her said that it was nearly nine in the morning. The watch was powered by batteries; it never ran down. Where was Randolph Paul? She looked at the date. Eight, it said. The eighth.

Is that right? She felt her breath, ragged and uneasy. She looked at the calendar printed inside her cheque book. The eighth of November, 1974, was a Friday. Friday? That's impossible, she thought. She began to pace up and down the beach. The watch must have counted wrong. But how could it have? It had been all right in October. It counted thirty-one days and started over again, and October had thirty-one days. But it couldn't be Friday. That would mean that she had been unconscious not merely a few hours, but over a day. It would also mean that she had missed Randolph Paul. She stared out into the inlet. There was still not a sign of a boat anywhere.

If I'd been out for over a day, she thought, I'd feel terrible. I'd really be sick. But I feel fine. She stretched her muscles, testing herself. She felt perfectly strong and healthy. I've lost a day somewhere, she thought. That's crazy. But if I've missed him, really missed him, how the hell am I going to get out of here? You walk, that's how, she answered herself. She opened her map.

The nearest useful place seemed to be a small circle called Port Franklin. The map legend told her that the small circle meant "post office." All right, that's the place to shoot for, but how? If she tried to cut directly through the bush due northeast, she'd have to cross a point labeled: Mt. Langly, 4324 ft. No, she thought, don't want to go over *that*. She frowned, looked up at the secondary growth forest stretching away to the southeast around the inlet. Yes, if she could walk in a vast semi-circle . . . But the question was, how far had they logged it off? She looked back at the map. If they'd logged as far as this beautifully named river—the Lull—she could get through, follow it down to Lull Lake. And then there was a trail marked in, crossing to the Tsitsiqua River which she could follow to the edge of the Langly Channel, then along the channel to Port Franklin. Five miles on the map was roughly the width of her thumb. She measured out forty miles. Two days, she thought. Unless there's some place I can't get through.

She repacked, then stood staring out into the inlet. Nothing. Just that broad expanse of uncommunicative water gleaming in the sun. She turned again to the totem poles. They continued to stand as enigmatically as ever, staring out to sea just as she had been doing a moment before. Can it be this simple? she thought. Pack up and walk away? If they'd logged as far as the Lull River, she'd be all right, could pick her way through secondary forest growth, keeping the inlet in sight on her right, but if they hadn't, she'd end up in dense bush growing directly to the edge of sheer cliff. No way she could follow the inlet then, no way she could get through without a compass. Except by sheer fool's luck.

I have matches, she thought, a sharp knife, warm clothes, my tent. I've got food left: bread, sardines, cheese, powdered milk, granola. I can drink the waters of the Lull and the Tsitsiqua. If it takes only two days, or even three or four, I'll be all right. There's no excuse for starving to death in British Columbia, not even in November. She shouldered her knapsack, adjusted the straps, but then continued to stand in the morning sunlight, listening to the bird songs. She found herself reluctant to begin walking; not that she was afraid, but that something important had not yet been settled. "Alone," she said out loud. It's what she'd wanted, what she must have been planning deep inside herself the whole time. Suddenly her thoughts were interrupted by another elusive wisp of memory, turning up unexpectedly like a forgotten old photograph among familiar objects at the bottom of a drawer; these trees, this beach, these totem poles, this long house—all seen from a vantage point thousands of feet in the air. She felt the shock of it pass through her body. There's more, she thought. It's not over yet. Her spirits lifted, and she felt light and joyous. She began to walk up the beach toward the forest.

After an hour she was working hard. She'd forgotten how difficult it was to get through logging slash: old branches crisscrossing high off the ground, many of them rotten and ready to snap. She could either lower herself down between them and crawl under, or she could test each carefully, edging out across the larger logs, balancing. Either way it was taking her a painfully long time to cover even a few yards. She was whistling to herself, a children's song: "Sally go round the sun. Sally go round the moon." She had just skirted a huge growth of devil's club, stopped now to strip off her poncho, wash her mouth out with water. Sweat was burning her face and sides. Then she realized she must have seen other trees like this one, that she must have passed at least three or four of them: small, silvery trees with widely spaced scars in their bark. She ran her fingers lightly over the deep cuts. The paws that did this must have been enormous, she thought. The claw marks went right up the tree for at least fifteen feet. Must be old, she told herself, must be from last spring.

She stuffed her poncho into a side pocket on her knapsack and began to pick her way along, testing. The log seemed sturdy enough. She crossed it quickly, paused. You've got to keep watching, Leslie, she told herself. It's important. Step on rotten wood, slip down between these crisscrosses, break an ankle, and you will be finished, no way you'd ever get out of here. She edged forward, and saw the black droppings on the ground below. Now *that* was fresh. Her skin prickled. All right, she thought, I see it. But what can I possibly do about it?

It took her another hour to admit to herself what she had known all along: that she was being followed. The sun was high and hot now. Fighting off a growing panic, she settled onto a log. Oh, he's good! she thought. So good she'd almost convinced herself that she'd been imagining it. She'd stop, and there would be nothing to hear but birds and insects, but she'd start to walk again, and there it would be, like a ghostly echo of her own movement from further in the bush, snapping branches. Twice now a low huffing noise. I didn't know they did that, she thought: that they stalked people. She turned her head slowly, searching the bush around her. And it was like the outcome of a bad dream. He was waiting for her not fifty meters away: a dignified gentleman in a dark-brown coat. His head was tilted slightly to one side.

The hair rose on her neck, on the backs of her arms. "Hey!" she shouted. He looked at her a moment longer, his head tilted as though in amiable curiosity. Then he slowly lowered himself onto all fours and walked away into the bush. He looked just like a Sendak drawing, even to the powder puff tail. She sat frozen, her mind empty of anything except a focused point of fear.

Then she took the weight of her knapsack on her shoulders, stood, and began to walk. Here was something like a trail, a cleared area for at least a hundred meters. She was moving slowly, whistling as loudly as she could. He's seen me now, she thought. Surely that's enough. They're supposed to be shy. They're supposed to run away if you make any noise. She crossed a log, jumped the few feet to the ground, and looked up to her left. He must have stopped to wait for her; she'd practically walked right into him. If she'd been at her desk in the library, he would have been closer than the card cata-logue. Her chest emptied and then, after a distinct pause, her heart re-engaged with a solid smack at the base of her throat. "Good morning, mister bear," she said out loud.

He was immensely familiar; there must have been hundreds of children's books with his picture in them. And he was also immensely alien; there was no way any picture, any imagining—even the bears in the zoo—could have prepared her for his solidness and immediacy: his enormous size, the massiveness of the muscles in his shoulders, his huge round paws. His ears were small and curved, his eyes, tiny and personable. A voice in her head was saying, just as though telling a story to a circle of children: "Leslie looked at the bear. And the bear looked at Leslie." Then, without any conscious plan, she began to sing to him: a simple quiet melody without words that rose up from somewhere inside her.

What happened next was so strange that she knew she should never tell anybody about it. The bear was listening to her. She knew he was listening to her. He tilted his head to one side. Then he yawned. She could see the pink tongue, the enormous yellow fangs. With great dignity he turned from her, looked back once, and walked away into the forest.

ELLEN STARED AFTER RANDOLPH PAUL'S GILLNETTER; on the bright water it was a distant dark spot, moving away, her last link to the known and safe world. Although the afternoon sunlight was not warm, she was sweating, waiting stupidly in Susan's windbreaker, Susan's knapsack on her back, Susan's gumboots on her feet. What am I doing here? she thought again. She was drawn so tightly into herself that she didn't seem able to form consistent consecutive thoughts, could only stand stiffly, suffering, like an animal.

". . . been here today," Mrs. Mackenzie was saying. "Look." Ellen saw the footprints. "Sometime today. If it was from yesterday, the high tide would have washed them away."

"Maybe she's still around," Ellen said. "Why didn't he wait?"

Mildred shrugged. "He probably thinks it's our problem now. She's a white girl, eh? Come on."

They began to walk toward the totem poles. Ellen tried to detach herself, see them as works of art, but she couldn't do it. Suddenly, harsh voices: "Alan! Ellen! Alan! Ellen!" Ellen stopped, the breath torn from her. "Ravens," Mildred said, laughing. Ellen saw them go up: black wings.

"Mildred!" Ellen said in a small voice, "Something strange is happening to me."

"What?"

"I don't know. It's like a . . . I can feel a pull." She closed her eyes.

"Don't drive it away. Let yourself feel it. What is it?"

"It's like a pull . . . It's . . . We're supposed to go that way." She pointed. "Mildred, what's happening to me?"

"Don't worry so much about what's happening to you. Don't think about it . . . Over there, eh? All right, come on."

Ellen followed dumbly. They shed their knapsacks in the shelter of trees. "Look," Mildred said. "That's where she camped." The marks of the tent. "She didn't bother to make a fire."

"I don't want to go on with this," Ellen said. "I want to go back."

"No way. Randy won't be back till tomorrow."

"It's like . . . This is like what Alan used to feel when he was a little boy. It's terrible."

Mrs. Mackenzie took her by the back of the neck. "Breathe down into your lungs. All our breath is up in your shoulders. That's right. Down. Breathe down all the way to the bottom of your stomach . . . Don't worry about your eyes. Don't try to stop them. Just let them go like that."

"It started happening so fast! I didn't think it would be so fast!"

"Sometimes it happens so fast you can't do anything. Just hang on, eh? All right." She let go of Ellen's neck. "Where are we supposed to go?"

"Over there. That way."

They walked without speaking, Ellen leading, the old woman behind her. The trail was easy to follow; someone had been over it recently. But it took them over an hour to reach the cabin. "We're supposed to come here," Ellen said.

"Yes?"

Ellen was hugging herself. "Someone was crying here. I can feel it."

"Good. Anything else?"

"Sadness. There's terrible sadness." Ellen felt the tears in her own eyes. She blinked them away.

She sank down onto the ground, rested her back against the cabin, and looked down over the small beach strewn with rocks and logs. Mrs. Mackenzie was peering about, swinging her head as though she were sniffing the air. Her lips seemed to be moving. Crouched, she looked like a great heavy animal, a cow perhaps, sensing danger. Stiff, swinging head. "What are you doing?" Ellen yelled.

"Shhh."

Ellen drew her knees up and hugged them to keep from shaking. She couldn't think clearly. "I'm going back," Mrs. Mackenzie said. "You stay here!"

"No!" Ellen wanted to jump up and run, but she couldn't move.

The old woman looked frightened now. She was crouched even lower, still peering about, her head bobbing in a jerky awkward way, an inhuman way, that Ellen found totally terrifying. "No. Have to go. Have to go fast. No time. Just sit. You'll know when to come back." And she was immediately running, shuffling sideways, crablike, in an angular crouching jog, back the way they had come.

"Mildred!" Ellen called. She moaned to herself. Her face was stiff. Her jaws were aching. Slow tears were running freely down her cheeks, and the world was blurring before her. For the first time, she voiced the terrible idea that had been growing in her: she's brought me here to die.

Then, without any sense of movement, she was on her feet, the sound of it still clear in her ears. Somewhere, very far away, had been a rifle shot. It seemed impossible to her that she should know with such certainty that's what it had been, but she knew it: a rifle shot. The dark confusion was gone. She could think again. What's going on? What am I doing here?

She looked around. The cabin was an ordinary cabin. An ordinary human being had built it. She ran her hand over the wood. Someone lived here. Or lives here. There are people. A rifle shot. Someone hunting. Is there someone hunting? "What am I doing here?" she said out loud. She stepped forward a few paces and looked out over the water of the inlet. She felt the sadness again, all around her. Oh, she thought, it's for me. It was my sadness all along. "I don't understand," she said. "I don't know what I should do."

The words came out without her planning them: "I should have been a girl!" But that's Alan speaking, she thought. The confusion was terrible, like something tearing apart inside her. "He never understood it," she said, "why he shouldn't have been born a girl. When he was little, he used to pray, 'Oh, please God, make me a girl!' And then, when he couldn't have that, he didn't want anything. He turned in on himself. He made a prison around himself." Tears were running down her cheeks, and she didn't seem able to stop them. "He couldn't love anybody, because he was in love with the girl in himself."

She stopped, amazed at what she had just said. "He loved the girls who were reflections of himself. His sister. Sandy. But he couldn't reach out and touch them. And then I came along. I was the girl he'd been in love with. He always thought that what was inside him was so terrible that no one could stand to look at it. He hid what was inside him. But what was inside was me. And now I don't know what to do. People come to me. I don't know why they come to me. It's frightening. Betty and Jeanie and even Susan wanted something from me. Oh, I can't go on like this. I'm not really a girl." She covered her face with her hands and sobbed.

"I don't know what I am anymore than Alan did," she said. "The only thing that Alan was ever able to do was look at things, to see them. And I can do that too. I always see even when I don't want to. But what can I do with it? Help me!" she cried out. "Show me the right way. Show me how to live. Show me who I am." The pain of the tearing inside her was so fearful she could no longer stand up. She pressed her arms into her stomach and folded to the ground, crying. After a long time, the pain left her.

She stood and felt peaceful. She'd stopped crying. "Help me," she said quietly to the growing darkness. "Make me wise."

She began to walk the trail back to the village. For the first time since she'd left Vancouver, she felt calm and unafraid. And then she heard another rifle shot. She froze, listening, her skin tingling. Hunters, she thought. But very far away. She began to walk again until she came to a point at which the trail opened out above the inlet. She stopped to look seaward. Below her the rock face fell sheerly down to the water. The sun was a sinking red ball, spotting the sea before it in brilliant drops. Monet would have loved to paint this, she thought, looking. She breathed deeply. She felt peaceful but absolutely alone.

She stood, watching, until the sun had set. It left behind it a red light; eventually that too was lost, and the sky turned a sombre translucent grey. I could almost believe that I've been here before, she thought, that I've stood here before in just this way and watched the sun set. She'd forgotten why she had come; she'd forgotten

Mildred Mackenzie. She began to feel a melancholy detachment (and that too was somehow familiar) as though she'd become lost in the way that Jeanie had been with no way to get back to the world of ordinary people. Then, from high overhead, she heard a single mournful cry. She felt the thrill of it in her stomach, and her sadness was gone immediately, leaving only the detachment. She now knew that she was waiting. She looked up and saw two geese flying far above her.

Her first thought was that she'd seen geese in formation before, but never just two of them like that. The cry was repeated, that single, painfully beautiful note. And for the brief time that the cry lasted, the geese were closer. She was aware that she was standing where she had been, firmly on the ground, that they were where they had been, high above her, but superimposed a moment on that awareness was another one, that they were much closer, as though seen through a telescope. How odd, she thought. It's like a transparency, a surrealist collage. One of the geese cried out again, and this time they were so close she could see the feathers on their long outstretched necks. Unbidden, her mind began to recite the verse that Alan had learned from Jeanie:

> Grey goose and gander,
> Waft your wings together,
> Carry the good king's daughter,
> Over the two-strand river.

And she would not have believed that anything could have taken her with so much force. She was spun out, tearing, riding high upon her own scream. Below, the trees were falling away. She struck and hung a moment on a curtain of hideous pain; then she was through it, she was torn apart. The incredible high wind was rushing over her feathers. She could see all of Johnston's Inlet below, as small as if it were on a map. Above, the stars glittered insanely in a sky that was perfectly black. She could not comprehend this speed; already they had chased down the sun over the bright curve of the earth. And then below was a wet blue ball, half in shadow, split night from day. And it was even colder where they were going, riding this expanding sky, even faster. She stretched her long neck and cried out. She was flying. Or she was falling.

ALAN WAS BEING DRAGGED FORWARD THROUGH THE MUD. He could feel the strong hands under his arms. He tried to sit up. "No, not yet," he heard Mrs. Mackenzie's voice. "You're too weak yet." Something was in his mouth. Salty. His face fell again into the mud. He raised his head and spat. His stomach contracted. He had mud in his mouth. And something salty. He had been moaning, he realized now, a droning inarticulate sound. He was being drenched by cold slanting rain. Then the memory began to come back. "Mildred!" he said, or tried to say, "I was flying!"

"Don't talk yet." She was a black form in front of him. He could just make her out. She was stripping off his clothes. "I have to wash you with leaves."

Suddenly, with horrible fear, he realized that he wasn't Ellen any longer. And he wasn't Alan either. He was both of them.

He grabbed Mildred's waist. "What's happened to me?"

"Wait, wait," she said. "You're not ready."

"What's happened to me?"

It was too dark to see her face. He heard her sigh. "Alan," she said, "listen. Before there were two, there was one. It's the one that bites its own tail." He could see the pale patch of her hand drawing a circle in the dark. "It's always there, behind everything. It's male and female before they were separated. That's where you are now."

"Ah . . ." he said, sobbing. He knew that it was blood in his mouth. "What am I going to do?" he said. "What can I do?"

"You'll know. There's nothing more I can teach you. You're free."

"Free!" he said. And he began to cry bitterly in his loneliness and terror.

WITHOUT ANY SENSE OF MOVEMENT LESLIE WAS ON HER FEET, the sound of it still clear in her ears. Somewhere, very near to her, there had been a rifle shot. That sound was unmistakable. And ravens were going up, black wings, screaming, and nothing she could understand; harsh cries just at the edge of meaning. Her heart was pounding. She was as poised as if she were crouched for the start of a race. The rifle shot like a starting gun. The sound of it seemed to be echoing in the bush, but then she knew it was only echoing in her memory. She exhaled.

A hunter, she thought. He had to get here from somewhere, and he has to get back. I can save myself a forty-mile walk. She was disappointed. Well, I could always sit down here quietly again and he'd never see me.

She'd found a trail and had been following it for several hours. At first it had run along near the edge of the inlet, exactly as she'd wanted it to, but then, a few miles back, it had begun to cut inland. She'd stayed with it, hoping it would swing again back to the sea, but it hadn't. She'd stopped to rest, wondering if she should backtrack or cut straight through the bush to water. She knew that she had to stay near water or she'd get hopelessly lost in this repeating world where evergreen forest continued to mirror evergreen forest, nothing much to distinguish one reflection from another, until she'd been made uneasy by a growing sense of false familiarity, and only the position of the sun to assure her that she wasn't again where she had been an hour before.

Don't be a damn fool, Leslie, she told herself. At least try to find him. She worked her arms through the shoulder straps of her knapsack and began walking. It was difficult to tell which direction the sound had come from; it had rung in the air all around her. She walked as quietly as she could, listening. But there was nothing that sounded like men, or a man. She almost didn't notice him, could easily have walked right by, his khaki coat and rain hat blending with the colours around him. She stopped, alarmed. It was as though he'd been waiting silently for her. He held a rifle in one hand as casually as if it were a stick. "What the hell *you* doin here, boy?" he said angrily.

He was an Indian, she saw that first, and then that he was an old man. He could have been sixty or he could have been eighty, round and solid, his feet spread. He was looking at her with an expression of unrestrained sour dislike, his mouth turned down at the corners like a carving meant to portray hostility. "What the hell you doin here?" he said again. She couldn't answer. Her mind was a scattering spray of thoughts, most of them useless. She couldn't say, "I'm lost," because she wasn't lost. She couldn't think of any way to summarize her situation. "I missed my ride back," didn't sound right. Why had he said, "What are *you* doing here?" as though he'd met her before? And had he really called her "boy"?

"Never seen a white man couldn't find somethin to say," he said conversationally, as though addressing an invisible companion. Then to her, "You guys are great for talkin, hey?" He was looking at her with such absolute distaste she thought he might be considering shooting her. He walked directly to her. She could smell sweat and whiskey. He leaned into her face and said, "What the hell's the matter with you, boy?"

She realized that she'd been stopped, staring. "I'm walking to Port Franklin," she said, the words tumbling out.

He made a sound. It could have been "Yeah?" But then it might have been something else. He scowled. He started to walk off. And then he paused and looked at her again. "Nothin there."

"I thought there was a post office there."

"Back last winter, old man died."

"Oh," she said. Pull yourself together, Leslie. He's going to think you're not right in the head. "I'm trying to get back to Adagalis or Huyatsi."

He did not ask the obvious question, "How did you get here?" He stared at her. It was not hatred, more like a profound annoyance as though she were a bothersome insect that had just crawled out of the bush to bite him. "I'm goin to Adagalis," he said and walked away. And then he yelled at her: "Come on, boy!" She jumped forward and ran after him.

He walked purposefully for about a hundred yards inland. He pointed at the ground. There was a huge dark splash of liquid. Leslie looked with a growing sickening fascination. Blood. "In the guts," the Indian said. "I can't shoot a damn anymore. Body's different now. Too many years back. I'm old now." His voice was angry. He sat down on the ground, leaned against a tree. He laid the rifle down, the barrel pointing away from them.

The blood was dark brown. It was mixed with another substance, a darker brown, thick and vile. Shit, Leslie thought. Blood and shit. "What is it?" she said.

"Deer," he said as though it were perfectly obvious. "He's runnin now. We go after him now, he just keep runnin. He run all the way to Bella Bella." He smiled bleakly at his own joke. "We wait now. It hurts him, hey? He's sick now. He gonna lie down to die."

Leslie sank to the forest floor. She slipped her shoulders out of the knapsack. She waited, numbly. The passage of time had become meaningless; it could have been ten minutes or a half-hour before the Indian spoke again. "Never could talk English much. All our kids talkin English now. Nobody talkin our language anymore. What's your name, boy?"

"Leslie."

"Leslie." He repeated it thoughtfully. "Billy is what they call me, hey? White man's name." He spat. His expression now was close to hatred. She looked away. "Old drunk Indian, hey? Old now. Too many years." He grabbed the rifle from the ground and stood up abruptly. "Not goina die in that damn hospital. Huyatsi. Goina drown." He walked away.

She worked quickly into her knapsack and scurried after him. Looking back, he said, "You sound like a sick moose, boy." Something in his face, a kind of contraction, told her that he'd meant a joke. She smiled. She began to walk carefully and quietly behind him. He pointed down. More blood.

They tracked the blood through the bush. She thought it must have been over an hour. He stopped and pointed upward. Black wings, moving away. Raven. "He's curious," he said softly. "He's always goin to see what's happened." The raven settled into a distant tree; Leslie could see the irritable speck of black.

"He's layin down over there," the Indian said in a voice barely more than a whisper. "He's layin down sick there. He's listenin. You wait."

She waited, stiff with tension, her breathing shallow. She watched him walk forward with maddening slowness toward the tree where the raven was also waiting. Then she couldn't quite make him out anymore. She heard the shot. She closed her eyes. "Oh, God!" she said. "You come, boy!" he yelled.

The buck's eyes were open. It looked surprised. It had been thrown down on its side. The first shot had come low in the belly, and parts of the intestines were leaking out. The second shot had gone through the head. "I shoulda got you the first time," the old man said to the deer. "I'm sorry . . . Come on, boy, we got to do it quick. The tide's comin up, hey?" He was already turning the buck over.

She knelt next to the Indian, unsure what she could do. He was making a long cut up the length of the belly. At the chest, the blade met cartilage. She saw the strain; the old man was beginning to sweat. He cut all the way to the neck. Then he was chopping away at the deer's sexual organs. She closed her eyes. Oh God, I can't stand it! she thought. But then: yes I can. She looked again and he was cutting around the anus. She could not yet see the deer as meat; it was an animal being violated, its bright, precise insides opened to daylight. He was cutting the windpipe. He was reaching inside and cutting away the diaphragm, cutting away the organs, pulling on them. It's like me! she thought. I'm full of organs like that, those lungs and loops of intestine. The blood spilling out was not the colour she would have expected, but dark, nearly maroon. She should be helping, but she didn't know what she could do. She'd cleaned fish, but she'd never gutted an animal before. And suddenly the old man had seized her wrist. He was staring into her face. "What was it?" he said. "What come for you?"

I don't know what he means, she thought. But she did know what he meant. She couldn't look away. "Geese," she said, "two geese."

"Good," he said, "I seen it on you, but I didn't believe it. You're a white boy . . . They took you, hey?"

"Yes," Leslie said. She remembered it all. And of course she'd remembered it all along. "They took me."

"What come for me," he said, "was the eagle. He come for me like this: Chaaaaaaaa!" Leslie jumped at the sound of the scream. "He grab me with his claws. He pull me up. He take me away. He drop me down in the snow. I'm bleedin, hey? I'm covered with ice. And they're workin on me. They're singin for me." He stared at her a moment, then said, "Come on, come on."

She didn't know immediately what he wanted, but she figured it out, helped him pick up the deer and turn it over and shake it. All of the guts came tumbling down to the ground. "We goina bury all this," he said.

He didn't speak again until they had begun to drag the deer toward the sea. "How you know to come up here?" he said.

"My grandfather lived up here. He had a cabin a few miles from the village where nobody lives now . . . And I saw him. He's dead, but I saw him."

"Dead people comin back sometimes. Not good."

"I thought he wanted me to come up here again."

"I knew him."

Leslie stopped walking. "You did?"

"Yeah. He was livin in that cabin years back. Yeah. He was a real nice white man. The only one. He was tellin us the truth and we weren't listenin to him. He was tellin us, 'Don't listen to those ministers. They tellin you lies.' But we listened to them. He was tellin us, 'Don't move down to Huyatsi.' But we went. Too many years now."

"You really knew him?" Leslie couldn't believe it.

"I knew him. My father knew him . . . Come on, the tide's comin up." They began to drag the deer again.

"When I was a boy like you," he said, "my grandfather take me down to the water. In the winter, hey? And he say, 'You go in that water. And when you come out, I'm goina beat you with . . . branches, hey? Don't know how to say it in English . . . That's how I get strong. Too many years back now. My body's different now." He stopped walking. He was sweating. "I was listenin to those ministers. I was goin to that church at Huyatsi. I was sayin the Lord's Prayer, hey? And then I lost it. They never came back to me. Damn fool. Now drunk old Indian. Too many years back now."

She stared at him. "Don't be sayin the Lord's Prayer, boy," he said. "White man comes up here and it all goes away from us. Now nobody's talkin our language no more. I got no people no more. Nobody listens to me no more. I'm old drunk Indian. Billy they say is what my name is. White man's name! Talkin to these young kids now is like talkin to a stone. I got no people no more.

"Come on," he said. "Tide's comin up." And they began to walk again.

"Not goina die in that hospital at Huyatsi," he said. "Goina drown." He sent her a strange, careful look. "Don't know why, but you're one now. They made you. Never know why they do that. Some people don't want it. I didn't want it. But they come for me . . . And we're always dyin hard, boy. Because we're not like other people. We're not really human."

"What?" I don't want to hear this, she thought.

"When we're dyin, it's always real hard. We're always dyin real hard. It always hurts us real bad. Like this." He dropped the deer and began to dance. He danced forward a few steps and then back. He sang. Then he said, "Like this we're dyin, and everythin's shakin. Everythin's shakin because we're dyin so hard." He danced again. "Like this. Ooooh, ooooh, ooooh! And people are hearin it shakin, and they say, 'Oh, it's the old man dyin. And he's shakin everythin because he's dyin so hard.'"

Leslie didn't speak. They dragged the deer. They came out of the bush. Below them lay a small cove. The sun was setting: long oblique rays of red light. "Boat," the Indian said. He pointed. She saw it, drifting away. She'd never seen anything like it outside of a museum: a dugout canoe. It was drifting away fast. She stared hard at the old man. "High tide," he said. Leslie let the deer fall. She ran down the beach to the edge of the water.

A steady cold wind was blowing across the inlet; it sent sea-chop scudding to froth at her feet. How far? she thought. How many pool lengths? Five? Six? She couldn't be certain. In pool water it would have been easy for her, but this was the water of Johnston's Inlet, so cold that even at the height of summer it could freeze a swimmer to death in minutes. Her father had told her stories of swimmers, good strong experienced swimmers, who had tried these waters. The cold had eaten them up, had destroyed their will, and they'd sunk without a trace, without a struggle, without even crying out for help. This is crazy, she thought, just a crazy whim. It isn't a life-and-death matter. We'd get back without the boat. But she'd already shed her pack and begun to strip off her hiking boots.

"Hey, boy!" the Indian yelled. She glanced back at him once. And then she threw her boots behind her, high onto the beach. She would need all the rest of her clothing. She pulled up the hood of her windbreaker, tied the string under her chin. Important to keep the neck warm. She'd read that somewhere. And she should have gloves. But of course she didn't have gloves. Her hands would be the first to go. She began to wade into the water. The coldness of it burned at her feet, incredibly, worse than she would have imagined. Can never remember pain, she thought. Only pain can remind you of pain.

It was the canoe, she thought, the sight of it out there. Might be one of the very last. That's why I'm doing it. (Because she still didn't know why she was doing it.) To bring it back to him, to say with that gift, "It's not your time yet. The old world is not yet deserting you, piece by piece." Somehow that was worth it, worth risking her life. But it's for me too, she thought. She waded in up to her thighs. She pushed herself down and began to swim. From that moment she began to die.

I have to do everything wrong, she thought. In this water you don't swim, you float and conserve your body heat. But she had to strike out fast, warm herself fast with activity, and hope she could make it. The action would cut her time down. How long? Ten minutes? Twenty? Sprint, she told herself. She was pulling; it was what she knew how to do. It was right, perfectly right. The joy in her was like a fierce song.

She stopped swimming a moment, raised her head, and looked. Immediately her teeth began to chatter violently. She had underestimated how fast the boat had been drifting away. Not even halfway there. She began to swim again, thinking, how long? How many minutes? The heat would be lost first from her hands and feet, then from her arms and legs, finally from the core of her body. Her internal temperature would begin to drop. She would lose feeling. And then her will would begin to go. She would want to fall asleep. She knew all of these things. She must remember.

She looked again. Her teeth weren't chattering anymore. Dangerous, she thought. It's beginning. How long had she been swimming? How much longer? The boat was within a hundred meters. But it was moving away from her fast, terribly fast. She had no choice now. If she turned back, she'd die before she made the shore. The pain was lessening. Dangerous, she thought, dangerous. She struck out again. Swim hard, Leslie. You've only got a couple of minutes to get on to that boat.

When she looked again, the boat was a dark shape riding above her. There was the bow line, trailing. She reached for it. Her fingers wouldn't close on it. Oh God! she thought. She pulled hard and was alongside. She reached up. The canoe teetered crazily. Don't pull it over on you, she told herself. But instead of panic, she'd begun to feel that it was all just a little bit silly, even funny. She thought she'd just hang there on the side for awhile and drift while she caught her breath. The water wasn't so bad. Peaceful just to hang awhile.

No! a voice inside her said. It's happening to you. *Get in the boat!* Her hands weren't working properly. She pressed with her wrists and pulled. The boat lurched. How? she thought. How do I get in? To try to think clearly was an immense effort. If I could just rest awhile . . . No! You've got to get in that boat. Not over the side. You'll turn it over on top of you. Over the bow. It's the only way. She swam around to the bow, reached up. The boat sank deep in the water. She pulled, got a leg over. Do it now! she told herself, and pulled. The canoe was rocking, but it was not going to turn. She was in. She was lying on her belly on the bottom. She turned over. Slanting rain had begun to fall. It felt warm on her face, but she knew that it wasn't warm.

Rest, one voice said. I'm dying! the other voice said. How long had she been swimming? How much longer did she have to live? She was not shaking; her teeth were not chattering. She rolled over and got her knees under her. With every second, the strong wind from across the water was taking more of her body heat away through wet clothing. It wouldn't be too bad to die now, she thought. It would be almost glorious in a way, a fitting finish for Leslie Cameron Fraser. She wanted to lie down on the bottom of the canoe and rest. Maybe that was a good idea. Maybe she'd feel better in a few minutes.

No! You're dying. And nothing in the boat to wrap herself in. At the stern was an ancient outboard motor, tilted up with propeller blades clear of the water. She tried the catch that would release it, drop it down into action, and her hand would not work. She smashed her hand down on the side of the motor, twice, hard. "Stop that!" she said out loud. She looked and her palm was covered with blood. She didn't feel anything.

She should put her hands in her armpits, but she couldn't work the zipper on her windbreaker. It's too hard, she thought. Everything's too hard. But, pushing with the tops of her wrists, she worked the windbreaker up her chest, then her hands under her wet sweater. Soon it would be too dark to see the cove. There was a paddle in the canoe, but she'd never be able to paddle back in time. Up the creek without a paddle, she thought, and giggled. Maybe if she could sleep for a while . . .

No! She tried her right hand again. It worked now, after a fashion, clumsily as if it were a hook. The outboard motor fell into place. Now what? I know how to operate these things. Pump it up. Start, choke, pull. And it wouldn't start, of course, not the second time or the third time. But it started the fourth. I can still make it, she thought. The throttle full on, she aimed for shore. She giggled again. They always say the return trip's faster.

She managed to cut the engine in time. He was already wading out in his gumboots and grabbing the bow line. And she was stumbling out of the water, up the beach. "I'm dying," she said, and giggled.

"Yeah," he said.

Perhaps I can lie down now, she thought. And, moving quickly, he continued what he must have been doing all the time she'd been in the water. He'd been skinning the deer. How absurd! she thought. That's silly. Then he was stripping her wet clothes off her. "Good strong boy," he said. "Good." She felt like a child being undressed for bed. She raised her hands docilely over her head so he could get the sweater off. And then the shirt underneath.

"Huh!" he said, surprised. "A girl. You're a girl."

She was naked. She wasn't even shivering. And he was wrapping her in the deer hide. The underside was slick with fat, and it was hot from the deer. It was burning. "Ahh, ahh!" she said.

"Fire," he said. "Got to make fire." He'd been gathering brush. She crouched, pulled the hide more tightly around her, and watched him. She began to shiver. I'm going to live! she thought.

He waded out to the boat and brought back a can, doused the brush with it. The fire went up with a thump, the crackling of wet wood. Her teeth were chattering. She was shaking. And her sense was coming back. She knew now how dangerous that silly sleepiness had been; she fought it. I'm going to live, she thought again. The joy of it seared her.

The heat of the fire. And the deer hide. If he'd merely put me in dry clothes, I would have died. My internal heat would have been too low to warm myself. She was shaking.

"A girl," he said. "A good strong girl." And then he said an Indian word. It sounded like "pakakla."

"Yes," she said, "I'm a girl."

The sun had set, leaving behind a translucent grey. The slanting rain fell. The smoky fire, the crackling of the wet wood, the slick fat of the deer. And she was shaking. The carcass was dark. The muscles beneath the skin. The dugout canoe was waiting. The years that were left.

Epilogue

IT ISN'T JUST A PROBLEM OF LOOKING AND SEEING, Alan thought. If it were, then it would all be simple enough. It's that you've got to forget everything anybody's ever told you and then look . . . and see. He'd been told that his eyes were grey. He had also been told they were green or hazel. But now the broad forceful light of the shop was presenting a colour to him that was clear and unmistakable, and he still couldn't find a name for it. He was delighted by the clarity in the mirror: there was a precise dark ring around each cornea. The whites were not white but marked with a minute tracery of blood vessels. He could see pores, hairs, veins. For the first time in my life, he thought, I like my own face. I'm not comfortable with it—no, and probably never will be— but it's me.

He still wore his hair as Ellen had done, and he neither tried to show it off nor to hide it, merely brushed out the ash-blond curls every morning. It's probably the hair that upsets people the most, he thought, the people in shops who call me "Miss" and then look again, startled. He rather liked the streaked hair, but when it grew out, he didn't think he'd bother to get it done again. He wore a mix of Alan's and Ellen's clothing: Ellen's blouse, Alan's pants, Ellen's shoes. At first the freedom had been maddening—that he could have worn anything—Alan's work shirt with a skirt of Ellen's, or a dress, but then the ordinary world had begun to close around him again, and he'd known that he was limited by it. He hadn't yet defined precisely the extent of that limitation. No, he thought, I'll never be comfortable, but that's OK. I can live with it. He turned away from the mirror.

He collected the coffee pot, carried it to the small pink lavatory at the back. He still enjoyed these few minutes in the morning before Kurt or Trish arrived. He cleaned and filled the coffee pot, carried it into the reception room, and plugged it in. Then he turned to look out the window where the snow was falling, white and fat, muting the street and softening it. Even the high rise that was filling up the vacant lot seemed lovely now, and oddly redeemed, by that layer of white.

Tricia walked in quickly, her long skirt swirling dramatically. She was all in furs . . . coat, mittens, and a small hat cut like a baby bonnet. Alan laughed. "What, love?" she said absently.

"You looked like the heroine of a Russian novel . . . coming in like that, all in furs, out of the snow."

"Snow," she said and sank heavily into a chair opposite him. "It won't stick. Be gone by noon." She briefly rested two long fingers (pointed pomegranate-coloured nails) on her forehead.

"Scotch?" he said.

"Gin. I swear to God, Alan, I'm going to have to learn to wait for the weekends. I just can't take it anymore." She lay slumped in an inelegant pose, her legs spread, the high heels of her boots resting on the floor, her feet tilted back. "You'd think by my age I would have learned some common sense, eh? . . . Oh, I didn't get you any coffee. Sorry, love."

"That's all right. Don't drink it anymore."

She grinned. "Don't be so pure. You make me feel old."

She carried her coffee to the reception desk, opened the appointment book. "Oh God! Another full day . . . Oh and your sister's coming in."

"Which one?" He looked over her shoulder. *Betty Kovaran*, the entry read, *Cut—Style*.

Trish walked to her station and began to fluff her hair in front of the mirror. "Do you think I'm too old for all these curls? Oh God, I never wanted to live past twenty-nine."

Their eyes met in the mirror. "It doesn't matter how old you are," he said.

They simultaneously turned away from the mirror to look at each other; inexplicably they both began to laugh. "That's what Donna says too. You seem happier."

"Not exactly happier, but . . ." He shrugged.

"You must have found somebody you like, eh?"

"No, but at least I don't think it's impossible anymore."

He touched her shoulder lightly, but what he'd been planning to say was lost in the bang of the door: Kurt arriving with a shout, "Well, children, winter, eh?"

"It must be nine," Trish said.

"Ah, Alan, dear boy, you always have the coffee on. How nice of you! Such a joy to work with. And so beautiful too. What more could I ask? . . . And here it is snowing and not even Christmas. But it won't stick." He turned on the stereo; the top-forty rock station filled the shop. The phone rang.

"Here we go," Trish said, running for it. "Page of Cups . . ."

Betty arrived. She was shaking snow from a broad-brimmed hat. She wore a plain black jersey and sleek jeans over her high-heeled boots.

"I've got too damn much hair, Alan."

"You want it really short?"

"No, just above my shoulders maybe. Something simple that I don't have to set."

He swept her dark hair into the shampoo basin. She lay with her eyes closed—that familiar face—his sister. "What have you been up to, Betty? I haven't seen you in awhile."

"Oh, I've been so bloody busy I haven't had time to turn around."

He lathered her scalp. He could see the faint blue veins in her closed eyelids. She wasn't wearing much makeup, just mascara and lipstick. "How's Gary?"

"Christ, he's so busy too that we practically have to set up appointments to see each other. I think he's happier. He's not making the money he was before, of course. But I think he feels better about what he's doing."

"How about you?"

"It's no joy working. I didn't really think it was going to be, but if I'm going to school next fall, I've got to make some money. This mortgage has damned near killed us."

The shop had come to life around them. The music on the stereo, the door opening and closing, the phone: ". . . not today, I'm afraid. Who usually does your hair?"

"How nice to see you again, my dear boy. Oh my God, snow, eh? And not even the end of December."

"Next Tuesday?"

Alan set Betty up at his station and began to cut her damp hair. "Didn't know what I was getting into," she said. "The idea seemed so exciting, but, my God, the work! Can you imagine me plastering, Alan? But I'm not afraid of the neighbourhood any more. Of course for Gary, it was just going home. Don't know how I'm going to like having his parents so close though. How about you?"

"I don't know. I'll work here awhile."

"Forever?"

"No, not forever. I may go to school too. Back to art school."

"Oh," Betty burst out laughing. "Amy called me. How did you do it? What on earth did you say to her?"

Alan laughed too. "She was ready to believe me. She *wanted* to believe me. It didn't matter much what I actually said."

"She's been talking about this trip for years. Jeanie must be pleased."

"That's putting it mildly. We're going to celebrate. She's taking me out to lunch today."

"Oh, she's taking you, eh? That's marvellous."

He was studying her hair. "How about bangs?"

"Yeah, I suppose. Not Cleopatra, eh?"

"No, of course not." He began to cut again.

"Alan," she said. Their eyes met in the mirror. "What *are* you going to do? Have you decided to be a man after all?"

He shrugged. "I have a male body."

"I thought you'd be happier as a woman."

"I probably would be, but . . . I don't know, Betty. I really don't. I'm just feeling my way along."

LESLIE STOOD AND WATCHED THE SNOW fall through one of the high windows in the children's section. Now that she was coaching her father's club, she did her swimming in the evenings. But the old habit of morning thoughtfulness persisted; she brought it to work with her, and for the first hour or so it was hard to get anything done. It's all right for now, she thought, but in the spring I'm going to start swimming alone again. Early and alone. And the snow was muting everything. Under it, the city was being transformed into a magical countryside. The children on their way to school, passing the window in lumpy clothes that disguised their sexes, had seemed like festival-goers, their voices obvious with delight, throwing snowballs, years away from the adult world where snow would be merely a nuisance. Almost Christmas, she thought.

Four new children's books lay on her desk. She had been trying to write reviews of them for the next selection meeting. She sat down and looked at the books with distaste. It's ridiculous, she thought, that I should be able to predict so accurately what's inside merely by the origin of the publisher. New York, New York, New York, New York. All of them. And what she had written so far applied to any of them: "Teenage 'problems' books. Teenagers don't read them, but younger kids do. Set in New York City or eastern United States. Written to formula—slick. Superficial characterization. Didactic. Phony solutions. Too easy." But if she fleshed out these comments into four specific reviews, she knew what the other librarians would say. "Oh, but the kids like them."

No, she thought. It's got to stop somewhere. There are more than enough of these books already. No more. Not in my branch. Not in the whole system if I have anything to do with it . . . although I probably won't be able to have that much to do with it. They can leave their damn slick little books in New York City. Maybe they have some use there. She began to write, thinking, I'm not going to be very popular. And here was Ted, walking toward her desk with that uneasy I-want-something smile fixed on his face. He was wearing a natty grey suit, well-cut to disguise his spreading mid-section. He'd begun to let his beard grow in again. His round pink chin was shrouded with a fuzzy down. "Busy day?" he said.

"Not particularly. Trying to get these reviews written."

"Really snowing, eh? Unusual for this time of year . . . Well, Leslie," his voice was overly hearty, "how are you feeling these days?"

"I'm fine." She looked at the round, questioning oval of his face. I don't feel the least bit sorry for him, she thought.

"That's good. That week off seemed to have set you up again. I was worried about you before that. You seemed a little . . ." he hesitated, searching for the properly neutral word, "edgy."

"Yeah," she said. "I was a little crazy."

He laughed uneasily. "But you're feeling better now?"

"I'm feeling fine."

"That's good. Leslie . . . ah . . . how about dinner?" She didn't answer. "We haven't had a good talk lately and . . . Well, you were planning to eat tonight, weren't you?"

I could tell him I'm coaching in the evenings now, she thought. But no, that's pointless. She tried to frame her words into a diplomatic sentence. Finally, she gave it up and said, "I'm not the woman for you, Ted."

"What?"

"I said, I'm not the woman for you. I'm not the kind of woman you need. You're wasting your time with me."

He didn't speak for awhile. His eyes were blinking rapidly. Then he said, "That's pretty direct, eh?"

"I suppose so."

He sighed and looked at the window where the snow was falling. "You know, I always knew it, I guess. Just thought that maybe . . ." He shrugged. "Friends?" he said.

"Of course we are." She was surprised to discover that as soon as the possibility of romance had been cut away she was prepared to like him, did in fact like him. And, absurdly, he was holding out his hand to her. She took it.

Without speaking, he walked away. She heard his rapid footsteps on the stairs.

He'll get over it, she thought. There are girls who will think he's very sweet. He is sweet, but not for me. She looked down at the books on her desk. Here I go. Four solid pans. Probably futile, they'll buy them anyway. But somebody's got to say no. It's funny. I never thought I'd be a gadfly.

"IT'S MELTING," JEANIE SAID SADLY.

"Yeah," Alan said. "It'll be gone by this afternoon. It's supposed to rain tonight."

"Someday I'm going up north where there's a proper winter," the girl said. They were walking rapidly up the street through snow that was turning to slush. "Maybe it will snow while we're gone. I'd like that. It's going to be really neat. We have a tent and everything.

I wish you could come too . . . Mildred says we're going to find the good powers, the ones that are on my side. I didn't know there *were* any on my side. Are there some on your side, Alan?"

"Oh, yes," he said, laughing, "a few . . . Hey Jeanie, where are you taking me?"

"I've got to return some books."

"We're going all the way to the library?"

"It isn't far. There's a restaurant just up the street."

"All right, but I've only got an hour, you know."

"So do I," she said. "Wow, it's really great isn't it? I didn't think Mom would ever go away. It's all she can talk about. The Bahamas. She's being pretty silly about it."

"Yeah, I imagine she is. I was really surprised that Mildred passed inspection."

"Oh, you should have seen her, Alan. She was all dressed up when she came to the house. She just looked like anybody else. Mom was very impressed. She said, 'That Mrs. Mackenzie seems a sober and responsible woman. I'm sure she'll take good care of Jeanie.'" She giggled. "She's a little scary though, isn't she? Did she scare you? She says we're going up the coast . . . I've never been there. It's going to be really neat." She stopped walking and looked at Alan with grave eyes. "I guess I'm really scared."

"So was I. It doesn't hurt you to be scared."

They began walking again, reached the library, stamped the snow off their feet, crossed the adult section, went down the stairs. "Hi, Leslie," Jeanie said to the boy behind the desk.

"Hi, Jeanie," the boy said, looking up from what he'd been writing.

Here was Jeanie bringing an older girl into the library, a blonde with clear grey eyes like Jeanie's. Must be an aunt.

He looked and felt it rushing through, between the shelves of books, like a cold high wind, moving out, into a perfectly black sky glittering with stars. He could not comprehend this speed;

already they had chased down the sun over the bright curve of the earth. Below was a wet blue ball, half in shadow, split night from day. It was even colder where they were going, riding the expanding sky.

She looked and felt it rushing through, between the shelves of books, like a cold high wind, moving out, into a perfectly black sky glittering with stars. She could not comprehend this speed; already they had chased down the sun over the bright curve of the earth. Below was a wet blue ball, half in shadow, split night from day. It was even colder where they were going, riding the expanding sky.

The girl was a boy.

The boy was a girl.

Alan and Leslie saw each other.

Afterword

IT'S BEEN TWENTY YEARS since *Two Strand River* was first published, and now, upon the occasion of its reissue by HarperCollins, I can't resist the opportunity to say a few words about it. I've often been asked, "How did you come to write it?"—or, as it has sometimes been put, "How *on earth* did you ever write something like *that*?" It is, I must admit, a pretty weird book, although I suspect that it will appear far less weird now than it did in 1976.

By the time I emigrated to Canada from the United States, I'd blocked out a body of fictional work in which I planned to explore the experience of people my own age or somewhat younger—the sixties kids—and I'd already created fully developed characters and partially developed plots for what would turn out to be four out of the five books in the cycle. But there was one book I didn't know anything about. It didn't even have a title, and I thought of it simply as "the sex reversal novel." The idea for it had come to me while talking to friends in a movement not yet called "feminism" but rather "women's liberation," and much of what the women's liberationists were saying made sense to me personally. The dictum that has since then become commonplace—"the personal is the political"—was freshly minted, and I was trying to see everything I did as political. What could be more personal, I thought, and therefore more political, than a novel with fully embodied human beings with their problems seen from the inside? So I decided to write a novel about a girl who should have been a boy and a boy who should have been a girl.

Alan in *Two Strand River* is not me; in fact, he bears almost no resemblance to me. But one thing we do share is an ambiguous relationship to gender. I was raised by two women; for the first few years of my life, I had no contact other than the most superficial with men. As a small child, I didn't know with absolute certainty what sex I was. People told me that I was a boy, but I didn't quite believe it. I'd never seen anyone other than myself entirely naked, and I believed that one's sex was determined by clothes and hair length—or at least I tried to believe that, but I sensed, obscurely, that there must be something more to it than that. I asked my mother how boys were different from girls. "Their bodies are different," she said. That didn't make any sense to me; I thought she meant the *stuff* bodies were made of, and I couldn't see that I was made of anything different from what a girl is made of. I can remember staring at my hand and trying to see how it looked any different from a girl's hand. I thought that if I grew my hair long and wore dresses, I would turn into a girl, and there were certainly times when I would have much preferred to be a girl, and I couldn't understand why I wasn't allowed to be one. I didn't want to be a girl all the time, but then I didn't want to be a boy all the time either; I thought it would be nice if I could decide day-to-day, depending on the mood I was in. I was well into grade school before I learned what we called "the facts of life."

As a general model for child rearing, my childhood has hardly anything to recommend it, but it did have a positive side: it made me thoughtful and watchful—characteristics that are useful for a novelist—and it left me with a deep inner conviction that gender is something that is, or can be, quite fluid. That conviction is the central strand of *Two Strand River*, but there are other strands as well.

When I first came to Canada, I lived in Alert Bay—an island community with a largely native population some three hundred miles northwest of Vancouver—while I wrote about Boston in the late sixties. (Even at the time it struck me as ironic that I should be living in Alert Bay and writing about Boston.) Once I got over a monumental case of culture shock, I fell in love with the Bay and knew that I would have to write something about it, and, a few years later, I did—a novel about an American draft dodger (or "resister," as we preferred to say) who emigrates to Canada and ends up teaching in a place that looks suspiciously like Alert Bay. I have never in my life written anything as turgid—as downright unreadable—as that wretched book; there's no plot to speak of, and it's built largely of internal monologues as the protagonist drinks coffee (in the morning) or beer (at night) and stares out the window (it is always raining) while asking himself a series of dark, koan-like questions: Should I have left the United States? What am I doing here? Where's *here*? Who are these people? What are *they* doing here? Is this really Canada? What does it all *mean*?

I knew that I'd failed to write anything even remotely interesting about my experience in Alert Bay, and I wanted to try again. Dozens of resonant incidents floated around in my memory and wouldn't let me go. There was, for instance, the night at a potlatch when an old man sitting next to me began to explain what was going on. He told me that the figure on the dance floor was the Bookwus, a human being who has returned to nature, gone wild. "See how he's digging with his feet?" he said. "He's looking for cockles on the beach." We watched the Bookwus for a while, and then the old man said something that struck fiercely at my mind: "You know, when I was a boy, all this was *real*." As I was getting ready to write *Two Strand River*, I thought: What if everything that old man remembered were *still* real? What if it had never stopped being real?

I'd been doing my best to answer a set of questions much like the ones the protagonist of my rotten Alert Bay novel had asked himself, and I'd been reading Canadian history and Canadian fiction and everything I could find about the B.C. coast. I'd read Boas and Barbeau, and *Guests Never Leave Hungry* and *I Heard the Owl Call My Name* and *The Curve of Time*; of course I'd read Atwood's *Surfacing* and *Survival*. The novel I was about to write, I decided, was going to be *Canadian*, by God. It wouldn't have a single American in it, and it would be set in Vancouver and up the coast.

I was sharing my life then with a children's librarian, and, if there is a profession that calls forth a more passionate—even evangelical—commitment from its practitioners than children's librarianship, I don't know what it is. So, naturally, I found myself reading a lot of children's literature. My book would be, I decided, an adult fairy tale. I would model it on the variety of tale that begins: "There was once a king and he had three sons..." In these stories it's most often the youngest son, or daughter, the one with the flaw, who successfully completes the magical tasks and wins out at the end. So my girl who should have been a boy would have two older brothers; like Cinderella's, her mother would be dead. I'd come to see my protagonists as mirror images of each other, so the boy would have two older *sisters*, and his *father* would be dead. I began making notes, creating biographies for each of them. She would be—of course—a children's librarian, and something boyish—an athlete, a swimmer so she could dive into the waters of the psyche. And he would be—well, why not?—a beautician. So I interviewed a swimmer and a beautician.

I was still strongly under the influence of writers I'd read back in the late sixties when I—along with innumerable other counter-culture freaks—had been trying to reinvent the world. Gary Snyder's *Earth House Hold* had been my Bible, and I'd read Mircia Eleade on shamanism and learned that shamans in many cultures are androgynous, and I still took Carlos Castenada straight, having not yet twigged to the fact that he's not an anthropologist but a novelist. Then, within weeks of beginning *Two Strand River*, I happened upon what, oddly enough, turned out to be exactly the right book at the right time: Iris Murdoch's *A Severed Head*. I'd always preferred reading realism, and, in everything I'd ever written, I'd always striven not merely for realism but for gritty, tell-it-like-it-is, *forensic* realism. I wasn't sure what Murdoch was doing, but it sure as hell wasn't realism. I'd never read anything quite like that crazy book. Oh, my God, I thought, she'll let her characters do *anything!* I wondered what would happen if I let my characters do anything.

I sat down at my typewriter in the summer of 1975 ready to begin my novel. I'd named Alan and Leslie by then, and I knew in a vague, general way their back stories—or, as we would have said in the sixties, where they were *coming from*. I didn't yet have much of a plot, but I planned to find that out as I went. It would, I was sure, take me at least a year to write a first draft of the book and maybe another year after that to kick it into shape. I wrote the first few pages quickly, hardly pausing to think. I kept waiting to hit the usual blockages I'd always experienced in my writing, but there didn't seem to be any. Then, within days, my characters jumped up into full-blown reality and took over, and I realized that I'd lost control of the book—even worse, that I'd never had any control to start with. I didn't feel like the author. I felt like somebody taking dictation.

It was the closest thing to automatic writing I've ever done in my life. My problem was not figuring out what was going to happen next; my problem was trying to keep up with what was already happening. I'm a fast typist; for long stretches of time, I was typing as fast as I could get my fingers to move. I typed every day from eight-thirty in the morning to four in the afternoon and left the typewriter exhausted. And then, as I lay around in the evening trying to recover, my characters wouldn't let me alone but kept on talking to me. I fell asleep with them talking to me, and I woke up with them talking to me. I gave up any pretense of knowing where the book was going or what it was about. Every morning I thought, "What are those crazy people going to do today?"

Dozens of times during the writing of *Two Strand River* I had panic attacks. A great sluice of words would be pouring through me from some obscure source that didn't feel like *me* at all, and I'd stop momentarily, my fingers hovering over the keys. I'd be sweating, and I'd feel my heart racing, and I'd think: oh, my God, you can't write *that!* Then I'd remember Iris Murdoch, and I'd make a deal with myself: go ahead and write it; you don't have to show it to anybody—and I'd go ahead and write it. The first draft took me six weeks. That draft, with only minor revisions, was exactly what was published by Press Porcépic in 1976.

Two Strand River was widely reviewed and, by and large, warmly received—although not without criticism. Nearly all the reviewers—even the most sympathetic and perceptive of them—tried to read the book as realism; read that way, it simply won't go, so I was trounced for relying too much on "coincidence." And there were a few reviewers who loathed the book and said so. My favourite pan bore the headline, GROSS MISUSE OF WRITING TALENT, and another reviewer called the book a soap opera—a comparison accurate enough to make me wince. There were a number of my friends who didn't like it either; one told me that he was only sorry that my first published book hadn't been one of my *serious* novels, and another said that trying to read it had been "like drowning in taffeta."

It's easy enough to see things wrong with *Two Strand River*. The reviewers pointed out its flaws, and many of these had, of course, already been noticed by the author. To start with, the book is just so *excessive*. And why do *all* the major characters have to have something radically wrong with them? Couldn't some of them be—well, just plain normal? And why are all the straight people such jerks, and why are they painted so broadly, often to the point of caricature? The obsessive attention to details of clothes and hair and makeup frequently overwhelms the story, and there are too many internal monologues, and the book is overloaded with symbols (count, for instance, the number of times mirrors are mentioned), and there are just too many references—to folklore and fairy tales and Mother Goose rhymes and children's literature, to the Tarot, to painters and artists, to North American native mythology in general and Kwakiutl mythology in particular—all of it boiled up into a great Jungian stew.

Whatever's wrong with *Two Strand River*, there's also something right with it, because there have always been readers who have not merely liked the book but have loved it and responded intensely to it—and I know this because they've told me. Novelists (at least obscure novelists like me) don't usually get much personal response to their work, but I've received letters and phone calls and private, passionate tributes offered to me after readings, and these are hardly ever about any of my other novels, are almost always about *Two Strand River*, and I continued to receive them for years after the book was first published, and occasionally I still receive them now. And what these people have wanted to tell me is not something about my writing but something about *themselves*—how the book touched them, affected them at a deep level. To such response I can only be grateful; I certainly can't take much credit for it because I don't feel much like the author.

I want to be clear about this. I am certainly *responsible* for *Two Strand River*. I was the one who sat there typing frantically to get it onto the page, and most people would probably argue that those voices dictating to me had to be coming from somewhere inside myself—and that's probably true enough—but that isn't how I experienced them. I've never felt that eerie sense of displacement from the center of the work—from authorship—more strongly than when General Publishing was planning to reissue *Two Strand River* in its *New Press Canadian Classics* series in 1982 and I read it again for the first time in nearly six years. Until then, I'd always thought I'd rewrite it if I had the chance, but I soon realized that if I tried to rewrite *any* of it, the entire construction would fall apart, and then I would have to rewrite *all* of it and it wouldn't be the same book, so, even when I was tempted, I rewrote nothing. I cleaned up the spelling mistakes, tightened the punctuation, cut padding and repetition, and restored the ending—approximately the last two pages—that I had originally written. Except for this afterword and the acknowledgements, this edition is identical to the 1982 edition.

There has never, to my knowledge, been a serious critical study written of *Two Strand River*, but I was pleased to see it described by the editors of *Magic Realism and Canadian Literature* as "widely regarded as among the best works of magic realism in Canadian writing," and I've heard from time to time that the book has been taught at both the high school and the university level—most recently in my own university.

Shortly after I received my first full-time appointment at U. B. C., I got a phone call in my office from a student in the English Department asking if I would mind talking about my work; she was, she said, studying one of my books in a course. That gave me a moment of magic realist vertigo similar to that experienced by my characters: in one part of the university *I* was teaching, while in another part of the university somebody was teaching *me*.

No, I wouldn't mind talking about my work, I said, but if she were in the English Department, then surely she must have heard of the intentional fallacy, and so, I suggested, she should take whatever I had to say with a grain of salt. What book was she studying? *Two Strand River*, she said. Of course that's the one it would be, I thought, but I had a hard time imagining a university course with *Two Strand River* on its reading list. We chatted for a while, and I couldn't help asking her what, exactly, was the title of the course she was taking.

"Marginal Literature," she said. We finished our conversation, and, after I hung up, I laughed for ten minutes.

Even though many of the characters in *Two Strand River* live their real or imaginative lives on the margins of society, I have always thought that there is something in it which is not marginal at all, but central. In the early eighties, the daughter of friends of mine called me up and said she was writing a book report on *Two Strand River*. Could she ask me some questions about it? She was, the best I can remember, fourteen at the time.

She asked me how I came to write it, and I gave her an abbreviated account of what I've just said here. Then she asked me what it all meant. As helpful as I was trying to be, I didn't have—and I'd never had—the faintest idea of what it all meant, so I threw her question back at her: "What do *you* think?"

She answered without a moment's hesitation: "I think it means— whoever you are, that's OK."

I can't imagine how it could be put any better.

Acknowledgments

My place names "up Island" are imaginary and are not meant to correspond one-to-one with any locations that could be found on a map of British Columbia.

The book that Amy has been reading (pp. 111) is Richard Green's *Sexual Identity Conflict in Children and Adults*. The career of the shaman "Billy" is strongly based upon accounts in Marius Barbeau's *Medicine Men on the North Pacific Coast*. Extremely useful to me as background material was Ruth Benedict's *The Concept of the Guardian Spirit in North America*.

The Mother Goose rhymes used here I learned by hearing them recited and may differ from versions in this or that particular book. A version of "The Red Ettin of Ireland" (from which Jeanie quotes, p. 34) as well as one of "Mr. Fox" ("Be bold, be bold..." etc., pp. 180) may be found in Joseph Jacobs' *English Folk and Fairy Tales*; the verse that has upset Amy (p. 28) is from Segal and Sendak's *The Juniper Tree*; Leslie's bedtime reading (p. 66) is the first paragraph of W. W. Tarn's *The Treasure of the Isle of Mist*; the pictures referred to on p. 171(and other references, passim) are from Robert Louis Stevenson's *The Black Arrow* illustrated by N. C. Wyeth; the verse and illustration Leslie associates with Susan (p. 127 and passim) are from Christina Rosetti's curious *Goblin Market*, illustrated by Arthur Rackham.

The editors of *Magic Realism and Canadian Literature* mentioned in the afterword are Peter Hinchcliffe and Ed Jewinski; the book is the *Proceedings of the Conference on Magic Realist Writing in Canada*, University of Waterloo/Wilfrid Laurier University, May 1985, and was published in 1986 by the University of Waterloo Press.

I'd like to thank Judi Saltman who opened the door to children's literature for me, Jamie and Flora Guenther and Ginger Eckert who made my experiences up the coast possible, Rod Paterson who helped me obtain background material on Northwest Coast shamanism, Rhiannon Paterson who told me what it all meant, Henry Tabbers and Mary Ann Franson who helped me prepare the revised 1982 edition, and Ferron, Nena Boax, Bonnie Strickling, Jim Silverman, Michael Williamson, and John Crouch for their support and friendship while I was first thinking about *Two Strand River* and writing it. And I would particularly like to thank those readers who have shared their personal responses with me.

Keith Maillard

February 1996
Vancouver